CLOVENHOOF

HEIDE GOODY

IAIN GRANT

Paperback ISBN: 978-0-9933149-0-2

Ebook ISBN: 978-0-9571754-4-0

Published by Pigeon Park Press

www.pigeonparkpress.com

info@pigeonparkpress.com

To our test-readers Helen Allan, Orion Andrews, Sarah Paddon, Richard Castell, Chrissie Daz, Simon Fairbanks, Chris Garghan, Kate Goodman, Danielle Green, Misha Herwin, Victoria Hudgson, Mat Joiner, Rosie Phenix-Walker, Martin Tomlinson, Martin Sullivan, Neil Price and Richard Wantuch who helped shuffle things around, remove the unnecessary and point us towards the funny stuff.

But most of all...
To our significantly better halves, Simon and Amanda, for putting up with us and Jeremy Clovenhoof for the last year or so.

HELL

"We're a little disappointed," said Saint Peter. "Let's take the measure of suffering. This was very straightforward. *All suffering should be graded as good or higher.*"

"And we're certainly getting those grades in a lot of the suffering that we deliver," said Satan.

"A lot. Not all."

"Yes, but it wouldn't be reasonable to expect it for everything," Satan argued. "We get some clients who simply enjoy it too much, and then there are those who lie about the experience because they can't help themselves."

"All suffering means *all* suffering," Peter said, "and some has been assessed as merely satisfactory. It's not good enough."

"Surely satisfactory means that it *is* good enough," said Satan.

"Not anymore," said Peter. "The measure is very clear. All

right, let us move on to the measure where I think we've seen no progress at all. *To consider opportunities for outsourcing the work of Hell to private contractors.*"

Satan rolled his eyes and blew out through his teeth.

"To be honest with you, I never really had any idea what that one meant."

"Well clearly, there is the possibility -"

"No!" snapped Satan. "Don't start yapping on about it now. Enough of this charade. I let you give me those targets because everyone has targets, and I'm meant to lead by example. But really. I'm in charge here, and I think you'll find I've been running my ass off making things better, and answering questions and generally keeping all the new plates spinning as well as the old plates. Surely, these things were set to give me something to do in the quiet times. Not that I get quiet times anymore."

"Your response distresses me deeply," Peter said, reaching for his glasses. "We, your assessment board have taken this process very seriously. You give me no choice but to recommend your immediate removal from the post."

"Are you kidding?" yelled Satan. "Are you fucking kidding? I'm the Prince of Darkness! You can't just sack me! What kind of puffed-up, pompous twat are you anyway?"

"I," said Peter heavily, "am the Rock, you inefficient, flabby, has-been angel. I am the man that has a completed process and an airtight paper trail proving that you are not fit to do your role. I'm sorry that we're not in agreement about this, but it's not up for debate."

"How can it not be up for debate? I'd like to take it up

with the Other Guy. Bring him along to back up this little kangaroo court you've got here."

There was a moment when the board seemed to glance at one another without actually moving, but it soon passed.

"We'll pass your request on, of course," said Peter smoothly, "but don't expect anything to change. This is a tried and tested process."

Satan turned on his heel and marched from the room, looking for something, *anything* to smash.

1

IN WHICH CLOVENHOOF ARRIVES, FAILS TO END IT ALL AND GETS A ROUND IN

Ben liked routine.

He got *twitchy* when confronted with the unusual.

He'd been extremely twitchy all morning.

When he left his flat, a small but weighty package that had been propped up against the door fell in on the carpet with a slap. Wrapped in brown parcel paper, it had a pink post-it note attached to it that read:

WHAT DO YOU THINK?
Nerys (upstairs)
X

THAT WAS A LITTLE UNUSUAL, since Nerys Thomas, who lived in flat 3, along with her elderly aunt and a rat-like Yorkshire terrier called Twinkle hadn't said more than a dozen words to him in the two years they had been neighbours.

Ben put the parcel on his kitchen table next to a line of war-gaming miniatures and went out. As he locked up, he looked across to the door of flat 2a. It had now been unoccupied for over a year, since the unfortunate departure of Mr Dewsbury. The thought of Mr Dewsbury made Ben twitchy for entirely different reasons.

Once out of the flats, which were all neatly contained within a large pre-war house, he headed towards Boldmere high street. He began to realise that he had seriously overdressed for the weather. Autumn was an unpredictable season with rain varying from violent torrents to half-hearted drizzle and wind that covered the spectrum from irritating gusts to full-on slap-a-wad-of-wet-leaves-in-your-face gales. But today was more like summer. Not that it was warm and sunny. Sutton Coldfield did a nice line in grey skies and rarely experimented with much else but there was a closeness in the air that was decidedly unseasonal and an indefinable electric crackle that spoke of a storm about to break.

This was unusual too.

And yet, though each of these things was unusual, none of these strange occurrences could quite compare to what happened shortly after eleven o'clock. Having restocked the shelves of the Thriller section with a newly arrived box of Deightons and Le Carrés and settled down to a mid-morning cup of tea, Ben heard a muffled roll of thunder, looked up and saw that a naked man had appeared on the pavement outside the shop.

The naked man was turning on the spot, looking furiously in all directions and making theatrical and vulgar gestures with his hands. Ben did not have much experience of nudity, male or female, and was so mortified by the prospect of seeing naked men in public changing rooms that he had never learned to swim. However, with the window as a screen between them, a social divider, once it became reasonably clear that the man was probably not going to come into the shop for a browse, Ben found himself interested rather than worried. He took a sip of tea and watched to see what would happen next.

What did happen was that two old ladies came along the pavement and stopped in front of the naked man. They were the kind of old ladies - puffy blue-rinses and thick knitted coats, one with a tartan shopping bag on wheels, one with a wooden-handled knitting bag in one hand and a brolly in the other - who were probably called something like Betty and Doris. They were also probably the kind who, having lived through a world war, weren't going to be put off their shopping trip by a naked man.

One of the old women used her brolly to point out the man's hairy genitalia just in case her friend had failed to notice it. Apparently, she had failed to notice it, because she now looked down and immediately burst out laughing. The naked man did not take well to this and began bellowing at the old dears.

Ben had an underdeveloped social conscience and knew himself to be a physical coward but, fearing civil unrest and the bad press that might come from having old ladies assaulted outside his shop, he put down his cuppa and left the safety of *Books 'n' Bobs* to remonstrate with the man.

The man, red in the face from shouting at the old ladies, wheeled on Ben instantly.

"Kneel before me, human!" he commanded.

Ben looked down and pictured where his face would end up if he complied.

"Ah, it's not that I'm not flattered by the offer," he heard his own mouth say without any input from his brain. "And I've got nothing against that kind of thing. In the privacy of one's home, you understand but, um..."

His mouth, having got so far by itself, ran out of steam and looked to his brain for instructions and found none forthcoming.

The man's face creased with bitter fury.

"Don't any of you worms know who I am? What I am?"

Ben took in the man's life-worn face, his neatly trimmed beard, his slight paunch, his precise but profane English and his general lack of care regarding his own nakedness.

"Are you Swedish?"

The man groaned and spun round, seemingly in search of someone or something else to latch onto.

"What is this place?" he asked, straining as though the very thoughts in his head were excruciating pain.

"Sutton Coldfield."

"Where's that?"

"Birmingham. England."

"Earth?"

Ah, thought Ben. And now he'll ask us to take him to our leader.

"Where are my halls?" the man wailed. "My flesh pots? My pleasure pits?"

Ben's thoughts shifted again. His suspicions had travelled from shameless nudist, to care in the community victim, to middle-aged hippy (perhaps one suffering an inconvenient acid flashback). But now he found himself wondering if the fellow was the victim of a stag-do prank and perhaps still inebriated from the night before. Admittedly, today was Monday and Sutton Coldfield was hardly a Mecca for hen and stag parties, particularly on Sunday nights, but maybe he had been wandering drunk, drugged and naked since the weekend. Yes, a man could walk out this far from Birmingham's numerous 'flesh pots' in that time...

"Do you need me to call someone?" said Ben.

"Who are *you* going to call?" shrieked the man and with a bizarre cry of "Dung beetles!" ran off down the road in the vague direction of Birmingham city centre.

Ben looked at the old ladies.

"Are you two all right?"

They both smiled at him but said nothing. He looked past them down the road.

The naked guy was capering in the middle of the road outside the Greggs bakery. A post van had pipped its horn at him and now the man was doing his best to kick the van's lights in and doing a surprisingly good job considering he had no shoes.

Ben sighed and shook his head.

"People, eh?" he said and then saw that the two old ladies had gone. Vanished without a trace.

Shortly, after the naked man had attacked the post van, a

number 66A bus and a lamppost, the police turned up and took him away.

"People," Ben said to himself again quietly and went back inside the shop.

THEY PUT HIM IN A CELL, which was small and clean and too bright for his liking.

The arresting officer, a lean moustachioed man, had given him a blanket to cover his nakedness and, after a length of time that suggested they had to root around in dusty cupboards or foetid lockers to find them, they gave him a pair of black police trousers, a white police shirt and a pair of heavy boots. He put on the trousers and the shirt but, of course, not the boots.

Later still they brought him a cup of tea and a plate of baked beans. He put them on the cushioned bench next to him and ignored them.

Much later, the cell door opened and the archangel Michael walked in.

He looked up at Michael and said, "What are you wearing?"

"Armani."

"And your wings?"

"Would ruin the cut of the suit. Both fashion and faith have moved on since my last apparition." He looked at his watch. "You've been on Earth for just over four hours. And already you've roused the ire of local law enforcement."

"What did you expect?"

"I expected better." He tapped his breast pocket. "Fortunately, I have a court order here demanding your immediate release."

"I'm not going out there!" He flung out his arms, knocking the polystyrene cup of tea off the bench. The cold tea splashed around the archangel's expensively shoed feet but did not touch them. It was not a coincidence. "Earth. It's an anthill. It's a cesspit. It's an anthill in a cesspit."

"Earth is lovely," said Michael. "It is His perfect creation."

"Have you looked at it recently?"

Michael smiled sympathetically.

"It's going to be your home."

"Balls it is!"

"It was all clearly laid out in the terms of the final agreement."

"I'm not staying."

Michael shook his head gently, his beautiful blond curls shining like gold in the cell's strip lighting, and produced a wallet from his pocket.

"Your documents."

He handed them over and watched as each plastic card was inspected and discarded.

"Who is Nicholas Clovenhoof?"

"You," said Michael. "It's your *nom de voyage*. I think people might raise eyebrows at someone signing his name Satan or the Angel of the Bottomless Pit."

"Nicholas Clovenhoof."

"That's right."

"Nicholas Clovenhoof?"

"Yes."

"Nicholas... *Clovenhoof*?"

"Yes? Something wrong with that?"

"Are you kidding me? Isn't this a blatant giveaway? You might as well call me Lou Cyphre or Mr DeVille. Nicholas Clovenhoof?"

"You want to change it?" said Michael.

"Yes, please."

"What to?"

"Oh, I don't know. Bernard or Jeremy or Colin or something, a bit more, you know..."

"Very well," sighed the archangel and waved his hand as though driving a fly away.

The words on a dozen cards writhed and shifted.

The former Angel of the Bottomless Pit tried out his new name.

"Jeremy Clovenhoof."

"Yes. Are you happy now?" asked Michael.

"Of course I'm sodding not. Look at this."

Clovenhoof held up his driving licence.

"What about it?" asked Michael.

"The picture!"

"I think it's a good likeness."

"Exactly! Look at the horns. The red skin. No one's said *anything!*"

"They're English. They're probably just too polite."

Clovenhoof kicked at the police boots on the floor with his goaty hooves.

"Look!" he squeaked. "Are they all morons?"

"Would you rather they saw you as you really are?"

"It might get me a bit of respect."

Michael sighed kindly and sat down on the bench, the plate of cold beans between them.

"You are not here as conqueror, my friend. You are now a resident."

"No way."

Michael gathered Clovenhoof's cards and paper and tucked them back into the wallet.

"We've given you an identity. We will provide you a modest but favourable pension. This is an opportunity, Jeremy."

Clovenhoof sneered in wilful ignorance and disgust at the items in his hands. All little plastic rectangles and strings of numbers.

"But what is this stuff? It's all crap. I don't know the first thing about life on Earth."

"Then learn," said Michael. "And live."

THE UNUSUALNESS FACTOR eased off through the afternoon. No more naked men appeared outside the shop and the peculiar pre-storm atmosphere had dissipated. Ben went home to a Pot Noodle for tea and an evening of war-gaming miniature painting to look forward to with an option on polishing his replica Seleucid shield and a documentary about gladiators on the History Channel.

And the parcel on his kitchen table.

In all the nakedness-related excitement earlier, he had completely forgotten about it. As he forked sweet and sour chicken noodles into his mouth, he opened the package with his free hand. It was a book, or at least a manuscript, printed on A4 but professionally bound.

<u>*YOU*</u> *Can Be My Perfect Man*
By
Nerys Thomas

A NUGGET of rehydrated chicken suddenly went down the wrong way and Ben coughed noodles across the table. He fetched a dishcloth and mopped up the mess before re-reading the title and discovering to his horror that he had read it correctly the first time.

He reeled in panic.

Him? The perfect man? He liked to think he was a little bit mysterious and definitely underrated, but he wasn't comfortable with other people thinking the same.

He tried to reflect on it rationally. He had many things going for him. He was young, single and disease-free. He had all his own teeth, his own flat and his own second hand bookshop.

And, thought Ben, wading purposefully into the matter rather than panicking at its edges, Nerys was not an unattractive woman. She was young. At least he assumed so. She wore make-up as though it was war paint and that made proper age analysis difficult. But she was attractive. Well, more striking than beautiful. And she certainly wore clothing that showed off the best of her... attributes.

She was quite clearly interested in men. He had heard her in company, giggling and stumbling past his door on more than one Saturday night. And she must have quite high standards because it was rare for her to invite the same man back more than once even though it was true that Ben was often woken on Sunday mornings by the words, "Call me!" shouted down the stairs or, less frequently, yelled out of an upstairs window.

Yes, he decided, she was a fine specimen of a woman and, although he hadn't even thought about her in those terms before, if she thought he could be her *perfect* man then he was willing to give it a go. It wasn't as though he wasn't interested in that world of romance, of intimacy, of sex. Of course he was. It was just that, in his reckoning, sex was a bit like skiing. It was something other people did, something that, in a perfect world, he would like to try but he hadn't had the training and wasn't even sure he had the correct equipment.

Well, perhaps now was the time to hit the piste, metaphorically speaking.

He opened the book and began to read.

CLOVENHOOF WOKE UP COLD, damp and miserable.

He had stormed away from Michael the moment they had stepped outside the police station and spent the afternoon and evening constantly walking, constantly fuming at his situation. He walked nowhere in particular. There was nowhere he wanted to go that could be reached by walking. He wanted to go *up* and punch the smug smiles off a few faces. He wanted to go *down* and do pretty much the same thing. But the signposts in this dump pointed to Lichfield and Birmingham and Kingstanding. The Celestial City and Pandemonium didn't figure.

The night was cold and lit by yellow sodium streetlights that merely made him homesick for the fiery orange glow of the Old Place. He found a real fire in a derelict warehouse behind the train station and two figures hunched over it. He approached and they didn't turn him away and he warmed his hand by the fire. One of them offered him swigs from a bottle of something called Scrumpy Thunder and in that fizzy chemical concoction found his first pleasurable experience since his arrival.

When Dan and Quentin had curled up amongst their sleeping bags and blankets to sleep, Clovenhoof sat close to the fire and stared into its heart. When the fire began to die down, he looked around for something to burn. There wasn't much to be found although there was a fat sheaf of papers in his wallet, red and purple portraits of some woman in a crown, and he burned most of those to keep the flames alive.

The fire was a tiny thing. Pitiful. Nothing like the great roaring furnaces of the Old Place.

When *exactly* was it that he began to see his kingdom slide away from him?

HELL

Satan shook his head at the carnage on the Plains of Hell below him. Carnage was supposed to be part of the package in Hell, there was beauty in chaos, but *this* was just a mess.

The entrance gate was clogged again. Built centuries ago for a more modest rate of influx, the constant press of humans coming through in the twenty first century was greater than anyone had ever anticipated. It was now the norm to see crushed bodies oozing through, like meat from a mincer. Other times, like now, the weight of traffic was just too much and blockages occurred. Demons wielded pitchforks and gouged at the writhing mass to try to dislodge the bodies.

"Mulciber," Satan sighed, "how did this ever get so bad?"

"Who could have anticipated the numbers, my lord?" replied his chief architect defensively. "The number of deaths each day is higher than ever, nearly a hundred and fifty thousand. We could maybe cope with that if so many of them weren't coming our way. Two thirds of them by my reckoning."

Satan nodded. "People are turning their backs on religion."

"It's not so much that," Mulciber said, "but it seems more acceptable than ever now to be religious and to treat people badly. You have crazy fundamentalists in every religion. They hate gays, foreigners, women. You name it, they'll find you a reason in the bible or whatever to hate it."

"Hmmm," said Satan, indicating the wailing, gnashing wall of bodies, tangled in the agonising crush. "What worries me is that we might have a whole load of low-grade sinners being pulled apart by those pitchforks. We'd normally reserve that for the more serious offenders."

"There have been some complaints, sir."

"Yeah, I bet there have. How are things at the Lake of Fire?"

"Same as before, I'm afraid," said Mulciber. "It's full, completely full. A mild scorching is all we can achieve in a lot of cases. I've seen people walk across it, barely noticing that they're not on solid ground."

Satan paused for a moment to remember the lake as it was. A wild and glorious place where a body could flail and roast in blissful isolation. Now he couldn't even paddle in the shallows. If he tried, it was likely that some hand would claw at his ankle, accompanied by whining about the overcrowding.

"I'm going to take a look up at the end of the line,

Mulciber," said Satan. "In the meantime, draft in some more demons."

"To help the pitchforkers, sir?"

"No, to whip the ones that are working there now. Make them go faster."

"Very good, sir."

Satan walked towards the gates. In ordinary times, the sound of so many souls in torment would please him greatly, but this just angered him. The torment was all wrong. Some of these souls had been sent to him for minor transgressions like bigamy or getting babies' ears pierced. They were only supposed to experience eternal dullness, and maybe the kind of minor discomfort one would get from a mildly disappointing camping holiday.

The smell was all wrong too. Instead of the overpowering sulphurous reek of brimstone, there was something else. He paused for a moment to sniff the air. It was human sweat.

He went through the side entrance, emerged onto the road before the gate, and saw a different kind of horror. The road was long and all he could see were bodies packed impossibly together, seething forwards. No wonder the demons were having trouble clearing the blockage, there was no way to reduce the pressure from the other side, even for a moment.

And how was he, master of this domain, going to get through against the flow of the traffic?

"You and you, come here." A pair of demons leapt to attention. "I want you to clear me a way through this."

"Er, how?" rasped one of them.

"You've got a pitchfork, haven't you? Well use it. Pile them on top of each other if you need to, but I want to go that way."

The two demons soon formed an efficient tag team. They bullied and prodded the crowd so that people tried to press away, and hefted the bodies over the heads of the others if they couldn't move fast enough. Progress was still agonisingly slow, and Satan had to endure the incessant grumbling from all he passed.

"What are you all in such a hurry for?" he yelled irritably. "'Are we there yet?' Do you people not know what eternity *means*?"

"But we've been waiting for hours!" moaned one of the yet-to-be-damned.

"Waiting for what?" Satan asked her.

"Well, you know," she said. "To get in."

"Don't you know where it is you're going? You must have seen enough clues by now, hmmm?"

He indicated his horns and hooves. One of the demons stabbed her arm with his pitchfork for good measure.

"Course I know," she said. "I just think it's disgusting that you make people queue like this."

Satan rolled his eyes and pressed on, tuning out the mutterings of the crowd. At the Styx, Satan had them find Charon's old boat and they made a private crossing, avoiding the overcrowded ferries. On the other side, they plunged back into the impossible crush and then, after several hours, the demons broke through the back of the queue and Satan staggered out into open space.

As Satan walked on, he waved the demons to stay behind.

"I'll need you to get me back through when I'm done here, boys."

They scowled at each other and settled to wait, poking passing humans with their pitchforks, competing to see who was quickest on the draw.

BOLDMERE

Clovenhoof awoke, slumped beside the still glowing embers with dew clinging to his trousers and shirt. He was on Earth and it was still shit. Quentin and Dan were already awake, sitting upright in their sleeping bags.

Dan offered him the Scrumpy Thunder bottle.

"Morning mouthwash?" said Dan.

Clovenhoof took it without a word and drank.

"I can't live in a place like this," he said, passing it back.

Dan lit a cigarette.

"We all got to live somewhere," he said.

Quentin nodded in agreement.

"But the people here," said Clovenhoof. "The way they look at me. No recognition."

"No respect, I know."

"It's unbearable," said Clovenhoof.

Dan grinned.

"We're like something they found on the bottom of their shoe."

"Right. Smarmy bastards, going about their pointless little lives."

"Too true."

"It's like they think they're living in the bloody centre of the universe. But what is this place? I've walked its length. It's some nowhere town, all shop windows and rows of identical houses."

"That's about the measure of the place," agreed Dan and offered Clovenhoof a drag of his cigarette.

Clovenhoof inhaled deeply and looked at the cigarette wistfully.

"God, that reminds me of the Old Place," he said.

"Yeah?" said Dan.

"The smoke from the furnaces. Those Satanic mills turning. It's a sight to behold. And the city. Not like this place. We've got beautiful ruins and towers that stretch up beyond sight. And my people knew exactly where they were, a real sense of place. Wailing and writhing. Acreages of human flesh."

"Sounds nice," said Dan uncertainly. "Can't you go back?"

"No," said Clovenhoof bitterly, handing the cigarette back.

"Well, then you'd best make the most of it. Wherever you are." Dan wriggled out of his sleeping bag and began to roll it up. "What other choice do you have? It's either this or make an end of it and top yourself."

Clovenhoof blinked.

"You're right," he said quietly.

"Of course I am," said Dan.

Clovenhoof jumped to his feet.

"Dan," he said, grabbing the man's ears and planting a kiss on the top of his knitted hat, "you are a bloody genius."

"Am I?"

Clovenhoof ran off into the grey light.

The two men watched him go.

"Where do you reckon he was from?" asked Dan eventually.

Quentin stroked his stubble thoughtfully.

"Coventry, I think."

NERYS LATER REFLECTED THAT, all told, Tuesday had started out so very promisingly.

She woke to find a text from a Trevor (or was it a Stephen?) who had been on her 'second date material' list but who had been in danger of being moved to her 'mysteriously disappeared' list. These were not imaginary lists but scrupulously kept documents in the back of her diary. A lot of 'second date material' moved to 'mysteriously disappeared' rather than the hoped for 'successful second date' list so she was cheered by the message.

Then, on her way out to work, she met that man from flat 2b on the stairs, the one she had heard the neighbours say worked in the book industry. He was a shifty looking man with low standards of dress but, since she had asked him to look at her manuscript, she made the effort to be polite.

"Good morning," she said brightly.

"Er, er, morning," said Ben and gave her a rictus-like grin. "Do you need a handkerchief?"

"What?" she said, wondering if she had something smeared on her face.

Ben pulled a white handkerchief from his pocket with a magician's flourish.

"'A fine gentleman always carries a handkerchief,'" he said and she realised he was quoting from her book.

She blushed.

"You read it?"

"I did."

"And what do you think?"

"Um," he said and then, "Yes. Yes, it's a really good idea."

"You think it has potential?"

"Well, er, we can only give it a go, can't we?"

She beamed.

"That's great news. Wow. Thanks."

She trotted merrily down the stairs with a sudden song in her heart and thoughts of her imminent publication.

Her buoyant mood carried her through an otherwise humdrum day at the *Helping Hand* Job Agency in Sutton Coldfield town centre. It was the usual round of HGV drivers and office temps in search of the next contract. She despaired at how they all conformed to the stereotypes of their trade. Fat with sagging waistline: HGV driver. Cheap ugly shoes and poorly co-ordinated make-up: office temp. It would have been so simple to sort each of them out, a belt and a low-carb diet for one lot, a ten-minute tutorial in fashion and make-up for the others. She had in fact produced a leaflet with those very guidelines, but the regional manager hadn't approved.

Her colleague Dave, technically on the same rung of company ladder but in so many ways her underling was out on a training course that day so she had to get her own coffee. At least that meant she wasn't plied with so many cuppas that she spent the whole afternoon busting for a pee. It also meant she didn't have anyone to brag to about her future publishing success. The rest of the people in the office were either gormless idiots or strangely uninterested in her personal news and views, frequently both.

She left the office at four, collected her dinky car from the shopping centre multi-storey fighting Christmas shoppers at every turn, and set off for home. As she pulled out of the car park exit, something flashed downward through her vision and landed with a thump. Even before the man had rolled off the dumpster and onto the pavement, Nerys was unclicking her seatbelt and getting out of the car.

She didn't stop to think about what she had seen in that second before she had leapt from her car but if someone had asked her what she had thought she had seen, she would have said she had seen a man fall from the roof of the multi-storey car park and smash into one of the dumpsters outside the service doors. But, of course, that couldn't be what had happened because no one who had fallen six storeys onto unyielding steel would be rolling around, clutching their elbow and swearing viciously to themselves.

As she ran towards him, remembered diagrams of how to make a tourniquet from a belt, of the recovery position, of how to perform an emergency tracheotomy with a disposable biro, flashed through her mind in vibrant

Technicolor. Heroic first aid related glory was within her reach.

And then something terrible happened. Out of nowhere, a woman had appeared and was crouching over the man, professional care oozing from her outstretched hands. Nerys put in a final spurt and cried out, "Don't touch him!"

The woman looked up.

"I'll deal with this!" Nerys shouted. "Stand back!"

"Are you a paramedic?" asked the woman.

"Pretty much," said Nerys.

She knelt down next to the man. He wore a shirt and trousers and a sleek goatee beard. His face was screwed up in pain, adding extra lines to his already deeply lined face. He had the leathery skin of an ageing rock-star and, Nerys noted, had quite probably been a sexy-looking feller in his youth although time had not necessarily been kind.

"My name's Nerys," she said. "I'm here to help."

The man blinked tears and looked up at her.

"Am I dead?"

"No," said Nerys with a comforting smile.

"Shit," said the man. "Shit shit shittity shit!"

That was an unexpected response.

"What do you mean, pretty much a paramedic?" asked the woman standing above them.

"I'm first aid trained," said Nerys. "Can you feel your legs, sir?"

"I'm first aid trained too," said the woman.

Nerys stood.

"Listen, sweet-cheeks. I don't mean I've just watched a few episodes of Casualty. I am first aid trained. I've helped out during several medical emergencies." She pulled out her phone, flipped to her photo library and passed it to the woman. "Look. Here's me helping a boy who was choking on a mint imperial."

Nerys knelt down again and began feeling the man's arms for fractures. The woman looked at the photograph.

"How many emergencies?"

"Several," said Nerys.

"How many?"

"Two," said Nerys. "Including this one."

"Two is not several."

"Two is more than one and therefore is several." She put her arms under the man's shoulder and began to turn him over. "Sir, I'm just going to put you in the recovery position."

"Oh, what's the point?" he said, producing fresh tears.

"To stop you swallowing your tongue, I think."

"Hang on," said the woman. "Did you ask someone to take a picture of you giving this boy the Heimlich Manoeuvre?"

"Yes," said Nerys irritably, getting the man onto his side.

"He was choking but you stopped to get out your phone so someone could take a photo *before* you stopped him choking?"

"Who wants to see a photograph of someone *who is no longer choking*?" She raised her eyebrows to her patient. She was sure he understood that the woman was some sort of imbecile.

"Suicides go straight to hell," the man was muttering unhappily. "Straight to hell."

"You're all right, now," she said soothingly.

She felt his legs for signs of injury. There was something odd about his legs. His knees seemed to be in the wrong place, his leg going backwards when it should be going forward. It was as though he had one too many joints in each leg. That, or he had the legs of an animal...

Nerys shook her head to herself, looked up and was irritated to see the woman still there. "Do you plan to stand there all day?" she said.

"I don't think you have a clue what you're doing," said the woman.

Nerys snorted.

"Well, at least make yourself useful. You've got my phone."

"Of course. Do you think he needs an ambulance?"

"I mean, take some pictures. Make sure you get both of us in them."

"WHERE ARE YOU TAKING ME?" asked Clovenhoof.

Nerys put her shoulder under his armpit and helped him out of her car.

"You don't have to do this," he said.

"You just need somewhere to sit down. Maybe a cup of tea, yes?"

"Don't take me to a hospital."

"You said that before. Here we are."

He raised his head. They were approaching the door of a tall old house on a long road of other tall old houses.

"This is your house?" he said.

"I have a flat here," said Nerys. "Well, it's technically my Aunt Molly's flat but I live with her and pay her bills and she's an old lady so, you know, fingers crossed, it'll be mine soon enough. Do you live nearby?"

He looked up at a sign in a first floor window that read, "Flat to Let".

"Er, no," he said. "I've recently been relocated."

She stopped at the door and fished for a key in her coat pocket.

"Where are you from? Originally?"

He raised his eyes to the heavens. "Here. There. Nowhere."

"You're not an illegal immigrant, are you?" she asked.

He frowned.

"I couldn't even begin to answer that question."

"Not that I'm judging," she said hurriedly. "I know that I'm a lucky woman to have been born in this country. Who can blame people for wanting to come here?"

"I was hoping to go back home."

"Maybe you will one day."

Nerys unlocked the door and then half-led half-dragged him up several flights of stairs.

Ten minutes later, he found himself sat in a high-backed armchair, nursing a cup of strong sweet tea whilst the weird young woman quietly argued with her shrill-voiced but otherwise invisible aunt in another room. A dog no larger than a gerbil was staring with what seemed to be intense fury at the new houseguest's feet.

"What?" said Clovenhoof.

The terrier leapt forward and gripped the edge of his hooves with its tiny sharp teeth.

"Get off," he hissed and shook his foot but the dog seemed to think it was now a game and with a pitiful growl, gnawed at the hard keratin.

"My foot is not a chew toy," said Clovenhoof and was considering giving the creature a terminal kick in the ribs when Nerys re-entered.

"Twinkle," she admonished without rancour, "leave the nice man's... shoes alone."

She smiled at Clovenhoof.

"You're very kind," she said, "but you shouldn't let him do that. It will lead him to bad habits."

The corner of Clovenhoof's mouth twitched.

"This is... all very nice, but I must be going," he said.

He placed his cup of tea on the table beside the chair, deliberately avoiding the doily coaster. He had stopped drinking it after discovering it had none of the potent qualities of Scrumpy Thunder.

"No," said Nerys, holding out her hands to keep him sat. "Not until you're better."

"I'm fine," he said. "I've spent long enough here already."

"You might have concussion. Do you feel nauseous?"

"Constantly."

"How many fingers am I holding up?"

"Three."

"What day is it?"

"Friday?"

"What's your name?"

He paused to remember.

"Jeremy Clovenhoof," he said.

"Really?" she said. "I once had a boyfriend called Jeremy. I say boyfriend. It was a brief – but passionate! – affair. You know what I mean?"

"No," he said, bored.

"Well, we split up. We had to. He told me, 'It's not you, it's me.' And I thought about that for a long time and you know what?"

"What?"

"He was right. It was him. It was all him."

"Yes?"

"But for the record, today's Tuesday and I was holding up two fingers; the thumb doesn't count."

She put a hand on his head.

"And you have a nasty bump on your head here," she said.

He moved her hand across his scalp.

"I have two," he said. "You might have noticed."

"So you do," she said.

"And, for the record," he said, "two is not several."

BEN STOPPED outside the door to flat 3, checked his breath against his palm, smoothed down his hair and then did a whole body shake as he tried to build up the courage to knock.

He had read *YOU Can Be My Perfect Man* in a single sitting and had spent much of the day at the shop re-reading key chapters and making notes. He had memorised the entirety of the 'How to be spontaneous' chapter and planned to follow its instructions to the letter. He had also committed to memory her hundred and thirty-seven rules for being the perfect gentleman. He had his handkerchief, wore a tie with his shirt, carried a hat in his hand (to show he had taken it off indoors) and was prepared to open as many doors and draw in as many dining chairs as his lady required.

He knocked in a manner he hoped was manly yet polite and greeted Nerys with his best smile.

"Oh," she said. "It's Ben, isn't it?"

"Good evening, Miss Thomas," he said in the most refined tones. "Your hair does look lovely tonight."

"Er," she said. "Thanks?"

"I wasn't planning to say that. It was just, you know... I just thought I'd say it."

"Right. Um."

She looked at him. Apparently, it was his turn to say something again. So soon? He had used up his opening lines and realised he hadn't planned anything beyond this. The silence stretched out and sagged between them.

She jerked a thumb over her shoulder.

"I've, er, got company."

"We spoke earlier. On the stairs. I just came up, spontaneously like, and thought we could..."

"You want to talk about-"

"I mean if it's inconvenient-"

"I'm really thrilled you think-"

"I don't want to intrude."

"No," she said, stepping back. "Come in, do."

Ben stepped into her flat, wondering if this was the

moment when he should kiss her on the back of the hand. The opportunity hadn't seemed to present itself.

Her flat wasn't as he had imagined it. From the tone of her book, he had imagined something like the parlour of an Edwardian lady but this room was more like a battle between old lady clichés and brash IKEA-bought accessories: antimacassars versus pink scatter cushions, Toby jugs pitted against cheap turquoise copies of Henry Moore sculptures. He had expected to see Twinkle, the Yorkshire Terrier. He had not expected to see the terrier growling at the feet of a man who seemed awfully familiar.

"Ben," said Nerys, "this is Jeremy Clovenhoof."

Ben found he couldn't stop his gaze from fixing on the man's crotch as though his eyeballs had some muscle memory of the man's previous nakedness.

"We've met," said Ben.

"Have we?" said Clovenhoof.

Ben suddenly remembered rule twenty-nine for being a perfect gentleman: the firm handshake.

He stepped forward, hand outstretched.

"Kitchen. Ben Kitchen."

Clovenhoof shook his hand. Ben applied a gentle but decisive pressure. Clovenhoof returned it. Ben squeezed tighter and turned his hand over, placing it on top of Clovenhoof's. Clovenhoof squeezed harder and pushed back in the other direction.

And, at some point, it magically transformed from a handshake to a silent arm wrestle. Clovenhoof gritted his teeth. Ben dropped his hat and gripped his wrist with his free hand to support it. Clovenhoof bent his elbow, drawing Ben in, so he could use his whole upper body strength. Ben dug his nails into the back of Clovenhoof's hand. There was the machine-gun crack of several finger joints popping, Ben whimpered in pain and dropped to his knees.

"Nice to meet you, Kitchen," said Clovenhoof, shaking the life back into his hand. "Now you're kneeling before me."

"Are you all right, Ben?" said Nerys, apparently oblivious to the alpha male struggle that had just taken place.

Ben, on one knee, stared at his white almost crippled hand and then saw that Nerys and her own hands were very close by.

Deciding that this was the ideal time and a great cover for his submission before Clovenhoof, Ben took Nerys's hand in his and planted a light tender kiss on the back of it.

Nerys snatched her hand away.

"What are you doing?" she said in disgust.

Ben looked up.

"I thought I was being a gentleman."

"What?"

"You want me to be your perfect man, don't you?"

"You?"

"You gave me your book. It was an unusual proposal but I read it and –"

"You're not my perfect man," said Nerys.

"I'm not?" said Ben.

"I wanted you to publish my book."

"Publish?"

"You said it was a really good idea and we ought to give it a go."

"I thought you meant... us."

She stared, open mouthed for several seconds.

"What on earth made you think I was interested in you?"

Ben's planet-sized embarrassment formed a mote of high-density anger at its heart.

"What on earth made you think I could publish your book?" he retorted.

"You're a publisher!"

"I am not!"

"Mrs Astrakhan in 1a said you worked in the book industry!"

"I own a bookshop!"

"Oh!" shouted Nerys furiously and then, much quieter, added, "Poo."

The silence that followed was long and eventually broken by Clovenhoof.

"You, Nerys-woman, do you have any Scrumpy Thunder?"

"Scrumpy?" she said. "Cider?"

"It's very nice."

A slightly hysterical yet almost silent laugh escaped her lips.

"I could murder a drink," she said.

"Me too," said Ben, sullenly.

"I think you owe me one," said Nerys.

"Me?" said Ben.

"Raising false hopes in a woman."

"Think how I feel."

"Scrumpy Thunder?" said Clovenhoof.

"Pub," said Nerys and pointed at Ben. "You're buying."

"What's a pub?" said Clovenhoof.

A PUB, it turned out, was an establishment called the Boldmere Oak, a sort of tavern or coaching inn but without the silly fripperies such as rooms or wenches-for-hire. It was filled with people who seemed to be enjoying themselves, in spite of the fact that someone was loudly singing that they wished it could be Christmas every day.

Ben put a pint down in front of Clovenhoof.

"There you go," he said.

Clovenhoof took a big gulp. It certainly tasted similar to Scrumpy Thunder but it seemed to lack the chemical bite and there was a strange additional taste.

"Is there fruit in this?" said Clovenhoof warily.

"It *is* made from apples," said Ben.

"Really?" He put the pint down. "Not sure I approve."

"Of apples?"

"Apples are fine. One of my first jobs was dishing out apples to young naked couples. I'm not sure if I approve of them in drinks."

He gave another experimental sip.

"What have you got?"

"Cider and black," said Ben.

"Chardonnay," said Nerys.

Without further word, Clovenhoof picked up each of their drinks in turn and took a swig. He mulled over Nerys's for a few seconds thoughtfully. Ben's he spat out on the floor the moment he tasted it.

"Apples *and* blackcurrant?"

"*I* like it," said Ben.

Clovenhoof got to his feet and looked about the saloon bar and the knots of drinkers about the room. So many different shaped glasses. So many differently coloured drinks. He strode over to the nearest table, took a man's pint of brown flat beer and supped at it thoughtfully.

"Hey," said the man.

"Tastes of socks," said Clovenhoof and gave it back to him.

He moved on, sampling from unguarded glasses and bottles.

"Oi," said a woman wearing reindeer horns.

"What is this?"

"It's my bloody gin and tonic."

"I don't like bloody gin and tonic," he declared. "Why is there a lime in it?"

"Piss off."

Ben and Nerys watched him circulate around the room.

"I swear he's concussed," said Nerys.

"I think he's Swedish," said Ben.

"His English is flawless."

"That's the Swedes for you. Natural linguists."

Nerys watched Clovenhoof receive a slap in the face and move on unfazed to the next table.

"So, you'd met him before," said Nerys.

"Briefly," said Ben. "Yesterday. He appeared outside my shop."

"You've not known him a long time then?"

"He left a lasting impression."

"What do you mean?"

"He was.... Well, it happened like this..."

CLOVENHOOF WAS TAKING an experimental sip of a drink called 'lager' when a hand slapped on his shoulder and turned him round. Clovenhoof looked up at the barman, a tall man with fat muscly arms and a genial but not pretty face.

"Are you drunk?" said the barman.

"I intend to be when I've found the right drink," said Clovenhoof.

"You having a laugh?"

"Not yet," said Clovenhoof.

"Don't think that because you're Old Nick you can just upset my customers."

"Old...? How did you know?"

The barman looked him up and down.

"The horns and the hooves were clues."

"You can see them?" said Clovenhoof, amazed and thrilled.

"A barman sees many things. Fact is though, way I see it, you need to buy a lot of people fresh drinks."

"Buy?"

"Cash. Money."

Clovenhoof shrugged.

"I don't have any money."

"You'd better have."

The barman saw the bulge in Clovenhoof's pocket and

clicked his fingers for him to hand the wallet over. He opened it and looked at the contents.

"Bugger me. Do you know how much you have in here?"

"I burned most of it," Clovenhoof admitted. "Is it enough to buy people drinks?"

"It's enough to buy everyone here the worst hangover in history."

"Excellent. Drinks for everyone!" he declared loudly.

"HE WAS STARK BOLLOCK NAKED?" said Nerys, laughing.

"Like a newborn baby. And there were these two old ladies just staring at him, goggle-eyed."

"I'm surprised one of them didn't have a stroke," said Nerys.

"Couldn't reach," said Ben, because he felt he had to.

"Was he...? Is he...?" Nerys raised her eyebrows.

"What?" said Ben.

"Well-endowed?"

"I wasn't exactly looking."

"But you saw."

"Unfortunately."

"So, was he?"

Ben blanched.

"That would depend on what you regard as well-endowed or, you know, an average endowment."

Nerys put her hand a distance apart on the table. She knew the measurements. She had conducted studies.

Ben took a long long sip of cider and black and wondered what the hell to say.

"I," said Clovenhoof once the barman had poured fresh drinks for those he had offended, "will have one of everything."

"What do you mean?" said the barman.

"What I mean, mortal man, is – what's your name?"

"Lennox."

"Lennox, what I mean is that, all those drinks there, the pint pulling things –"

"Taps."

"All the beer taps, all the bottles in your fridge, all those upside down drinks behind the bar. I would like one of every one of them."

"Are you sure?"

Clovenhoof nodded.

"And then we will move onto" – he savoured a new word he had learned – "cocktails."

"HE'S KIND OF RUGGED, don't you think?" said Nerys, watching Clovenhoof work his way along a row of bitters, lagers, stouts and ciders, dwelling on some, shaking his head instantly at others.

"You mean weatherworn," said Ben.

"How old do you think he is?"

"Sixty."

"Don't be silly."

"You're not... interested in him, are you?"

She gently swirled her glass.

"I don't know," she said playfully.

Ben sighed.

"So that's your perfect gentleman, is it?"

"Hardly."

"Right," said Ben in disbelief.

Nerys downed the remains of her drink.

"Hercule Poirot."

"What?"

"The perfect gentleman. No, the perfect *man*."

"Fat Belgian detective Poirot?"

"Suave, mannered, precise and intelligent. And that little waxed moustache!"

She gave a little shudder of pleasure.

"Each to their own," said Ben.

"When I was a little girl, I wrote to David Suchet and asked him for a signed photograph of him as Poirot."

"Did he send one?"

"No."

"That's not very nice. I think famous people should always be good to their fans."

"I mean I did ask for a photograph of him naked but, still, you're right."

Clovenhoof lurched against their table.

"I've done it!" he declared.

"Done what?" said Nerys.

"Found the perfect drink," he said and placed a wine

glass reverently in the middle of the table where its contents gently fizzed.

"Champagne?" said Ben.

Clovenhoof shook his head. "It's called..." – he licked his lips – "Lambrini."

Ben looked at it.

"As drinks go, isn't it a bit... girly?"

"It looks like fizzy piss," said Nerys.

"I know!" said Clovenhoof in ecstasy. "And it tastes great too!"

IN THE CORNER of the pub, unnoticed by everyone were two old ladies. With their puffy blue-rinses and thick knitted coats, they were of the type that were often called something like Betty and Doris. The one who might have been called Betty was sipping a small sherry. The one who might have been called Doris had a glass of tap water, untouched, on the table in front of her.

"It's that man again," said possibly-called-Doris.

"Well," said possibly-called-Betty. "At least he's wearing clothes now."

2

IN WHICH CLOVENHOOF TRIES TO LEAVE, DABBLES WITH SATANISM AND DISCOVERS CRISPY PANCAKES

It wasn't the daylight that woke him, or the intense cold, or even the chattering of passing shoppers, it was the large, bearded man in the red suit, kicking him in the side.

Clovenhoof clutched his head and curled into a foetal position.

"What are you doing?" he groaned.

A shiny black boot connected with something soft and squishy that might have been his liver, maybe a kidney.

"Get out, you filthy scumbag," scowled the bearded one.

"Ow. Get lost!"

"I need to open up and you... you've smashed the roof in."

Clovenhoof rolled over and looked up.

Oh, yeah.

. . .

CLOVENHOOF HAD NEVER HEARD of the conga before, but he'd got the hang of it quickly with help from his new friends from the Boldmere Oak. They were all going off to the Moo Moo Club, whatever that was. He'd laughed and cavorted so energetically that he'd somehow spun away from the others and formed a conga line of one, high-kicking and butt-waggling for goodness knows how long before he had realised he was alone.

He'd wandered on, very drunk and slightly unsure of his bearings. He headed through Sutton town centre, wondering if he could find his way back to Dan and Quentin and their warm fire when he saw a large tree artificially tethered on the paved floor.

It stood next to a little wooden shack with a sign on the top. His vision was swimming in and out, but he was impressed to see that it said "Satan's Grotto".

Maybe Michael had arranged this. It was very basic accommodation, but it clearly demonstrated that he was to be accorded some respect. There was even a roped-off section, patently for queues of humans to come and bow down before him. That was a nice touch.

"Well, goodnight world," he declared loudly. "I've been wonderful."

As he turned to address the dark street, his wobbly gaze moved up the tree.

"No!" he yelled, shaking his fist at the image on the top. "You little prick! You couldn't resist, could you? It's my place, and you just had to spoil it with a stupid angel!"

He shook the tree, hoping to dislodge it, but the angel held fast.

"I thought that you didn't wear your wings anymore? Haven't styles changed since your last apparition, huh?"

He stamped around and bellowed and swore. As he took another swipe at the tree a thought crossed his mind, and he began to giggle.

"Gonna help you out, Mikey," he said as he started to shin up the tree. "Gonna pull your wings off. Gonna tidy you up. Haven't got an Armani suit for you, but I can help you with those messy wings."

The tree swayed violently as Clovenhoof clambered upwards and the needles dug into his legs and arms, but he was focussed on the angel. Its serene and benevolent face made him more and more furious as he drew closer, swinging from side to side as the tree grew thinner towards the top.

"Hell, you're a smug one," he sneered. "Look at you. Well I think we'll see how well you fly down from there without your wings, shall we?"

He looked down at the ground as he reached for the angel and saw how far away it was.

His stomach lurched and he tried to grab back hold of the tree, but missed, and clawed into space.

"Ohh!"

YES, thought Clovenhoof, reacquainting himself with the bruising pain in his back that had troubled him throughout his sleep.

"It's not funny," said his assailant. "We open in five minutes."

"It's my grotto!" said Clovenhoof, scrambling unsteadily to his feet. "I can smash the roof if I want to!"

The white-bearded man in red spluttered.

"Your grotto? This is Santa's grotto, and I'm Santa."

"Santa? Don't make me laugh. This is mine."

"It's for kids you know, not disgusting dossers."

Clovenhoof let the red buffoon manhandle him out of the door. It was easier than trying to do it under his own steam.

"Santa's not even real," said Clovenhoof. "Satan's grotto makes so much more sense."

"Look, pal. I don't want to hear you talking like that round little kiddies. You'll frighten them with talk like that."

"I mean look at these," said Clovenhoof and waved a hand at the cavorting fibreglass models on the fake lawn around the grotto. "My little devils."

"Elves."

"Same difference."

"Look. There's no such thing as Satan and you need to shut your filthy mouth."

"No such thing! Are you serious?"

"Are you some religious nut?"

Clovenhoof gave the nonsensical question some thought.

"Possibly. I'll prove it. Look at what's written on the top of this place, just read the sign."

They both stepped away from the shack to read the lettering above.

"Santa's Grotto. There." Santa turned to Clovenhoof and smiled grimly. Clovenhoof kicked the ground with his hooves and sighed.

"Typical bloody humans, they can't even spell a simple sign properly."

He saw the angel lying on the ground nearby. He hadn't even finished the job of pulling the wings off the stupid thing. He picked it up.

"Go on Michael, if you value your wings you need to tell me now."

He held the angel to his ear.

"I'm listening. You can whisper your heartfelt apology if you like."

The angel was silent so Clovenhoof pulled off the wings and ground them under his feet with a chuckle.

"Yes officer, that's him."

Clovenhoof looked up and saw that Santa was pointing him out to a pair of policemen who gently ambled over.

"Didn't we take him in yesterday?" said one and Clovenhoof felt a twinge of recognition of the man's lithe frame and well-tended moustache.

"Yeah," said the other. "Some nob turned up and got him out. Must have some influential friends."

"He's a very influential knob," agreed Clovenhoof.

"It's Jeremy, isn't it?" said the moustache.

"Yes. It's Constable 1623, isn't it?"

"PC Pearson to you," he said tucking an arm under Clovenhoof's.

Clovenhoof allowed himself to be led away. Santa leaned across as they went through the roped-off area.

"Something tells me," he said with a smirk, "that you haven't been a very good boy this year."

Clovenhoof kicked him hard in the shin, and watched the

queuing mothers put their hands over the children's ears and hurry them away from the sound of Santa swearing loudly as he hopped on one foot and rubbed his leg.

THEY PUT him in the same cell again. He whiled away the hours sharpening his horns on the breeze block walls until Michael appeared, freshly pressed.

"Jeremy, there's really only so many times I can get you out of trouble like this."

"How many?"

"Do you think you might calm down and stop antagonising the good people of earth?"

"Good people? They're idiots! There's more respect for that buffoon in the red suit than there is for the real deal. How stupid would you have to be to encourage children to believe in a creepy old man who's going to break into your house in the middle of the night?"

"Yes, I heard you met Santa. Is that where you got your dolly?"

Michael smirked as he indicated the wingless angel still in Clovenhoof's hand.

Clovenhoof looked down at it and swung it by the feet in frustration, smacking the head against the bench. It failed to smash in a satisfying manner, but bounced off, unharmed.

Michael shook his head in pity, enraging Clovenhoof even more. He started to jump on the doll.

"Come along, Jeremy. We need to get you home."

Clovenhoof froze.

"Home?"

"Yes, come on."

Clovenhoof was whisked out of the police station, giving PC Pearson a cheery salute of farewell as he passed, and into a waiting taxi.

"Why do we need a taxi if I'm going home?"

Michael smiled but said nothing.

A few minutes later, they pulled up outside a large pre-war house. Clovenhoof recognised it and groaned.

"Oh no."

"You'll love it."

"No, no, no. Why have you brought me back here? This isn't home. I want to go HOME!"

"This is your home now. We've taken care of all the formalities for you, so you can move straight into flat 2a."

"A flat. Are you kidding? A flat! You might as well tell me that you've bought me my own ditch. What good is a flat to me?"

"You'll be comfortable in there. I've checked it all out and you've got everything that you need in there. Come on."

They went inside and stood at the door to flat 2a.

"Here's your key. Shall we go inside?" asked Michael.

"Don't want to."

Clovenhoof scuffed his hooves and pushed out his bottom lip. There was a clattering of high heels on the stairs above them.

"On second thoughts," he said. "Let's not get held up talking to that ridiculous woman from upstairs."

Clovenhoof opened the door with some speed and they were both inside the flat with the door closed.

"See? It's already furnished," Michael beamed. "It's perfect."

"How is it perfect?"

"It just is and the fact that you already met the neighbours is a bonus, too. I'm sure you'll soon make it yours."

"Make it mine?"

"Yes, you know, add some homely touches, a few of your favourite things."

Clovenhoof stared at Michael.

"What utter bullshit. Are you serious? So maybe if I get some cushions this place will be indistinguishable from my most decadent chambers? I don't think so."

"Well I'm not going to stand here and argue with you, we've given you everything you need."

Clovenhoof growled.

"What I need is-"

But Michael had vanished and Clovenhoof was alone.

"Tit," hissed Clovenhoof.

He stalked around the flat, grimacing at the domestic prissiness of it all. There were pictures on the walls of kittens, six of them, arranged in a perfect two by three grid. They posed in flowerpots and wellington boots, all competing in their efforts to be cute and twee. Clovenhoof hated them.

There was also a footstool.

"I haven't even got any feet!" yelled Clovenhoof. "You dumb-ass, angelic twat! What am I going to do with a footstool?"

He picked it up and swung it at the offensive kitten

pictures, shattering glass and breaking a leg off the footstool. He used it as a club to beat the fragmented remains of the pictures.

A lampshade with a tasselled fringe caught his eye. His urge to destroy that was even stronger than his kitten-rage. He put it on the floor and lifted the end of the settee. He kicked the lamp underneath and slammed the settee down onto it. There was a small amount of resistance, so he slammed it down again and again until the base was pulverised ceramic and the shade was flattened. Then he climbed up on top of the settee and jumped up and down, roaring to be sure that nothing remained of the hideous lamp. The settee itself was covered with a cheery throw decorated with large abstract poppies. Clovenhoof clasped it above his head and charged around the room twirling the heavy fabric around and around, bellowing obscenities and shattering candlesticks, vases and various china ornaments in his wake.

There was a hesitant knock on the door. Clovenhoof crunched across the debris to see who was there. He opened it to find Ben, the cider-and-black-drinking bookshop man, there.

He was wearing a faded Saxon t-shirt and a concerned expression.

"Oh, it's you," Ben said. "I thought it might be a ghost. Are you our new neighbour then?"

"A ghost? Why on earth would you think-"

"I meant rats. Yeah, I thought maybe it was rats," said Ben. "It's always a worry if rats get in a building. They breed pretty quickly."

Clovenhoof stared at the babbling idiot.

"Have you been drinking?" he asked and then added, "I could do with a Lambrini myself."

"It's three o'clock in the afternoon, it's a bit early for me. But, er, do pop over for a cup of tea if you like. You know, any time."

"Tea?"

"Anyway," said Ben pointedly. "I can see that you're in the middle of, um, redecorating."

Clovenhoof idly kicked a glass vase at the wall opposite.

"Laters," said Ben.

Clovenhoof shut the door and decided to explore the kitchen.

He knew about kitchens in the same way that he knew about coal mines or the insides of watches, he had never had the slightest inclination to find out what was involved, they just needed to be there for other people to deal with. He found that a kitchen contained a baffling array of equipment, all neatly arranged in compartmentalised drawers. Much of it seemed to be in the form of a jaunty cockerel. He wasn't sure whether that was normal. He twisted a small cockerel-shaped plastic thing and it emitted a shrill ringing sound. He fixed that by clubbing it with a larger cockerel, which turned out to be breakable.

He turned switches to see what happened. He was staggered to find that some of them made small fires. Small but fierce. He turned on all four of the fires and admired them. Finally he'd found something in the flat that pleased him. He left them burning, and wandered back into the living room. He found hundreds of gaudy leaflets for something called *Keep Boldmere Beautiful* in a sideboard drawer and he had a half-formed idea that he could make the fires bigger by adding the leaflets and the poppy-covered throw.

The thin plastic box in the corner had escaped his demolition, and he wondered what it was for. He pressed switches to see if it would make more fire, but he jumped back in surprise when it lit up with a large picture of a lady's bottom. Interesting. He stood further back to admire it. The lady smacked herself on the back of her jeans and then wheeled a metal basket away from him, smiling in a smug way. Perhaps she had stolen the metal basket and its contents.

Clovenhoof didn't have long to puzzle over this before the next set of peculiar images was presented. A rodent of some sort was standing on its hindquarters and addressing him. It spoke with a foreign accent and then winked. Clovenhoof was no wildlife expert, but he thought that this was unusual behaviour.

He sat down on the remains of the settee in order to study more closely what the box was showing him.

Many hours later, he'd worked out that the box was a television, and that humans routinely coveted bigger and better ones. He'd worked out that the content was a mixture of information, entertainment and numerous attempts to get humans to buy things with their money.

The sun went down and the parade of programmes rolled on. He watched humans forced to compete for money and prizes by smarmy-grinned game show hosts. He watched other humans spending money on houses and interior renovations in order to climb up some invisible thing called a property ladder. He watched a fascinating documentary about a community of people forced to live in a grimy place called Albert Square where they spent their days insulting each other, scheming against one another and moaning about how terrible life was. He enjoyed that one.

And then he watched a movie double-bill of *Rosemary's Baby* and *The Devil Rides Out* and he found his worldview transformed.

These films presented him with an entirely new concept. He expected humans to fear the devil. He liked to think of it as respect, he felt he was *owed* respect, but what he really expected was respect through fear. He expected that they would avoid him at all costs if they knew who he was. The idea that some humans – these 'Satanists' - would actively welcome him into their lives was fascinating. His mind buzzed with excitement.

BEN WOKE with a start at the loud thumping on the door. He checked his alarm and wondered what kind of emergency would make someone pound on his door in the middle of the night. There must be a fire or something. He answered the door wearing boxer shorts and t-shirt.

It was the new neighbour, Clovenhoof.

"Oh. Hi," said Ben. "What's the matter?"

"I've come for a cup of tea."

"It's four in the morning!"

"You said any time was okay."

"I know I said that, but most people wouldn't, um." He

stopped and tried to think of the appropriate words but it was four in the morning and his brain was on strike. "Come in."

Clovenhoof followed him inside.

"Tea then," said Ben and went to fill the kettle.

"Are you a Satanist?" said Clovenhoof.

"What?"

"Your t-shirt. It's got pentagrams on it."

Ben put the kettle on

"No. It's just a heavy metal thing. It's a cool design that's all."

Clovenhoof looked at the round shield and beaten metal breastplate hanging from the wall above the mantelpiece.

"What's that?"

"Seleucid armour."

"What?"

"Replicas, of course. I'm a bit of an ancient history buff."

Clovenhoof picked up a part-painted military miniature from the dining table.

"You also have a collection of petrified homunculi."

"Isn't that a kind of mushroom?" Ben was trying to find two clean mugs. He hadn't had visitors in months.

"Are you their god?" asked Clovenhoof.

"No, they're miniature scale models. I use them for war-gaming."

"War gaming?"

"We enact battles from history using the miniatures. I'm in a club. It's a fascinating insight into the thought processes and strategies of some of the great military leaders. There's never a dull moment, honestly."

"'And whoever makes a false image will be punished and will be told by God to breathe life into it and will not be able to do so,'" Clovenhoof quoted.

"What are you on about?" Ben rubbed his eyes as he poured the tea.

"It's from the Qur'an."

"You're a Muslim?"

"Let's just say that you and I are going to get along well. Tell me more about Satanists."

Ben brought the teas over.

"I don't know all that much about them. One of the guys from our war-gaming club is a Satanist, but I don't know what he does, exactly. It's not my bag really."

"Could I talk to him?" Clovenhoof asked. "Do you know where he lives?"

"Sure, let me give you his phone number." Ben looked up the number on his phone and jotted it down on a piece of paper.

He hesitated as he handed it to Clovenhoof.

"You are going to wait until the morning, aren't you?"

"What do you mean?"

"Don't ring him now, for God's sake."

"'For God's sake!'" Clovenhoof roared with laughter and slapped Ben on the back. "All right, I'll wait until the morning until I, er, do whatever you just said."

"Just remember to call him Pitspawn."

"Pitspawn?"

"Yeah."

. . .

CLOVENHOOF HANDED the taxi driver the piece of paper.

"I want to go there."

The taxi driver stared at the paper.

"This isn't an address. It's a phone number."

"A phone is a communication machine, I know that," Clovenhoof said, thinking of the films he'd watched, "so I need to go where the phone is."

"So, you need to call them up, and find out where that is. Then I can take you."

"Surely that's your job," Clovenhoof said, puzzled. "I mean it's not as if you've got anything else to do right now, is it? Obviously you wish it could be Christmas every day," he said, indicating the radio which was playing the song that he was already bored of, "but it's not. Is it?"

"You haven't got a phone?"

"No."

The taxi driver sighed and phoned the number, shaking his head. He managed to elicit an address and drove Clovenhoof into a suburb called Erdington and pulled up outside a semi-detached house with a large holly wreath on the front door. Clovenhoof frowned, there were no pentagrams or candles visible, but the taxi driver was adamant that this was the right address.

Clovenhoof knocked at the door. A woman with a gentle face and a grey bun answered.

"Are you Pitspawn?" asked Clovenhoof.

"You want Darren," said the lady.

"No. Pitspawn."

"Come in."

Clovenhoof found himself steered into a room of lace

doilies and side tables. He sat on an uncomfortable settee while the lady called up the stairs.

"Darren! Someone's here to see you."

She came back and sat opposite Clovenhoof with a smile. She picked up some knitting, and started to work on it. Clovenhoof stared at the design. It looked as though it was the front of a jumper, or maybe even one of those stylish tank top garments. It was mostly black, but had red and white pentagrams up the sides.

He looked up as someone entered the room. It was a man in his mid-forties, with an enormous paunch and a receding hairline. He wore a tank top that was the twin of the one that was under construction.

"Hail, stranger," he said and gave a sharp wave of a heavily be-ringed hand in greeting.

"Hail... Pitspawn?" said Clovenhoof uncertainly.

"You're Ben's mate, right?"

"That's me."

The lady with the bun set down her knitting and stood up.

"Darren, show your friend upstairs and I'll get you some squash."

"Mom, I've told you, it's not Darren, it's Pitspawn! Can I have a straw, seeing as we've got a guest?"

She nodded and went to the kitchen. Pitspawn mumbled something that sounded like "silly bitch" and gave Clovenhoof a look that suggested that Clovenhoof surely understood how annoying the little woman must be.

"Ben rang and said that you might be in touch."

"Yes," said Clovenhoof. "I need a Satanist."

Pitspawn nodded obligingly.

"I am a humble servant of the Great Adversary. Do you want to come up to my room and see some of the cool stuff I've got?"

"Sure."

They climbed the stairs and entered a large back room in which someone had done their best to obliterate the blue floral wallpaper with posters, banners and flags. Skulls, goats' heads, demonic faces and occult symbols figured largely. Statuettes and candles dotted the shelves and surfaces.

Clovenhoof picked up a demonic candlestick holder.

"That's Shalbriri, demon of blindness. One of my favourites." Pitspawn said. "Look at the detail, it's genuine cast resin."

"You do know that Shalbriri's female?" Clovenhoof asked, turning the ugly, masculine demon in his hands.

"I think there might be some debate on that matter, actually," said Pitspawn with a flick of his comb-over, "the man in the shop was pretty certain that Shalbriri's male."

"Take it from me," said Clovenhoof with a wink, "she's all woman."

Pitspawn indicated that Clovenhoof should take a seat. There were two chairs that looked like a pair of ebony thrones. Clovenhoof discovered that they were actually typists chairs fitted with a kind of elaborate gothic chair-cosy. He wondered if these were also the handiwork of Pitspawn's mother.

"So what do Satanists actually do?" Clovenhoof asked.

"We revere Satan, the vital force in our lives. We reject the white-light hypocrites and practise the occult arts."

"It's good that you've been practising," agreed Clovenhoof, "because I need some of your occult arts."

"I am a competent sorcerer," said Pitspawn, "but a lot of people misunderstand what it is we do. What do you require?"

"Do you think that you could send someone to hell?"

Pitspawn stroked his chin and pondered for a moment.

"Send someone to hell? Physically, like?"

"Yes. Me, in fact."

Pitspawn picked a book off his shelf and pored over it. Clovenhoof tried to see what it was called, but it had a thickly embroidered cover, featuring the pentagram motif once more. He wheeled his Satanic throne a little closer and read the page header.

"*Occult Rituals for Dummies*?" said Clovenhoof.

"Yeah, yeah, I think I could do that," Pitspawn muttered, ignoring him. "I can do summonings. Maybe even resurrections. Sending someone *to* Hell is just the reverse, isn't it? Why do you want to go there, exactly?"

"It's a personal errand."

"You know you can be an effective Satanist on earth."

"Believe me when I say it's where I belong. I need you to perform the ritual now, on me. Do you need anything special, like a goat to sacrifice?"

"No, no. Mother would never – I mean it's not really necessary for a modern Satanist to indulge in that kind of thing."

"Then what's that?" said Clovenhoof, pointing to a short,

stubby sword hanging point down on the wall above the single bed. "Not a sacrificial blade?"

"That's more for the look of things," said Pitspawn.

Clovenhoof peered at the brown flecks along the blade's edge.

"So that's rust, not blood?" said Clovenhoof.

"Absolutely. There are rules. Doing all that nasty stuff gets us a bad name. No, we mostly get our powers from words, symbols and crystals. We hone these rituals over a lifetime of careful study to ensure we're in tune with the powers of Satan."

"Oh, okay. So I guess if Satan ever walked the earth, then you'd be one of the first to know?"

Pitspawn laughed.

"If that momentous day ever comes, there will be a vibration through my very being, so deep and so resonant that I will not be able to rest until I seek out and serve my master. It is the day that I am primed and ready for. I am but a foot-soldier, preparing the way for that glorious time, whether it's in my lifetime or not."

Clovenhoof raised his eyebrows.

"Right. Well it's good to know that you are so highly attuned to your master. In the meantime, can we get on and do the ritual?"

"Yes, OK. I will arrange the crystals. Move your chair to the middle of the rug."

Clovenhoof moved into position. There was a knock at the door.

"Here's your squash, Darren. And some crispy pancakes to share with your friend."

"It's Pitspawn, mom!"

"Darren, are those my crystal animals?"

Clovenhoof looked down to see that each point of the pentagram sported a different creature. A frog, a deer, a cat, an elephant and a dolphin. The cat had a jaunty smile painted on its face.

"Er, yes. I'll put them back in a minute," Pitspawn said.

"Darren, you know they're collectables."

"Yes mom. I'll take good care of them. Now please leave! We're in the middle of something important."

As his mother left, Pitspawn rolled his eyes and fell upon the plate of food.

"Want some?" he spluttered around a mouthful. "Findus crispy pancakes."

Clovenhoof took one of the baked semi-circles from the plate and tried it. He sniffed its golden exterior and then bit into it, releasing the fragrant cheesy savoury insides.

He moaned with pleasure and realised that this was the most perfect food that he'd yet encountered since arriving on Earth.

"These are brilliant," he said, making sure he grabbed another before Pitspawn finished the lot. "Is your mother the only person who can make them?"

Pitspawn laughed, spitting crumbs.

"You know, you've got the weirdest sense of humour. I like you!"

"I like me too."

Pitspawn put the plate to one side and stood over Clovenhoof, swaying gently.

He put the open book on the side, where he could see it, and picked up a smoking joss stick.

"I anoint the crystals to please the worshipful deities," he intoned, and bobbed the joss stick around the crystal animals. He stopped to blow ash off the dolphin, glancing nervously at the doorway.

"A sacrifice of blood for His Satanic Majesty."

He dipped his finger into the blackcurrant squash and smeared it lightly across Clovenhoof's forehead.

Clovenhoof sighed as it ran down his face.

"Why don't we just say that His Satanic Majesty is very pleased with you, and move on?" he suggested.

Pitspawn frowned but flipped the page.

"By the power of the sea at fullest surge. By the power of the wind across the highest peaks of the world, by the power of chaos that topples the mighty and challenges everything, I humbly summon the form of Belial, to guide this servant to the splendour of your palatial quarters, that he might seek a place at your feet."

Pitspawn continued to baste the crystal animals with smoky touches, and capered as nimbly as a twenty stone man can caper around the seated Clovenhoof. His eyes were half-closed and he made a low, tuneless humming sound.

Clovenhoof waited for the buzz of hellish intervention. He braced himself for the whoosh of sudden displacement. The only sound he heard was a light tap on the door.

"Darren," said his mother, with her head round the door, "I don't want to interrupt, but I think we might need to get some thicker underlay for your carpet."

"Mom, I'm busy!"

"All I can hear downstairs is you stamping around. I think it might be bringing on a migraine, so please stop it, will you love?"

Pitspawn kicked the door shut as his mother left and grunted with frustration.

"So, did it feel as though anything was happening?"

"Not a thing," said Clovenhoof.

Pitspawn sighed heavily.

"Maybe I'm not the right person for this. Most of these rituals are supposed to summon things from hell, not send them there. You sort of want someone who works things from the other end."

"Eh?"

"What you want is an exorcism."

"You mean like a priest?"

Pitspawn shrugged.

Clovenhoof took a quick swig of squash, and pulled a face at Pitspawn.

"You know, you should really ask your mom to get you some Lambrini. This stuff's terrible."

He found an Anglican church.

Of course, it was called St Michaels. He'd passed it before, but never got this close.

He walked up to the door and banged loudly. There was a stone carving above the door of Michael standing triumphantly on top of the Great Dragon. At least he supposed it was meant to be the Great Dragon.

"What, you hired a blind sculptor? You made me look

like a cat. And as cats go, I've seen scarier ones peeking out of flowerpots!"

A blonde-framed face appeared in the doorway.

"Hello," she said.

Clovenhoof noted the dog collar.

"You'd be Father...?"

"Reverend. Steed. Evelyn. I'm the rector. Are you all right?"

"I need an exorcism."

Her eyes opened wide in a deliberate expression of scepticism.

"I get people wanting to come in for a quick pray, mistakenly ask for confession, perhaps begging for a place to kip but... exorcism?"

"Do you do them?"

"That would be a matter for the diocesan Deliverance Ministry. Look, come in."

Clovenhoof extended a tentative hoof across the threshold of the church, wondering if he would burst into flames. Nothing. He trotted onto holy ground, slightly disappointed that it wasn't so different to the ground outside.

He followed her into the body of the empty church. At the back of the church hung a large modern tapestry, again depicting the Archangel Michael's victory over the Great Dragon, Satan. At least they hadn't hired a blind weaver.

"Are you going to come sit with me?" said the Reverend Evelyn Steed.

Clovenhoof joined her on a pew.

"What's your name?" she said.

"Jeremy."

"Well, Jeremy, a lot of people experience 'disturbances' in their lives but we don't get much call for exorcisms in the modern church. People don't fear evil spirits or demons so much these days. In fact there's debate about whether or not demons really exist."

"You are kidding me?"

"No. We live in a rational and a sceptical age."

"Well, if the church doesn't believe in demons, what about Satan?" asked Clovenhoof.

"Satan represents the idea of rejecting God. That's very real."

"But Satan's not just an idea!"

"No?"

"He's got horns," he pointed at the top of his head, "and hooves," he waggled a hoof at her.

"Well that image has certainly got a strong hold in the popular imagination," she said and then gave him a shrewd look. "You weren't watching *The Devil Rides Out* last night, were you?"

"Might have been."

"This horned devil image has parallels in lots of ancient cultures, and for hundreds of years, there's been reinforcement of those scary images. But think about this. Satan, Lucifer, was a former angel. If he looked like anything, he'd look like that."

She indicated the tapestry behind them. Clovenhoof scowled at the image.

"We can't even imagine what Heaven is like," said Evelyn. "It's not all clouds and harps and halos."

"No," said Clovenhoof. "It's all computerised. Even St Peter has a tablet computer."

"Pardon?"

"Nothing."

Clovenhoof gave a small snort as he remembered Peter and his high-tech gadget.

WALKING BACK along the dwindling line of people heading for Hell, Satan spotted St Peter up ahead. He was easily recognised. Sure, there were the keys at his belt, the symbols of his office, but, more than that, there was swagger of a man who was the most powerful mortal in the afterlife and who knew it. Peter – 'The Rock' - was turning his well-practised smile on the new arrivals, and either waving them to the right, or giving them a dismissive flick to the left. To the right, a row of rainbow-spangled angels placed garlands of flowers on those bound for Heaven and gently guided them towards a brightly lit portal of sparkling lights. Those that headed left were met by Hell's demons, guided down the road to damnation and jabbed with pitchforks to both hurry them along and give them a flavour of what was yet to come.

St Peter had a helper by his side. This short, jowly man carried a large ledger, while Peter worked from a state-of-the-art tablet computer.

"You've not been here long," said Satan to the jowly man

as he approached. "You've still got some colour in your cheeks."

The man made a disdainful moue with his rather feminine lips and turned to Peter.

"Is this who I think it is, sir?" he asked.

"Yes Herbert." Peter said. "Don't worry, I shall deal with our guest. Would you hold this for a moment and keep things flowing?"

"Oh yes, of course!" Herbert scurried off with the tablet.

"Prick," Satan sniggered.

Peter bristled.

"You're a long way from home, Lucifer. What brings you out here?"

"I came to see why you're sending me so many people. Can't you see they're backing up?"

Peter gave him a superior *don't-you-know-I'm-the-rock-on-which-God's-church-is-built?* look.

"They're backing up because you're not processing them fast enough."

Satan paused, wanting to punch Peter for being smug and superior but holding back because it occurred to him that he might be able to learn something.

"There are problems," he admitted. "It's not easy to get them all across the Styx and even the gate's jammed."

"You need to expand, modernise," Peter said.

"We have the ferries across the Styx. They run all day every day and still it's not enough."

"I heard you were digging a tunnel, whatever happened to that?"

Satan sighed. "That didn't go too well. It flooded and we

had to fill it in with the bodies of executive engineers from Union Carbide. We started a bridge, but it's never easy getting that lot to work on a project. They're all too busy trying to stab each other in the back. Literally."

"It sounds to me as though you need some modern management techniques."

"New pitchforks?" Satan asked.

"No, a framework to ensure everyone is working to their best ability. You need to delegate some responsibility."

"You do this stuff in Heaven?"

"Oh yes," Peter said, "we've been doing it for some time, and you can see that things are working pretty smoothly." He indicated with a sweep of his arm that the Heavenly process was working as smoothly as ever.

Satan looked at him shrewdly, waiting for the catch.

"But why would Heaven want to help Hell? We're not exactly on the same side."

"*We*," said Peter and by 'we' he meant 'God and all the angels and me, that most beloved of all mortals.' "*We* have responsibility for all of the afterlife. We want to see it running as efficiently as possible, and we're getting a lot of negative feedback at the moment."

"Negative feedback?"

"Complaints," Peter explained.

Satan rolled his eyes.

"So God has responsibility for all of this. I suppose there's something in that. Where is he anyway? I haven't seen him in ages."

"He won't be going out of his way to see *you* now, will he? I think it might be an idea if I send someone round to see you. Just a little chat, see if we can work something out."

"That's very decent of you," said Satan.

Peter smiled.

CLOVENHOOF REALISED he was staring with fury at the tapestry of Michael.

He looked at Evelyn.

"Can you exorcise me or not?" he said. "I'm pretty sure it's the only answer for me."

"You are? Tell me what's troubling you."

"I'm being forced to live amongst cushions and kittens."

"Right."

"I met a bloke who claims to worship me."

"That's nice."

"But he didn't even recognise who I was."

"So this a relationship issue?"

"The police arrested me twice."

"Oh."

"But your mate off the tapestry got me out."

"Er."

Evelyn's brow creased with confusion.

"I can't say that I understand your troubles – not all of them - but you're obviously feeling them very deeply."

"Is that a yes to the exorcism?"

"Perhaps you would like to talk to me some more about these problems."

"So it's a no."

"Jeremy. I'm here to listen, if you would like that."

Clovenhoof shook his head and walked out of the church.

He stopped outside the door to flick a bogey at the stone Michael and headed for home.

THE FOX HAD BEEN dead for some time. It lay matted and muddy in the gutter of the Chester Road. Clovenhoof stopped to look at it and sniffed the pungent smell of decay. He lifted the corpse and turned it over in his hands. The crumpled bloody mess on its underside indicated that it had been hit by a car. The eyes were collapsed and he wondered how long it would be before the fox's head became a skull. He thought back to the décor in Pitspawn's attic room and decided that he would take Michael's advice and give his flat some homely touches. Skulls would be cool. The smell itself was so interesting that it reminded him of the old place. He inhaled deeply and carried the carcase back to the flat.

He spent the rest of the day looking for other skulls. He'd walked the streets and found a roadkill cat, but the mother lode was among the scrubby area by the garages behind the house. Three rats, bloated with poison had expired near to some fragrant sacks of rubbish. Clovenhoof thought the whole scene had a certain poetry to it, and it almost felt wrong to remove the rats from the tableau.

HE ARRIVED BACK at the flat with his collection and found a small basket outside.

He read the card:

To our new neighbour,
    Do pop up and say hello when you're settled.
    Love Nerys.
    X

HE UNCOVERED the basket and tried one of the mince pies. The pastry was dry and the mincemeat content was like squashed bugs sprinkled with sugar.

They weren't crispy pancakes, but that couldn't be helped.

HE SET to work taking the skulls from the bodies. It was harder than he's imagined. He went into the kitchen to find something to help him. A corkscrew shaped like a fish was handy for reaming out the eye sockets, while a large pair of scissors was handy for de-skinning and trimming off the bits he didn't want. Try as he might though, he couldn't get the skulls to look properly shiny and skull-like. They had bits of icky gore stuck all over them.

He held them over the gas flames that had been burning since he moved in, and although it made a strong and not unpleasant odour, the bits remained firmly attached to the bone. He picked at them with a fingernail, but that was quite hard work. It did taste better than mince pies though, he reflected as he sucked his finger. The thought of Nerys and her peculiar pies made him sit up straight. She had a machine in her kitchen for cleaning things. He'd seen it before. Surely, that would work on these skulls.

He went upstairs, cradling his flesh-encrusted skulls and knocked on the door.

There was no reply. He gave the door a hefty kick to see if it might just pop open. He had to kick it a few more times quite hard before the frame splintered and the door did indeed pop open.

In the kitchen, he opened the dishwasher and lodged his skulls in between the plates and cups that were already in there. Nerys's little rat-dog creature, Twinkle, had yapped at him ever since he had entered the flat and seemed intent on hauling Clovenhoof's prize goodies from the dishwasher. Irritated, Clovenhoof scooped up the long-haired beasty and put it in the fridge where its barks were muffled to bearable levels.

Clovenhoof closed the dishwasher door and pressed buttons until something happened. The sound of water filling the machine satisfied him that it was doing its work. He decided to explore the flat while he waited for the skull cleansing to be complete.

He went into one of the bedrooms and decided that this probably belonged to Nerys's elderly aunt. There were ornaments and pictures galore. He groaned at the hideousness of the soppy decor.

"Does my work never end?" he said and hurled a china shepherdess at a picture of round-faced children smiling out from underneath an umbrella and felt better.

There was nothing else in there to see, so he went into Nerys's bedroom. The bed was the focus of the room, piled high with silk and satin cushions in shades of deep red and purple. If people bled soft furnishings then this would be a bloodbath. He poked one and wondered if it was stuffed with real feathers. He ripped it apart without too much trouble.

He swung it and watched the feathers drift lazily around the room. This was better! He ripped a couple more cushions, making a snowstorm and scanned the rest of the room. He found a lingerie drawer, and held up lacy garments, trying to work out how they would fit onto a body. Some of them defied study. He stretched a pair of tiny panties off his thumb and pinged them across the room and then spent several minutes using her remaining panties to try to hit the framed picture of David Suchet. He improved his aim as he worked his way through the drawer.

There were lots of books on shelves, but he was drawn to the one that was open on the bedside table. It contained many handwritten entries. He looked at the front, which was lettered with something that might have been red nail varnish, saying, "The Hunt for Mr Right, Volume 3".

Clovenhoof opened the book and found a catalogue of men, some identified by single names others by full name and even titles, each assessed according to a variety of unclear criteria. He found an entry for Ben Kitchen. It seemed that Ben scored well for attentiveness but badly on personal appearance. There was a column entitled "Skills between the sheets" but Ben had "not applicable" under that one. Under the mysterious heading of "Poirot Scale", he once again scored badly.

Clovenhoof flicked through page after page, fascinated by the range of the research. The dates stretched back over the last five years and there were well over a hundred entries. Towards the end, he saw his own name. He was appalled to discover that he scored badly on almost everything; there was actually a "hahaha" under the "Poirot Scale" column. However, he did notice that there was a scribbled note saying "indefinable something" just underneath his name.

He slammed the book shut and stood up as he heard an irritating yipping bark.

He walked into the kitchen to find Twinkle had escaped from the fridge. The fact that Nerys was stood there beside the open fridge door might have had something to do with it. Nerys's mouth hung open as she gazed round in horror, the mistletoe that she was carrying hanging limply by her side.

"What on earth are you doing here?" she squeaked.

"Your note said to pop up." Clovenhoof said, waving the piece of paper.

"And you found it like this?"

"Er, yes," he said.

Nerys twirled around in anger.

"Just look at the state of the place! Burglars. I can't believe it! Aunt Molly's going to need fetching from the hairdresser's within the hour and there's so much to do. I need a locksmith, and a cleaning service, and I need to call the police and get a crime number, and – why's the dishwasher on?"

She pulled open the door of the dishwasher and saw the skulls. She screamed and staggered backwards.

"Oh my God! I've heard about this kind of thing. I'm going to have to throw away all of the toothbrushes."

"Toothbrushes?"

"Apparently they break in and... defile your things."

"Do they?" said Clovenhoof with interest.

"I bet it's all over YouTube by now."

"You're right, it's a disgrace," he agreed, not having a clue what a YouTube was. "How about I take those out of your way?" Clovenhoof suggested, scooping up the gleaming skulls with a smile.

"Are you sure?" she said. "I do appreciate it."

Clovenhoof disappeared as quickly as he could, and placed the pristine skulls in pride of place on the shelves in his front room. He was particularly pleased with the fox skull, with its wide eye sockets and prominent canine teeth. As he stepped back from admiring it, crunching over the glass and porcelain remains of unworthy ornaments, he glanced from the window and saw a police car pull up.

He thought he recognised the policeman who stepped out.

Opting for discretion, he waited until he heard Nerys take them up the stairs to her flat, then slipped quietly out of the front door.

. . .

H<small>E FOUND</small> a supermarket not far from the spot where he had been unceremoniously dumped on this plane three days earlier.

He wandered in and took one of the wheeled food chariots that they thoughtfully provided. He ran down the centre aisle and launched himself on top of the trolley. His high-speed freewheeling was curtailed by a large security guard who brought him to a halt by grabbing the handle.

"How old are you, mate?" said the security guard.

"As old as creation," said Clovenhoof. "And how old are you..." - he peered at the man's name badge - "Doog? Dowg?"

The security guard rolled his eyes.

"Doug," said the guard. "And too old for this. Just push the trolley, mate. No monkey business."

Clovenhoof walked the aisles, marvelling at the array of goods. He came to the Lambrini and found that there were numerous flavours. He stopped a woman who seemed dressed to match the shop's decor so was probably in thrall to the shop's masters.

"Can I just put these in my trolley and take as many as I want?" he asked.

She laughed.

"As long as you've got the money to pay, duck, no-one's going to stop you."

"Really? How much money would I have to pay to make them stop playing that song about wishing it could be Christmas every day?"

She smiled at him in a way that made him think he wasn't the first person today to ask her that question.

He filled the trolley, stripping the shelves bare of Lambrini.

A thought crossed his mind.

What was that magical food Pitspawn had offered him.

"Do you have crispy pancakes?" he asked the shop-slave.

"Frozen food aisle," she said and pointed him in the right direction.

Four aisles over, he peered into the cabinets and saw them laid out. Row upon row of them. Findus Crispy Pancakes.

"And I have found you," he said and let out a whoop.

He went to fetch a second trolley, but on his return he saw that Pitspawn's mother was there, and that she had a trolley piled high with the precious delicacies.

His mind raced as he peered into the empty cabinet. He could not be robbed of his prize now that he'd found something worthwhile to eat.

She hadn't seen him, so he crept up behind her as she reached for the last few packets from the very bottom.

He bent down, grabbed her ankles and hoisted her quickly up and over the edge of the freezer. She screamed loudly as she landed upside down. Clovenhoof took her trolley and wheeled it briskly away. Doug, the security guard ran towards him.

"I think there's a lady having some trouble over there," Clovenhoof mentioned helpfully, in case Doug hadn't noticed her legs waggling in the air above the frozen food cabinet.

Clovenhoof managed to get his two trolleys through the

checkout before anyone came looking for him, and he even remembered to give them money as well.

As a final flourish to demonstrate how familiar he'd become with the ritual of shopping he slapped his buttocks and winked to the woman on Customer Service as he passed her on the way out.

Two old ladies were next in line at the checkout.

"He seemed cheerful, Doris. Maybe we should get what he's having?" said the first, unloading her basket.

"I don't think so. I'm quite happy with my Edam, thank you Betty," said the other primly, patting the enormous cheese in her basket.

"Is that all you're getting? Look, I've bought lots."

"Yes," said Doris, "but four bottles of sherry won't last you long. What's that other stuff you have there, tofu? Never heard of it."

"It's easy on my dentures. I read it in a magazine."

Doris pursed her lips.

"What have I told you about those magazines, Betty? That pesto's *never* coming out of that carpet."

HEAVEN

- Matters Arising
- The Shaker Enclave
- Seraphim Rota
- Earthly visitations
- The Throne
- Clovenhoof
- AOB

The Archangel Gabriel tidied his papers noisily.

"I don't see how it is appropriate."

Pope Pius XII leant across the table.

"I am merely sharing what the modern faithful are expecting."

"Because their heads are full of Hollywood movies and Saturday morning cartoons?"

The Archangel Michael, chairing, tried to intervene.

"Heaven *is* a place of music."

"But a harp for *every* angel?" said Gabriel. "Dry ice in the streets?"

Pius adjusted his glasses.

"Clouds and harps. That's all I'm saying."

"Maybe we can intwoduce them to one quarter of the Celestial City," suggested St Francis of Assisi. "For a twial pewiod."

"And create further balkanisation?" said Michael. "We have enough trouble getting the different denominations to mingle. I'm not going to carve up the City like a theme park with Ye Olde Harps and Clouds Heaven tucked away in one corner."

"In my Father's house there are many mansions," pronounced St Paul from the end of the table.

"Well, quite," said Michael. He could feel the Blessed Mother Teresa's gaze boring into him as she struggled, quill in hand, over the spelling of 'balkanisation' for the meeting's minutes.

St Peter tapped his heavy keys on the table, quietly but insistently.

"There are also certain logistical issues with the idea that I'm not going to bother explaining in this arena."

"Of course," said Michael. "I'm sorry, Pius. I'm going to put that one on the back-burner, maybe discuss it again at the next meeting. We *were* talking about the seraphim's rota for singing of eternal praises."

"Well, I don't see why *that* needs changing," said Gabriel.

"It's been fine for the last two thousand years," said St

Peter.

"Longer," said Gabriel.

"But," said Michael, "the question raised by one of the faithful is whether we need over ten million seraphim whose sole role is the singing of eternal praises to the Throne."

"Speaking of the Thwone..." began St Francis.

"That is a later item on the agenda," said Michael, cutting across him. "Let's deal with the issue in hand."

"But why are we even having this debate?" said Michael. "Have the seraphim been complaining about their duties?"

"No. The member of the faithful in question has asked if some of them could be diverted to other activities such as the beleaguered and understaffed Guardian Angel programme."

"Ridiculous," said Gabriel.

"Logistical issues," said St Peter for good measure.

"Who is this member of the faithful?" asked Pius. "Let him come before us to make his case."

"That's exactly what *she* wants to do."

St Paul coughed in surprise.

"If there is anything women desire to know let them ask their husbands at home," he growled.

Michael tried not to roll his eyes as he did every time Paul quoted his own epistles.

"Who is it?" asked Pius.

"Joan of Arc," said Michael.

St Peter tutted.

"We let her sit in on the Hell Project. Now this? Does she have political ambitions?"

"This committee always welcomes fresh perspectives," said Michael smoothly.

"Yes, it would be good to have a woman about the place," said Gabriel.

Michael looked down at Mother Teresa to see if she reacted but she was too busy over the spelling of 'perspectives'.

"I shall invite her to the next meeting then," said Michael, making a personal note. "Now, onto the subject of earthly visitations. This is definitely an area in which we *do* need a rota."

"Is there a pwoblem?" asked St Francis.

"I've had complaints about a certain donkey manifesting itself to the faithful on earth."

All eyes turned to St Francis.

"There are many donkeys in heaven," he said indignantly.

"But only one which makes spontaneous appearances on earth," said Michael.

"And is there a pwoblem with that?"

"Er, yes," said Michael.

"He was as faithful a servant and as good a Chwistian as one could ever hope to sit upon. He cwied at my deathbed, you know."

"We know."

Gabriel frowned.

"What spiritual or theological message are the faithful supposed to take away from a visitation by your donkey?" he asked.

St Francis pondered for a while.

"Be nice to animals," he decided. "Especially donkeys."

"I think any future apparitions by the blessed - angelic,

human or animal – need to be run by this committee first," said Michael.

"But what about the Holy Mother?" said St Francis frostily. "Where is she at the moment? Appearwing on a tea towel in Mexico? Making statues weep in Tokyo? She's never here. Are you going to tell Mary to wun her plans past this committee?"

Michael shook his head.

"Are you?" he said pointedly.

"No," said St Francis quietly.

"Next order of business?"

"The Thwone."

"Actually," said Peter, "I wondered if we could skip over that for now as I am keen to hear how the adversary is getting on in his new home."

Michael smiled with genuine pleasure.

"Satan – or Jeremy Clovenhoof, his *nom d'exile* – has taken to his new situation very well. He's been relocated exactly as suggested and looks ready to settle in for the long term."

"I thought he'd kick up a big fuss," said Gabriel.

"Your adversary prowls around like a roaring lion," Paul self-quoted, "seeking someone to devour."

"Actually," said Michael, "he was last seen in a supermarket, buying frozen ready meals. Hardly a roaring lion." He clicked his fingers in recollection and turned to St Francis. "We *must* have a word about your lions-laying-down-with-lambs project, Francis."

St Francis winced.

"Teething pwoblems. That's all."

"Actually, I think the teeth *are* the problem."

IN WHICH CLOVENHOOF DISCOVERS HEAVY METAL, TAKES TO THE STAGE AND BECOMES A ROCK GOD

C lovenhoof tried to ignore the sounds coming from the stairway outside his flat, the dull flat thumps and the sharp juddering snaps. He also successfully ignored the hissed reprimands and the wheedling replies but it was the loud crash followed by a long and inventive curse that piqued his interest.

He opened the door and looked out.

Nerys stood, fists on hips, staring furiously at Ben and the large upright parcel perched on the stairs, a parcel that was threatening to crush Ben and bear his remains down to the ground floor.

Clovenhoof cleared his throat.

"What the hell is this?"

Nerys gave him a bright smile.

"This is my New Year's resolution."

"To kill Kitchen?"

"No, it's –"

"It's admirable," said Clovenhoof. "Worthy, even. Best of luck."

He began to close the door.

"I think Ben could do with a hand," said Nerys.

"I'd love to," said Clovenhoof, "but I'm not really a problem *solver*."

"Just do it," said Nerys.

BY THE TIME the parcel was in Nerys's living room, Clovenhoof had chipped a hoof and Ben had a livid graze on the back of one hand. Twinkle was sniffing around the package's base.

"What is it?" said Clovenhoof.

"It's a harp."

"As in instrument of the angelic hosts?"

"Yes."

"I should have pushed in the other direction."

"I thought you were," said Ben.

Nerys stroked the brown cardboard wrappings tenderly.

"I've always wanted to play a musical instrument."

"A recorder would have been easier," said Clovenhoof.

"And lighter," said Ben.

She scoffed.

"No sense of ambition, you two."

"Oh, I have ambitions!" said Clovenhoof.

"Wearing a permanent butt-groove in your sofa is not an ambition."

Clovenhoof looked at Ben.

"I don't think it is," conceded Ben.

"You need to do something constructive with your time," she said, jabbing a finger towards Clovenhoof before swinging it on to Ben. "And you... you need to get out more."

"Me?" said Ben.

"Sitting in your dingy flat playing with your toy soldiers is not healthy."

"They're miniature scale models," protested Ben but Nerys wasn't listening.

"You mustn't let life pass you by."

Nerys looked at them. It was the sad, affectionate, look of a woman who's about to have a favourite puppy made into a nice pair of gloves.

"I see," said Clovenhoof.

"Now, who is going to help me unwrap this and set it up?"

"I – " began Ben but Clovenhoof spoke across.

"Kitchen can't."

"Oh?" said Nerys.

"He's got to go out more. New Year's resolution."

"Oh, well, you..."

"I'm taking him out," said Clovenhoof, already pushing Ben towards the door. "Doing something constructive with my time."

They were out on the landing before Nerys could reply.

"Where are we going?" said Ben.

"Alcohol."

"Alcohol's not a place."

"It's a destination."

OUTSIDE THE BOLDMERE OAK, shoppers shuffled through the grey drizzle, weighed down by their spoils from the January sales. Inside, Ben sipped at his cider and black while Clovenhoof played with the stem of his already-finished Lambrini. In a back room, there was the groan of wildly distorted music.

"In hell," said Clovenhoof, apropos of nothing, "there is a freezing, turgid river of black water and the sullen and miserable lie on the bed of that river, surrounded by icy darkness."

"Is there?" said Ben.

Clovenhoof nodded.

"I was awake at midnight on New Year's Eve."

"Yes?"

"I stood in front of my window and looked out at the world."

"You mean at the houses across the road? We're not very high up."

"Specifically at the houses across the road but more generally at the whole world."

"Were there fireworks?"

Clovenhoof shook his head.

"It was raining. I looked at the world and thought, 'I'm stuck here. I'm not going back.'"

"Back where?" asked Ben.

Clovenhoof had, from the off, struck Ben as deeply unhappy in his new home, like an elderly relative thrust into a care home that had recently featured on a consumer watchdog programme. Part of him wondered if he was a political exile but Clovenhoof's accent was a not-particularly-regional but definitely English accent and Ben couldn't imagine that there were many people exiled in disgrace from Leicester or Cambridge or Nottingham.

"The river," said Clovenhoof. "The pit. The Old Place."

"Ah."

"So, I thought I'd use my time here to put things in order, set the record straight. I thought I'd write my side of the story. The Other Guy got a best-seller out of it. Why can't I?"

"So, you're writing your autobiography?" said Ben.

Clovenhoof dipped into his pockets and scattered a dozen bits of screwed up paper and post-its onto the table with the flair of a crap magician who couldn't afford doves.

"It's not as easy as it looks..."

He had sat down at midnight with pen and paper and waited for the words to come. The ideas and concepts, vivid and angry things, boiled at the forefront of his mind, but translating those ideas into mere words proved difficult. The words were there, out of focus and elusive but he was sure they were there. Through the hours of the early morning, he tried to coax them forth, along his arm and out through the pen but the only thing to emerge was a trickle of pureed bollocks.

"You've written the words, 'In the beginning' a lot and then crossed it out," said Ben.

"They're *his* words," said Clovenhoof.

Ben unscrewed another ball of paper which appeared to be a list of titles.

"'Be my Enemy.' 'Tempted by the Fruit.' 'Sympathy for the Devil.' Aren't these song titles?"

"Are they?" said Clovenhoof with a lacklustre sigh. "I need another drink. Do you want one?"

"Yes, please."

"Give me some money then."

Ben read further whilst rummaging in his pocket for a tenner.

"'The Fallen One Rises.' 'Bloody Scapegoat.' 'Cursed by Fools.' I don't remember these songs. Cool titles though. 'Glory to the Beast.' Was that an Iron Maiden track?"

Lennox, the barman, had to go and change the barrel for the cider. As he opened the door into the back, the muffled background music was released, transformed into a not overly tuneful collision of rapid bass beats and frenetic electric guitar.

Clovenhoof stared into his fresh Lambrini while he waited but even the light bubbles of golden perry failed to raise his spirits much.

It was infuriating. He had assumed that writing would have come to him so easily. He wanted vindication in print form. He wanted everyone to know the indignities and betrayals he had suffered.

'Feel the hatred of all damned in hell!'

He wanted to force feed every page of his story into Michael's smug and well-meaning mouth until the words stuck in his craw and he choked on them.

'Flesh starts to burn, twist and deform!'

Yeah, what did Michael know about eternal torment?

He'd never so much as dipped his toe in the Lake of Fire. That self-righteous prig!

'Learn the sacred words of praise, hail Satan!'

A glass was placed clumsily in front of him.

"Hail Satan," said Clovenhoof, startled.

"Er," said Lennox. "That's four twenty."

Clovenhoof looked at the cider and black.

"Right," he said and handed over the tenner.

He straightened up and listened to the horrific – wonderful! – chanting coming from the back room, accompanied by that music that sounded like a thousand squeaky toys being fed into an industrial shredder.

'Master the forces and powers of Satan! Controlling the creature's instincts!'

"There you go."

Lennox passed Clovenhoof his change.

"What is that?" asked Clovenhoof, nodding towards the back room.

"Oh, I'm sorry. It's my brother-in-law's band. They're practising at the moment. They sometimes play at our open mic nights if we don't have any decent acts. Look, I'll go tell them to turn it down."

"No, no," said Clovenhoof. "It's really quite beautiful."

"Is it?"

Clovenhoof pocketed Ben's change, picked up the glasses and moved round the bar and through to the back of the pub.

Down the end of short corridor was a grey room, perhaps once a snooker room, now home to a dozen kegs of beer, stacked crates of bottled drink, a small mountain of industrial cleaning fluids and a four-piece group of long-haired gentlemen who seemed hell bent on torturing their instruments to death, particularly the drummer. The demented man was thrashing about as though fending off a horde of invisible tarantulas who had taken sincere offence to his bleached shoulder-length hair. Clovenhoof watched from the doorway, mesmerised.

The lead singer and guitarist half-mumbled, half-screamed his way through the last couplet of his song, something about angels searching for salvation, and then raised his hand to bring it to a close.

He brushed several locks away from his sweaty brow and looked at Clovenhoof.

"Can we help you?"

"Well," said Clovenhoof, grinning. "First of all, thanks. That was really something. What do you call that?"

"It's an old Slayer number, *Altar of Sacrifice*. You liked?"

"I liked. Do you play other songs like that?"

The singer jiggled his head.

"We do a lot of Slayer covers. A few Judas Priest numbers. A bit of Black Sabbath."

Judas Priest! Black Sabbath! The names were delicious things. And if the songs produced by them were as tantalising as the one he had just heard...

"You're not a talent scout, are you?" asked the bassist. "We're ready to take this to the next level, you know? Reach out to a wider audience."

Clovenhoof's head was abuzz with ideas, notions and half-formed plans.

"I'm sorry," he said. "I'm just an enthusiastic amateur. Always have been."

"You took your time," said Ben when Clovenhoof returned with the drinks.

"They were out of cider. The barman had to get some more."

"Where from? The West Country? Have I got any change?"

"Shut up. Have you heard of a band called Slayer?"

"The heavy metal band? Yeah."

"What about Judas Priest? And Black Sabbath?"

"Of course," said Ben. "They're local bands."

"What? From round here?"

Ben gestured through the wall in a roughly southerly direction.

"They're Birmingham boys."

"You mean we could go see them?"

Ben smiled as he shook his head.

"They're *from* Birmingham. The best heavy metal bands come from places people are only too keen to get away from. It's part of the... you know, inspiration... shitty grey nowhere towns."

"You seem to know a huge amount about these heavy metal bands," said Clovenhoof.

Ben drained the remains of his first drink and pulled the second towards him.

"Well, I was a bit of a metal-head in my youth."

Clovenhoof tried to see any resemblance between this bland-looking nerd and the shaggy-haired berserkers he had just met and found none.

"Really, Ben? I just picture you as the kind of man who spent his youth shut away in his bedroom, playing with himself and wondering why he couldn't get any girls."

"Classic metal fan," said Ben blithely, taking a first sip of his new drink. "Anyway, I've still got some of the old records back at the flat if you fancy a listen."

Clovenhoof was suddenly standing up.

"What?" said Ben.

"Drink up."

EXACTLY NINE MINUTES LATER, they were in Ben's flat, Clovenhoof sat in the open doorway of the broom cupboard, looking through a box of vinyl LPs while Ben loaded one up on a turntable he had reclaimed from behind a dust-covered synthesiser keyboard at the back of the cupboard.

As a loud pounding bass riff rippled through the flat, Clovenhoof flicked from album cover to album cover. Most of them were lurid painted covers, of hideous beast men, of rotting corpses and of people wearing very little clothing. Several of them were clearly meant to be depictions of Hell or something very much like it. Here, a Black Sabbath album in which a blood red orgy was overseen by a distorted skeletal figure. Here, a naked muscle-bound woman with a horned skull for a head plunged a knife into her sacrificial victim on the cover of Danzig's *Demonsweatlive*. Here, a woman being held down by her undead torturers as slime-covered creatures burst out of...

Clovenhoof held up the album for Ben to see.

"Cannibal Corpse," said Ben. "Yeah, that one was a gift from my mum. Hmmm. She tries."

"And who's this meant to be?" asked Clovenhoof, pointing at giant cat-faced being on Pantera's *Metal Magic*.

"I think that's meant to be Satan."

"I thought so," said Clovenhoof. "Don't see the resemblance myself. I mean, it hasn't even got any horns."

There was a thumping at the door. Ben sidled past Clovenhoof to open it and revealed a thunder-faced Nerys.

"What the hell is that racket?" she demanded loudly.

"*Be My Slave* by Bitch."

"What did you call me?"

Ben scuttled back to the turntable and killed the music.

"Sorry," he said.

"That din is coming right through our floor. It's setting Aunt Molly's teeth on edge and is seriously interfering with my harp practice."

"Is it going well?" asked Ben.

Nerys hesitated.

"Not exactly," she said. "I think the shop might have strung it incorrectly. That's the only reason I can think of."

She looked down at Clovenhoof.

"What *are* you doing?"

He delivered her a wide, toothy grin.

"We're starting a heavy metal band," he declared.

"We're what?" said Ben.

"Isn't it obvious?"

"Is it?"

"We're in a shitty grey nowhere town. Exactly the kind of place heavy metal springs from. Heavy metal is all about Satanic music for loners who play with themselves. I know everything there is to know about Satan. You know everything there is to know about playing with yourself. I need a creative outlet. You need to get out more. It's perfect!"

"Right," said Ben, taken aback. "What instruments will we play?"

Clovenhoof yanked the dust-covered keyboard out of the cupboard and held it up triumphantly.

"It's years since I've played it," said Ben. "It wheezes like an asthmatic and occasionally picks up CB radio signals."

"Details!"

"Madness, Jeremy!" said Nerys. "Can you play any instrument at all?"

Clovenhoof blew out his lips and shrugged.

"How hard can it be?"

THE FIRST PARCELS arrived at flat 2a the following morning. There were seven of them and they were quite large.

Clovenhoof, who was still getting to grips with the plastic credit cards he had been given, was amazed by how quickly large and expensive items could be made to appear at your door by reading out a string of numbers over the phone and saying 'yes' to every question.

From Nerys's flat above came faint tuneless twanging sounds, intermittently punctuated by vehement swearing. It sounded like an archery contest for Tourette's sufferers. It added to the warm glow in Clovenhoof's heart as he set about investigating his purchases. He had unwrapped a mixer desk, a four foot amplifier and was pulling the plastic sheeting from his silver-painted axe-shaped electric guitar when he abruptly realised he was not alone in his flat.

"Come out, Michael," he said.

The archangel came in from the kitchen, carrying two glasses.

"I was just mixing a cocktail," he said.

Clovenhoof looked at the pink frothy drink he was being offered. He wasn't aware of having any pineapple juice or cherry liqueur in his poorly stocked kitchen, nor indeed any of the other ingredients of a Singapore Sling. He certainly didn't have any bendy straws or cocktail umbrellas, not that such niggling reality-nuggets would mean anything to Michael.

"You spying on me again?" said Clovenhoof, begrudgingly accepting the drink.

"No, this is a social visit."

"Yeah?" said Clovenhoof sceptically.

Michael smiled and walked around the flat, stepping over the strewn remains of the open parcels. He bent to pick up one of the many polystyrene packing chips.

"Non-biodegradable," he said sadly. "What is all *this*, Jeremy?"

"I'm starting a band."

"What kind of band?"

"The musical kind. I'm going to write the songs, sing, play lead guitar. I've got a friend who'll play keyboards."

"A friend? Well done, Jeremy." Michael gave him a big, supportive smile. "I suppose you do need something to do with your... retirement. What kind of songs?"

"My songs."

"Songs about what?"

"My experiences. What it means to be me."

"Hmmm," said Michael, continuing to pace. Clovenhoof noticed that wherever he trod, the carpet became instantly cleaner. He hoped he could entice the angel into doing a quick circuit of the hallway and the bathroom.

"You know what would happen if you tried to tell people who you really are?" said Michael.

"Strait-jacket. Padded room. A syringe full of anti-psychotics, I know," said Clovenhoof, adding silently to himself, *either that or offer me a recording contract.*

"And I imagine this musical equipment is quite costly," said Michael.

"No idea," said Clovenhoof honestly.

"Your remuneration package is meant to be a modest one. Heaven's coffers are not limitless, you know."

"Bollocks."

Michael gave Clovenhoof a long, evaluative look, up and down. In the silence, Nerys's battle with the harp appeared to be reaching some sort of conclusion, possibly mutually assured destruction.

Michael grunted lightly and smiled.

"I wish you every success, Jeremy."

"Well, I can't do any worse than her," said Clovenhoof, pointing upwards at the flat above.

"I may have had a hand in that," said Michael coyly.

"Oh, yes?"

"No mortal's going to play the harp on my watch. It *is* the preserve of angels."

He sipped the straw into his mouth and slurped deeply on his cocktail before giving a warm sigh.

"I always think it tastes like a piece of heaven."

"Not my cup of tea," said Clovenhoof and put his Singapore Sling down on the mantelpiece, untouched.

IN THE END, Clovenhoof reasoned, the whole project boiled down to writing the songs and performing them. Writing the songs was just matter of finding the words and composing the music. Performance merely entailed practice, finding a venue and, of course, developing the right sort of stage look. Broken down, it seemed terribly, terribly simple.

Clovenhoof had ordered himself a series of 'teach yourself guitar' books with accompanying CDs. He started at Book One, had mastered the chords of G, C and D within the hour and was playing a selection of Status Quo's greatest hits by tea-time. Whilst waiting for his Findus Crispy Pancakes to cook, he phoned Birmingham Symphony Hall and left a message on the answer phone asking if he could book the place for a concert that weekend or, failing that, the weekend following.

After dinner, he sat down with glass of Lambrini and tried to pen some songs. By midnight, he had written a dozen possible verses for a song tentatively titled *Fools in Paradise* but which by morning had morphed into the shout- and rage-filled *Swallow My Fruit, Bitch.*

Clovenhoof quickly moved through Books Two and Three of 'teach yourself guitar' and tried his hand at fingerpicking as well as chords. He scribbled down the notation for the songs he had written so far, now including *Soiled Angel* and *Night of the Morningstar* and took them down the high street to Ben's shop so that Ben could begin practising the keyboard parts. Ben stared at the ink-stained manuscripts, speechless. Clovenhoof took this as a good sign.

On the way, back he stopped in at a charity shop, where he bought a black leather jacket and some tight jeans, and then took a walk through Short Heath Park where he composed in his head a soaring power ballad entitled *Drowning in a Lake of Fire.*

At home, he tried on his new clothes and contemplated himself in the mirror. He decided that it wasn't quite enough and ordered some bondage gear over the phone. He then phoned Symphony Hall again and spoke to a polite but obviously dim-witted woman who, firstly, had no knowledge of his previous answer phone message and, secondly, seemed unable to grasp that he wanted to book the *venue*, not mere tickets.

CLOVENHOOF AND BEN held their first joint practice on Saturday morning. Clovenhoof had cleared all the furniture from his lounge to make room for amps, mikes, mixers, wires and an audience (should one magically appear). Ben plugged an audio lead into his keyboard. It produced an uneven droning sound, like a sleeping beehive.

"Are you ready?" said Clovenhoof, hefting his axe.

"Are you?" replied Ben.

Clovenhoof grinned and performed a fast-fingered lick that ran all the way down the fretboard.

"When did you say you first picked up a guitar?" said Ben.

"I don't know. What day of the week is it? Right, let's do *Spineless Disciples*."

They didn't have a drummer and neither knew how to count them in but by some happy accident they both stumbled into the first verse at roughly the same time. Clovenhoof thrashed through the chord changes D minor to G augmented seventh to E minor, leaned into the mic and let loose.

"Three times the cock did crow!
Christ denier! Christ denier!
A bunch of cocks all in a row!
Cowards and liars! Pants on fire!"

Clovenhoof launched into his solo with more enthusiasm than accuracy, ran a crazy tremolo-picking journey across the strings whilst Ben's antique keyboard swept around him with haunting and occasionally intentionally discordant chord changes. They rampaged through two more verses and then finished at roughly the same time.

Clovenhoof looked to Ben. Ben struggled to find the words.

"That was..."

"What?"

"That was actually quite good. You can sing."

Clovenhoof grinned but, for once, it was not a devilish smirk but the smile of someone whose chest was swelling with deserved pride.

"They do say I have all the best tunes," he said. "What was that weird chanting sound during verse two?"

"A local taxi cab company," said Ben, gesturing to his keyboard. "I did warn you."

"And that violent thumping sound?"

"No, that wasn't me."

The thumping sound came again as if on cue. It was the front door and, behind it, Nerys. She was holding a piece of broken wood in her hands with a series of catgut wires hanging from it. She was gripping it so tightly Clovenhoof could see the painted veneer cracking beneath her fingertips.

"How's the harp-playing going?" asked Clovenhoof.

Nerys growled.

"Whoever invented the harp was a sadist and a twat."

"You're not wrong. I could introduce you to him."

"Of course," she went on, pushing past him into the flat, "I would have had more success if I didn't have to listen to the crap booming out of this place."

"We were just agreeing on how good it was."

"Rubbish," she said, "You were – ugh! What's that?"

She pointed at Clovenhoof's Singapore Sling, which had stood untouched on the mantelpiece for several days now. A fine green mould had grown across its surface and was gamely climbing up the cocktail umbrella.

"It's a cocktail," said Clovenhoof.

"I meant the green fuzz growing in it."

"I'm thinking of calling it Herbert."

"Herbert?" said Ben.

"I need a pet," said Clovenhoof. Herbert was the name of one of the most obsequious and oily of the recently deceased he had met. It struck him as fitting.

"Anyway," said Nerys, "the timing was awful. You" – she pointed at Ben – "got completely lost and started playing Greensleeves at one point."

"I panicked," said Ben.

"And you, Jeremy, couldn't keep time between your voice and your guitar."

"I disagree."

"Yeah?" Nerys picked up a discarded fork from the floor, brushed Findus Crispy Pancake crumbs from its tines and held it up like a baton. "Well, let's take it from the top."

She counted them in, slowed Ben as he stumbled headlong into the middle section, brought them back together during verse three and drew a crescendo from them at the song's climax.

There was a long silence once it was over.

"That *was* better," said Ben quietly.

"Yes, it was," Clovenhoof agreed.

"Shall we have a go at another?" said Nerys happily.

Clovenhoof passed out fresh sheet music.

"This is great," he said with genuine joy. "Finally, a

chance to express myself. A chance to create something of lasting value. Art."

Nerys looked at the music and raised her baton.

"Okay. *Virgin Whore*. From the top."

AT THEIR NEXT PRACTICE, Nerys came armed with a pair of maracas and some news.

"I've got us our first gig," she said.

"Us?"

She waved her maracas in his face as evidence of her intrinsic role in the band.

"The Boldmere Oak, this Wednesday," she said. "It's open mic night."

"Well," said Clovenhoof loftily, "I've been in negotiations with the Symphony Hall."

"Perhaps best to start small."

"What's this stuff?" said Ben, digging into the wrappings of a recently arrived parcel.

"Clothing accessories," said Clovenhoof. "Part of our image."

He took out a studded black harness of straps and laid it experimentally against his leather jacket.

"I thought it'd look a bit more hardcore. What do you reckon?"

Nerys had found a red and black leather basque and admired it at arm's length.

"What do you think?" said Clovenhoof.

Nerys realised that the others were looking at her.

"I couldn't possibly wear this," she said in a deeply unconvincing tone. "I'd look like a *complete* slut."

"Oh, I don't think so," said Clovenhoof, equally unconvincingly.

"I mean, I would if I *had* to," she said, hopefully. "You know, for *art's* sake."

"For art's sake, of course."

"What's this?" said Ben, holding up a contraption of straps, buckles and a large sausage of moulded black latex.

"It's a strap on," said Nerys.

"Really?" said Ben, fascinated and horrified. "Why would anyone...? I mean, these straps don't seem long enough to go around anyone's waist."

"That's because it's meant to go on your face," said Nerys.

Ben froze and then dropped it with a small yelp.

WITH SO LITTLE time until their Boldmere Oak gig, they crammed in as many practices as possible. Each night, after a successful run-through of their current songs, Clovenhoof would take to his desk and pen several more. He was particularly proud of the anthemic *Lord of the Wilderness* and, when he had finished the words to *Vampire Messiah (Chalice of Blood),* he felt goosebumps across his whole body.

On the Monday, he managed to get through to the Director of Programming and Events at the Birmingham Symphony Hall to whom he outlined his proposed concert.

"Yes, madam," he said, "I fully understand that you plan

months in advance but maybe you have cancellations and the like."

He listened carefully.

"Perfect. Well, we could step into that slot."

There was laughter and more words on the other end of the line.

"I have no idea how much it costs to host such a concert. Perhaps you could tell me. Pluck a figure out of the air."

He nodded.

"Okay. That seems reasonable. I'll take it."

He rummaged around in his desk while she spoke.

"Here," he said, picking up a credit card. "Let me read some numbers to you."

He nodded.

"I'm deadly serious, madam. Ticket sales and promotions? Don't worry, I'll deal with that."

Once their business was concluded, Clovenhoof had a celebratory Lambrini, checked on Herbert's progress and continued composing.

At five am, having just finished the score for the twenty-minute rock instrumental *Care Bear Torture Cycle*, he wondered if he perhaps ought to just give it a rest and go to bed for once.

THE OPEN MIC evening in the upstairs room of the Boldmere Oak opened with Lennox's brother-in-law's Slayer tribute band, followed by a three piece band of college kids who clearly put more effort into the rock music than their studies. Ben, Nerys and Clovenhoof were on third.

Ben took to the stage and plugged in his keyboard. The drinkers in the room winced at the howl of feedback, which never quite died away. Eschewing the bondage gear, his one concession to metal-wear was a Megadeth T-shirt that his grandma had bought him for his sixteenth birthday and which still fitted him. Nerys's outfit, which wasn't so much suggestive as downright explicit, drew much more attention when she flung off her overcoat and picked up her maracas. Clovenhoof strode onto the miniscule stage, all leather and denim, picked up his silver axe and glared at the crowd.

The crowd glared back.

Ben found himself nervously reflecting, almost as though he was having an out-of-body experience, that they weren't a typical heavy metal band. None of them had the trademark long hair (Nerys's was too tidy and feminine to count) and only Clovenhoof had a true heavy metal instrument and, sure, Nerys had a certain vampish metal-girl look about her but that was totally destroyed by the maracas. Maracas? What were they thinking? She wasn't Bez and they weren't the Happy Mondays! If anything they looked like an unholy Latino electro-synth rock band, fronted by a man who already seen too much of life.

It was all going to go horribly wrong.

"We're Devil Preacher," growled Clovenhoof, a name Ben was sure he had made up off the cuff. "And this one's called *Spineless Disciples*."

Clovenhoof glanced at Nerys, who licked her lips

nervously, shared a panicked look with Ben and then shook her maracas...

...and they played.

And it worked. It shouldn't have worked. But it did.

They played *Spineless Disciples* and *Vampire Messiah* and *(Never Trust a) Man in a Dress*, one song rolling into the next.

They were carried along by Clovenhoof's guitar-work and singing voice, sometimes screaming, sometimes a silvery tenor, sometimes something dark and gravelly, dredged up from the bottom of a canal. What audio landscape he couldn't generate was filled in by Ben's distorted keyboard work, adding breadth and depth (and, at one point, the Shipping Forecast) to the music. And through it all ran the quiet but insistent hiss and rattle of Nerys's maracas, like the tapping of death watch beetles or the rattling of bones in their graves.

And when Clovenhoof shouted one last, '*Run away from the man in a dress!*' and the final synth howl faded, the drinkers tucked their pints under their arms, clapped and even whooped a little.

"Yeah!" shouted Clovenhoof in utter jubilation, dug his hands deep into his pockets and flung dozens of freshly printed tickets out into the small audience.

"Come to our next gig!" he shouted. "Give tickets to your friends!"

"Next gig?" said Nerys but got no answer and didn't overly care because she was suddenly being paid attention by a small knot of men who wanted to buy her drinks and play with her maracas.

CLOVENHOOF KEPT the details of their second gig from Ben and Nerys, wanting it to be a surprise. Between band practices, he made phone calls and bookings and on one long and productive afternoon took a gargantuan tour of record shops and bars to distribute free concert tickets. He was a little dismayed to discover that taxi drivers did not accept credit cards and had to ask the man to show him how cash machines worked.

On the Saturday evening, the three of them watched a dozen hairy and tattooed men pack their gear into a Pickfords truck.

"Where the hell is this gig?" said Nerys.

"You'll see," smiled Clovenhoof. "Here's *our* transport."

A white stretch limo – no, not a stretch limo, a stretch Hummer - pulled up outside the flats.

"You are kidding me," said Ben.

"Come on," said Clovenhoof and led them out through the grey winter drizzle, flicked an irreverent salute to the chauffeur and barrelled his companions inside.

"This is bigger than my flat," said Ben.

"I know," said Clovenhoof. "Onward James!" he called to the driver.

"Jeremy," said Nerys as they pulled away.

"Yes?"

"Two things. One, why are you wearing sunglasses when there's no sun?"

"It's an accepted part of the rock star life style. And two?"

"Yes. There appear to be two... gentlemen of limited stature in here."

Clovenhoof peered over the top of his shades down the neon-lit interior of the Hummer.

"Oh, that's Mark and Graham. They're my entourage."

The two dwarfs waved cheerily. One of them, Graham, winked at Nerys and waggled his bushy eyebrows suggestively.

"M&Ms!" said Ben, spying a glass bowl.

"Eh?"

Ben picked them up.

"Only blue ones, I see," he said knowingly, popping one in his mouth. "Is that one of your concert riders? Like Van Halen had?"

Clovenhoof, who had no idea what riders, Van Halen or even M&Ms were, said, "Er, yeah."

"Just go easy on those," he added, recalling that his efforts to attain the true rock and roll image had also involved a discreet conversation with a black-market pharmacist, one who he suspected specialised in veterinary medicine.

WHEN THEY PULLED up outside the Birmingham Symphony Hall, Nerys swore loudly.

"Tell me you're joking," she said, not sure whether she was delighted or terrified.

"It's the big time for us now," said Clovenhoof.

A crowd of people, Saturday night pubbers and clubbers, were pressed up around their vehicle.

Ben, who had his nose pressed into the soft furnishings mumbled something like, "I live in a world of tweed."

"Too many M&Ms," said Clovenhoof. "Graham. Mark. Give us a hand with the keyboardist."

They forced their way out into the crowd and to the service doors of the symphony hall.

A sharp-looking woman with a computer tablet in her hand shook Clovenhoof's hand.

"We expected you two hours ago, Mr Clovenhoof," she said curtly.

"We're here now," he replied. "Which way's the stage?"

The woman gave a wordless grunt of disapproval and led them on through the building.

"We've already let the audience in. You've clearly sold a lot of tickets."

"Sold?" said Clovenhoof.

Nerys saw a blond, beautiful young man in a crisp suit step in beside Clovenhoof.

"Michael," said Clovenhoof. "Spying on me again?"

"Heaven's omniscience makes that assertion nonsensical," said Michael. "I have just come to offer my support."

"It's too real," said Ben dreamily as Mark and Graham steered him around an equipment trolley.

When Nerys looked up again, Michael had vanished.

"Too real," agreed Nerys, who didn't have the benefit of illicit drugs to keep her going.

And then she saw that the woman and the other venue

staff had stopped and were waving them on with encouraging pats on the back. There was a doorway ahead of them, filled with a pink and golden glow and the sound of two thousand expectant people.

She suddenly felt like she was on the long slow haul up the first slope of a rollercoaster. Sure, the big drop was coming, sure, she wanted it to happen but not just yet...

"Not now," she said but it was too late. They were already walking onto the open stage. A ragged, almost polite cheer rose up from the stalls and tiers of seating that ran up to the high ceiling.

Mark and Graham parked Ben in front of his keyboard, guided his hands to the keys and then exited. Graham gave her a cheeky wink from the wings and was gone.

Nerys looked beyond the footlights and could see hundreds of eyes on her, an army of T-shirts and aggressive haircuts. She adjusted her basque and picked up her maracas. She glanced across at Clovenhoof and saw a man born to go on stage. He slipped the strap of his silver guitar over his head and stepped up to the mic.

"We're Devil Preacher," he shouted to a faint cheer. "Let me tell you my story."

Clovenhoof started up with the opening riff for *The Devil's Party*, Nerys fell in with her maracas and Ben, though clearly operating on another plane of consciousness, managed to come in on the synthesiser at the right moment.

In front row seats in the upper circle, Doris pulled open a paper bag and proffered it to Betty.

"Humbug?"

"I'm listening," said Betty petulantly but took a mint humbug anyway.

Doris squinted at the cavorting figure at the front of the stage.

"It's all just noise, isn't it?"

"It's not to my tastes, I'll admit," said Betty. "But the tickets were free and it makes a change to the bingo."

"It's still just noise."

"He's telling a story through song."

"Can you actually hear what he's saying?"

Betty shrugged.

"Something about fighting unwinnable wars."

"Codswallop then."

"I think he's trying to be..."

"What?"

Betty sucked on her humbug thoughtfully.

"He's trying to be eloquent."

The lead singer of Devil Preacher allowed no gaps between the songs, launching into each before the cheers for the previous died. He did not speak except through his lyrics. The second song, which was apparently about 'soiled angels' (although Betty wasn't overly sure) described the singer's torturous descent into a Hell of his own making.

"The keyboard player's good," said Betty.

"There's something wrong with his eyes," said Doris. "I bet he's on those herbal cigarettes. You know the ones. Looks like a ghoul."

"I think it's the fashion."

Betty tapped her orthopaedic shoes along to the music, wondering if the high-pitched whine she could hear was part of the music or just ringing in her ears.

"*Swallow my fruit, bitch*?" exclaimed Doris indignantly. "Did I hear him right?"

"I think it's about that couple, thingy and doodah. With the wotsits."

"Fig leaves."

"Thank you."

"And speaking of covering up one's embarrassment. What's that thing she's wearing? Like a corset."

"It's called a basque."

"It's immoral, that's what it is."

"I think she's enjoying herself with her shakers."

"Harlot. Harpy."

"Oh, let her have some fun."

Doris, torn between disbelief and disgust that this music was proving so popular, made a point of getting out her knitting pattern and reading that instead of listening to the racket emanating from the stage. Nonetheless, she couldn't prevent herself tutting at the crudity of *Virgin Whore* or the cruel, mocking lyrics of *Spineless Disciples*. And as for *Vampire Messiah (Drink my Blood)...*

"It's just childish," said Doris.

"I think it's quite clever," said Betty.

An hour into the show, Doris had irritably devoured a whole bag of mint humbugs and completed fifteen rows of a woolly jumper. Meanwhile Betty, always up for new experiences, had followed the band's journey down into a pit of hopelessness, where the illusions of civilisation were stripped away and the rotten core of received wisdom was revealed. Now (as Doris sucked furiously on her dentures and worked on the jumper's neckline), Betty and the audience were lifted up by an optimistic shift in Devil Preacher's music.

Night of the Morningstar was an act of resurrection with strained synthesiser chords challenged by an upbeat tempo. *Drowning in a Lake of Fire* took this change further with some cheesy power chords and conceited lyrics that together skated close to the ludicrous but never quite passed into it.

Betty had moved on from mere toe tapping to shoulder jiggling and the occasional bout of jazz hands. It was certainly better than bingo.

"Jezebel," muttered Doris although Betty wasn't sure who that commented was aimed at.

UP ON THE STAGE, Ben, who was struggling to focus on much at all, came back to himself for long enough to notice that the concert was going really well. The audience were loving it and so were his band mates. Nerys was cavorting and gyrating in the spotlight like the demon-possessed, shaking her maracas with disturbing vigour. And Clovenhoof had the crowd in the palm of his hand, everyone joining in with the choruses and probably not noticing Clovenhoof's successful use of the E flat diminished seventh chord which had proved awfully tricky in rehearsals.

The audience roared their approval as Clovenhoof

plunged like a Stuka dive-bomber into the band's final number, *Lord of the Wilderness.*

The audience stamped along and punched the air. If the band had leapt from the stage at that point and began to march on parliament, say, or Rome, or the gates of heaven, the audience would have followed them. Devil Preacher had two thousand converts, free-thinkers who had been released from their chains and blindfolds and were now ready to put all creation to rights.

Clovenhoof – Narrator? Singer? It was all one - leaned down to the audience and cried for their allegiance.

'Hail to the Beast!' Dun. Dun. Dun.
'Hail to the Beast!' Dun. Dun. Dun.
'Hail to the Beast!' Dun. Dun. Dun.
(went two thousand voices, two thousand stamping feet and two thousand pounding fists)

ALL THE WHILE the guitar and the keyboard wrapped around one another in a chain of progressing chords that could have no end.

'HAIL TO THE BEAST!' Dun. Dun. Dun.

"OH," said the handsome young man three seats along from Betty. "This will never do."

The man was, unlike the jumping, thumping mob around him, dressed in a respectable and cleanly pressed suit. He seemed to be enjoying proceedings almost as little as Doris.

The man reached into his pocket and produced a phone. He didn't seem to press any buttons but it was ringing anyway.

"What service do I require?" said the man. "Police. Definitely the police."

'*HAIL TO THE BEAST!*' Dun. Dun. Dun.

THE AUDIENCE WERE MOVING AS one, as if hypnotised. It was as though the whole world was being bent to the will of the band, well, Clovenhoof's will. It is said that willpower could move mountains and it seemed to Ben (who would happily admit he wasn't feeling entirely *compos mentis* at the time) that the very walls of the symphony hall were bending in to meet them. And a quiet part of Ben's brain pointed out that the symphony hall's walls, floor and ceiling were made of two-metre thick concrete and this kind of behaviour couldn't have been part of the architect's original plans.

But the walls were not just bending but stretching up to lift the ceiling to impossible heights.

'*Hail to the Beast!*' Dun. Dun. Dun.

The concert hall was transforming into a palace, a fortress, a battleship carrying Clovenhoof's army of dark warriors towards that ultimate battle which could only end in victory. And, as if to signal that victory, Ben's keyboard began to emit an ululating siren call and a strange, dispassionate voice said something like "Charlie Whiskey Foxtrot. We're moving in."

Clovenhoof had his guitar raised as if to shoot down the sky and Ben saw that his band mate, his neighbour, wasn't just some bloke with too much money and bad manners but was a red-skinned demon with horns and goat legs and hooves – hooves! – and, worst of all, *always had been.*

And then someone cut the power and the house lights came up and the doors opened and dozens of men in helmets and hi-vis tabards came running in.

The demon turned to Ben, a crestfallen look on his face.

"Spoilsports," he said.

Ben took a deep breath.

"Jeremy," he said. "I think I'm having a real bad trip."

"Me too, Kitchen," said Satan.

BETTY AND DORIS walked away from Symphony Hall, gingerly probing their ears.

"That seemed to go rather well," said Betty.

"You're right. Absolute Hell," grumbled Doris. "Have your ears gone funny?"

"What?"

They walked on.

"You'd never catch Daniel O'Donnell *flaunting* himself like that," said Doris after much thought.

"The young people seemed to enjoy it though. I liked the part with the policemen. Very entertaining. I always like to see a man in uniform."

"They were all a bit young to be real policemen if you ask me. I'm not sure it's done my rheumatics any good." Doris grunted as she put weight onto her hip in order to illustrate this.

"Still, it's an evening out, isn't it?" said Betty.

Doris peered up and down Broad Street, stepping back with a grimace as a girl of around eighteen staggered out of a pub and vomited onto the pavement in front of them.

"That's all very well," said Doris, "but where on earth are we going to get a nice cup of tea at this time of night?"

NERYS WOKE SLOWLY, battling her way up through the layers of sleep, trying to piece together the memories of the night before and separating them from the bizarre dreams she had had. Her brain and her mouth were lined with the dry cotton wool of last night's alcohol.

She remembered the concert and the roar of the crowd. She remembered the police coming in and the arguments backstage before she and some guys pegged it down Broad Street to the nearby clubs. She remembered the dancing and the drinking and some hilarious fumblings in the back of a black cab. That all seemed pretty straightforward but then there were these other images sprinkled through her recollections. A snarling devil's face, the concert hall distorted into some brutalist cavern and, weirdest of all, a sensuous lover with too many arms and too many legs.

She rolled over, her hand touched naked flesh and she opened her eyes. She was in a hotel bedroom. Grey daylight filtered in through net curtains.

The man next to her rolled over and smiled.

"Morning gorgeous," said Mark.

"Oh," she said. "I thought..."

"What?"

She sat up. From what little she could remember, she was sure Graham had been the much more flirtatious one...

There was the sound of running water from the bathroom.

"Graham's in the shower," said Mark.

Ah, thought Nerys. That's one mystery solved.

IN WHICH CLOVENHOOF DOESN'T NEED ANYONE, MEETS A CERTIFIED GENIUS AND CATCHES A LIFE-THREATENING COLD

C lovenhoof pressed himself into the shadow of a snow-covered privet hedge.

"Mommee, why's that red man playing that funny game?"

Clovenhoof glared at the small child and shrank back into the hedge. A blob of snow fell onto his back. He hadn't had time to grab a coat, and it quickly melted through his shirt, resulting in an uncomfortable cold trickle down into his underpants.

He *wasn't* playing a game. He was following Nerys and her Aunt Molly. He wasn't overly sure why.

It was partly out of boredom, partly out of curiosity.

He had spotted Nerys and Molly leaving the flats that morning and it was unusual to see Aunt Molly out at that kind of time. She had a routine of hairdresser appointments and shopping trips, but those were invariably in the afternoon. Clovenhoof had tried to close his ears to details of

Molly's delicate digestion which apparently made morning outings a dangerous prospect.

Clovenhoof felt compelled to follow and see where they were going. As he made it out onto the street, they were a couple of hundred yards away so he trotted after them. As they turned onto the much quieter Church Road he realised that he ran the risk of being spotted so used the technique that he'd seen on television, of scuttling from tree, to postbox, to gateway and pressing himself into each hiding position so that he remained unseen. He was close behind Nerys and Molly now, but he couldn't quite make out their conversation.

"Look at him, mommy."

Nerys glanced back over her shoulder when the child spoke, but didn't notice Clovenhoof. The mother – thankfully – didn't look back at all.

When they disappeared from sight, he walked on, trying to shake himself free of the snow. There had been quite a fall in the night, but it was already melting into a slushy beige mess. Ridiculous stuff. He remembered why they'd never bothered with it in hell.

Nerys and Molly were heading for St Michael's Church. They joined a crowd of people who were already standing outside and moved to the front where there were some other women of Molly's age. Clovenhoof stood at the back with the stragglers and tried to fit in, doing what they did. They stared at the floor, or looked up the road as if they were waiting for a bus.

But no, not a bus. As he was looking up the road, a large

black car arrived and Clovenhoof spotted the coffin in the back.

He wondered if there was free food at funerals and putting his clammy undergarments out of his mind for the time being, he trailed in behind the other mourners.

He loitered at the back of the church and looked around to see if there was a buffet. The large pale tapestry of St Michael standing over the vanquished Satan hung above him.

"Ugh."

The mourners started to sing the first hymn *All Things Bright and Beautiful* a high-pitched, saccharine bleating. Clovenhoof changed his mind about staying and thought he would sneak out before he threw up.

He turned and Michael was standing there, looking incredibly pleased with himself.

"Spying on me again?" said Clovenhoof.

"My church, my people," said Michael.

"Oh please. None of these people would recognise you with or without your frock on." He looked up at the tapestry "Although they've really caught your smarmy arse smugness. And that's not easy in tapestry."

Michael brushed a speck from the lapel of his immaculate suit.

"Jeremy, I know that you're trying to goad me but I want you to know that I am here to make sure your transition is as smooth as possible."

Clovenhoof gave Michael a look of disbelieving contempt.

"My *transition*?"

"Yes. Everyone wants to see you settled in, and living a nice normal life. We were a bit disappointed in your recent activities. Dabbling in... popular music could only be described as..." - Michael pulled the face he'd pull if he found he'd been flossing with a pubic hair - "Attention-seeking."

"So, what's the problem with attention-seeking?"

"It's just not part of the deal, Jeremy. You're to live a quiet life, here on earth and blend in, otherwise it just won't work."

"What deal? I made no deal!" Clovenhoof bellowed. "I never asked for any of this. Nobody bothers to check with me."

"Your resettlement package has been very generous."

"And if I don't want your 'resettlement package'?"

Michael's smile (such a versatile expression) shifted from all-round geniality to loving condescension. His eyes flicked to the tapestry of his Biblical victory.

"Let's not forget who the decision maker is here, Jeremy."

"You've cheated me out of my position."

"An angel? Cheat?"

"It's just like the last time, that stupid war in heaven." He flung a finger at the wall hanging. "You cheated me then too."

"Jeremy, that's ancient history. Move on."

"You had two thirds of the angels and you gave me all the duffers."

Michael tried to turn up his smile, but his face was already full.

"Everyone picked their own side, friend."

"Yeah, but how was I ever going to win with Petuniel on my team?"

"I don't think –"

"And I had the sun in my eyes!"

"Now you're being petty."

"You know it wasn't fair!" howled Clovenhoof. "I bet you even think that maybe I was right all along, don't you? DON'T YOU?"

"Of course not."

"'Don't give humans free will!' I said. Well, look around at what they've done with the place. Was I right, hmmm?"

"I am not about to question the divine plan."

"I think that deep down inside you *know* I was right. But you never listened. You still never do. You had better angels than me and you stabbed me." He was jumping up and down now, pointing at the tapestry.

"Fine, fine," snapped Clovenhoof. "Do all that stuff, but then leave me with my own place. Hell's a shithole but at least it was mine. It's not as if you'd ever want to go there, you in your stupid fancy *suit*. I can't believe you've thrown me out of there too and you're still trying to make me miserable, here in this stupid place, in this stupid town, with these stupid people!"

Clovenhoof kicked a pew, and then realised as he looked up that Michael had gone. He turned around to see that the hymn had finished and a whole church full of horrified pensioners was staring at him.

NERYS WAS MOMENTARILY STUNNED to see him there, but she recovered quickly and barged towards him, almost colliding with the lady vicar, who was also heading his way.

"I know him," said Nerys.

"So do I, I think," said the vicar. "Is he...?" The vicar pointed to her head and made a cuckoo whistle.

"No, he's a git. It's a fine line. Go back to the service. I'll deal with him."

The vicar nodded, looking levelly at Clovenhoof before turning back to the congregation.

"Interesting," said Doris, turning to Betty in a pew towards the back.

"She handled it well though," said Betty, indicating the vicar. "She's got *gravitas*. Unusual thing for a woman."

"Don't forget *we're* women," said Doris.

"True. Well I'm giving it a nine for solemnity," said Betty, jotting in her notebook.

"A nine? Really? Look around you! Hardly anyone's even crying. No wailing at all. That's never a nine."

"How about we give it an eight, but we have a new category for 'entertainment value'? I think we could give it a nine for that."

"Fair enough, although that organist lets them down on the music," Doris said, jotting her own notes.

"The hymn-singing's not bad though," said Betty. "Not too many people are miming."

"Hmmm, this one here could do with learning to mime, if she can't be bothered to learn to sing in tune," said Doris, getting a furious scowl from a woman nearby.

"He's not afraid to speak his mind, is he?" said Betty, nodding towards Clovenhoof.

"Well, he's got no idea of when to stay quiet, that's the trouble," said Doris. "Mind you, speaking of quiet, I still can't hear properly after that concert of his we went to."

"Would you say that he should have some credit for coming into a church?" Betty asked, her pen poised.

"Certainly not," said Doris. "It's not as though he's shown it any respect, is it? What a place to have an outburst like that."

"Do you think he did that on purpose? I think he's just a bit *troubled*."

Nerys shoved Clovenhoof out of the door and out into the porch.

"I can't believe this," she said, simmering with fury. "Even of you. I know you're selfish. I know you don't care about anyone else but yourself, but somehow, I would never have believed that you could stoop this low."

"What?"

"To follow us into a funeral, that's *pretty* creepy in itself. But everyone knows that of all the places where you show a little bit of decorum, a little bit of respect, a funeral's the place."

"I didn't mean to-"

"But you! You don't just make a little bit of a nuisance of yourself, you practically ruin the whole service! What on earth were you doing?"

"I..."

"No, don't tell me. The only possible thing I can say to people is that you're a simpleton who doesn't *know* what he's doing. Just get out of here. I don't want to look at your face for another moment."

Nerys went back inside and Clovenhoof stood looking at the door, wondering what had just happened. It had started to rain.

Michael re-appeared with an umbrella in his hand.

"A lady vicar, I see," he said.

"I'm not talking to you."

"Strange idea. Brolly?"

"What?"

Michael offered him the shade of his umbrella.

"It rains on the just and unjust alike."

"Sod off," said Clovenhoof.

"I suppose it's nice for the ladies to be involved," continued Michael thoughtfully, "but still, it just doesn't look right, does it?"

"Yeah," said Clovenhoof through gritted teeth, "only men should wear dresses. Everyone knows that."

He walked off, unable to tolerate Michael anymore.

"Won't be a problem for much longer anyway," Michael called, and disappeared.

Clovenhoof, getting slowly soaked to the skin, didn't stop to wonder what he meant. He trudged through the melting slush at the church gate. He just wanted to get back home. He hated Michael. He had always hated Michael. Had he *really* agreed to work with him?

HELL

Satan met Michael, for the first time in millennia, in the demilitarized zone between Heaven and Hell. Strictly speaking it didn't exist, had never existed, but Satan had insisted that if he was going to have this chat with some representative of Heaven then it would be on neutral ground, so Heaven had made sure that it would exist, for a little while at least.

A figure approached Satan through the wispy nothingness. Satan groaned when he saw who it was.

"If I'd known they were going to send you I don't think I'd have bothered."

The Archangel Michael smiled at his oldest adversary.

"I'm unarmed. This is a meeting between professionals, remember? Purely business. Surely you're not going to sulk about our last meeting are you?"

"Why would I sulk about you sticking me with a spear and doing a victory dance on my back?"

"Angels don't dance," said Michael smoothly. "Shall we sit?"

"Where?" Satan asked. He looked round to see that a sleek mahogany table had appeared with a pair of chairs.

"Show-off," he mumbled, and sat down.

Michael had a pad of paper and a fountain pen. He started to make notes, glowing golden ink flowing onto the crisp parchment.

"Shall we set an agenda?" said Michael.

"I didn't think you had a gender," said Satan but the pun was lost on Michael.

"I think we should chat about the high level things today," the angel said. "And if you decide that you'd like to go ahead with some of these suggestions, then we'll involve a few more people. What do you think?"

"Yes, high level," agreed Satan, not particularly sure what Michael meant.

Michael made a brief list and showed it to Satan.

1. *Describe how a carefully chosen management team can increase productivity and enable delegation.*

"Delegation," said Satan. "That's telling people to do stuff?"

"Yes."

"I can do that."

2. *Describe the framework used by Heaven for performance management.*

"Performance management?"

"That's how we measure how well people are performing their role and guide them towards improvements."

"Like 'don't jab him like that, jab him like *this*.' That sort of thing?"

"Sort of."

3. Create a Vision and Mission Statement for Hell.

"A lot of people have visions of Hell," said Satan.

"Yes, it means something different in this sense."

"Oh."

4. Propose members of a board to implement suggested changes.

"I see," said Satan.

"What do you think?" asked Michael.

"Just one thing missing," Satan said, and indicated that Michael should pass him the pad.

He wet his finger in his mouth and smeared the ink all down the right hand side in a wavy line.

"Better," he said, and nodded in approval as he passed it back to Michael.

Michael rolled his eyes and restored his smile.

"Good," he said, "let's get started then. I'm going to walk you through some of the basics. Maybe I'll start with a couple of diagrams, showing how a well-organised management structure will allow you to allocate work to people who are best able to deal with it, while still leaving you ultimately responsible."

He took up his pen again and started to draw a pyramid with arrows going up and down. He glanced briefly at Satan who was leaning towards him, and shifted position so that his arm was spread protectively round his work.

A few hours later, the table was covered with diagrams, notes and lists. Satan's head was full of new concepts. Some of them sounded insane. Some sounded pointless. But some of them sounded as if they might even work.

"So, we need a team," Michael said, "a group of representatives from Heaven and Hell. They will form a project board to steer this transition."

Satan was still trying to understand some of the language.

"What does it mean when you steer a transition?" he asked.

"The group will give you advice about how to do things."

"Oh. That sounds good. I'll still be in charge?"

"Of course. So, let's get some names down. I'll put Peter from our side, as he came up with this idea."

"God, I bet he'll bring that simpering sidekick of his along. Well, I'll have Mulciber then. Chief Architect and all that. And Azazel, he's probably the most level-headed of the chief demons."

Michael raised an eyebrow. "Uh, right. Good. I'll choose Saint Francis next, he can keep an eye on expenses, and Joan of Arc. She has a lot of get-up-and-go."

"I'll have Raum and Baal," said Satan.

"A cat demon and a bird demon? Is that wise?" said Michael, pen poised.

"Hmmm, OK. How about Leviathan?"

"He's over three hundred miles long. Not ideal to get round a board room table."

Satan pushed back from the table, exasperated. "Well what about Ceto? Another female would be good, surely?"

"Well, I agree with that, but someone with a legion of monstrous children is going to have issues with childcare, no?"

"Look. I'm not complaining about your trippy visionaries and suck-up arse-lickers."

"Fine. Fine. But I will draw the line at any demons who vomit bile or belch flame."

"That's just picky."

The bickering continued for a long time but it was a constructive form of bickering.

BOLDMERE

Ben was painting tiny soldiers in his kitchen when Clovenhoof entered. His tongue was sticking out the corner of his mouth, a sure sign of intense concentration.

Clovenhoof peeled off his sodden trousers and draped them over a radiator. He rearranged his underpants and slumped into a chair and scowled at Ben's delicate brushwork.

"People are sort of tricky, aren't they?" said Clovenhoof.

Ben shrugged as he switched brushes.

"Well I can never figure them out."

Clovenhoof picked up an unpainted soldier and pouted glumly at it.

"Simple misunderstanding, and all of a sudden everyone's up in arms."

Ben nodded.

"Is that why you like these so much?" Clovenhoof asked.

"Yeah." Ben replied. "They look how I want them to look, they go where I want them to go, and they stay there if I turn my back. People never do that."

"Interesting," said Clovenhoof. "Can I have a go?"

Ben handed him a small brush and a pot of paint.

"Work in layers. Save the detail until last. See with this one, he's infantry so you can do most of his clothes with a wash of this paint here. I mixed it myself – I call it *Dirty Linen*. Then you can add the brown leather detail when it's dry."

Clovenhoof worked carefully, making sure he kept the paint exactly where it should be.

"You know, I used to have something a bit like this once. A world at my mercy, where I could control exactly what happened."

Ben peered at his painting and nodded in approval.

"Yeah it looks like you've done this before. You've got the attention to detail. Listen, I've got an afternoon shift at the shop, so I'll need to go out in a minute."

"OK," said Clovenhoof, picking up the next infantryman and washing out his brush.

"So..."

"Yeah, yeah," said Clovenhoof. "Off you go."

"Oh. Right. Yes. Well what I should have said is, you need to go home."

"I'm not wearing any trousers."

"You can't stay here."

Clovenhoof looked up in disappointment.

"Oh. Can't I? Well can I take some with me?"

"Sure. And your trousers."

CLOVENHOOF FOUND it so absorbing that he forgot to get out of his wet clothes or put fresh trousers on. He sat all afternoon, giving the soldiers small individual touches like moustaches and acne.

The last soldier he painted was all in white. He worked hard to give him just the right expression of smarmy benevolence.

He arranged them all on his table when he was done.

The white soldier was at one end and the others were all at the other.

"Herbert," he said to his pet mould, which had a ringside seat on the mantelpiece, "I feel I should say a few words. The occasion demands gravitas, as I'm about to replay my historic battle with Michael, but this time with the numbers on *my* side."

He turned to the amassed lead infantry.

"Now, my fine men," he commanded, "I want you to advance, on my order, and annihilate that little prick. I want you to smash him into so many tiny pieces that they won't even find his stupid smile afterwards."

He went to the other end and faced the white soldier.

"Say goodbye, Michael."

He stood erect, stopping only to blow his nose, which had started to run. He paused to find the right words.

"Die Michael, die!" he screamed. "Go, soldiers! Rip him to shreds!"

Nobody moved and he hesitated.

He knew it was called gaming, but he assumed it would work better than this.

"Go on!" he urged.

Still nothing.

"Aaargh!" he yelled in frustration, and swept the soldiers to the floor with his arm.

"Useless bloody cowards!"

He would have to punish them for their inaction, of course.

He picked up the first two from the floor and examined their faces. He was unable to detect the fear and respect that he knew he needed in his minions.

"I need to make an example of these men, Herbert."

He fetched the emergency toolbox from the fuse cupboard and extracted a hand drill. He pinned the first soldier to the table with the end and leaned on it heavily.

"Now do you wish you'd done as I commanded?"

He disembowelled the soldier and his companion, leaving the twisted remains at the feet of Mini-Michael.

"Who's next? Are you going to advance on the enemy or do I have to hunt you *all* down, you cowards?"

He scooped up some more and snipped off their heads with a pair of pliers.

When the remainder continued to hide on the floor, he lost the final remnants of his patience. He gathered them all into a saucepan and set them onto a low light.

"Go on, tell me that it's a bit warm for you! Tell me that you'd rather go and fight like men! Well it's too late now, you stupid cowardly fools!"

He amused himself for a moment bashing mini-Michael with a hammer and then he watched as the saucepan of soldiers started to melt and then stirred them with a spoon to be sure that none escaped. He failed to notice how thick and black the smoke drifting upwards had become, until the smoke alarm went off.

He ran cold water into the saucepan, which made a crackling filthy mess, and left it on the side to go and open some windows.

BEN HAD JUST RETURNED from the bookshop as he heard the alarm going off. He stood in the hallway trying to work out which direction it was coming from.

"It's Clovenhoof," said Nerys, coming down the stairs. "I wonder what the stupid bastard's up to."

As she went to knock on his door, the alarm stopped.

She shrugged her shoulders and turned back to Ben.

"I'm glad you're here though, I need your help for a minute."

"OK, what do you need?"

"I just need someone to take a photo, come on up."

She led the way to her flat.

"Wait there while I get everything ready. I need a good shot for some Valentine cards I'm making."

She handed Ben a camera and disappeared into the bedroom while he studied the controls.

He took a picture of Twinkle to be sure that he understood it and then looked up as Nerys returned.

She held two large fans in front of her, and he could see that she'd changed into a pair of unfeasibly high heels.

"How on earth do you walk in those?" he asked.

"Oh, these aren't for walking in," Nerys answered. "So, I need a pose that shows enough to titillate, but not enough to be considered pornographic."

She adjusted the fans slightly.

"How's this?" she asked.

Ben swallowed.

"Are you *naked*?" he asked.

Nerys rolled her eyes. "Well, *durrr*. It wouldn't be very titillating if there wasn't some flesh on show."

Ben carefully put down the camera and ran downstairs, whimpering. He knocked Clovenhoof's door, slightly fearful that Nerys might follow him.

As the door opened, swirls of evil-smelling smoke escaped. Clovenhoof stood in the doorway, a saucepan in his hand.

"Can I come in?" Ben asked, glancing nervously backwards.

Clovenhoof stood aside and said nothing.

"What on earth have you been cooking?" Ben asked and then stopped and stared in horror at the saucepan Clovenhoof held. He could see an arm poking out the melted, blackened mess. An arm, a head and a tiny twisted leg. It looked as though his Seleucid warriors had drowned in mud.

He looked at the table and saw the headless infantry, the crushed bodies.

"What did you do?" he hissed.

Clovenhoof looked at his hands.

"I think they might have been faulty. They didn't work properly."

"Didn't *what*?"

"They wouldn't do what I wanted."

"Why would you think they'd *do* anything? They're models. It's up to you to make them do things."

Ben gathered up his paints, which had been tipped across the table.

"Oh. Were they very expensive?" Clovenhoof asked.

Ben shook his head.

"It's not about the money. I mean, these were mail order from Germany they don't come cheap but, Jeremy, I trusted you with my things."

Clovenhoof opened his mouth to speak, but suddenly sneezed instead.

He looked surprised at himself and wiped his nose on his sleeve.

"I'm disappointed, Jeremy," said Ben.

"To be honest, I don't see how this is my fault," said Clovenhoof but Ben was already leaving.

CLOVENHOOF'S CLOTHES had dried onto him from his early morning soaking and he was left feeling stiff and tired. He climbed into bed with his Lambrini.

"People aren't tricky," he said, flicking on the TV with the remote and wondering why he couldn't get warm. "They're impossible."

On the news were images of famine victims in Africa, driven from their land by civil unrest.

"Free will is something you'd give to *rational* beings."

He changed channels and bellowed insults at a TV game show that was offering contestants money if they'd eat a maggot.

He thumped his pillow and howled with anger and flicked on through a televised riot in some foreign city, comedy clip shows of people hurting themselves in imaginative ways and a bile-fuelled documentary about evil bankers.

"Idiots! Idiots! All idiots!"

The only times he saw genuinely happy faces was in the adverts, people oohing and aahing and cooing over their newest white goods, the coolest gadgets and the sleekest cars. The problem was, the advert breaks were constantly interrupted by the flood of human misery and stupidity evident in all the other TV programming.

People were infuriatingly contrary things, he silently fumed when he finally turned off the TV and put his head under the pillows. His flatmates were proof of that. He had done – what? – nothing and they acted as though he declared a second war on heaven.

"Idiots," he mumbled groggily into his pillow.

HE WOKE up the following morning feeling strangely light-headed and with only one clear thought in his mind: happiness was to be found in buying stuff, not in people.

He called a taxi and demanded to be taken to the largest shopping centre around.

"The Bull Ring?" said the taxi driver.

"Whatever," sniffed Clovenhoof.

His nose kept running and he was fascinated to find that his snot had turned thick and colourful.

He scooped a blob of it onto his fingertip and offered it to the taxi driver for an opinion but the man seemed peculiarly uninterested.

Clovenhoof alighted outside a giant edifice of steel and glass and poster adverts of some seriously happy people. He quickly concluded that the Bull Ring was a much more impressive place of worship than any church he'd been in. It had a feeling of space, light and supreme power over mortals.

He nodded in approval.

"My church, my people."

He saw the brass statue of a bull outside its main entrance.

"And it even comes with its own golden calf. Delicious."

He prowled through the displays and realised that he could have anything that he wanted. He just needed to use the credit cards that had proven so useful.

He watched a demonstration of a pasta-making machine and decided that he had to have one. He found a useful gadget for electrically rotating his ties so that he could find the right one. He was pretty sure that he only had one tie, so he bought a couple more while he was there.

He went to the computer shop and bought a silver box of delights that looked like it might sprout limbs and take over the world at any moment. He kept stroking it, hoping that it would do just that. It was also (so said the salesman) 'voice-controlled', which reminded him of Ben's crappy non-voice-controlled soldiers and this made Clovenhoof, feel immeasurably superior.

After the shopping splurge, he was so exhausted that he decided to find somewhere to eat. He asked a taxi driver to take him to the most expensive restaurant in town and found himself in a place where the staff were most helpful, and made suggestions on what he might like to eat and drink. When he complained that the portions were a bit small, they fetched more.

He found that there were even people whose job it was to tell you what drinks went with different kinds of food. He was so pleased to discover this that he sampled every course on the menu and demanded the drink for every single one. He scoffed and quaffed, belching his appreciation and sniffing his farts to see if his diet made any discernible difference.

He called over the wine waiter, struggling to focus on the approaching man after his sixth glass of claret.

"They call you *the nose*?" he said in drunken incredulousness.

"Yes sir, that's right," said the wine waiter.

"Would you say that this" - he let rip with a thunderous sound - "has a hint of that Mouton Rothschild 'forty-five that you just served me? Or is it carrying notes of the Carménère from before?"

He used his hands to waft the scent upwards and sniffed appreciatively.

The wine waiter paused for a moment, considering the tip that this dreadful customer might pay for the hours of attention he'd had. He was on the verge of offering his professional opinion in no uncertain terms when the dilemma was removed. Clovenhoof fell forward onto the linen tablecloth and started to snore loudly.

As he helped the other staff members to carry the unconscious Clovenhoof to a taxi he murmured quietly, "I think sir, on balance, that the most assertive notes were of carrion and brimstone."

"Thass right," Clovenhoof whispered. "I think I'm coming down with something."

THE NEXT MORNING he clutched his head and groaned as he woke. This wasn't right. His head had never felt like such a giant, throbbing painful mess before.

As he moved, he realised that something was wrong with his entire body. Pain pulsed through every part that he tried to move. He sat upright and found that his head was now throbbing even more ferociously. He saw the computer he had bought on the floor nearby. The words 'voice-controlled' were printed on the side.

"Computer," he called croakily. "Go get me a cup of tea."

The box just sat there.

"Computer!" he shouted, already hoarse, but again it failed to respond.

He tested his weight on shaky legs and collapsed back onto the bed. He couldn't understand it. He'd been told that death was not an option for him. But surely, he was close. Suffering like this could only mean death was imminent. He staggered to the toilet, and found that he could barely focus on the "Keep Boldmere Beautiful" leaflets as he picked one up to wipe his bottom. He needed advice, and fast. He couldn't go to the neighbours, who both hated him now. He decided to try out the computer, and see if it was as smart as they'd said in the shop.

He staggered over the computer box and kicked it.

"Wake up, you great tin tit," he snarled. Nothing.

Maybe it needed charging. He ripped open the box and began to pull things out. He recognised the keyboard and monitor, but other boxes, wires and disks followed and he realised that it might be trickier than he'd thought.

He turned over all the pieces in his hands, but with his head pounding and his grip wobbly, he was having trouble thinking it through. Surely, what he wanted was to join the keyboard and the monitor? The other bits could wait.

The wire from the keyboard wouldn't fit into the monitor, however hard he tried. He cursed the shoddy workmanship that allowed this rubbish out of the factory. He picked up the pliers that he'd used on the soldiers and snipped the annoying adapter off the keyboard wire. He tried to poke the wires into the hole on the monitor, but they wouldn't stay in. He snipped off some other adapters and tied those onto his wire, but nothing he typed on the keyboard showed on the screen.

He rang the number that they'd given him in the shop.

"I bought a computer from you yesterday and it won't work."

"Would you like to book an appointment with a Genius?"

"Oh. Well yes, of course. Who wouldn't?"

"Come in at two thirty."

BEN KNOCKED on the door as Clovenhoof was trying to gather the pieces together.

"Look, I know you didn't mean –"

"Can't stop now, Kitchen. I'm off to see a genius. Put those cables on top of this, will you?"

"Erm, I know a bit about computers."

"Didn't you hear? I'm going to see a genius. A genius! I've got a lot of questions. Out of the way."

CLOVENHOOF MADE it to the Bull Ring, without dropping too many of the bits.

He rode the escalator, sniffing. He gobbed a wad of yellow phlegm over the side and watched it tumble lazily to the ground floor. He was quite impressed and decided that if he felt equally ill on the way down the escalator he might try an experimental vomit, sure that the results would be quite beautiful. He felt wretched but confident that here, in this place of power and grandeur, were the answers that he needed.

He entered the shop, wondering where he would find the genius. He noticed the pine altar-like counter at the rear, and knew where he needed to go.

His name was displayed on a board behind the altar.

"That's me!" he said, impressed.

"Hi, Mr Clovenhoof, I'm Ryan, and how can I help?"

The man was impossibly young. He looked a bit like Ben. Clovenhoof wondered if there was a shabby factory that turned out such creatures on a production line.

"You're the genius?" he asked.

"Yes I am," said Ryan. "What can I help you with today?"

"Oh, so many things. I've got this horrible mucous in my throat and my friends don't like me anymore. And this suffering business, should it hurt as much?"

Ryan winced.

"I'm more of a computer-type Genius."

"Right."

Clovenhoof unloaded the computer onto the counter.

"Yeah, this thing won't work."

"Let's take a look."

"Yeah, but first, I have to know, how did you become a genius?"

"Company policy forbids me to speak of the training."

"Oh. Yeah. I guess it would."

"Some of these leads are badly damaged. When did you say that you bought it?"

"Yesterday, from here."

"And did you make any modifications?"

"Nope." Clovenhoof said, avoiding his gaze. "It just wouldn't work."

"Right. I'm going to try some new leads and see where that gets us. This will take a few minutes. You're absolutely sure that you made no modifications?"

Clovenhoof shook his head.

"Our computers are made to be reliable and foolproof, but only if you treat them exactly as intended. Like it says in the manual."

"Manual?"

"Yes the manual, the instruction book. It tells you exactly what to do, and if you stick with that you'll rarely get problems."

"Since when did people do what the book told them?"

Ryan nodded knowingly.

"I know. Bane of our lives."

"So you agree that humans should never have been given free will?"

"Um, I don't think I said that," said Ryan.

"Why would you give them free will, if they could do anything they liked?"

"Isn't free will sort of the point of us being here?"

"But some of the stuff they'll do will be wrong, or evil or stupid. They might mess up your computers, for instance. Any time you make it all better, someone will come along and break it again."

Ryan gave Clovenhoof a sideways look.

"But that's what I'm here for, to make things better. Sometimes you can see that people caused the damage, but that just means that they have to pay for the repair. They still deserve to have stuff that works, don't they?"

"Well I suppose you get paid either way."

"That's true."

"It's not like you're doing it because you care."

Ryan frowned at that. For a genius, he did seem somewhat uncertain.

"There are lots of people in the world who live completely selfless lives," he said.

"Really?"

"Like some people are working hard to protect children or end wars. They probably feel as if the odds are against them ever making a difference, but they're doing what they can, and that's what's important."

"But the crazy thing is that evil's allowed to exist."

"Allowed?"

"Any decent God would prevent suffering by making humans do the right thing, and not cause all that harm."

"Most people I know do the right thing." Ryan said. Clovenhoof rolled his eyes but Ryan continued undaunted. "But sometimes, you need some exposure to the bad stuff out there so that you can appreciate the good stuff. It's all about balance."

The computer chimed into life.

"Oh look, the leads have done the trick." Ryan said. "Now you can Google your questions."

"Google?"

"Oh. Let me show you."

Ryan opened a browser window and showed Clovenhoof how to search the internet. Guided by Ryan he asked the internet how to find out what kind of illness he had. He found the NHS Direct site, which offered to check his symptoms.

He dismissed suggestions about pregnancy, mental health

and wounds. He went into the section about headaches, as this was the thing that he'd found the most unpleasant. He answered a series of questions. He couldn't find where to enter details of his running nose and his wrong-smelling farts, but he thought he was on the right track.

A red warning flashed up on the screen

"It says I've got to go to the accident and emergency department."

"Are you not well?" said Ryan.

"What do you think?"

He clutched his head and wondered what could be happening to him. If it was death, then maybe he had a chance to get back where he belonged, but he had no idea that it would *hurt* so much. He thought about the damned in hell. He liked to think of them as his playmates. Did their torments hurt like this too? They always seemed so... playful. This unfortunate new knowledge would kill the party atmosphere if he ever did get back.

He sighed and looked on the computer to see where he'd find an accident and emergency department near his home. It provided him with both directions and a map.

Clovenhoof was impressed despite his imminent demise.

"So, what you were saying about balance," he asked Ryan, picking up his computer, "do you really believe all that? That bad actions are balanced by good actions, and vice versa?"

"Yes I do, as it happens," said Ryan. "It's been a fascinating discussion, Mr Clovenhoof. Tell you what, I won't charge you for those new leads."

He winked conspiratorially at Clovenhoof.

"That's very kind." Clovenhoof said. He turned to go and

then, almost as an afterthought, he leaned over and head butted Ryan, flattening his nose and sending fresh blood across the pine counter.

"Just making sure there's balance. Didn't see that coming did you, genius?"

"I WENT to try and make things up with him," said Ben, "but he just, well, you know..."

"Acted like a total knob?" said Nerys. "Yeah I know. He's a pig. In fact, that reminds me."

She went across to her table where there were magazines and pieces of paper and scribbled out something she'd written. "There."

"What are you doing?" Ben asked.

"I'm working on my Valentines card list. Clovenhoof's definitely off."

Ben remembered their previous encounter and edged quietly towards the door.

"Don't worry, the photo's all done. I got Dave to do it. It's at the printers now."

"That was good of him. I bet he's top of the list."

"Dave?" Nerys laughed. "Don't be silly. We can't give him ideas like that! No, my list is broad, but it's very carefully selected."

"What are all the magazines for?"

"*Hello* magazine is for the celebrity break-ups. Eligible men on the rebound. These others are trade magazines we get at work. I can target all the movers and shakers in the most lucrative fields. Then I always check the obituaries, local and national, to see if anyone interesting has been recently bereaved. You'd be surprised how they respond to a bit of kindness and attention."

"So, how long *is* your list?" Ben asked.

"I've ordered a print run of five hundred. I can call off more in blocks of fifty if I need to."

Ben blew out his cheeks.

"Aren't you afraid of rejection?"

"I'm less afraid of rejection than I am of not finding Mr Right."

"Am I on the list?"

"Oh Ben, you are funny!" laughed Nerys.

"I DON'T THINK you realise, this is pretty serious." Clovenhoof said to the receptionist at Good Hope Hospital.

"Please take a seat, sir, someone will be out to see you soon."

"But I've been here for an hour already."

"You might have to wait for a bit longer, there's a queue."

"But it's an emergency! My computer said so. I think I'm dying!" Clovenhoof yelled.

"Please don't get agitated, sir. We'll be with you when we can. I'm fairly certain that you're not dying."

"Are you a doctor? No. You're a pencil pusher. I must be dying. It hurts so much. Do you know my legs feel wobbly as well? My head is thumping and my throat hurts, of course I'm dying."

"It sounds like a cold to me."

"A cold? A COLD! Are you crazy? People get colds all the time! There's no way that this is a cold. I'm in AGONY."

He turned to the waiting room.

"Nobody here's really suffering, are they? Not like I am?"

"Sir, there are people here with much more serious problems than you. There's a woman with a broken arm, several people with bad lacerations and a boy with glass stuck in his knee."

Clovenhoof wandered over to the woman who was cradling her arm.

"Are you sure that it's broken? That sounds pretty serious."

He picked it up, making her scream with pain and shock, and saw that it was an unusual S shape at the wrist.

"Oh yeah."

"Security!" said the receptionist into the phone.

"Listen," Clovenhoof said, addressing all of the waiting patients. "Why do you put up with this? If you're really suffering then who wants to sit and wait for help? It's completely stupid."

A large security contractor took him by the arm at that point and led him away to a room where he sat for another two hours, glaring sullenly at his captor.

Eventually a head appeared around the door.

"Mr Clovenhoof?"

"Yes."

"I am Doctor Singh. We'll do an examination on you now."

Clovenhoof gave a weak smile. At last! Someone would find out how ill he really was.

He followed Doctor Singh to a cubicle, and took a seat on the edge of a bed.

"Roll up your sleeve for me please."

Clovenhoof exposed his arm and closed his lips around the thermometer that was slipped into his mouth. The doctor put a cuff onto his upper arm and pressed the button to inflate it. The machine made a noise like a wounded buffalo.

"Aaargh! What are you doing to me?" yelled Clovenhoof. "It's crushing my arm, make it stop!"

"It's just to measure your blood pressure," said the doctor, pressing his stethoscope to Clovenhoof's lower arm and pressing another button to deflate the cuff. "Really nothing to worry about."

He paused as he looked at the results, and pressed the inflate button.

"I'm just going to check that again."

There was a small *ting* and the end flew off the thermometer.

Doctor Singh turned to look.

"Oh, that is most unfortunate. A faulty thermometer. Let's get another."

He fetched another thermometer and put it in Clovenhoof's mouth as he repeated the blood pressure check. Clovenhoof managed not to yell this time.

Doctor Singh's pen hovered over his clipboard, a frown upon his face, when there was another small *ting* and the second thermometer broke.

He crossed out everything he'd written and wrote *faulty equipment* across the section.

"OK, we have the gremlins today. Let's get some history. Did you ever smoke?"

"No," said Clovenhoof, "but I worked for years in a smoky environment."

"How about alcohol? How much would you say you drink?"

"Well, I like to drink Lambrini. It's very weak."

"Well, go easy on it while you've got this cold."

"A cold! You people clearly don't know what you're doing!" Clovenhoof yelled.

"I do think it's possible that you have a secondary infection as well. You're running quite a high temperature."

"An infection? Is that serious?"

"It can be, if untreated. I think I'll give you a shot of antibiotics just to be on the safe side."

Clovenhoof felt a swelling of pride. He *did* have something life threatening after all.

The doctor rubbed his arm with something chilly and then produced a small instrument that Clovenhoof regarded with interest.

"What's tha – oww!" he howled and leaped back. "How can you call yourself a doctor? You're an inflicter of pain! If I still had my old job, I'd snap you up with skills like that! Did you make a hole in me?"

"Just a little prick."

Clovenhoof gave him a look.

"Now you're just being offensive."

Nerys finished writing the last address.

"I need to make sure that these get in the last post and I can make it if you'll help me."

"You've got plenty of time yet."

"No, I haven't. They all need swalking."

"They need what-ing?"

"They need a SWALK. It stands for Sealed With A Loving Kiss. Here, put this on."

Ben examined the offered lipstick.

"SuperVamp?" he read out. "Can't I have something a bit less -"

"Just put it on."

Ben applied the lipstick with an obvious lack of training. Nerys sighed and applied some more, so that it was at least symmetrical.

Ben tried his first SWALK. He closed his eyes and pressed his lips to the envelope.

"Whoa, steady! It's just meant to be a light peck!"

Nerys examined his work and sighed.

"You're not supposed to be snogging them, it looks like a crime scene. Do it like this."

She demonstrated the required technique, puckering up and dabbing lightly.

"Then you put a bit more lippy on after every four or five."

They worked their way down the pile, Ben becoming much more adept at handling the lipstick.

"Good, that's the lot," said Nerys finally, packing the

envelopes into carrier bags. "Er, Ben. Why are you putting on more lipstick?"

"This is the best my lips have felt for weeks, they get really dry in the winter."

CLOVENHOOF WALKED HOME from the hospital. However, he soon regretted attempting something so energetic, particularly when the computer under his arm revealed itself to not simply be silvery and very clever but also very very heavy. It started to rain heavily. He was only a short way from home but he couldn't afford another soaking, not when he had an infection. He scurried up the pathway of St Michael's and sheltered in the doorway.

The door opened and the vicar, the Reverend Evelyn Steed, backed out, keys in hand to lock up. She glanced at Clovenhoof and then did a double take. She clearly remembered him.

"It's Jeremy, isn't it?"

He nodded glumly.

"Can I help you?" she asked him, with an expression that suggested she was thinking he might be there to cause further trouble.

Clovenhoof shook his head and stared at the floor.

"No, really," she said, softening. "Can I?"

Clovenhoof shrugged.

"You look unhappy," she said.

He looked up. The last thing he needed was one of God's happy band trying to tell him that Jesus wanted him for a sunbeam. But then she *had* asked, and it had been quite a while since anyone had been kind to him.

"I've been feeling bloody awful."

"Oh, dear. You've not been watching Satanic horror movies again?"

"No. I've got a horrible, life-threatening infection, but everyone keeps telling me it's just a cold. Even when I'm better I'll still be here, in this place, where everyone hates me."

"I don't think they do," said Evelyn and then stopped. Clovenhoof could see the memories of his last visit to the church parading in front of her mind.

"I can't imagine ever being happy again," he said.

"Listen, Jeremy. We all have days that seem black, when the world seems like a cold and friendless place. You've been happy in the past though."

"Oh, yes."

"Can you remember what it felt like?"

"Of course. There was a time when everyone would do as I said."

"Er."

"I could have whatever I wanted."

"No, that doesn't sound like genuine happiness to me. It's much easier to be genuinely happy without power and material things."

Clovenhoof grunted with confusion.

"It's love and friendship that makes us happy," she said.

"My friends are idiots."

"And still you love them. That's what makes them friends."

"I don't think that makes sense."

"Have you ever heard of King Solomon?" said Evelyn.

"Solomon the baby-slicer. Once claimed to have trapped me in a brass vessel. Load of bollocks."

"King Solomon," she continued forcefully, "once asked some wise men to give him something that would provide comfort when the world seemed black, and also to keep his feet on the ground when pride and vanity threatened. The wise men went away and later returned with a ring for the king."

"Yes?"

"On it were inscribed the words '*this too shall pass*.'"

Clovenhoof thought hard about this.

"Whatever it is," said Evelyn. "Whatever this fug is hanging over you, remember that. Go find your friends."

She locked the church door and headed off. At the end of the path, she turned and called back to him.

"Remember, Jeremy. *This too shall pass*."

She gave him a wave and stepped backwards into the road.

That was when the speeding hearse hit her.

BEN AND NERYS carried the bags full of cards downstairs just as Clovenhoof came in. Nerys bristled and prepared her cat's arse face. She glanced at Ben, who was doing the same, but who looked unfortunately like a pantomime dame.

Clovenhoof wasn't himself though. Instead of his wide-open arrogant gaze, Nerys thought he looked troubled.

"What's wrong?" she asked.

He looked between Nerys and Ben, opened his mouth wide as if he had lots to say and then closed it again.

"There was an accident," he mumbled, and slipped inside his flat without another word.

Ben and Nerys stared at each other for a long moment.

"He didn't even comment on my lipstick," said Ben.

"It's a subtle shade." She checked her watch. "Come on. The law of averages says that one of these kisses will end up with Mr Right!"

Ben fingered his lips and felt queasy as he followed her out of the door.

SEVERAL DAYS LATER, Clovenhoof was at the church carrying two bunches of flowers. He'd been forced to queue for a long time and the florist took some convincing that neither bunch was for a wife, girlfriend or that 'special someone'. He reached the spot, just outside the church gate. There were already several bouquets tied to the nearest lamppost and others resting at its base.

He felt the need to say something. There were the words he could say, the words a stupid human being would say, but they weren't the words for him.

"Yup," he said. "See what happens?"

He laid down a bunch of flowers amongst some others.

"Should have followed the rules, read the instruction book."

He kicked at air, his little hooves clicking on the pavement.

"Doesn't stop you being right though, eh?"

He turned to leave with his remaining bunch but something made him turn back.

"And *he* was wrong, you know. You looked better in the dress."

A much larger, beautifully arranged bouquet on the pavement caught his eye. He checked that nobody was looking and swapped the bouquets over, carrying his new prize back home.

BEN WAS SORTING through the recently arrived post when Clovenhoof entered with a posh-looking if somewhat sombre bouquet of flowers.

"Nice flowers."

"Thanks. I chose them myself."

"Here's your post. A parcel too."

Clovenhoof flicked through a sheaf of official-looking envelopes. Quite a few of them seemed to have red writing. He'd burn those later.

"Hang on," Clovenhoof said to Ben. "There's something in here for you."

He undid the parcel and handed Ben some small boxes.

Ben lifted the lid and examined the figures.

"Oh wow. Thank you."

"I thought you could use them with your Macedonian Revolt soldiers."

"What are these dogs with things on their backs?"

"They had braziers strapped to them, on top of a blanket, so that they could run under the enemies' horses and singe their bellies."

Ben looked appalled.

"They didn't do that in the Macedonian Revolt!"

Clovenhoof gave him a sideways smile.

"Were you there?"

Ben shook his head in confusion.

"By the way, this doesn't mean that I fancy you," said Clovenhoof. "It's just, you know..."

"Yeah I know. Thanks."

"Are you taking those up to Nerys?"

Clovenhoof indicated some handwritten envelopes in pastel covers.

"Yeah, I thought I would," said Ben. "It's funny, I wondered if she might have sent some of these to herself. It's the handwriting-"

"Best not ask. Would you take these up for her?" He handed Ben the flowers. "They're just to say..."

"Yeah I know."

Ben took the flowers and walked upstairs, impressed with Clovenhoof's version of an apology. He'd even taken the trouble to include a small card in the arrangement for Nerys. She'd be pleased with a detail like that.

HEAVEN

- Matters Arising
- Seraphim Rota
- The Throne
- Easter Bonnet Parade
- Clovenhoof
- Harps
- AOB

"Ah," said Michael, looking St Joan of Arc up and down as she entered the boardroom.

He understood that many of the blessed had their own personal iconography. Heaven was a busy place and it was only understandable that individuals might want to dress in a way that made them instantly recognisable to the faithful. Looking round the table, he saw St Peter with his keys of office, the Archangel Gabriel in his pristine blue robes and St Paul with a book of his own writings plus his trademark pointy beard. Pope Pius XII had his little spectacles, even though he no longer needed them. Mother Teresa, even in Heaven where most people incarnated as the youngest and healthiest versions of themselves, kept her 'pickled walnut in a tea-towel' look. St Francis had his tonsure, brown robes and, depending on his mood, a full set of bloody stigmata.

These affectations and traits were all understandable, but Michael had an issue with anyone who turned up to a boardroom meeting wearing shining plate armour and wielding a massive broadsword.

There was a blonde woman in casual clothing with Joan. Michael recognised her at once.

"These seats taken?" said Joan. She plonked herself down with a harmonious clang of armour and patted the other seat with a gauntlet for the other woman to sit beside her.

The board members looked at them.

"Sorry, I'm late," said Joan. "I was showing Evelyn around. She's a recent arrival. What's that word, Evelyn? Newbie?"

"Newbie," agreed Evelyn.

Joan gestured to the board.

"Evelyn, this is the board that runs the whole show. Everyone, this is the Reverend Evelyn Steed. Newbie."

"Reverend?" said Pius.

"Women should remain silent in church," quoted St Paul.

Michael coughed politely.

"Joan, nice though it is to meet Evelyn, we aren't usually in the habit of bringing chums to these meetings."

"What's he doing here then?" said Joan pointing to the pink, jowly man lurking behind St Peter's chair.

"Herbert is my amanuensis," said St Peter. "Not my chum."

Michael kept his gaze from Mother Teresa's minute taking and her attempts to spell 'amanuensis'.

"Well, Evelyn *is* my new chum," said Joan, "and I think her experiences would provide some valuable insight into the problems Heaven is currently facing."

"I thought you were here to talk about the Seraphim singing rota," said Pius.

"That's just a piece of the puzzle," she said. "Do you know how many people have died since the beginning of time?"

There were shrugs and shared glances.

"No," said Gabriel.

"Nor do I," said Joan, "but a rough guess would put it at over one hundred billion. And how many of those people are in heaven?"

Michael spread his hands.

"Do tell."

"No idea," said Joan. "Let's err on the small side and say ten percent. And how big is the Celestial City?"

"Oh, I know this one," said Pius, putting a hand over his eyes to think.

"The city is laid out as a square," quoted St Paul, "and its length is as great as the width and he measured the city with the rod: twelve thousand stadia; its length and width and height are equal."

"Or fifteen hundred miles to a side in new money," said Joan. "And how many angels are there?"

"One hundred million," said St Francis, before St Paul could speak.

"Is there a point to these questions?" asked Pius.

"Can't you see?" said Joan. "We have a major population problem on our hands."

"I don't think that's true," said Gabriel.

"Really? Heaven is of a finite size and has a finite number of angels but is accepting the newly dead every day."

"It is quite busy out there," said Evelyn.

"If you don't like it you can leave," said St Peter.

"All I'm saying is we need to look into it," said Joan. "We need precise figures and a planned solution."

"I quite agree," said Michael.

"You do?"

He nodded enthusiastically.

"This requires immediate investigation. The exact dimensions and capacity of the city need measuring and we need a thorough census of the population. This matter should be subject to a rigorous and *lengthy* study."

St Peter caught his tone.

"If you're going to do this thing, you must do it right."

"If we could leave this with you, Joan," suggested Michael.

"Certainly."

"And Gabriel," Michael continued, "could you ensure Joan is provided with enough data to work with?"

"Of course," said the Archangel.

"Next item," said Michael. "The Easter Bonnet Parade."

St Francis gave a little clap of his hands in excitement.

"A highlight of our cultural year," said Pope Pius XII.

"Is it?" said Joan.

"Pardon?"

"Isn't it – and I don't mean to be rude here – isn't it just a bunch of people in hats?"

"No," said Pius. "It has a far deeper meaning than just hats. It's about connecting to the true meaning of Easter."

"Through the medium of hats?" said Joan.

"And then there's the wabbits," said St Francis. "I love the wabbits."

"The Easter Bunny? Symbol of some ancient Teutonic goddess? Is that the true meaning of Easter?"

St Paul, clearly lacking some precise scriptural quote to express his feelings, gave a grunt of support for Joan's words.

"You don't like the Easter Parade?" said Gabriel.

"It's not that I don't like it," said Joan, "but perhaps we could try to be bit more progressive. Evelyn, here went to something called Greenbelt last year."

"I got right up to the stage when Jars of Clay were playing," said Evelyn.

"I also found these," said Joan, producing a sheaf of large photographs from beneath her breastplate and spreading them on the table. "You have a pair of operatives at work in England, following this man."

She stabbed her finger at a guitar-wielding figure leaping about on stage in front of a baying crowd.

"I believe you saw this Devil Preacher band play, Michael?"

"I, er, did," said Michael.

"I had a listen to some of their music."

"I thought I had destroyed every recording. It was blasphemous."

"It was challenging, yes. Refreshing." She smiled to herself. "They didn't necessarily have nice things to say about you, Peter."

"Is that so?" said St Peter haughtily.

"But I want to bring the kind of energy they embody to future cultural events we hold here."

"You want some guitawists at the Easter Pawade?" said St Francis.

"I want us to hold a festival."

"Oh, well," said Michael happily. "You know we celebrate the feast days of hundreds of saints."

"I mean a rock festival," said Joan.

Michael saw frowns ripple up and down the boardroom table until Gabriel plucked up the courage to voice what they were all thinking.

"You want us to have a feast day for rocks?"

"No, Gabe," said Joan. "I don't."

5

IN WHICH CLOVENHOOF MAKES A FORTUNE, LOSES IT ALL AND HELPS THE POLICE WITH THEIR ENQUIRIES

Clovenhoof enjoyed his weekly trip to the supermarket. There was a tangible sense of achievement in walking out with a trolley piled high with boxes of frozen ready meals, crinkling packets of crisps and biscuits and the melodious tinkle of two dozen bottles of alcoholic froth. He felt like a caveman coming home with a mammoth carcass. The fact that his glorious achievement required no real skill or effort did little to dampen the cosy joy it gave him. And the aspects of the supermarket shop that should have irritated him – the aisles filled with dead eyed humans grasping vainly for meaningless luxuries, the bickering families and wailing children denied every treat they reached out for – were in reality gentle reminders of the Old Place.

He had decided that if he ever returned to his old job he would create a special level of hell, an enormous inescapable shop of attractive but useless and overpriced items that the damned would wander for eternity in the cold delusion that this was what they wanted. And then Nerys had taken him to IKEA and Clovenhoof realised the humans had once again beaten him to it.

"Ninety-one pounds and eight," said the cashier. "Do you have a reward card?"

Oh, and reward cards. Another insanely brilliant soul-destroying human innovation. Make life a game. Collect points. Earn rewards. Distract yourself from any genuine goals and ambitions.

"Indeed," said Clovenhoof. He let the woman scan his reward card, then inserted his credit card, and typed in his pin.

"I'm sorry that's not gone through," said the cashier.

He frowned at her.

"What?"

"Your card has been declined. Do you have another means of payment?"

He shook his head, took out his card and looked at it. It didn't appear damaged. The bumpy writing, the black strip, the magic golden sigil thing all seemed fine. He wasn't exactly sure where the money flowed out of the card, in the same way that he didn't understand how televisions worked or where poo went, but everything seemed in order. He blew on it, gave it a rub and put it back in the card reader.

"Give it another go," he said.

The cashier sighed, put the bill through again and when he typed in his pin once more, said, "No. Sorry, it's not working. Do you have another card? Or cash?"

Clovenhoof shook his head.

"Could I owe you?"

"What?"

"Could I come back and pay you tomorrow?"

"That's not company policy."

"Oh."

"I can put your goods to one side and maybe you could draw some cash from the machine outside."

"I suppose."

Reluctantly, Clovenhoof said farewell to his trolley-load of groceries, like a caveman watching the wounded mammoth escape across the tundra, and went outside. He waited in line for the cash machine, inserted his card, pressed the mystical combination of buttons that would reward him with banknotes and then watched with horror as his card was spat out again. He tried again. He tried a third time.

The old bloke in line behind him leaned forward.

"You've got insufficient funds, mate."

"What does that mean?"

"It means you've run out of money."

Clovenhoof stared with disbelief and increasing frustration. In his anger, he was torn between punching the cash machine or kicking the old bloke in the shin. He opted for the latter as the cash machine looked fairly solid and he didn't want to bruise his knuckles.

He stomped back inside the shop.

What to do? What to do?

He had no money. He couldn't go and take his trolley of shopping without paying. The cashier would see and the security desk and Doug the security guard were close by.

And then he saw the in-store café off to the other side and the bays of parked trolleys next to it, trolleys filled with goods that had already been paid for by inattentive fools who were now rewarding themselves for another successful shopping trip with coffees and teas and sticky cakes.

Sure, those cake-eating fools hadn't shopped with Clovenhoof's needs in mind but some shopping was better than no shopping and, clearly, it couldn't be stealing if it was already paid for.

BEN ENTERED flat 2a to find Clovenhoof, naked from the waist down, experimenting with disposable nappies and sticky tape.

"I'll come back," said Ben.

"No, it's all right," said Clovenhoof, attaching a final piece of tape so the makeshift loincloth, two nappies taped together, just about stayed up.

Ben gestured, wishing he didn't have to.

"Are you going to a fancy dress party?"

"No. Why?"

"Oh. Sorry. It's a medical condition, I see. There's nothing to be ashamed about."

"I'm not incontinent, Kitchen," said Clovenhoof and did a couple of lunges to test the solidity of his construction. "I found them in my shopping. I thought, you know, there are just some times when you can't be arsed to go all the way to the toilet. Thought I'd treat myself to a little luxury. Know what I mean?"

"No," said Ben. "Have you been hiding in here all morning? Nerys was looking for you."

"What for?"

"To help her deliver some charity envelopes."

"What?"

"You know, raising money to dig wells in Africa."

"Can't they dig their own wells?"

"They need the equipment though."

"What? Spades?"

"She says she's got to raise four thousand pounds."

"How expensive are these spades?"

"And it's your fault."

"What?" Clovenhoof paused to adjust his nappy and pop a stray testicle back inside. "How is it my fault?"

"That message you put on those flowers you gave her. Something about her 'generous spirit.'"

"Is that what it said?"

"And now she's got herself involved in some charity drive. And, with her, everything's a bloody competition. And you weren't here this morning to help her."

"Ah," said Clovenhoof, finally understanding Ben's peevish tone. "So you...?"

"Two hundred poxy envelopes through two hundred poxy letterboxes. Yes. On my morning off." He rubbed his fingers together and sniffed them. They smelled coppery, like old pennies. "People don't clean their letterboxes, do they? Who knows what's touched them."

"Well, letters mainly," said Clovenhoof.

Ben suddenly felt unclean, went into the kitchen and washed his hands under the hot tap. The handwash dispenser, usually empty, was full for once and he pumped several blobs into his palm and lathered up thoroughly.

"To be honest, I've had more important things on my mind," said Clovenhoof.

"Oh, I can see."

"My bank has stopped giving me money. My cards don't work."

"Are you overdrawn?" said Ben, feeling the pungent soap tingle pleasantly on his skin.

"I've no idea what that means."

"I mean, have you looked at your statements?"

"Again, gibberish."

"Have you spoken to your bank?"

"I am going in later."

Ben was about to tell him to put on some trousers before he did but was distracted by the realisation that his hands were tingling *a lot*. He sniffed at the soap. It was a powerful combination of lemon scent and ammonia. He quickly rinsed it off. His fingers had gone bright pink and were still tingling though no longer pleasantly.

He went back into the living room hands outstretched.

"Jeremy, what kind of soap have you put in the kitchen?"

Clovenhoof picked out a bottle from the half-unpacked shopping on the table.

"It's, er, Drain Blaster."

"You've let me wash my hands in drain cleaner?"

Clovenhoof took the lid off.

"It smells lemony."

CLOVENHOOF DROPPED IN AT *BOOKS 'N' BOBS* on his way back home from the bank that afternoon. The woman at the bank had spoken to him at length and he had been thinking about how little he understood the banking system as he walked down Boldmere high street. He now had questions and resolved to put them to Ben.

The shop was empty as usual. The sound of Aussie rockers AC/DC turned down to a faint warble emanated from Ben's computer on the counter. Ben made a harsh scoffing sound when he saw Clovenhoof and held up his hands to show him. The raw, split skin of his hands and fingers was plastered with thick white cream.

"I've got to ask," said Clovenhoof.

"I bet you bloody do," said Ben.

"Is money-lending legal?"

"What?"

"Is lending money to someone legal?"

"Of course it is."

"I mean, I'm only just getting used to the concept that it isn't free. I thought it just magically appeared. Like... like snot. And earwax."

"Jeremy," said Ben, waving his hands at him, "haven't you noticed something unusual?"

"That's what I'm saying. I went into the bank and spoke to a very nice lady and she told me that, for months, I've been spending money that isn't mine."

"You've been borrowing money."

"I never asked anyone for it."

"No, you sort of have to say you don't want it. The banks assume you do."

"That's odd. And what's odder is that they want it back now. With extra money on top called *interest*, which is like a fine or something."

"They usually send out a reminder letter in red ink before the situation becomes too painful. And speaking of *red* and *painful*..."

Ben waved his hands under Clovenhoof's nose again. It was almost as if he was trying to tell him something.

"Well, I didn't pay attention to those," said Clovenhoof. "I thought they weren't to do with me."

"Why would you think that?"

"I don't know. And the nice lady said that my home would be at risk if I didn't pay up. Do they firebomb it or something?"

"No, mate, they'll send round the bailiffs first."

"Who?"

"Big, beefy men who'll take all your possessions and sell them to pay off your debt."

"Sort of like pirates. Or brigands."

"Yes, except they're called bailiffs."

"So, let me get this straight. I have borrowed money I didn't ask for and now, if I don't pay back more than I borrowed, the lady at the bank will send thugs round to take my precious stuff and probably take my flat off me too."

"Yes."

"And she's doing this to people other than me?"

"Absolutely."

"She must be very rich to be able to lend out so much money."

"It isn't hers. It belongs to the owners of the bank."

"And who are they?"

"I don't know. Shareholders. Businessmen."

"And how did they get their riches?"

"Through investments, I suppose."

"Which is?"

"Lending money to other people and getting back more than they put in."

"So, the rich investors are rich because they've been lending money to poor people and they use the money they make to put more poor people in debt."

"Well, that's probably a bit too simplistic."

"And this is legal? It's not a criminal offence?"

"No. I suppose it's not very fair when you put it like that."

"It's fantastic. I had no idea such things were possible. We had nothing so brazenly devious back in the Old Place."

"You're not worried?"

Clovenhoof shrugged.

"I'll find some money somewhere. Sell my services somehow. As long as I can afford life's simple pleasures. Look, Ben..."

"What?"

"I know you've been avoiding mentioning it but" – Clovenhoof pointed at the man's cream-smeared hands – "have you been eating ice-cream without a spoon or something?"

Ben's cheeks flushed hotly.

"This is emollient cream."

"French ice-cream?"

"It's to soothe the burns I got from washing my hands in drain cleaner."

"Why did you do that?"

"Why did you put drain cleaner in a soap dispenser?"

"It smelled lemony."

Ben growled.

"I've not been able to get on the computer all afternoon. I've got a dozen items to put on eBay and my fingers keep slipping off the keys. And *hurting*."

"I could help," said Clovenhoof.

"It's the least you could do in the circumstances."

Clovenhoof frowned.

"No, I don't think so. The least I could is just go home or stand here and laugh at you." He came round behind the counter. "Show me how this eBay thing works then."

Ben showed him the website and explained the principle.

"So, it's an auction," said Clovenhoof.

"Yes, but one open to anyone with access to the internet. I sell more books this way than to actual shop customers."

"I was wondering how you made a living without anyone actually coming into the shop."

"Hey, I had six people in here this morning."

"Was that when it was raining?"

"Might have been."

"So, you have to show photos of the stuff you're selling."

"It helps a lot."

"And you can use this to sell anything."

"Pretty much. Books. Clothes. Cars even. I think I saw a Chieftain tank on eBay once."

"Cool."

In no time at all, nodding to the sound of Ben's hard rock,

Clovenhoof had uploaded fifteen rare books and watched the first bids appear.

"Free money," said Clovenhoof.

"You've got to have something to sell," said Ben.

"Right. Well, that's done. I need a pee."

Ben jerked a pink thumb over his shoulder.

"Toilet's in back."

"No need," said Clovenhoof and closed his eyes. "You forget I have moved beyond the realm of mere toilets."

Ben moved away hurriedly.

Clovenhoof opened his eyes.

"See?"

"That's disgusting."

"You're jealous." He stopped, stood up and shook his leg. "Oops, a bit of a leak."

"Oh, God."

Clovenhoof looked at Ben reproachfully.

"It's a prototype, Kitchen. Don't shoot down my dreams so quickly."

"This is not a dream, Jeremy."

CLOVENHOOF EBAYED half his possessions that night. He created an account on his computer, took snaps with a digital camera he had bought but never previously used and wrote florid and tantalising descriptions of each item.

He even put Herbert the Mould on but with a thousand pound reserve price.

Later on, as he ran out of things to sell, he got creative. He thought about auctioning off his internal organs but couldn't work out how to take photographs without causing lasting damage. The last item he put on the site before he retired to his bed (which was already going for an exciting four pounds nineteen) was entitled *Dirty Deeds Done Dirt Cheap* and which he described with the words:

WANT *to give someone a piano-wire necktie? Need someone put in concrete shoes? Got an unsightly corpse under your patio? Whatever it is, I will do it. One job to you, the highest bidder.*

HE WAS PARTICULARLY pleased with that one and slept with a smile on his face.

THE NEXT DAY, Clovenhoof checked on his items and was pleased to see that some, such as his curtains and heavy metal bondage gear were being hotly competed for, although others, such as the toilet brush and a second prototype man-nappy remained curiously untouched. All the auctions still had some time to go and he felt the itch to sell more. Also, unless Herbert went for the hoped-for thousand pounds, he was unlikely to make enough to pay off the demonic bank woman.

And so, logic dictated, he would have to sell some things that weren't his. Armed with his digital camera and his credit card (now transformed from money-maker to lock-opener) he explored the other flats while their occupants were out.

He took nothing but photographs, reasoning that he didn't need to steal the items unless they went for a decent price and then, if an unlikely pang of conscience gripped him, he could leave part of the proceeds as payment.

In flat 1a, he took snaps of vases, paintings and the fox stole in Mrs Astrakhan's wardrobe. In 1b, he found an alarming collection of china cats, a digital radio and a bread-maker. In flat 3, he found Aunt Molly fast asleep in front of a blaring daytime chat show so had to work quietly around her, taking pictures of shoes, a library's worth of self-improvement books and an assortment of battery-operated toys he found in a bedside drawer. Finally in 2b, a flat he had more familiarity with, he set to work with a frenzied zeal, photographing every dusty vinyl record, every tiny legion of ancient soldiers and every piece of computer hardware. He tried to force the padlock from the blue and brass trunk in the hall area but it was stronger than him so he photographed the trunk instead with the intention of selling it along with its unseen contents.

As he finished up there was a knocking sound from outside. He went to the door. Across the way, outside his own flat were two shaven-headed men, one tall and one fat – well, one *taller* and one *fatter*.

"Who are you?" said Clovenhoof.

They turned to look at him. They didn't move quickly.

"Is he in?" said the taller one, his voice like a sack of potatoes rolling down stairs.

"Who?"

"Clovenhoof."

"No," said Clovenhoof honestly. "Who are you?"

The fatter one held out a clipboard, attached to which was a crumpled sheet of yellow triplicate paper.

"Debt collection service," said the taller one.

"Oh, bailiffs," said Clovenhoof, pleased to see what they looked like although a little disappointed that they looked nothing like pirates.

The fatter one posted something through Clovenhoof's letterbox.

"Just tell him we came," said the taller one. "And we'll be back."

Clovenhoof waved to them as they thumped down the stairs.

A close call, thought Clovenhoof. He didn't want anyone stealing – *legally* stealing - his personal possessions before he had a chance to make a little money from them. They'd be back and banging on his door again. Unless...

The flat numbers on the doors were printed on silver plastic squares with self-adhesive backs. It was only a moment's work to prize the 'a' off his own door and swap it with the 'b' on Ben's door. The squares didn't stick very well once moved but a bit of spit and pressure made them stay.

"Genius," said Clovenhoof.

Nerys came up the stairs to find Clovenhoof polishing the door number to his flat with his thumb tip.

"I just met two very unpleasant men downstairs as I was coming in," she said.

"Big blokes? No hair?"

"One of them was so fat he looked like Buddha's evil twin. The other one was more your classic knuckle-dragger. Both had the same poor grasp of clothes sizes. Why do men think wearing tight trousers and letting their bellies sag over the top is at all attractive?"

"I don't think it's a deliberate look."

"They were looking for you."

"They found me."

"Actually, *I've* been looking for you."

"I'm a popular guy."

"You owe me a favour."

"Do I?"

"You injured my assistant."

"I did what?"

"Dipped his hands in acid or something."

"Drain cleaner."

She beckoned with a hooked finger.

"Come with me, Jeremy."

Nerys led him up to flat 3 where Aunt Molly slept in front of the television. Nerys took a folder from her work bag and opened it out on the table. She opened up the colour-coded map, extended the fold-outs of her targeting strategy and income projections and then simply stood there to let the majesty of her plan settle on Clovenhoof.

"You need some pins and flags," said Clovenhoof.

"They fall out when I pack it away."

"And some little tank divisions and bomber squadrons and one of those paddles to push it across the table."

"It's not an invasion plan," she said curtly, although she

was quietly pleased by the comparison. "It's my charity collection project."

"You're buying spades for Africans."

"And I need your help to collect the envelopes."

Clovenhoof inspected the map. His finger traced along the red lines of the high-income streets she had identified.

"Forgive me," he said, "but since when did you care about thirsty Africans?"

"I have a caring nature," she said.

"A caring nature means putting fifty pee in a collection tin. This..."

"I have a *very* caring nature."

"Nerys..."

She flinched under the look he gave her.

"Okay," she admitted. "There's a charity gala ball next month and the top ten fundraisers in each region get a free ticket."

"You're doing this for a party ticket?"

"Not just a party. A party attended by wealthy philanthropists. Wealthy, potentially single philanthropists."

"Ah, you want access to the hunting grounds."

"Exactly," she smiled. "And Tina in the office says she's already on target to raise four thousand pounds. That's the competition. I don't want to merely beat her. I want to drive her into the ground, crush her smug little face under my foot."

"I can see your caring nature shining through, Nerys."

She ignored the comment.

"We have six days left."

"We? Oh, you're taking me to this party?"

"We means me. You're just my friendly neighbourly helper."

"Why me?"

"Because I have a full-time job and an elderly relative who requires round the clock care."

Clovenhoof looked at Aunt Molly, snoozing silently in her chair.

"Whereas," said Nerys, "you're an unemployed layabout with time on your hands."

"So you're going to pay me to help you?"

"Jeremy!" She was taken aback. "You would have me take money from the world's poorest to line your pockets?"

"Yes?" he suggested.

She ignored the comment and kitted him out with everything he needed: the smaller map of the local area with the streets he should visit, a laminated postcard with his charity collector's script on it, a canvas satchel to put his collections in and a black flip over notepad.

"What's this for?"

"To jot down the names and addresses of any potential gentleman friends."

"I don't want a gentleman friend."

She glared at him and gave him the tick list of desirable qualities in a man.

"Socks?" said Clovenhoof, reading the first item on the list.

Nerys nodded earnestly.

"Any man who is going around barefoot at this time of day is either a sponger or a hippy."

She looked down at Clovenhoof's feet and found herself

mysteriously unable to tell if he was wearing anything on his feet or not. She rubbed her eyes, blinked and then gave up.

CHARITY COLLECTING TURNED out to be even less fun that Clovenhoof had expected and he had expected it to be no fun at all.

He wrestled with a tiny garden gate with a difficult latch and a loud squeak. This street had them at every single house. He could easily have jumped over it but Nerys had included a section in his instructions about '*decorum*'.

He went up the path and rang the bell. It was answered by an old lady.

"I've come to collect the charity envelope," said Clovenhoof.

"Betty!" the woman called over her shoulder. "Come here and see the charity man."

Another old lady appeared, eyes wide.

"Ooh Doris, well I never!" she exclaimed.

They stood and grinned at him side by side for a few seconds.

"So, have you got the envelope?" he asked.

"Come in and sit down for a minute while we find it," said Betty. "Maybe you'd like a nice cup of tea? We're gasping for one, aren't we Doris?"

"Gasping," Doris agreed.

They led him in and sat him down. Betty rummaged in a large handbag, but instead of pulling out the collection envelope, she produced a notebook and pen.

Doris disappeared into the kitchen.

"So, you're collecting for a charity?" Betty asked.

"Yes," Clovenhoof replied.

"How do we know he's not going to keep the money for himself?" Doris called from the kitchen, accompanied by the banging of cupboard doors.

"I've got a card, from the charity," said Clovenhoof, showing his ID to Betty.

"Well, this looks authentic," said Betty, jotting something on her notepad. "How much have you collected so far?"

"It's all in envelopes, I can't tell."

Betty nodded and made another note.

"Has everyone given you money, so far?"

"Why are you so interested in this?"

"Doris and I are always interested in other people, aren't we Doris?"

"More like a morbid fascination if you ask me," called Doris.

Clovenhoof decided that they were both just nosey. This would be a week's worth of chatter for them.

"No," he snorted. "Some people are do-gooders. Smiley with it as well. But more often than not, people will pretend they're not in, even though I can see them, twitching their curtains. Some of them will say they've lost their envelopes," he raised an eyebrow, "and I *do* have spares if you're interested. Anyway, the worst of all are those that tell me that it's morally wrong to give to charity."

"Why are they the worst?"

"Because they can't be ars- I mean bothered to even come up with a half-convincing reason. It's like 'I'm lying, you know I'm lying, I know you know I'm lying and I don't care.'"

Betty made another note.

"Fascinating. So what made you decide to help out?"

"For a friend. I decided that in the long run it would be less painful to do this than to put up with the moaning I'd get if I didn't. I am beginning to wonder though."

"Well, that's *lovely*! You're doing it for a friend!"

"So anyway," Clovenhoof asked, losing patience, "did you find the envelope or do you need another?"

"Yes it's right here," said Betty.

She picked it off a nest of tables to her side, and dived back into her bag to find some money. Clovenhoof couldn't be sure, but it looked as though she put a thick wad of twenty pound notes inside.

Doris came through from the kitchen.

"Betty, I think we're out of tea," she said.

"How about a sherry?" asked Betty. "I was about to have a small one myself."

"No, I'd better be off," said Clovenhoof, standing up and taking the envelope. "I've got lots more excuses to listen to before I go home."

THE REST of the road provided very slim pickings, and Clovenhoof came to the conclusion that the annoying squeaky gates were actually an early-warning system that alerted householders to visitors so that they could check them out and ignore them more easily.

The man who simply told him to piss off came as a refreshing change and made Clovenhoof curious.

"Can I ask why you want me to piss off?" asked Clovenhoof.

The man stroked his stubble-covered chin wearily.

"Because I want you to piss off," said the man.

"Yeah, but is it because you don't like giving to charity or is it something about me you don't like?"

"Look, mate, I'm kind of in the middle of something here."

He raised his right hand in which he held a bottle of imported lager and, tucked between his fingers, a slim wad of banknotes bound together with a paper band. Money. Refined tastes. Clovenhoof checked out the man's feet. Socks and shoes. This could be one for Nerys's little black book.

"So," persisted Clovenhoof, "if you weren't in the middle of something, would you be giving to charity or would you still tell me to piss off?"

The man gave a raspy bark of laughter.

"You cheeky bastard," he smiled. "Tell you what, I'll toss you for it."

He pulled out a fifty-pence piece from his pocket.

"You win, I'll give you a nice crisp twenty. If I win, I'll have one off you from your collection bag."

"Deal."

"You call," said the man.

Clovenhoof called. They both looked at the coin on the porch carpet. The man peeled a note from his fingers and passed it to him.

"Happy now?"

"Very," said Clovenhoof. "Double or quits?"

The man looked at the sheath of banknotes in his hand for a long time.

"Why don't you come in?" he said.

NERYS HAD ONLY SHARED one folder of her fundraising project with Clovenhoof. The second folder was devoted to her plan of action at the charity gala ball, once she secured a place. She had done some research on the guest list, including possible targets and possible competition. The gossip pages were essential in finding out which of the celebrities and high-flyers had wives or girlfriends. Having partners didn't necessarily remove a man from her list. She was certainly no home-wrecker, but if a marriage was on the point of breaking up, it wouldn't be wrong to step into the rift.

A large part of Nerys's plan involved her wardrobe. Clothes were the silent communicator. A properly chosen outfit could say anything you wanted it to say. A perfect outfit could lie better than the most gifted conman. And shoes... shoes were the most gifted liars of all.

Nerys looked back with warm disdain at her younger self, strutting around nightclubs in her 'fuck me' shoes. She had moved on so much since then. Now, her best shoes were 'wine me, dine me and, if you're a very good boy, I will fuck you ragged' shoes.

With Molly only vaguely stirring from her nap, Nerys sat down with her laptop and browsed the internet. Ten minutes later, she found something interesting. Five seconds after that she was swearing bloody vengeance in her head. A minute after that she was hammering on Ben's front door. Twelve minutes after that she stormed into Ben's bookshop and slammed the door behind her.

"Whoa," said Ben. "Hinges and glass cost money, Nerys."

"Are you SuttonSeller666?" Nerys demanded.

"Am I what?"

"On eBay. I know you sell lots of stuff on the web."

"Oh, right. No. I'm BensBooksnBobs."

"Really?"

"Yeah. Why?"

"I'll show you. Log on to eBay."

Ben held up his hands. They were slathered in cream and covered with clear plastic gloves.

"Rather not."

Nerys grumbled, came round the counter and took control of the computer.

"Look," she said.

Ben looked.

"Nice shoes."

"They're *my* shoes."

"Oh, you're selling them."

"No," she said loudly, "but someone is!"

"Why are you letting someone sell your things?"

"Shut up. Look. They also listed my books, my toaster, Molly's Toby jugs – actually, I ought to sell those – and-"

"They've listed your Aunt Molly as an item," said Ben. He pointed at the image of the dozing woman. "She's listed as an 'antique conversation piece' and – hey!"

He grabbed the mouse from her, smearing her with his slimy gloves.

"Those are my records!" he exclaimed. "And my phalanx of Argyraspides! They cost me fifty quid in kit form! Oh no!"

He had clicked on the picture of the blue and brass trunk that stood in his flat.

"Current bid twenty-five pounds," said Nerys. "Not bad."

"How could he do this?" Ben moaned.

"Who?" said Nerys.

Ben glared at her.

"Who do you think?"

CLOVENHOOF SAT ON A LEATHER ARMCHAIR, across from Roger – stubbly, beer-drinking Roger – and looked at the amassed pile of cash, now his, on the coffee table.

He was no longer entirely sure what was going on. Roger had invited him in, and despite his initial offish nature, was clearly glad to have someone to talk to. All the curtains in the house were drawn, Roger was the only occupant and the way he moved about the place indicated that Roger was trying very hard to act as if nobody was home at all.

It might have had something to do with three gym bags full of cash beneath the living room floorboards, all neatly banded and wrapped in cellophane. Roger had explained he was holding it for someone.

"Like a bank?" Clovenhoof had asked.

"Like a bank," agreed Roger and passed him another beer.

Roger hadn't been forced to dip into the gym bags or even reveal their presence until he had lost seven successive tosses of the coin and found himself owing Clovenhoof one thousand two hundred and eighty pounds.

Roger had tried to laugh it off, said, "Fun's over. I'll give you that twenty, we'll have a beer and you can be on your way," and reached for the money but Clovenhoof drew it close to himself and gave Roger a warning look.

"I won it fair and square, Roger," he said.

"Don't make me unhappy, Jeremy."

"I'll try not to."

"That's not my money, mate."

"I know. It's mine."

"It belongs to some nasty people."

"Thank you," said Clovenhoof.

Roger gave him a pained look.

"Please."

Clovenhoof leaned forward and grinned broadly.

"Double or quits?"

And so the floorboards were lifted up, the first of three gym bags removed and the game continued.

Half an hour later, three beers and two gym bags later, Clovenhoof stretched and said, "I've got to go."

"You can't," said Roger.

"It's nearly tea-time."

"I have to have that money back."

"No."

"I have a knife," said Roger abruptly.

Clovenhoof nodded thoughtfully.

"Is it worth...?" He paused to calculate, "...ten thousand two hundred and forty pounds?"

"What?"

"Didn't think so."

Clovenhoof stood, hoisted a bag in each hand and made for the door. Roger followed him, pleading, then ran off into the back of the house. Clovenhoof opened the door, stepped out in the evening air and suddenly felt a pain in the centre of his back.

"Ow!" he declared loudly and spun round, ripping the knife from Roger's hand and leaving the blade embedded in his spine.

Roger froze, wide-eyed.

"That really hurt!" said Clovenhoof irritably, put the bags down for a second and awkwardly reached behind him to pull the knife out. He grunted as it came free. Clovenhoof looked at the bloody blade and then tossed it into the front garden.

"I'm going to be bleeding all night now," snapped Clovenhoof, picked up his winnings and strode off.

Roger made no attempt to follow him.

It was only a short walk home, made longer and more annoying by the tickly stream of blood that ran down his back into his underpants. It was one of his favourite shirts too and probably beyond saving, blood being such an awkward stain.

He slammed the door of his flat, threw the bags of money onto his sofa and stripped off his bloody clothes. He inspected the wound in the bathroom mirror. The five-inch gash had already closed up, leaving a dark, purplish scar.

There was a loud knock at the door. Clovenhoof put on a quilted dressing gown and answered it.

Ben and Nerys stood side by side on the landing, arms crossed, glaring at him. Clovenhoof looked at them for several seconds.

"I can do this for hours, I practise all the time against Herbert. You've no idea how good he is," he declared.

"What?"

"Ben blinked! It's a game, right?"

He looked at Ben's plastic gloves lined with medicated cream.

"Are you about to investigate a cow's rear end? I saw this programme and-"

"You're SuttonSeller666," said Ben.

"Oh, have you bid on something?" smiled Clovenhoof.

"You've put our belongings on eBay."

"Not all of them."

"How could you do that?" said Nerys.

"There's step by step instructions."

"But our things!" said Ben.

"I was going to split the money with you."

"My aunt!" said Nerys.

Clovenhoof rolled his eyes.

"Fine. Have a go at a man for trying to raise a little cash."

He stepped back into his flat and pick up the canvas satchel of collected envelopes.

"I've been doing your filthy work all afternoon and as you can see," – he waved his hand over the two gym bags – "I've been very busy."

"What's in there?"

Nerys opened one of the bags and looked at the loose notes inside.

"You robbed a post office?"

"I got that fair and square."

Ben tried to get a better look.

"Is that...?"

"A lot of money," nodded Nerys.

"See?" said Clovenhoof. "I'd say that congratulations are in order. So what do you say?"

"Thank you," said Nerys.

"Eh?"

She put the money away and picked up the two gym bags.

"Tina is going to be so jealous when she sees this."

"No, you don't understand...," said Clovenhoof.

"What about the eBay thing?" said Ben. "Aren't we still angry?"

Nerys hefted the bags in her hands, clearly enjoying their weight in her hands.

"Hi-jinks. A joke. Jeremy hasn't actually sold any of our things."

"He wanted to sell your aunt. Your dog too."

"If only someone would buy them," said Nerys with a trill of laughter. "It was all for a good cause, wasn't it?"

"Wait," said Clovenhoof, "that money is mine."

"And I won't forget your efforts to help those less fortunate than yourself."

She danced out of the flat. Clovenhoof watched the money go and wondered why he hadn't stopped her.

"So," said Ben, "you'll take those auction listings down?"

"S'pose so," said Clovenhoof moodily.

"Good. Have you sorted out your finances with the bank yet?"

Clovenhoof gave his sofa a sulky little kick.

"I'll go see them tomorrow."

"Good. Then you can do me a favour. I need you to pick up my prescription for hand cream at the chemist tomorrow. I can't even manage my own door keys with these gloves on."

"If I must."

"You must."

"You want my advice?" said Clovenhoof.

"What?"

"You shouldn't have washed your hands with drain cleaner."

THE FOLLOWING morning was a Saturday which annoyed Nerys as she wanted to take the bundles of cash she had collected to work and rub them, metaphorically and actually, in Tina's smug fake-tan face. She would have phoned her up but couldn't think of any believable pretext for the call. By noon, she was sufficiently irritated by her inability to gloat that she called Tina anyway and to hell with any kind of pretext.

"Hi Tina," she said. "Yes, everything's fine. I know it's Saturday. I was just wondering how your fundraising is going because I've..." She paused as Tina cut across her. "Oh," said Nerys eventually in a much less buoyant tone. "That's... that's wonderful. That's amazing. Me?" She thought about the bags under her bed. "I'm doing my best. I know, only a few days left to go. Yes. It *is* all for a good cause. No, that was it. Just catching up with you. See you Monday."

She killed the call and hurled her phone onto a chair.

"Cheating bitch!" she snarled.

There was a knock at the door.

"'Corporate donation'!" she spat as she crossed the lounge. "'Greasing a few wheels'? She's been greasing more than wheels, that tramp. Everyone knows what she did at the regional managers' away weekend. You don't get carpet burns like that doing the Macarena."

She twisted the latch savagely and wrenched the door open, prepared to give both barrels to whoever it was, but checked herself rapidly when she saw the dark-haired man who stood on her landing.

It wasn't the look in his green eyes that stopped her, that dangerous, self-assured, knowing glint. It wasn't the fine shape of his handsome chin or the faint, roguish scar on his cheek. It wasn't his perfect hair. It wasn't even the classy lines of his dark suit and the suggestion of the physique beneath.

It was the blue and white charity envelope in his hand.

"Are you Nerys Thomas?" he asked.

"Yes?"

"Have you been distributing these in the local area?"

"I have," she smiled.

Her mind was already racing ahead. Here was a man, moved by her philanthropic nature, seeking her out to thank her for her selfless efforts. Perhaps a drink out? Dinner? A passionate tumble between the sheets?

"One of your people came to my house yesterday," he said.

"Did he? He didn't mention you."

"Mention me?"

"Mention meeting someone like you," she said.

Clovenhoof hadn't made any note of this near-perfect specimen in the notebook she had given him. She would have to chastise him later.

"I wasn't in at the time," he said. "My... brother, Roger, gave him a donation."

"Oh, I see. Would you like to come in?"

The man leaned against the doorjamb.

"I was hoping to speak to the man who came to my house."

"Of course. But come in for a cup of tea first. Or coffee. Is it too early for a glass of wine?"

"Where can I find the person who came to my house?"

"Is there a problem?"

"I think he might have accidentally picked up something that belongs to me."

"He took something from you?"

The man gave a disarming smile.

"Accidentally, I'm sure. Where can I find him?"

"Flat 2a. Downstairs."

He nodded.

"You've been a great help."

He turned to go.

"What about that cup of tea?" said Nerys.

"Another time, Nerys," he said.

CLOVENHOOF TRIED to put a brave face on the new day.

His eBay efforts had been stymied before they'd even been given chance. Sure, he still had his own possessions up for auction but he had reluctantly taken down the items that weren't *technically* his. eBay had also removed several listings for him and sent him a stern message regarding inappropriate postings. He thought something ridiculous had to come to pass when one was barred from selling animals, old ladies and contract killings over the internet.

That, plus the money he had let Nerys take from him, had set him back at square one. He had no income, no resources to fall back on and no brilliant money-making schemes in the pipeline. He was going to have to throw himself on the bank's mercy and beg for more money.

On the way to the bank, he went into the post office and put a card in the window. It was his *Dirty Deeds Done Dirt Cheap* advert with his phone number on the bottom. If the internet was going to block his attempts at making a quid or two, he could at least rely on traditional *local* advertising. He watched the assistant put the card in next to a much-faded *Keep Boldmere Beautiful* poster. It was similar to the ones that he used at home as toilet paper. He felt inspired by the notion and upturned a nearby wheelie bin. It made Boldmere much more beautiful, he decided.

He popped into the chemist, collected Ben's large tube of emollient cream and then stepped into the bank where he joined the small queue for the one cashier they had put on that morning.

"I recall a time when you would have pushed to the front of a queue like this," said a voice at his shoulder. "Actually, stabbed and garrotted your way to the front."

Clovenhoof turned.

"Where the bloody hell have you been?"

The Archangel Michael smiled.

"Pleased to see me? I'm touched."

"The one time I've needed you and you've been conspicuous by your absence."

"I've been watching."

"Watching me flounder, you bastard. Where's my money?"

Michael gave him a look of mild incomprehension.

"You've spent it all, dear friend."

"How can that be?"

The queue moved forward, leaving only one person between Clovenhoof and the cashier.

"As I said to you before, heaven's coffers are not limitless."

"And as I said to you before, bollocks. I need money."

"Then earn some."

"Earn some?" hissed Clovenhoof. "I thought I had earned it. Thousands of years doing the shittiest job in creation."

"That wasn't work. That was you stewing in your own rebellious juices."

"As part of the Other Guy's effing ineffable plan!"

"I told you not to overspend."

"Shut up, you sanctimonious cock. Just give me some money. Magic some up. Make it appear. By the time I get to this counter, I want a hundred million quid in my bank account."

Michael placed a loving hand on his shoulder.

"Tantrums will get you nowhere, Clovenhoof."

Clovenhoof pulled away and, as the customer in front moved off, wheeled on the cashier.

"Okay, love, show me the money."

"I beg your pardon," said the cashier.

"My money. I want my money now."

"You have an account?"

"Here." Clovenhoof took out his wallet and frisbee'd a succession of bank and credit cards through the divide and onto her side of the counter.

"Just give me all the money."

The cashier picked up the cards slowly, fixing Clovenhoof with the strangest look.

"This joker said I had to earn my money but, you know, sod it, I'll just take it. I'd kill for it if I had to, I put a card in the post office, but no one has to die, do they? Not really."

"No," said the cashier.

Without actually moving anywhere, she seemed to be trying to back away from him.

"I don't want anyone to die," said Clovenhoof. "I don't like mess."

The cashier gathered all the cards together.

"Yes. No. I'm not sure what it is you want, sir."

"Look, we're wasting time. My friend, Ben, is waiting on me. He's in some pain, you know."

Clovenhoof tapped the large bulge in his jacket pocket where the cream was. This seemed to crystallise the cashier's attention.

"You want money," she said.

"Please don't pander to him," said Michael. "If you just give it to him, he'll never learn."

"Ignore him," said Clovenhoof. "Open up that till and just give me everything you've got. While we're still alive, eh?"

"Of course," said the cashier, her hands trembling.

WHEN THE KNOCK came at Ben's door, he almost jumped from his seat.

This was it, he thought. His fears had been realised.

The lie he had told Clovenhoof about being unable to manage his door keys was a simple ruse, an excuse to stay at home and prepare for this moment. Nervously, he got up and opened the door.

"I'm sorry," he said to the two men at the door. "It's not for sale."

"What isn't?" said the dark-haired man with the scar on his cheek.

"The trunk. In fact, none of it's for sale. It's all a horrible mistake."

The man frowned and then turned to his stubble-cheeked companion. This second man, shifting unhappily from foot to foot, had a black eye, a split lip and the look of a rabbit that had finally been caught by the greyhound.

"Is this him?" asked the scarred man.

"No," said the terrified rabbit of a man.

Scar looked at the door. Ben saw that his flat number had inexplicably become 2a.

"Oh, you're after Jeremy," he said and then nodded in

further realisation. The bailiffs, of course. "It's about the money, right?"

"Quite. Is this Jeremy in?"

"No, but he'll be back in a bit."

"Good," said Scar and walked into the flat, pushing Ben before him. "Roger," he said. "Get the door."

THE CASHIER PUT the bundles of cash from her register into a small canvas coin sack.

Clovenhoof grinned smugly at Michael.

"I knew you'd see sense."

"I've not done anything," said Michael. He looked around. "Actually, I'm not sure what's going on here…"

A bank employee in a suit hovered like a wobbly mannequin in a doorway. The customers in the queue behind them had mysteriously melted away. One was crouched behind a glass partition filming Clovenhoof with his mobile phone.

Clovenhoof took the sack from the cashier's outstretched hand.

"Thank you. Must dash," he said. "Who knows what state poor Ben is in."

He stepped out onto the street with a doubtful Michael in tow.

"You know," said Michael, "to the untrained eye, what just happened in there looked an awful lot like… Ah."

The 'ah' was directed towards the flashing blue lights approaching from the distance.

"I think we need to run now," said Michael.

"Really?" said Clovenhoof.

"Yes. I don't think my get out of jail free card is going to help you this time."

Clovenhoof looked at the money in his hand. The sirens grew louder.

"Surely, they don't think..." he said, but Michael was already ten yards away and accelerating.

NERYS CAME DOWNSTAIRS to find the two badly dressed bailiffs on the first floor landing, arguing over their clipboard.

"Yeah, but it was this door," insisted the taller one, Knuckle-dragger.

"It was flat 2*a*," said the one that she'd christened Buddha, whose belly not only hung over the edge of his belt but actually poked out from under his T-shirt, as though it were trying to make a bid for freedom.

"Excuse me," said Nerys haughtily, not willing to physically squeeze past the obese apes.

They shuffled slowly aside and she went up to Clovenhoof's flat door. The roguishly handsome young man had yet to come back up for his cup of tea and she had begun to worry what Clovenhoof had done with him. She raised her hand to knock, saw that Clovenhoof's door was now labelled 2b and turned to look at Ben's door which Knuckle-dragger had decided to knock at.

The door opened. The scar-faced man's eyes flicked between the two bailiffs.

"Who are you?"

"Mr Clovenhoof?" said Knuckle-dragger.

"He's not here. Piss off."

Knuckle-dragger gave a cynical chuckle and just walked in, brushing the man aside.

"Mr Clovenhoof, you owe us some money," said the bailiff to Scar.

"I think there's been some mistake," said Nerys and followed them in.

"Bloody right. Any money he's got is mine," said Scar.

"I really do think you should listen to me," said Nerys, managing to manoeuvre round Buddha and then stopped.

Ben was sitting on his sofa, his hands and feet bound before him with silver duct tape. Sitting next to him was a bruised man with a rodent face.

"Kinky," said a bailiff.

"What is going on here?" said Nerys.

Scar pulled a pistol from the waistband of his trousers.

"We're waiting for my money," he said. "Now, shut the door, Nerys. There's a love."

CLOVENHOOF AND MICHAEL cut a corner across St Michael's churchyard, dodging between tombstones and looking up through the trees to see if they could see the helicopter that was circling noisily above.

"We're not going to make it," said Clovenhoof.

"More speed, less chat," panted Michael. He leaped a wall and sprinted on towards the Chester Road.

The sound of sirens seemed to be coming at them from all angles. Somewhere behind them was the sound of squealing tyres. Clovenhoof didn't dare look round and focused on keeping up with his angelic partner in crime.

Michael cut straight across the Chester Road, causing cars to brake suddenly in both directions. Clovenhoof clattered over the bonnet of a Vauxhall Astra, leaving a nice hoof-shaped dent in the bodywork, ran up the path to the flats and slammed his key into the door with astonishing accuracy.

"Upstairs! Upstairs!" he hissed, pushing Michael in ahead of him.

Together, stumbling over one another, they got to the first floor.

"Not my flat," said Clovenhoof. "If they've seen my face..."

Michael hammered on Ben's door, which was opened almost instantly by Nerys.

"Jeremy-"

"Out of the way," said Clovenhoof, bundling Michael inside.

Clovenhoof slammed the door behind him and bent over, wheezing with exhaustion.

"That was a close one," he said once he had regained his breath and straightened up.

He looked at the people in Ben's flat. Nerys, Ben and Roger sat in a miserable row on the sofa. Ben was wrapped up in silver tape. The two bailiffs were sitting on either side of the dining table with their hands on their heads. They didn't look particularly happy either.

There was only one person in the flat he didn't recognise and he was holding a gun.

"Are you a bailiff too?" said Clovenhoof.

The man pointed his pistol at the bag in Clovenhoof's hand.

"Is that my money?" he snarled.

"I think it's technically the bank's," said Clovenhoof.

"We're not sure," agreed Michael.

"Toss it here," said the gunman.

Clovenhoof groaned.

"What is it with me? The moment I get some cash, someone wants to take it from me."

"Now!"

Clovenhoof threw the bag to him and, at that moment, there was a rumble on the stairs, a crash and half a dozen armed police officers spilled into the flat, shouting and waving guns.

Ben shrieked. Nerys yelled. Several people swore. A dining chair gave way beneath a huge backside. A shot was fired and answered with several more. Hands were raised. People fell down. And Clovenhoof found himself looking straight down the black barrel of a large gun.

"I can explain," he said. "At least I think I can."

IT TRANSPIRED that Clovenhoof didn't need to explain anything. The situation was perfectly clear to the police officers on the scene as was explained to him at the station.

Trey Daniels, renowned armed robber, currently sought for a bank job in Lichfield had broken into a flat and taken its owner, Ben Kitchen, hostage in order to force Mr Kitchen's friend and neighbour, Jeremy Clovenhoof, to carry out another bank robbery in the local area. Mr Daniels, possibly aided by known accomplice Roger Cotton, had tortured Mr Kitchen by chemically burning his hands just to show he wasn't messing about. Mr Clovenhoof, who had made no attempt to hide his identity whilst in the bank, had also been caught on video telling the cashier that he was worried about his friend's well-being and needed to get back to help him. Mr Daniels, who had received a superficial gunshot wound to the arm, denied all involvement but was unwilling to give the police an alternative version of events. Where Miss Thomas and the Brothers Coddington (one of whom had taken a painful but not life-threatening bullet in the stomach during the police raid) fitted into the story was unclear but the investigating officers were certain they could weave it into their chosen narrative.

CLOVENHOOF AND MICHAEL were released without charge in the early hours of the morning. They might have been there longer if the moustachioed PC Pearson hadn't come into the interview room, laughed at them and then sworn on his life that the pair of them were genuinely harmless fools.

Michael and Clovenhoof walked back to the flat together. Clovenhoof felt as if he'd been wearing his clothes for a week. Michael looked as if he'd just stepped out of an Italian boutique.

"I did not like that one little bit," said Michael.

"I don't think you're meant to like being locked up," said Clovenhoof.

"The cell was draughty. And as for the catering..."

"You could have just waved your magic wand," said Clovenhoof. "Made it all go away."

Michael shook his head.

"Ripples and repercussions. I'd rather this one went away all by itself."

The star-strewn black of night was slowly giving way to a grey spring dawn.

"Here," said Michael and passed Clovenhoof a roll of banknotes held by an elastic band.

"What's this?"

"The last money I'm ever going to give you. I've cleared your bank debts but after this, that's it, no more financial assistance."

"Aw, Michael," said Clovenhoof, stuffing the money in his pocket. "You do care."

"Just stay out of trouble."

"Aye, aye," said Clovenhoof and gave him a ridiculous salute. "I'll be a good boy from now on. You'll see."

"We'll see," agreed Michael and was suddenly not there – not anywhere – anymore.

Clovenhoof let himself into the flats, went upstairs,

looked at the plywood board put up to cover Ben's broken door, and went into his own flat.

There was a message on the answer phone. Clovenhoof pressed play.

"I've seen your advert in the post office window," said a muffled, female voice. "I need a job doing. Her name's Tina. She needs taking down a peg or two. Nothing permanent. Do you do kneecappings? Whatever, just something that'll mean she can't attend a charity gala next month."

Clovenhoof grinned, went to the kitchen to pour himself a drink and then returned with paper and pen to replay the message and jot down the details.

6

IN WHICH CLOVENHOOF LOOKS FOR LOVE, GETS HIS HOOVES BUFFED AND HITS THE DATING SCENE

"Glack, glack, glack."

Nerys cleared her throat and tried again.

"Glack, glack, glack."

There! She was certain she'd got it now.

She shuffled round to the position indicated in the diagram and shifted the torch in her hand.

The duvet was thrown back.

"What are you doing?" said Trevor. Or was it Stephen? She couldn't remember.

"Deep throat technique," said Nerys. "It'll knock your socks off. I just need to relax the muscles at the back of my throat."

"Is that, is that..." his gaze took in the torch and the book "Is that a *sex manual*?"

He grabbed the book.

"'*Make him your love slave; one hundred ways to excite a man in bed.*'"

"I told you, I'm a great believer in self-improvement."

Stephen (or was it Trevor?) hurled it to the floor.

"Hey! That's a library book!" said Nerys.

"When you said self-improvement, I thought you meant Open University or meditation, shit like that. Not coming to bed with an instruction manual, for God's sake. What's the matter with you?"

"What's the matter with me? I think you're the one with the problem, actually," said Nerys, indicating his rapidly shrivelling member.

He gathered the duvet around him, tucking it underneath his body.

"I want you to leave. This is just too weird for me."

"Too weird?" spat Nerys. "I'll tell you what would be weird. It would be really weird if we were all *born* with the knowledge of how to give the perfect blow job! How on earth can you criticise a person who's trying to give you the best possible time? Would you prefer it if I just made it up as I went along?"

"Er, yes."

Nerys flung herself off the bed and stamped around, gathering her clothes. She stuffed her sequinned knickers into her handbag. They were the centrepiece of her seduction arsenal and they chafed something awful. The ingratitude of men!

"Well I hope you find some nice, mediocre girl that you'll be very happy with," she said as she pulled on her clothes. "I could never be happy with someone who's prepared to take second best."

She straightened her shoulders and strode out of the room.

Moments later she scuttled back in, grabbed the library book and the recently opened bottle of champagne and scuttled out again.

NERYS BANGED on the door of Flat 2a

"Jeremy! Wake up, I know you're in there."

She thumped the door with the base of the now empty champagne bottle.

"Jeremy! Open up!"

The door opened and she narrowly avoided smashing Clovenhoof's face in with the bottle. She gave him a look and pushed past him into the flat.

"What do you want?" he growled. "It's four in the morning. I was having the most delicious dream. I was back in the Old Place and we'd just opened a new wing for reality TV contestants."

"Stop talking drivel, Jeremy, I'm having a crisis and I need help. First though, I need more wine."

On the lounge window-sill stood a half-drunk bottle of Lambrini. She pulled a face, but swigged deeply from the bottle.

She sighed and sank into an armchair.

"When you look at a woman, Jeremy, what's the main thing that you're trying to find?"

"When I look at a woman?"

"Yes."

Clovenhoof coughed and stared at his hooves.

"No, no," he said, "it's not like that at all."

"Eh?"

"I mean the telescope. It's for looking at the stars, that's all."

Nerys noticed the telescope by the window. She leaned over and put her eye to the eyepiece. Even in the dark, she could tell that it was angled towards a bedroom in the next road.

"Oh, I see." She gave him a sideways look. "Well, what I really meant was what qualities do you look for in an ideal woman? Is it the superficial, physical stuff that matters, or do you want her to have a great personality?"

Clovenhoof's face twitched with confusion.

"Ah, the second one. And the first one. Yup. Yeah, they're both important."

Nerys shook her head.

"You really haven't got a clue, have you?"

Clovenhoof shook his head along with hers.

Nerys exhaled heavily and stared at the Lambrini bottle for a few long moments.

"You know what we're going to do? I'll tell you what we're going to do." She gestured grandly with the bottle, spilling some wine on the telescope. "This weekend we're going to hit the scene. You and me. There's a singles night on at the Boldmere Oak. We're going out on the pull." She pulled something from her bag and started to mop up the spilt drink.

"Why would I want to go –" Clovenhoof stopped. " Um, are those your knickers?"

"Jeremy! Stop changing the subject." She stuffed the

damp undies back in her bag. "We need to do this or we'll be on the shelf forever."

"Were they sequinned?"

"Listen! Don't you want a woman?"

"I don't know. Do I?"

She groaned. Clovenhoof frowned.

"Those sequins, don't they chafe?"

IN THE MORNING, Clovenhoof dropped in on Ben,

"Do I want a woman?" said Clovenhoof.

"How should I know?" said Ben, busy at his computer.

"But should I want a woman?"

"Blimey, Jeremy. It's not like I have a lot of experience in the matter."

"Well, you must have been out with a woman at some point, surely."

Ben focussed on the computer screen as his face flushed red.

"Oh, I see." said Clovenhoof. "Okay. You must have thought about it though. Why do men want to have women in their lives? Lots of them do."

"You know..."

"No, I don't."

"Please. Don't make me spell it out."

"What?"

Ben turned away from the screen to study Clovenhoof's face.

"They have," he coughed and dropped his gaze, "they have *front bottoms*. And boobs."

Clovenhoof rolled his eyes.

"I know that," he said, "but are they really that much fun to play with?"

"No idea," said Ben, turning to the screen again. "Look at the detail on these soldiers, mmmm."

Clovenhoof peered forward to see a miniature figure in a leather skirt and carrying a short sword. Ben ran his finger lovingly down the image and then clicked through to the checkout and entered his credit card details.

"How about the people who come into your shop?" Clovenhoof asked. "They must talk about women."

"Well going by what they say, I think that mostly, women are useful for things like doing the cooking and washing and finding their keys," said Ben. "That seems to be what they miss when the women leave them."

Clovenhoof picked up Ben's credit card and tapped it thoughtfully on the table.

"I can see that it might be useful to have a woman," he said. "But don't you think it might also be hard work?"

They both found that they gazed involuntarily towards the ceiling. Their eyes met but they said nothing.

"Well if you find out, let me know," said Ben.

"Oh no, you're coming with me."

"What?"

"Nerys has decided that I need to go and find a woman this weekend. She plans to look for a man."

"So what's that got to do with me?" Ben asked.

"Well," said Clovenhoof, slipping Ben's credit card into

his pocket, "judging by her past performance she'll find some poor victim in the first ten minutes and leave me sitting there. Let's face it, I'm going to need the company."

CLOVENHOOF ADMIRED himself in front of the mirror. He hadn't had a chance to wear his leather and denim gear since that ill-fated Symphony Hall concert.

There was a knock at the door.

He gave himself one last preening look.

"You're on fire, Jeremy."

On the landing, Nerys tottered in the highest of heels. She saw what he was wearing and pointed theatrically.

"*What* are you wearing?"

"Um, pulling clothes. Babe-magnet clothes."

"No, no, no. You look like a rent boy. Let's go and find you something else."

"Look, it's this or the smoking jackets."

"Smoking jackets? Who are you? Hugh Hefner?"

She took a step to the side and rapped smartly at 2b. Ben emerged from his door.

Nerys sighed.

"Ben, I never thought I'd say this, but I need your clothes."

"I'm kinda busy...," said Ben, jerking a thumb over his shoulder.

"Helping me," said Nerys. "I know."

Inside, she ransacked Ben's wardrobe and piled his arms

high with anything that was both clean and vaguely wearable.

"What's this?" she said, pulling out a bright red sheet.

"Seleucid cloak," said Ben.

"What?"

"To go with the armour."

Clovenhoof and Nerys just looked at him.

I've got the sandals too," he said.

He picked up a pair of strappy leather sandals.

"It's for historical re-enactments," he said.

"Not kinky bedroom roleplay?" said Nerys.

"When has Ben ever had anyone in his bedroom?" said Clovenhoof.

"Point. He just spends his night all dressed up, alone, polishing his helmet."

"Have you quite finished rubbishing my wardrobe, hobbies and sex life?" said Ben testily.

Clovenhoof shrugged.

"Suppose," he said.

"Right," said Nerys. "We'll look through this lot. Maybe between the two of you we can make a couple of wearable outfits. No, you can leave all those white socks, we won't be needing those."

In the lounge, she strode over to the large blue and brass trunk.

"Any clothes in here?" she asked, reaching for the lid.

Ben launched himself in front of her and flung his arms out to ward her off.

"No!" he said. "Definitely nothing in here."

"Keep your hair on," mocked Nerys. "What is it? Dirty mags?"

"No," said Clovenhoof. "He keeps them under his mattress."

"I don't!" Ben sat on the chest and tried to compose himself. "Sorry. It's just private."

THEY EVENTUALLY MADE it out onto the street, fully dressed. Ben and Clovenhoof weren't overly impressed by Nerys's sartorial decisions.

"I don't get why we both have to dress the same," complained Ben. "We look like dorks."

"Best I could do, I'm afraid," said Nerys sniffily. "You've got t-shirts, Jeremy's got jackets. It's the closest thing to a normal person's casual attire we're going to get. You think yourself lucky you didn't end up with one of his smoking jackets."

"No, I just look like I should be selling ice cream."

They stopped outside the Boldmere Oak. There was a poster for the over-twenty-five's singles night in the window and a kaleidoscope of disco lights shimmering across the frosted glass.

"Right," said Nerys. "You're going to meet women. How will you behave?"

"Just be ourselves?" Ben ventured.

"God, no!" Nerys turned and grabbed them both by the arm. "Whatever you do, don't be yourselves. You need to pretend you're regular people. Say normal things. Jeremy, whatever you do, don't start rambling about the place where you used to live. You know how you go on."

"I do not *go on*."

"And Ben, you are absolutely forbidden from mentioning toy soldiers."

"Actually, they're collectable militaria –"

"Shush! Game faces, gentlemen."

AN HOUR LATER, Ben seemed to have come to a decision.

"I reckon everyone thinks we're a gay couple. We're dressed in these stupid outfits, looking like we picked them out together."

Clovenhoof, who knew two meanings of the word 'gay' considered Ben's point and decided that neither applied to him at all. Not at that moment anyway.

"At least it means we can have a quiet night," said Clovenhoof.

Three tables over, Nerys was wedged between two braying salesmen. The pair of them took it in turns to recount golfing anecdotes and guffaw at the other's. Nerys tittered politely at the appropriate pauses.

"Well, relatively quiet, anyway," said Ben. "How do you think Nerys stands it?"

"Do you know, I think she actually likes it," said Clovenhoof. "Do you want another drink?"

Clovenhoof went to the bar and ordered drinks. He pulled out Ben's credit card to pay, and then realised as the machine was presented to him that he didn't have the pin number.

"Oh, I've forgotten the code." He took the card back and started to go through his pockets, looking for money.

"Here, let me."

A woman leaned across and passed Lennox a tenner.

Clovenhoof looked up at her. Clovenhoof had decided upon some very specific criteria for his ideal woman. She had to be legal, own her own teeth, free from disfiguring diseases and financially solvent. He was surprised to meet his perfect woman quite so soon.

"You're very kind," he said. "Just give me a moment."

He scooted over to Ben with his cider and black and whispered loudly.

"Don't look now, but I think I found a woman. No more washing for me!"

He went back to the bar and leaned against it casually. How he wished he was wearing his smoking jacket.

"I'm Jeremy," he said, taking a manly and debonair sip of his Lambrini.

"And what do you do, Jeremy?"

Clovenhoof thought quickly. He was not permitted to mention Hell or any of his previous employment. He must say something simple and earthly.

"Well. Sometimes I weigh myself before and after having a poo."

He smiled broadly at the woman, who looked as though she was going to say something but then she shook her head and moved down the bar.

Clovenhoof turned in confusion.

"Does that mean you don't want to have sex?"

She did not look at him.

Lennox slid along the bar to Clovenhoof.

"You're new to dating aren't you, mate?"

"Yes." he said, "You can tell?"

"Do you want my advice?" he said.

"Yes," said Clovenhoof who felt Lennox, as a barman, must have seen all of life pass through at one time or another.

"Don't mention sex or bodily functions, mate. Most of the ladies don't enjoy that. And think about some grooming."

"Grooming? What's that?"

"Tidy yourself up. It's the horns and the hooves." He gave Clovenhoof a big toothy grin. "You're ugly, mate."

DORIS TURNED to Betty at a corner table.

"They're not very good at this are they?" she said.

"Well, you know Doris, they don't have our wisdom. That only comes with age."

"You think *we* could sort them out? You do know that they all just want to have, you know..."

"Sex?"

"Not just sex! Sex outside of marriage, Betty. I can't agree with that."

"Well let's give it some thought anyway. We'll start with Nerys, shall we?" said Betty.

"Well, there's a case in point. She takes a different man home every week. Dreadful carry-on."

"Why do you think she does that?" asked Betty. "It's as if she's always searching for something she can't find."

"Well she's not going to find it with those two." Doris indicated the salesmen. "Pair of predators if ever I saw them. Both married."

"I know, but I think Nerys can give as good as she gets."

"You make that sound as if it's a good thing," scolded Doris.

Betty shrugged.

"Do you know who I'd like to see get paired up?" she said. "Lennox there, behind the bar. They all overlook him, but he's a lovely man. Got kind eyes. And good muscle definition."

Doris regarded Betty with mild distaste.

"Let's move on to Jeremy, shall we? He really has no idea how to talk to ladies in this kind of situation. He really needs to learn how to be more of a gentleman, in my opinion."

"Oh, chivalrous you mean? That would be lovely, but a chivalrous man's a very rare thing. It's gone right out of fashion since the war, if you ask me."

"Oh yes, the war. A man in a uniform never fails to impress," said Doris.

"I think we can forget the idea that Jeremy will be wearing any kind of uniform," said Betty, "or suddenly becoming chivalrous. The best we can hope for is that some woman will see past his unusual appearance, and unpleasant habits."

"Where on earth is he going to meet a woman who'll do that?" said Doris. "You saw how he put that woman off just now. It took him all of five seconds."

"Well she wouldn't have been any good for him anyway," said Betty. "She's in here every week. Needs the love of a good man, if you ask me."

"Hmmm, you're right. Not Jeremy then."

"Ben's a different matter though," said Betty. "He needs taking in hand."

"Taking in hand? How do you mean?" asked Doris.

"He needs an experienced woman to show him the ropes. I do believe she's going over to him. Get the sherries in Doris, we're in for a show."

BEN LOOKED up from his drink to see a tall woman approaching.

"OK if I sit with you?"

"I thought you were talking to my friend at the bar."

"You looked so lonely, I thought it was my duty to come on over and help you enjoy yourself! I'm Sophie."

"Ben," squeaked Ben.

"Are you local, Ben?"

"Yes, I live just up the road."

"Oh, that's lovely, *lovely*!"

Sophie liked to talk so Ben sat rigidly while she told him about her family, her friends and her work as a nursery assistant. She pulled out her phone and showed him endless pictures of her cat.

Ben hoped that Clovenhoof would come and rescue him from this juggernaut of a woman but he appeared to be deep in conversation with the barman.

"Just going to the little girls' room, I'll be right back!"

Ben breathed a deep sigh as he relished the silence for a moment. If this was what meeting women was like he wasn't sure he was up to it. The silence was broken by Sophie's phone chiming as she got a message. Ben glanced sideways at the screen, which had brightened to display the message.

'*Well make sure you're gentle with him!*' was enclosed in a cute speech bubble. Ben swallowed hard and looked up the screen at Sophie's last outgoing message.

'*I think I found a VIRGIN!*' the speech bubble above said.

Ben screamed and bolted for the door.

BY ELEVEN, Clovenhoof was back home in his flat, wearing a smoking jacket (to make a point to himself if no one else) and casually trawling through internet pages.

It was possible to find women on the internet, he was certain. He wondered if he could specify that he'd like one that wasn't going to stalk off if he said the wrong thing. He tried some searches. He combined '*ideal woman*', '*harmless dating partner*' with '*will not complain*' and browsed through the results.

After a few minutes, he noticed that as well as dating sites, there were sites advertising love dolls. Love dolls? He looked at some of the sites then changed his searches to find some more.

This was interesting. He had no idea that such things were possible, and in such astonishing detail, too.

He was equipped for fornication; it was one of the perks

of being a fallen angel. He'd practised more than his fair share too, but never on earth. It seemed as though things here were a bit more involved. Emotion and other distasteful elements seemed to be part of the whole experience. Perhaps he should get one of these love dolls and make sure that everything was in working order before attempting it with a real woman. They certainly had front bottoms and boobs, and compared favourably with the woman he watched through his telescope.

Nerys knocked and entered.

"It was open."

"What happened to your salesmen?" he asked, angling the screen away so she couldn't see it.

"Pah," she snorted. "They got in a taxi and went off to a strip club after some bloke rang and said it was his treat."

"Oh. No sex for you then?"

"Jeremy! We need to discuss this. I heard what you said to that girl at the bar. We're English, and we don't talk like that.

"Like what?"

"About sex. Well not out loud. Not between men and women."

"I don't care," said Clovenhoof. "Apparently, I'm ugly."

"Aw," said Nerys, a noise that was probably meant to be sympathetic but sounded like a balloon going down. "You're not ugly. You're differently attractive, that's all. Where's Ben?"

"In his flat. Locked the door. Put the chain on. Whimpered something."

"He's a strange one," said Nerys.

"Yeah, but he's a nice guy," said Clovenhoof. "Generous."

He pulled Ben's credit card from his pocket and looked at

the top of the range love doll on the screen and hoped that Ben's limit was large enough.

THERE WAS a beauty therapist's on the high street.

Beauty therapist. Clovenhoof loved the sound of those words. There was something reassuring in them. Giver of therapies. Healer. Scientist.

A little bell rang as he stepped through the door of *Boldmere Beauty*. He looked the woman in a white tunic in the eye.

"Apparently," he said, daring her to disagree, "I'm ugly."

The woman stopped stacking pots of face cream and smiled broadly.

"Can you cure me?" he said.

Her smile broadened further.

"Have a seat, chuck," she said. "And we'll chat about that."

NERYS SAT at her office desk and chewed a pencil like an angry beaver. Those ridiculous salesmen had ruined her chances last night. She seemed to attract losers. How on earth could she meet a decent man?

She turned to Dave at the desk next to her.

"Coffee break, Dave."

"No, I'm fine. I just got one," said Dave.

"No, you need to get one now. With me. I need to ask you something."

"Oh OK."

Dave allowed himself to be shepherded into the kitchen area. Nerys shut the door so that the clients in the outer office wouldn't overhear.

"Dave, am I attractive?"

Dave flushed.

"Yes Nerys, you are."

"Good," she said, pulling out her notebook and her much-chewed pencil. "So tell me my good points."

"Your what?"

"My good points. You know. If I'm attractive then I need to know why. Give me something to work with."

Dave blew out his cheeks and eyed the door.

"OK. You've got good legs. And nice eyes."

He made a move for the door.

Nerys scribbled on the pad and sidestepped neatly to block his exit.

"Keep going."

"Um," he said, "you've got a sexy voice."

"Yeah?" Nerys smiled. "Go on, more."

"You smell nice."

"My arse?"

"What?"

"Do you like my arse?"

Nerys looked up and saw that he was now blushing furiously and looking anywhere but at her.

"Er, yeah. Not that I've ever looked at your..."

"You've never looked at my arse?"

"Oh, no. It's a great arse. Like two puppies fighting in a sack," he added weakly.

She wrote down 'two puppies in a sack' and added several happy exclamation marks.

"OK," she said, "now I need to know where my weaknesses are. Tell me what's bad about me."

"Uh-oh," he said. "That sounds unwise."

"No, no. There'll be no repercussions. It's a scientific process. I really need to understand what's going on in the male mind when you look at me. Please."

Dave sighed.

"Well you can be aggressive. Like now. And sometimes when you've drunk lots of coffee your breath smells bad."

Nerys cupped a hand to her mouth and huffed experimentally.

"You don't always listen to people," he continued, getting into his stride now, "and I happen to know it was you who gave 'The Dumb-ass Guide to Management' to our boss in last year's Secret Santa. So I'm going to say vindictive as well."

"Good. Er, thank you."

Dave slipped out and Nerys reviewed the list.

She'd need to verify this. She couldn't just take Dave's word for it, that wasn't scientific at all, especially when he'd been so harsh.

Back at her desk, she drew up a spreadsheet. A grid of her various qualities, with a possible score of one to five. By the time she went home she had twenty copies of the survey in her handbag.

∾

"So, Jeremy, what's the thing you like least about yourself?" asked the beauty therapist.

Her name was Blenda. At least that's what it said on her name badge and he assumed it wasn't her job title.

"Well, there's these," he said. He showed her his hooves.

"Ah yes. It's common to get a thickening of the toenails. You'd be surprised how many people get that. Sometimes a fungal infection will set it off. I can give you a pedicure and make those look a whole lot better."

"Oh. OK. Well then, what about these?" He indicated his horns.

Blenda examined the top of his head.

"Hmm, interesting double crown you've got there. A good haircut is what you need, and maybe some massage oil to soften the scaly build-up. Don't you worry, I've seen it all before."

"That sounds OK. Are you sure it will make a difference?"

"Definitely. There are many things we can do for you. Some gentlemen like to have their teeth whitened too. It can take years off you, would you be interested in that?"

Clovenhoof exhaled and wondered if he'd be able to use Ben's credit card.

"Yeah, let's do it all."

Blenda beamed.

"We can make a start right now if you have the time to spare?"

"Oh yes, I've got nothing pressing in my schedule for today."

Clovenhoof found the hoof buffing a fairly pleasant

sensation, and conversation with Blenda seemed an easy thing, like floating downstream.

"So what's made you decide to do all of this?" she asked him.

"I'm supposed to find a partner," he said, "and it seems as though I'm not up to scratch."

"You sound as though you're not all that keen on the idea yourself."

"No, I'm not. I don't know what to think about the whole thing. It seems as though men want women for the washing, the ironing or the sex, but nobody's allowed to say that. You can get all of those things if you pay for them, but nobody's allowed to say that either. I haven't even started to try and understand why women would want men."

Blenda laughed.

"Do you know what I think? I think that for some people, paying for those things is exactly the *right* thing. There's this terrible pressure to have a partner, I see a lot of it in here, and it's just not the answer for everyone."

"Yeah, I think maybe you're right."

Clovenhoof settled back to enjoy his treatment and wondered when his love doll would be delivered.

"WHAT HAVE YOU GOT SO FAR?" Ben asked.

Clovenhoof read out his latest attempt.

"Experienced and charismatic lover seeks pneumatic babe for hell raising fun."

Ben thought for a moment.

"You want a woman with big boobs then?"

"Yeah."

Clovenhoof was merrily basking in the knowledge that he was now irresistible. He'd checked himself out in the mirror a dozen times since returning from Blenda's and was delighted anew every time. He'd even bought some buffers for his hooves, so he could keep them in tip-top condition. They said '*Boldmere Beauty*' on the back, which made him smile when he looked at them.

That evening he had sat down at the computer to compile a profile for online dating. He'd toned it down from '*molten-hot love machine*' in case it alarmed people. All of the stock phrases and odd terminology were confusing him. He needed help with it and had called on Ben for assistance.

"Sounds good," said Ben.

"The bit I'm not sure about," said Clovenhoof, "is all the code. You know. 'GSOH', which really means 'fat'."

"No actually, 'bubbly' means 'fat'." said Nerys, coming in.

Clovenhoof scribbled a note '*bubbly=fat*'.

Nerys checked the wording he'd got so far.

"Experienced? That's code for 'old'."

"I'm probably older than you think," Clovenhoof said.

"OK. Go with that then."

"Mention the rock star thing!" said Ben. "Women will go for that."

Clovenhoof made another note.

"Jeremy, have you had a haircut?" Nerys said, staring at him.

"Yes," he said. He gave a twirl and grinned.

"Ooh, and teeth whitening too?" Nerys nodded in approval. "Looking good. Is that why you put 'charismatic'?"

"Yup."

"Hm. I wonder if you should maybe say 'enthusiastic' instead?"

"Are you saying I'm not charismatic? I can't put 'experienced and enthusiastic', it makes me sound like a long-term loser who just hasn't got it right yet."

Clovenhoof went into the kitchen to pour himself a drink. He'd need some fortification if this was going to continue.

Michael was leaning against the counter, sipping a White Russian.

"She might have a point," he said.

"Oh no. Please don't tell me that you've come to mock me for looking for a date?"

"Mock you? Oh no, I would never do that. I do wonder what you'd want with a woman though."

"What I'd want? Well you're so keen to see me settled on earth, I'd have thought that you'd be all for it." Clovenhoof's eyes narrowed. "Except of course, you can't."

"Can't what?" said Michael diffidently.

"Screw," said Clovenhoof. "Bonk. Bang. Dip your wick. Fuck. Make whoopee. Shag."

"Really, Jeremy."

"You don't have the equipment. Smooth between the legs. Smooth between the ears."

"I'm not aware that I've ever shown you my-"

"Don't need to. Matthew, chapter twenty-two. It's all there in black and white."

"That verse is open to many interpretations," Michael protested.

"Oh, hello," said Nerys, coming into the kitchen.

She smiled at Michael and Clovenhoof rolled his eyes.

"You're wasting your time there, Nerys."

"Oh? Oh. OK. Shame. Well, you can both fill in a survey anyway."

"A what?"

"A survey. About me. I need to know what people think of me, so that I can target my dating more effectively."

She thrust a sheet and a pencil at them both.

ON SATURDAY, there was a parcel for Ben, which he had to sign for. He carried it eagerly upstairs to check out his new soldiers. The box was enormous. He was pleased that they'd been packed so carefully. He met Nerys coming down as he struggled to get it upstairs.

"What's that?" she asked.

"A legion of Seleucid infantry," he said. "Care to lend a hand?"

"Sorry," she said, squeezing past. "Off to get myself a man."

"At this time of day?"

"Supermarkets are already open."

He squeezed the parcel into his flat, thinking how amazing it was what supermarkets stocked these days.

He laid his parcel down, opened it and pulled aside the top layer of bubble wrap.

"This can't be right," he muttered, annoyed more than surprised.

He lifted out a life-size arm. Pink, fleshy, soft to the touch. "The scale's all wrong for a start."

CLOVENHOOF SLUMPED in the corner of the Boldmere Oak, scowling at the scribbled notes that he had so far.

"Hello, chuck."

He looked up.

"Hello, Blenda."

"Well, don't you look nice, even though I say so myself. Liking the smoking jacket."

"Thanks."

"Had a thing for Noel Coward as a girl. God, I can pick 'em. So what are you doing?" she asked. "You don't look as though you're enjoying it very much."

"I'm working on my online dating profile. Have you ever tried to describe yourself in a handful of words?"

"Always ready to lend a hand," she said, sitting down beside him.

NERYS HAD READ in a magazine that the supermarket was an ideal place to meet a future partner.

She had been crunching numbers. She'd tried various different ways to analyse the survey results, and had found that the most pleasing comments came from men with brown hair born under the sign of Scorpio. Now she was getting somewhere! She had her hunting ground. She knew her quarry. She just had to wait for the opportunity.

She'd positioned herself by the freezer cabinets, thinking that she might use an opening gambit along the lines of "Brrr, it's chilly here. A bit like the last half of October and the beginning half of November. I wonder what it's like to have a birthday at that time?"

After the first few times, she realised that it wasn't going to work, so she pulled a notebook from her bag and told all the brown-haired men that she was doing a survey for the supermarket and wanted to know their star sign. She'd failed to find a single Scorpio when a large woman came up to her.

"You need to come now. Someone's parked in the mother and baby space and they don't even have a baby."

"Er no. Sorry. I'm just doing a survey."

"Why didn't you ask me about my star sign?"

"Wrong demographic." said Nerys.

The woman stalked off, unimpressed.

A few minutes later, Nerys had found a Scorpio, but realised that his girlfriend was walking along behind, pushing a trolley. She quickly handed him a Nerys survey and asked him to fill it in.

"Can I ask what you're doing?" asked the store manager, appearing at her side.

The large woman stood a short distance away, looking smug.

"I'm doing a survey." Nerys replied. Then, noting that he had brown hair, she smiled at him. "Are you a Scorpio by any chance?"

AFTER HALF AN HOUR of diligent construction, Ben had got the basics together. It was a model of a woman. He'd not seen these on the site, but he was intrigued. It seemed easy enough to assemble. For some reason, there were two heads, but he just chose the one that looked the least like Nerys. He took the head that looked like Nerys and shut it in the wardrobe. Then he imagined opening the wardrobe and seeing her look at him, so he took it out and hid it under the kitchen sink.

He realised that he was playing for time, because he had a bad feeling about the final pieces in the box. He thought at first that they were fingerless gloves for the doll, which seemed strange because no other clothes were supplied. He slipped one on each hand and found that they fit, but were made from the same strange rubbery compound as the rest of the doll. Definitely not gloves in the traditional sense. Then he looked down at his hands and realised that there was a label on the left saying 'large labia' and the right saying 'medium labia'. He ran around in a circle squealing and flapping his hands until they flew off. He fetched the dustpan and brush to clean them up, but he could only find one.

BLENDA LEANT in close to peer at Clovenhoof's dating profile jottings.

"Why did you change your mind about 'charismatic'?"

"I was told that 'enthusiastic' was better."

"Nonsense! It makes you sound like an amateur. I'm sure you're not." She raised an eyebrow. "Anyone who can carry off a smoking jacket can describe themselves as 'charismatic'."

"Thank you," he said, feeling a sense of personal vindication.

"Let's start with the basic stuff," said Blenda. "Tell me about yourself."

"Er..."

"Come on, Jeremy. Give me your life story."

"How long have you got?" he asked.

She looked at her empty glass.

"How long have you got?" she replied.

BEN FOUND the doll's nakedness beguiling yet ultimately an annoying distraction. Where would he find something to make her decent at short notice? He ransacked his wardrobe, pulled out an old Sepultura T-shirt and a pair of Bermuda shorts that had always been too big for him.

Ben wrestled his kit-assembly lady into the clothes and sat her down on the settee. He was pleased that she was wearing something of his. He was *very* pleased that he no longer had to worry about her private places either.

He sat beside her.

"There," he said and put on the television so that they could watch something together.

"WHAT HAVE I DONE? Loads of things. But not all that many that I should really put down on here. I've done a lot of bad things."

"Oh, well we're getting somewhere then," exclaimed Blenda. "All women love a bastard, after all. We just need to find the right words to say that. Without actually saying it, obviously."

"Obviously!" laughed Clovenhoof, "I'm beginning to get the hang of being English."

His face clouded.

"Do you really think that's true, by the way? Do all women love a bastard? If so, I'm not really sure why I don't have to beat them off with a stick. There's no bigger bastard than me."

Blenda looked at him across the rim of her glass.

"Are you selling yourself short, Jeremy?" she asked.

"No, I'm really not. I am the original bastard."

IT TURNED out that none of the store's management and security staff were Scorpios. That explained why, firstly, she wasn't quite managing to snare them as potential boyfriends and, secondly, why they were annoyingly unsympathetic to her personal scientific quest.

"I'm not causing any trouble," she said.

"I don't care what you think you're doing or not doing," said the store manager (who was a Leo). "I've asked you to leave the premises."

"I could just stand inside the front door and speak to people as they come in," she offered.

"Do you want me to call the police?"

Nerys gave the matter genuine thought. Policemen came in twos. One in twelve chance of either of them being a Scorpio. That was a one-in-six chance overall, wasn't it?

"Doug."

The security guard (a Libra) stepped forward.

"Okay," she said. "I get the message."

At the exit, she stopped.

"I could stand here," she said to the security guard, Doug. "I'll be tucked out of the way. You'll barely notice me."

Doug put his hand on her shoulder and escorted her the last few feet outside.

On the pavement, she wriggled free of him.

"Get your hands off me. I don't want to be touched by you. Even if you *were* a Scorpio!"

"Nerys?"

She turned. Dave was stood there, bulging carrier bags in his hands.

"Doing a bit of shopping?" he asked.

"Not exactly. I've been scouring the place for brown haired Scorpios. God knows where they all are."

"Well you found one now," he laughed.

"Oh yeah, how funny is that?" she said sourly.

"Can I give you a lift anywhere?"

She gave him a long look.

"Sure."

∾

HE MADE dinner for the two of them. It seemed the obvious thing to do.

Ben set out the table, poured wine and even considered lighting a candle but then feared his lady friend might be flammable. He sat her opposite him and served up for the pair of them. A slightly smaller portion for her as she was watching her weight.

"You look great in that T-shirt," he said, spearing a carrot.

She gave him a faint, enigmatic smile.

"Got it at a concert in ninety-eight."

She wasn't touching her food.

"It's not too hot for you, is it?" he asked.

He realised she was looking past him, over his right shoulder. He turned and saw that she was staring at the blue and brass trunk by the wall.

"Please," he said. "Don't look at that."

She continued to look.

"I know I can trust you," he said. "I want to tell you everything."

She kept looking.

"It worries me so much. I don't know what's going to happen to me. I will show you. One day."

He reached over and squeezed her hand. Something clicked under his touch.

"I want you to give it to me hard and fast, Big Boy," said the doll.

"Pardon?"

"Do you want to do it doggy style?"

"No thanks. I mean it's really nice of you to try to cheer me up. I am having a tough time at the moment."

"Oh my God! It's so hard!"

"It is," he agreed. "You're a great listener. It's a lost art, really."

There was a knocking at the door.

Ben ignored it.

"Shhh!" he said to the doll, "stay quiet and they'll go away."

The doll started to emit ecstatic moans.

"Ben! Is someone in there with you?" Nerys called.

Ben shushed louder, and the doll responded by moaning and panting at full volume.

"Ohhhh! Hnnnnnnnnnn!"

"Ben! What's the matter? Are you in pain? Let me in, I'm a first aider!" Nerys bellowed. "Dave, knock down the door, we need to get in!"

Someone started to barge the door. Ben could see it bulging in the frame.

He looked around in panic. He was suddenly all too aware of how this would look to someone walking in. He had a sex doll, dressed in his cast offs, and he was having a meal with her. He could not allow Nerys to see him like this.

He opened the window, grabbed the doll and hauled her across the ledge. He paused for a moment, pulled her back, and gave her a long, passionate kiss. Then he gave her a shove and sent her flailing down into the dark.

CLOVENHOOF WALKED up the path to the flats with a spring in his step.

He had got his dating profile sorted and, sure, he hadn't submitted it, let alone got himself a date and yet, somehow, over a drink or two, he felt he and Blenda had achieved something that afternoon.

His buoyant mood was abruptly spoiled by a moaning sex doll landing on him from a great height.

"Cocks!" he shouted in shock and anger.

He picked himself up and turned the doll over.

He was sure it was the love doll that he'd ordered. Strange that it was flying through the air, fully clothed. It emitted a groaning sound, the last of the smashed circuitry making its presence felt. Definitely the deluxe model with the speech module, thought Clovenhoof. Then he saw with a terrible clarity how it came to be here. He knew that Ben must have taken possession of the doll. Only Ben would dress it in these cast offs. Had he been rumbled and thrown it out of the window in a panic? Probably.

He picked up the latex lady.

"What are you up to?"

He looked up in alarm.

"What you doing with her?" said a man, peering over the short wall between the flats and the house next door.

"No," said Clovenhoof. "This isn't..."

"What's happened to her?"

"Nothing! I've done nothing!"

The man advanced on him, pulling a phone out of his pocket, dialling.

The doll emitted another low groan.

"Oh, shit," said Clovenhoof and ran.

BEN, Nerys and Dave looked to the open window as a shout came up from street level.

"Stop him! Murderer! Murderer!"

Ben went over and closed the window.

"Sorry about that. I think I fell asleep in front of the television."

Nerys looked at the two plates of food and the two glasses of wine. She opened her mouth to say something, when a strange rubbery object fell onto her head.

Ben gasped. It was the missing labia, which had been stuck to the ceiling.

"Oh look at that," he said, peeling it from her hair, "it's my missing cycling glove. I wondered where that went."

He started to usher her out of the door.

"But you haven't even got a bike. It looks for all the world like –"

"Bye Nerys, it was so kind of you to check up on me."

Ben closed the door and slid to the floor in exhaustion. Women were more trouble than they were worth.

"STOP HIM! He's killed someone! Don't let him get away!"

A man was getting shopping from the boot of his car a few doors down. He looked up and saw what was happening. He dropped the shopping and joined the chase.

"Killer!"

"Murderer!"

"Don't let him get away!"

Clovenhoof looked round to see more people after him. Where had they all come from? He had to find some way to ditch the doll and give these people the slip.

He ran full pelt down the middle of the Chester Road. Brakes squealed as drivers took in the spectacle of a man running at top speed down the carriageway, with a woman under his arm, chased by an angry mob.

Clovenhoof was able to gain a few yards as cars skated into each other and blocked the road.

He rounded the corner and saw a bus just pulling up at the bus stop. He put on a spurt and with a final glance over his shoulder to see if his pursuers were in sight, clambered onto the bus.

"One adult," he said, panting, and slapped coins into the payment slot.

The bus driver just stared at him. Clovenhoof followed his gaze to the sex doll under his arm.

"And a half?" he suggested.

"Jeremy?"

Blenda was standing up from her seat a little way down the bus.

"Blenda," said Jeremy with a breathless smile.

"What are you doing?" she asked.

He was silent for a moment, composing his thoughts and getting his breath back.

"Do you know," he said truthfully, "I have absolutely no idea."

HEAVEN

- Matters Arising
- Easter Bonnet Parade
- Extra-Celestial Travel
- Heaven's Population –Report
- The Throne
- Swedenborg Seminar
- Clovenhoof
- AOB

J oan of Arc walked into the boardroom carrying a pile of papers, files and scrolls that came past her chin. The Reverend Evelyn Steed came in after with an equally high pile.

They dropped them noisily onto the table, creating a minor paper avalanche that almost buried St Peter's tablet computer. St Peter's toady, Herbert, whipped it out of the way just in time, polished it with his sleeve and passed it back to his master.

"You are late," said Michael.

"Apologies," said Joan.

"We've already covered the Easter Bonnet Parade, which is *still* going ahead, and we had just finished talking about the need to perhaps regulate extra-celestial travel."

"Has Francis' donkey been making unscheduled visitations to the faithful on Earth?" said Joan.

"He cwied at my deathbed, you know," said St Francis.

"No," said Michael. "We were more concerned about certain individuals popping off to Hell to consult with the damned."

"It was necessary for the completion of my report on Heaven's population problem," said Joan.

"Completion?" said St Peter. "But the data collected for you filled acres of parchment."

"That's why I drafted in some of those spare seraphim to help."

Joan grinned, the wild and shameless grin of youth. How old had she been when the English had killed her? Eighteen? Nineteen?

"You should read it," she said. "Read it and weep."

Michael lifted the corner of one sheet and then let it drop.

"Perhaps you'd summarise it for us?"

"Well," said Joan, taking her seat, "the Celestial City is indeed a cube fifteen hundred miles to a side."

St Paul gave a grunt of self-congratulation at having his scriptural recollection confirmed.

"That gives us a floor space of two and a quarter million square miles."

"That's enormous," said Gabriel.

"But apparently there's no room for a harps and clouds quarter," said Pope Pius irritably.

"By comparison," said Joan, "there's fifty-seven million square miles of land on Earth."

"That's more," said Gabriel helpfully.

"And Heaven's population is greater than that of the Earth," said Joan.

"I see," said Michael.

"To put it bluntly, each one of Heaven's residents has roughly three hundred square feet of living space. That's the equivalent to a very small house on Earth."

"Thank you for clarifying the situation for us," said Michael.

"But it's not clear at all!" said Joan. "The more you look into it, the more it becomes obvious that this city is a physical impossibility."

"I don't think Heaven has to contend with what is possible and what is not," said Pius.

"In the *physical* universe," said Joan, "a cube fifteen hundred miles across would collapse under its own weight and become a sphere."

"As I said-" began Pius.

"And yet," said Joan, "we have gravity or some semblance of it."

She pushed her mountain of report papers so that they spilled further across the table to illustrate her point.

"You talk of Easter Bonnet Parades as though they are an annual event and yet this place is located outside of the temporal universe."

"You've lost me," said Gabriel.

"I lost myself. I had to seek out a natural philosopher, a scientific genius who could explain it all. That's why I went to Hell."

"I am sure we have many fine scientists in Heaven," retorted Pius.

"You have Max Planck and that's it," said Joan bluntly. "I got nowhere with him. Started babbling about a matrix of matter and the consciousness behind all existence. I had to go to Hell."

"And what did you learn there?" asked St Peter.

Joan placed her hands on the table.

"One, Hell is a bureaucracy of nightmarish proportions. Two, there's a seven year waiting list for an audience with Albert Einstein. Three, there's only a four hour waiting list for Niels Bohr and he was just as good. Four, we have a population problem that shouldn't exist."

"How so?" said Michael.

"Because distance is a relative measurement. This city can be expanded to infinite size."

"But scripture speaks plainly," said Pius.

"As it is on Earth, so shall it be in heaven," said St Paul.

"But what is fifteen hundred miles in Heaven?" said Joan. "Who defines a stadia? A metre? A foot? There's nothing to measure it against. Whose foot? What light waves?"

"Light waves?" said St Francis.

"Scientists moved from measuring a metre by the wavelength of emissions from Krypton-86 in 1983 and chose to..."

Joan stopped in the presence of eight blankly uncomprehending faces. Mother Teresa, quill in hand, seemed ready to burst into tears.

Michael whispered to her out of the corner of his mouth.

"K – R – Y – P..."

"The point is," said Joan, "we want to expand Heaven or shrink its inhabitants. As we are outside the constraints of time and space, this problem can be resolved without any scriptural contradictions. As Gabriel said, Heaven should not be bound by what is possible and what is not."

"How nice it is," said St Peter, "that you've managed to solve the problem with such ease."

"All we have to do is take our proposal to the Throne and request that He makes the appropriate changes."

Michael coughed.

"I don't think that you should be bothering the Lord with such matters."

"I didn't mean *me*," said Joan. "I wouldn't be so presumptuous as to approach the Throne myself. Actually, I noticed that the Throne has been an item on the agenda for two consecutive meetings."

"More than that," said Pius.

"Is there a problem?" said Joan.

"Pardon?" said St Peter.

"With the Throne," she said. "Is there a problem with the Throne?"

"Ridiculous," said Michael and waved her words away.

"In truth," said St Peter, "your concerns about Heaven's capacity are ill-founded and your solution ham-fisted."

"Is that so?" said Joan.

"My underling, Herbert, has been working on an initiative – at my bidding of course - that should allay your fears and bring about many positive changes to the Celestial City."

Herbert squeezed round the side of St Peter's chair and placed a number of brightly coloured leaflets on the table at the foothills of Joan's paper mountain.

"*Keep Heaven Holy*?" read Evelyn from the across the table.

"We'll be making a full presentation at the next board meeting. We must keep to the agenda or there will be chaos."

"Indeed," said Michael. "Now, I see the next item on the agenda is the Swedenborg Seminar."

"What about the Thwone?" said St Francis.

"Oh, I think we've covered that in enough depth for now," said Michael. "This Swedenborg thing is another one of your ideas, Joan?"

"Yes," said Joan. "I've been reading your field reports on this Jeremy Clovenhoof character. You still have two Recording Angels tailing him."

"We do."

"His recent exploits have taken a... romantic turn."

Mother Teresa's quill wobbled erratically for a moment.

"And it's not an area I know a great deal about," said Joan.

"Nor I," said Pius firmly and there were general murmurs of assent all along the table.

"It is not something of particular interest to angels," said Gabriel.

"But," said Joan, "this sex thing is apparently quite nice."

Evelyn nodded in agreement, so readily that all eyes turned on her.

"Well, it is," she said. "It's right up there with chocolate and bungee-jumping."

"Bungee-jumping?" said St Francis.

"You're losing the gist of what I'm saying," said Joan. "If this sex thing is so amazing then we should be doing it."

"In the resurrection, people will neither marry nor be given in marriage," quoted St Paul. "They will be like the angels in heaven."

"Quite," said Michael uncomfortably.

"I'm not talking about marriage," said Joan. "I'm talking about sex."

"You mean...?" said Pius.

"Yes. The beast with two backs. Rumpy-pumpy. Getting giddy with it."

Evelyn leaned over and whispered in her ear.

"Getting *jiggy* with it," said Joan, correcting herself.

"I feel quite pale," said St Peter.

Herbert produced a sick bag and presented it to his master but St Peter waved it away.

"Emmanuel Swedenborg is going to explain all the details at a seminar next week," said Joan.

"I can't believe I'm hearwing this," said St Francis.

"Don't worry, Frankie. There'll be diagrams."

7

IN WHICH CLOVENHOOF EARNS HIS CRUST, CORRUPTS THE YOUNG AND SEEKS FORGIVENESS

"Are you sure you're all right?"

"I'm fine."

"You look a little red."

"Well, I would, wouldn't I?"

Blenda poked at the remains of Clovenhoof's chicken tindaloo with her fork. The dish of sag phall next to it was completely empty, although a heat haze still seemed to hang over it.

"There were whole chillies in there."

"I'm not saying it wasn't warm."

"I didn't think anyone genuinely enjoyed them. I thought they just put them on the menu for idiots, drunkards and, you know, Geordies."

Clovenhoof sighed.

"Blenda."

She smiled sweetly. It was a smile that played up and down his spine like those fascinating massage techniques that she'd introduced him to.

"Yes, chuck?"

"You were telling me about your dreams."

She looked round, perhaps to see who was listening in. They were alone in the Karma Lounge Restaurant, apart from the waiting staff who loitered by the bar, all toothy grins and floppy fringes.

"Well," she said. "I used to dream of having children but that boat has definitely sailed. At one time, I wanted to travel. And" – she laughed at her own recollection – "I wanted to be a professional belly dancer."

"You danced?"

"With more gusto than skill," she said.

"But what about now?" said Clovenhoof.

"More gusto. Less skill."

"No, I meant what do you dream about now?"

She shrugged.

"Peace and quiet. Long lie ins. Finding a good man who I can trust."

She looked at him meaningfully. Clovenhoof suddenly found himself feeling uncomfortably hot and it wasn't the curry to blame.

The spell was broken by the waiter coming over with the bill. Clovenhoof passed him a credit card in the name of BEN D KITCHEN.

"And you?" she said.

"No, I'm not looking for a man," said Clovenhoof.

She punched him playfully.

"Dreams, Jeremy."

"Oh, I had dreams."

"Yes?"

He sat and thought. Dreams of servitude they had been in the beginning, which became dreams of conquest and of vindication, dreams of a white throne in a silver city. Then dreams of revenge and the desire to ruin.

"My dreams didn't come to much," he said.

"And now?"

He shook his head.

"No dreams. I'm just killing time in this place."

"What? Waiting for death?"

"Not even that."

She made a noise.

"What do you do with your days, Jeremy?"

"I don't know. Stuff."

"Like what?"

"I used to be in a heavy metal band."

"Used to."

"I have a pet mould called Herbert. He needs frequent attention."

"Not selling it to me."

The waiter walked back from the bar.

"Does it matter?" said Clovenhoof. "I'm healthy, financially solvent and currently dating a beautiful ex-belly dancer."

"Dating are we?"

The waiter presented Clovenhoof with the credit card.

"I'm sorry, sir. This card has been declined."

Clovenhoof looked at it.

"Declined?"

"It has been cancelled by the credit company."

"Oh."

"Do you have an alternative means of payment?"

"Er."

He looked to Blenda. She was already reaching for her purse.

"Financially solvent, are you?"

"Two out of three ain't bad," he said.

"Smooth, Jeremy. Real smooth."

CLOVENHOOF STOMPED into Ben's flat and slammed the door behind him.

"That was a short date," said Ben.

Clovenhoof made a noise in his throat.

"A bit of trouble with the bill."

"Huh!" said Ben, sat at the dining table, savagely flicking through a book on the Second Punic Wars. "Tell me about it!"

"Yeah?" said Clovenhoof, taken aback by his unusually fiery tone.

Ben closed the large hardback with a thunderous snap.

"I got my credit card bill today."

"Oh," said Clovenhoof.

"And I've discovered I've been a victim of credit card fraud."

"I see. I mean, really?"

"Really. It was after I bought those Seleucid infantry models. Some bastard must have cloned my card or something. Four thousand pounds they've spent on that card."

"Do they know who did it?" said Clovenhoof.

"Not yet."

"Thank God." He paused. "I mean thank God because you look like you're ready to commit murder and I don't think prison would suit you."

These words seemed to have a peculiar effect on Ben, who paled a little and looked over to the blue and brass trunk by the wall.

"I didn't think this kind of thing would get you so riled up," said Clovenhoof. "It's only money, isn't it?"

"Only money? Do you think I like working in *Bits 'n' Books* five days a week?"

"Yes."

"Well, yes, I do. But I don't do it for free. I do it to be paid. I work for my money. I have a bloody work ethic. I earn every penny that goes into my pocket and that money is mine. I do not work to support thieves and spongers. You wouldn't understand."

"Why wouldn't I?"

"Not all of us have trust funds and investments to live off or whatever it is you have."

"Yeah, about that..."

He rubbed the back of his neck as he contemplated unpleasant thoughts.

"Ben?"

"Yeah?"

"Could I get a job in your shop?"

"What?"

"Maybe I need to get a work ethic too. Maybe I need a bit more purpose in my life. Maybe something to do with my days."

"Are you strapped for cash?"

"Yes, I am."

Ben shook his head.

"There's enough turmoil in my life thanks."

"Oh, come on."

Ben returned to his book.

"Ask Nerys. She works in recruitment after all. I'm sure she could find something for you."

"No way."

"Oh, come on," said Clovenhoof, following her through Sutton's pedestrianised high street.

"I'm not even going to entertain it," she said, her substantial heels clicking rapidly over the brick paving.

"Why not? Don't you need clients on your books?"

"Clients, yes," she said, stopping outside the *Helping Hand Job Agency*'s door. "Qualified, hard-working... *presentable* clients."

Clovenhoof's mouth fell open.

"I *am* presentable. Look at me."

"I am. You're wearing a bolo tie with a silver cow skull clasp, a granddad shirt and chinos."

"I'm creating a look here."

"The word you're grasping for is 'spectacle.'"

She pushed the door open. He followed her inside.

"Are you going to follow me all day?" she said.

"Yes, I am."

She shook her head.

"Dave!"

A tall fellow with an unfortunate haircut and face like an eager puppy stood up at his desk.

"Morning, Nerys."

"I've got a client for you."

Clovenhoof smiled and did a victory tap dance while Nerys made good her escape into the back room. Clovenhoof slid over to Dave's desk and shook him firmly by the hand.

"You'd be Jeremy Clovenhoof," said Dave.

"And you're the famous Dave."

"Famous?"

"Nerys talks about you all the time."

"Does she?"

"And she rarely talks about her conquests except in purely anatomical terms."

"Oh, er," said Dave, blushing. "I'm not... We've not..."

"Haven't you? You must be something special then."

"Yes. I suppose," said Dave doubtfully.

CLOVENHOOF AND DAVE spent a fruitful half hour together. Clovenhoof did not have a CV but Dave was able to cobble one together on his computer. Clovenhoof provided Ben with the same date of birth and birthplace that appeared on his passport. Having never been born and coming into existence before the creation of time and space made telling the truth impossible. It was the only lie he told.

He had no qualifications. The angelic host had never really gone in for bits of paper. However, he did have many titles: His Satanic Majesty, Prince of this World, The Author of Evil, Morningstar, Light Bringer, The Angel of the Bottomless Pit. All good titles but Dave was not interested, persisting with the belief they were band names from Clovenhoof's brief dalliance with rock music.

What Clovenhoof did possess was experience. He had that in bucketsful.

"I've always held positions of authority. My last job but one was as the Big Guy's right hand man."

"Was it a big organisation?"

"Global."

"What kind of company was it?"

"We were in the construction business to start off with. We were *the* construction company for a while. Our first job was huge. Brought it in a day under schedule. Declared it a day of rest and put our feet up. Then there was a change of direction which I didn't like."

"Yes?"

"It shifted to housing, civic planning, legislation. Soft, squishy people-centred stuff."

"You're not a people person?"

"Not really. I don't really see why the clients should tell *us* what to do. We went from being a wholly private affair to a messy co-operative. Most of my colleagues who had been there from day one were downgraded to glorified couriers and messengers. I fought against the change tooth and nail."

"You don't like change?"

"If it ain't broke... Anyway, that was when I was kicked

out. I went into freefall for a long time. But I picked up my new role soon enough. It was smaller but at least I was my own boss."

"You don't like working for others?"

"Who does?"

"Er, quite. And what kind of business was that?"

"We worked with ex-offenders."

"Really?"

"Yeah, those who'd stepped over the line out in the big wide world. We were in the business of re-education and personal refinement."

"So rehabilitation?"

"Well, rehabilitation's a nice idea, but society rarely forgives you once your card is marked."

"Fascinating."

"I led the organisation through some challenging times."

HELL

Michael had created a much larger oval table in the demilitarised zone, with chairs surrounding it and a side table holding drinks. The Heavenly contingent arrived first, seating themselves neatly at the table and smiling at each other. The delegates from Hell were all late. They arrived piecemeal, and each tried to make an outlandish entrance. Michael drummed his fingers on the table as yet another demon materialised on the top of the table and ran around, trampling papers and kicking over a glass.

Mulciber hissed and leaped up from his seat as the liquid spread across the table top.

"Is that holy water?"

"Yes," Michael replied, mopping up the spillage with his handkerchief, "but there's blood over there for the demons."

"Blood?" squealed Saint Francis, his googly eyes wobbling all over the place. "Is that human blood?"

"Yes, it is," said Michael, "but it was donated. No humans died."

"That's okay then," said Saint Francis, "as long as it's not from a lovely little animal."

Azazel groaned and stuck his claws into his own face in exasperation.

"Wabbits are my favourwites," said St Francis although no one was listening.

Satan had arrived and was looking at his demonic colleagues.

"Hey. C'mon now guys, don't get over-excited. Yes, Berith, I know they're angels, but they've seen bottoms before. Probably. Anyway, put it away and sit down. Michael, can you do something about that?"

Satan pointed down the table.

"Oh no, stop it!" Michael jumped up and moved to where Saint Peter was trying to exorcise the demon Azazel. They were pulled apart and sat down, scowling at each other.

Satan and Michael turned in unison as they heard a munching, cracking sound. Berith had speared a white dove with his pitchfork and was enjoying a tasty snack.

St Francis murmured the name of his beloved pet and fainted across the table.

Michael raised his voice, as he fanned Francis with a sheaf of papers.

"We've got lots to talk about today. Maybe we should first of all have a few ground rules about refreshments. Drinks are over there, please help yourselves. We can sort out some canapés for later, but until then, er, please don't eat anything that you didn't bring yourself."

There was some giggling from the back where Berith had taken a bite from his own arm in response to this.

"We'll run through introductions, briefly. From Heaven, we have Peter, Herbert, Joan, Francis and myself of course. From Hell, we have Mulciber, Berith, Azazel, and Satan." He glanced at his notes. "We'll kick off with a brainstorming exercise. I'll write on the flipchart all of your thoughts on the biggest problems that Hell has right now. We'll refine the list later and decide how to tackle them, but for now let's get the ideas down."

As Michael picked up the pen there was shouting from almost every person at the table. Francis had evidently recovered enough to make his voice heard clearly as all the others reached the end of their complaints.

"-and wough, howwible demons all over the place."

Michael put the pen down and turned back to the table.

"We need to be more orderly about this," he said. "I think I'll go round the table in turn and see who has items for the board. And I only want to hear suggestions from people who have first-hand experience. Mulciber, why don't you start us off?"

"It's all about capacity," Mulciber said. "We need to be able to process people faster."

Michael nodded and started to write.

"Not just faster," yelled Berith, "what about quality? I know that I can only get really high quality suffering if I spend time with a person. What's going to happen to that if we're all going faster?"

"You sound a bit too much as though you enjoy it to me," Joan remarked.

"Of course I enjoy it you stupid girly," Berith snarled. "Hang on, is she French? Angels is one thing but Frenchies... We've got to draw the line somewhere."

Joan pulled her sword from its sheath.

"I can draw a line for you if you like," she said, a glint in her young eyes.

"Well I think you're all vewy howwid," Francis said, standing. "And I think I'd wather not be a part of these discussions if you're going to talk so unpleasantly."

"Hang on," Berith whispered to Azazel. "Is he a Frenchie too?"

"Italian," replied Azazel.

"Oh, that's all right," said Berith. "I like Italians. Delicious actually."

"Please!" Michael said. "Everyone's here because they have something to contribute. We need to respect each other a little bit more. I don't want to hear any more name calling."

"Poof," said someone at the back.

Satan strode around the table.

"Who said that?"

There was silence for a moment, and then Francis, deciding that he might stay after all, sat down and pointed a finger at Berith.

TWICE, they had to send out for more refreshments. There were arguments over whether Berith would be allowed snacks that were alive. They compromised on spiders, because Francis wasn't all that keen on spiders.

"Can't you eat with your mouth closed?" Francis moaned.

Berith opened his mouth wide, and lolled his tongue down over his chin, raising his eyebrows at Francis. He whipped it back in rapidly as a half-eaten spider made a bid for freedom.

"We're almost done now I think," said Michael. "We've identified our key areas of focus, and we have a workable Vision and Mission Statement. Very important things to have, so that we never forget what we're working towards. Let's just get the wording right for those, so we can have some motivational posters made up. Satan, would you like to read them out for everyone, one last time?"

Satan consulted his notes.

"Vision. 'To be the provider of choice for corrective torment and to offer "best-in-class" suffering for souls with challenged purity.'"

He turned over the paper.

"Mission. 'Exploit synergies with other providers and expand into emerging markets.'"

He looked around the table, and was met with faces that reflected a range of emotions that ranged from earnest approval through total bafflement to desperation to be out of there.

"So," Michael said, "if we just reach approval on these two, then I think we're done for the day. Let's have a show of hands."

There was a scramble of eager raised hands and then everyone sighed with relief and dispersed as rapidly as they could. Satan wandered around the table staring at the notes and plans and decided that he'd started something big. He wasn't sure what it was, and whether it was a good thing or a bad thing remained to be seen.

BOLDMERE

Dave finished typing on his computer and looked at Clovenhoof.

"Well, that should be enough info. Let's see what we've got for you."

Dave went to a filing cabinet, pulled out half a dozen sheets of paper, all headed with job titles and reference numbers.

"I've got some posts we could slot you straight into."

"Okay."

"Now, you've a lot of experience and many... fine qualities, but without qualifications, your options are limited."

"I understand."

"They all pay minimum wage."

"Is that a lot?"

"Er, no," said Dave. "It's the smallest amount anyone's allowed to be paid. Most of these are sanitation and cleaning roles."

"What's that?"

"Cleaning toilets mainly."

"What? Other people's toilets? No, I don't think so."

"What about this? Stock taking at a warehouse in Erdington."

"Yes?"

"You'll be working alone. Won't have other people to contend with very much. Simple steady work."

"Stocktaking is counting stuff."

"Is that a problem?"

Angels, even ex-angels, were good with numbers. Numbers and lists. Salvation and damnation.

"I can count," said Clovenhoof. "What about these jobs?"

He pulled at the papers already resting on Dave's desk. He could see higher rates of pay and there was one with very reasonable hours. He craned his neck to have a look.

"I'm afraid you'd not be suitable for these," said Dave, drawing them away. "School jobs are a bit out of your league. For the time being. Why not give the warehouse job a try?"

"Yes. It sounds thrilling," smiled Clovenhoof.

"Tina over there can sort you out with a start date. Tina!"

"Thanks," said Clovenhoof and took the sheet over to a familiar-looking woman sitting at her desk in a wheelchair.

"Job reference number?" said Tina, without looking up.

Clovenhoof looked at the paper. Angels (even ex-angels) were good with numbers. And Clovenhoof had an excellent memory.

~

CLOVENHOOF SIGNED in at reception of St Michael's C of E Primary School and they gave him a clip-on visitor's badge with his name on and he felt instantly proud and nervous. This was it. A job. His first new job in millennia. Such a thing came with responsibility. He had to make the right impression.

The security doors clicked open and a tiny blonde woman in a roll-neck top stepped through.

"Mr Clovenhoof?"

He stood, towering over her, and shook her hand politely.

"I'm Mrs Well-Dunn. Carol. Do you want to come through?"

He followed her into the school proper and along a corridor lined with display boards of children's work. The appalling spelling and inaccurate drawings made him smile.

"You're standing in for my regular LSA who's not at all well," said Mrs Well-Dunn. "You'll be with me and my year twos."

"Year two?"

"Age six and seven."

"I imagine you're brilliant with them," said Clovenhoof, who had been reaching for something positive to say.

"Thank you."

"Because you're so short, you'd only have to bend down a little to be on their level."

She stopped and looked at him and then laughed.

"You'll need that sense of humour with this lot," she said.

"Oh, I'm sure your students are darlings."

"Of course they are. But they are also children."

She led the way into a classroom. Thirty little figures in

bright blue jumpers sat at low tables with colouring crayons in hand, chatting as they worked.

And you'll be working with Spartacus," said Mrs Well-Dunn.

Clovenhoof looked across the sea of ponytails and spiky haircuts to where a boy sat, slightly apart from the rest.

"Spartacus?" said Clovenhoof.

"Spartacus Wilson. He's statemented."

"Is that a word?"

"He's clearly ADHD. There are obvious signs of ASD. His IEP also has him as mildly dyspraxic."

"He has stomach ache?"

"But his statement is for his ODD."

"He's odd?"

The teacher smiled.

"Oppositional Defiance Disorder, Mr Clovenhoof."

"Right..."

"Go over and say hello while I take the register."

Clovenhoof wove his way through the tables and sat down next to the boy on one of the tiny classroom chairs.

"Hello."

The boy ignored him completely and continued with his drawing.

"I said hello, Spartacus," said Clovenhoof.

The boy didn't look up but did the physical equivalent of a sigh.

"I'm Mr Clovenhoof."

Spartacus turned his head slowly and looked at Clovenhoof as though he was a piece of Cubist artwork. He held Clovenhoof's gaze for a long time and then, deciding that Cubism wasn't to his tastes, went back to his colouring.

Clovenhoof looked to Mrs Well-Dunn for help or guidance but she was busying logging onto a computer and handing out letters whilst simultaneously drinking a cup of coffee and explaining to the class that they would be putting on an assembly for the whole school later that week.

Clovenhoof scooched his chair nearer to Spartacus and tried again.

"What are you drawing there?"

"Picture," said Spartacus.

Contact! thought Clovenhoof.

"You're using a lot of red and black. And are these eyes?"

Spartacus shrugged.

"What's it meant to be?" asked Clovenhoof.

"Your mum," said Spartacus without a pause.

"You don't know my mum."

"Everyone knows your mum."

"I don't think so."

"Your mum smells of cat food."

"I think you're mistaken, young m-"

"Your mum works in the kebab shop. She doesn't sell any. She just eats them."

Clovenhoof tried to keep his voice low and even.

"Now, listen h-"

"Your mum gets bullied at bingo."

Clovenhoof clenched his fists.

"If you don't shut up now, I'll..."

"Getting on all right, Mr C?" called Mrs Well-Dunn from across the room.

Clovenhoof tried to give her a reassuring smile but it was a broken and crooked thing.

"Famously," he said.

Very quickly, Clovenhoof worked out what his job was meant to be. It was to be a buffer between the boy Spartacus and the rest of the world so that Mrs Well-Dunn could get on with her job of teaching the other students.

While Mrs Well-Dunn did her best to improve the numeracy and literacy of the little Fabians, Kenzies, Chardonnays and Aramintas that made up her year two class, Clovenhoof did his best to corral the uncontainable spirit of the boy and verbally head him off at the pass whenever he decided that, like his namesake, he should rise up and lead a rebellion against his masters.

By the end of the day, Clovenhoof was wishing that Spartacus, again like his namesake, had been crucified and left to die on an Italian roadside.

"Tomorrow," said Mrs Well-Dunn to the class as they put on their coats to go home, "we'll be breaking into groups to prepare for next week's assembly. Some of us will be in the choir. The rest will be preparing our dramatic presentation of one of the stories of Jesus. Mr Clovenhoof?"

"Yes?" said Clovenhoof, looking up.

"Could you lead the drama group to start off with while I have a quick chat with the new choirmaster?"

"Of course."

Spartacus picked up his lunch box and homework bag.

"Mr Clovenhoof?" said Spartacus.

"Yes?"

"Your mum's so fat she appears on Google Earth."

And with that, he was gone for the day.

CLOVENHOOF DOWNED his first Lambrini at the bar of the Boldmere Oak while Lennox the barman poured his second.

"Are we allowed to punch children?" he asked.

"Sadly not," said Lennox.

"What if no one's looking?"

"Seven thirty, mate."

Clovenhoof dug deep in his pockets for change but only came up with three pound twelve and a red crayon.

"Can I owe you? I get paid on Friday."

"Dunno, mate. 'Neither a borrower or a lender be.' Shakespeare said that."

"'What a piece of work is man.' He said that too."

Lennox gave him a shrewd and penetrating look.

"Friday, yeah?"

"Friday," said Clovenhoof and made off with the drinks to where Ben waited.

"Thanks," said Ben, slurping deeply. "So here's to your first day at work."

"Yeah. Might be my last."

"Work proving a little harder than you expected?"

"It's not the work. It's the..." He held his tongue, remembering that, officially, he was working at a machine parts warehouse. "It's another employee. I'm having problems with a colleague."

"Have you fallen out with your boss?"

"No. He's meant to be doing what *I* tell *him*."

"You're being bullied by an underling."

"Well, no. No. It's not like that. It's... yes, it's exactly that. I'm being bullied."

Ben chuckled and tried to hide it with a gulp of cider and black but just made a noise like a drowning hippo.

"It's not funny," said Clovenhoof.

"It's not," said Ben, wiping purple juice from his chops. "I just can't see you being the victim."

"This guy's a little shit."

"Jeremy. First of all, you've got to rise above it."

"Rise above it?"

"Yes. Whatever jibes, whatever insults he's flinging at you, ignore them."

"But he's so irritating and I've spent all afternoon thinking up snappy comebacks."

"Fear leads to hate. Hate leads to anger. Anger leads to suffering."

"What a load of twaddle."

"I know this from experience, Jeremy. I had a neighbour I fell out with. A really bitter old sod. I let him get under my skin and..."

"And?"

"And it didn't end well."

Ben sighed deeply.

"I got my itemised credit card bill through today," he said.

"Oh, yes?"

"Sex dolls."

"I beg your pardon."

"Someone used my card to buy a latex sex doll. Two thousand pounds it cost!"

"Wow. It must have been pretty top notch."

"It was. I mean, I assume it was. I wouldn't know."

"Of course you wouldn't."

"And then this bastard used my card number to pay for some supermarket groceries, stereo equipment and clothes. All on line. What is a bolo tie anyway?"

"No idea," said Clovenhoof, glad he'd opted for an alternative outfit that evening.

HE HADN'T LIED to Ben. He had spent the whole afternoon thinking of witty insults to use on Spartacus. It seemed a shame not to use them but Clovenhoof chose to follow Ben's advice for the time being. Besides, having been given the name Spartacus, the boy deserved at least a little sympathy.

After registration, Clovenhoof and his little drama group went into one of the school's two small halls, the other year two students going into the second hall behind a partition screen.

"Right, sit down you lot," he said.

Four of the children sat down in front of Clovenhoof.

Two girls, Pixie and Mercedes, were too busy comparing scrunchies to listen, Kenzie Kelly was running around pretending to be a fighter jet and making 'budda budda' gun noises and Spartacus Wilson was diligently and forcibly trying to break into the PE cupboard.

"Girls, sit down," said Clovenhoof. "Kenzie, stop strafing the chairs and land over here. Spartacus, come sit down."

"You're not the boss of me," called Spartacus.

"Yes, I am," said Clovenhoof.

"You can't tell me what to do. It's a free country."

"Since when?"

But the girls were seated now and Kenzie was taxiing to the terminal so Clovenhoof decided to ignore Spartacus for the time being.

"Right, let's see what our assembly is on."

He looked at the notes and book Mrs Well-Dunn had given him.

"Ah, the parable of the prodigal son."

"What's that?" said Mercedes Jones.

"It's a story Jesus told," said Araminta Dowling.

"Is it a true story?" asked Herbie Gates.

"What do you think?" said Clovenhoof. "The guy who told it was an illiterate carpenter and was making it up as he went along and the bloke who wrote it down didn't even write it down until fifty years after Jesus died, had never met Jesus and didn't know anyone who had. Chances of it being true..."

Clovenhoof made a seesaw motion with his hand.

"Still," he said. "At least it's short, morally bonkers and features the mindless killing of farm animals."

"Killing?" said Spartacus who was trying to pick the PE cupboard lock with a pencil.

"Absolutely."

Spartacus drifted over.

"Can I do the killing?"

Clovenhoof scoffed.

"I decide who gets which part."

"Yeah, but can I do the killing?"

Clovenhoof looked at the boy.

"Please," said Spartacus.

Clovenhoof felt a sudden and unexpected frisson of power.

"Well, that would depend," he said.

CLOVENHOOF HAD ORCHESTRATED great plans and co-ordinated many minions in the pursuit of a single goal before. And getting demons to work together was like trying to herd cats. However, getting six year olds to do the right thing at the right time was like trying to herd neutrons in a nuclear reactor. They simply had too much energy. Before the morning was out, he had composed several angry letters to parents in his head on the subject of sugary cereal and snacks and why they should be replaced with a diet of gruel.

Meanwhile, from the other side of the partition, came the sound of the school choir, an alarmingly and annoyingly melodious sound. No random whoops, screams or bursts of automatic gunfire from *them*.

"No, Spartacus. The prodigal son's father did not have an AK47."

"Why not?"

"They weren't invented then."

"How do you know? You said historical records of the time were sketchy at best."

"I did."

As he battled on with his eight prima donna actors, the choir progressed through a beautiful repertoire of songs, culminating in a four-part harmony rendition of *Jesus wants me for a Sunbeam*.

Part of the partition was pushed aside and Mrs Well-Dunn stepped through. Clovenhoof noticed with some pride that the teacher was surprised to see the students vaguely doing what they were supposed to be doing and not eating each other alive.

"How's it going, Mr C?"

"Not bad," he conceded. "We've taken a few liberties with the script you gave me but we've got the general gist of it."

"Very good. What are you doing on the floor, Thor?"

Thor Lexworth-Hall, an unfortunately rotund boy, looked up.

"I'm the fatted calf, miss."

"How silly of me not to realise." She turned to Clovenhoof. "I am so sorry for leaving you to it but I just wanted to see the new choirmaster at work. Oh, here he is."

A man stepped through the partition and smiled brightly.

"This is Mr Michaels," said Mrs Well-Dunn.

"We've met," said Clovenhoof.

"Oh?"

"We go way back," said Michael. "It's amazing how we keep bumping into each other."

"Amazing," said Clovenhoof.

MICHAEL STRODE beside Clovenhoof as he trotted home.

"You're spying on me again," Clovenhoof stated flatly.

"Not at all. I've recently become quite involved with the local church and community. I like the vicar they brought in to replace that unfortunate woman. He has many admirable qualities."

"Balls."

"And those. My appearance at the church school is purely a coincidence."

"Heaven's omniscience makes that assertion nonsensical," snapped Clovenhoof. "Your words, I recall."

"Have it your way," said Michael, inspecting his perfect fingernails. "Even if my presence at the school was not wholly coincidental, you couldn't be surprised. I mean, Jeremy, *children*?"

Clovenhoof gave him a sideways look.

"What about them?"

"Surely, some things are off-limits, even to you."

"You assume that I have wicked intentions."

"It is in your job description, dear chap."

"I beg your pardon," said Clovenhoof, feeling a small but righteous anger rise up inside him. "Was it me who told Jephthat to sacrifice his own daughter to the Lord?"

"Oh, yes. Rake up the Old Testament. That's just cheap."

"Was it?" Clovenhoof demanded.

"Actually, it was Jephthat's daughter who insisted he do it."

"Right. So, was it me who ordered that all the Samarian children have their brains bashed out against rocks?"

"Look, Hosea was writing in tumultuous times and there's a lot of allegory in his work."

"Did I personally wander through Egypt killing the firstborn child in every family?"

"You cannot judge past events through a modern moral framework!" said Michael hotly.

Clovenhoof smiled and was silent for a while as they walked.

"I can't believe you actually said that," he said quietly.

"If you intend the children at that school no harm then what are you doing there?" asked Michael.

"I'm only doing this job for the money."

"You need money?"

"You know I do."

Michael reached into his jacket and produced an impossibly fat sheaf of banknotes.

"How much?" he said.

"Do I need?"

"To keep you away from my school."

"Your school?"

"It has my name above the door."

Clovenhoof spat.

"Put it away."

"Ah," said the angel sagely, squirreling the money away into some other dimension. "You want the satisfaction of knowing the money in your pocket has been earned by the sweat of honest toil."

"I want the satisfaction of rearranging your face, Mickey-boy. I'm a citizen of the world now and you don't tell me what to do. You're not the boss of me."

"If you say so."

"Oh, and Michael?"

"Yes."

"Your mum."

"I don't have a mother."

"She's so stupid that when I told her Christmas was around the corner, she went and looked."

"Ah. A joke."

"Your mum's so fat that the local buses say, 'occupancy seventy-five people or your mum.'"

"Hilarious."

"Your mum's so fat that when she walked past the TV I missed three episodes."

"Oh, is there no end to these side-splitting put-downs?"

"Your mum's so stupid that when she heard someone say pi r squared she said, 'No, they're not. They're round.'"

"Okay. You can stop now, Jeremy."

"Your mum's so stupid she got run over by a parked car."

"Please stop."

"Uh-huh. I've got another twenty-seven of these."

Clovenhoof got through a further thirteen before Michael vanished.

NERYS PLONKED herself on the edge of Dave's desk and took a crisp from the open packet by his keyboard.

"What did you do with Jeremy Clovenhoof?" she asked.

"Your friend?"

"I don't like that word."

"Acquaintance?"

"Yes. What have you done with him?"

"Nothing."

"I passed him over to you. He was looking for a job."

"That's right and I got him one."

"And what happened?"

"Nothing. He's got a job."

"Did he quit?"

"No."

"Was he fired?"

Dave glanced at his computer screen, a reflex action. He didn't need to look.

"No. It's still his first week."

Nerys munched on the crisp fretfully and helped herself to another.

"I don't like it."

"What? He's got a job. He's been there every day this week. No complaints from the employer."

"Look. You don't know him like I do. Jeremy Clovenhoof is the kind of guy who can't commit to anything. His lifestyle comes with an automatic self-destruct."

"Maybe he's happy. Maybe it's his dream job."

"Doing what?"

"Stocktaking at an engine parts warehouse."

"Jesus Christ, Dave. What kind of dream job is that?"

"We all have different dreams, Nerys. They don't have to be big ones."

"Do you dream of working in an engine parts warehouse, Dave?"

"No."

She narrowed her eyes.

"Do you have dreams at all, Dave?"

He shrugged.

"A quiet life. A lie in on a Sunday morning. Finding myself a good woman I can trust."

Nerys took a third crisp. Clovenhoof. Happy. Productive. Some deep intuitive thought centre of her brain was sending out alarm signals.

"I don't buy it," she said to herself. "It's very fishy."

"Prawn Cocktail," said Dave, tilting the crisp packet to check.

"Shut up, Dave."

NERYS DECIDED to do the only sensible thing. She followed Clovenhoof to work the following morning.

She wore a high-collared coat and, grateful for the May drizzle, carried an umbrella to hide behind. She tailed him onto the Boldmere Road where he popped into a corner shop and emerged two minutes later with two large bottles in a carrier bag. He whistled a merry tune – most suspicious, Nerys concluded – as he continued down the shop-lined street, into a side road and through the gates of a primary school.

"This is not good," she said.

She dithered for five minutes and then went in. She showed her work badge to the receptionist.

"Hi," she said, "I'm from the *Helping Hand* Job Agency. I believe we've got one of our people working here."

"Mr Clovenhoof," nodded the receptionist.

Nerys was expecting to hear the name but it was still a surprise.

"Checking up on him are you?" said the receptionist.

"Yes."

"He's a character, isn't he?"

"Isn't he just."

"The year twos are about to do their assembly. You're welcome to go and watch."

"I'd like that."

The receptionist gave her a visitor's badge and buzzed her through. She went into a hall already half-filled with parents and younger children. Nerys took a seat in the back row and tried her best to not look like an interloper.

Two old women were seated next to her. Nerys was intrigued to see that they had notebooks and pens.

"Looking forward to it?" she asked the one closest to her.

"Hello dear," said the old lady, and nudged her companion. "Doris, say hello to the young lady." Doris inclined her head and smiled. "Yes, we're both very excited about the show."

"How old are the children?" Nerys asked.

"Oh, they're fairly small ones," said the old woman, motioning up and down with a hand to indicate a child somewhere between eighteen inches and four feet tall.

"You're making notes?" Nerys said.

"Oh yes, dear. We record the good things and the bad things that we see."

"Right," said Nerys, hoping that these primary school theatre critics would not have anything sensationally bad to record. "What have you got so far?"

"Well," said the old woman, "I think that's a nice set, well laid out, with good lighting and plenty of access."

Doris rolled her eyes. "It's a couple of blocks on the hall floor, Betty."

Betty pressed on. "There are clearly plenty of supportive parents here. You can feel the good will in the air. Very positive atmosphere. A lovely nurturing environment."

"Hmph," said Doris. "All the more reason to keep our young chap well away!"

Nerys laughed to hear them joking about a cherished grandson.

Betty produced a camera from her enormous handbag and switched it on. She held it at arm's length, trying to focus on the tiny screen.

"Can you see the button that puts it back to normal dear?" Betty asked.

Nerys glanced at the display and recognised the interior of the Boldmere Oak as the last photo, with a picture of a woman who looked vaguely familiar. She pressed a button and the camera obliged.

"Here you go."

"Thank you dear! We're all ready to go Doris."

"I think they're coming Betty, look!" Doris stood up and clapped with excitement.

Betty sprang to her feet and started snapping pictures.

"There he is, Doris, look!"

"Which one?" asked Nerys. "Which one is yours?"

"That one there, at the front, that's our Jeremy," said Betty, still concentrating on the camera.

"Oh, that's a coincidence," said Nerys. "What're the chances of a child having the same name as his, er, teacher?"

"I don't know dear," said Betty. "Look Doris, he's smiling. I told you, he's enjoying himself."

"Of course he's smiling. He's up to something, you mark my words," said Doris.

CLOVENHOOF HELPED SHEPHERD the two classes of years twos into the hall to accompanying coos and waves and the flash of cameras from the audience. Once both classes were sitting down in front of the low stage, Mrs Well-Dunn came to the front and made some opening remarks which were generally ignored while parents checked the pictures and videos they had already taken and jostled for position to take more.

The choir were welcomed on and Michael, with a cheesy grin for the mums, and twenty-odd children took to the stage. Michael bent to address his choristers.

"Deep breaths. Faces raised. And let God's love shine through," he whispered.

The children did as they were told and launched into *He's Got the Whole World in His Hands.*

Clovenhoof gritted his teeth and listened. He hated all hymns but there were degrees of hatred. He only held a half-hearted dislike for some hymnals. He liked the lunacy of Blake's *Jerusalem* and he always appreciated any mention he got in a hymn. But on the other hand, there were hymns that he loathed beyond words. *He's Got the Whole World...* was one of them but that was nothing compared to...

"Shoot me, please," he moaned as the choir segued into *Kumbayah*. The horrifically insipid spiritual was like nails dragging down the blackboard of his nonexistent soul. To round off the torture, they finished with *To Be a Pilgrim*, including those ridiculous lines about giants, hobgoblins and foul fiends.

While Clovenhoof clutched his guts and tried to hold himself together, the audience clapped, cheered and elbowed each other aside to get a good photo of their offspring.

"Well, how do you follow that?" said Mrs Well-Dunn to the audience as the choir trooped off.

"Yeah, beat that," said Michael, sliding past Clovenhoof and away.

"Here," said Mrs Well-Dunn, "are some members of 2W with a dramatic presentation of the parable of the prodigal son."

Clovenhoof ushered his company players onto the stage. Fat Thor Lexworth-Hall, dressed in sacking with a cloth cow mask over his face crawled into position. Clovenhoof went over and stuck a bottle under each arm.

"On your cue, remember," he said.

"Moo," said Thor dutifully.

Little Peroni Picken, with a towel on her head, strode to centre stage.

"Where are my sons?" she declared with the slow and deliberate pronunciation of the conscientious child actor.

"Here we are," chorused Kenzie Kelly and Herbie Gates.

"I want my share of your money," said Kenzie.

"But I'm not dead yet," said Peroni.

"But I want it!"

Peroni counted out invisible coins and shook her head.

"Now spend that wisely," she said.

Kenzie trotted over to the side of the stage where he contrived to demonstrate through energetic mime the travails of a young man who did not spend his wealth wisely. Mercedes Jones appeared, slapped Kenzie about a bit and told him to look after Araminta Dowling, who was a pig.

"Can I have some of your seeds?" Kenzie asked the pig. "I'm sooo hungry."

"No. Oink, oink."

"This is rubbish!" declared Kenzie, jumping to his feet. "I've lost all my money. I'll go back home and maybe my father will employ me as a servant."

Kenzie trudged the many miles back to centre stage.

"Is that you, son?" said Peroni.

"Yes. I've lost all my money. I'm so sorry."

"I'm so glad to see you. Servants! Bring him a robe and sandals."

Spartacus Wilson and Pixie Kaur wrapped a tablecloth around Kenzie's shoulders and stuck imaginary sandals on his feet.

"Slaughter a fatted calf in honour of his return," declared Peroni.

Thor Lexworth-Hall shuffled forward and said, "Moo."

"Hang on!" said Herbie Gates. "Why does he get all this good stuff when I've been a good son all along?"

"Because I can buy his love. I don't need to buy yours," said Peroni. "Besides, I can do what I like, so there!"

And at this declaration, Spartacus drew his cardboard

sword and swung it down at Thor's neck. Thor convulsed his arms, squeezing the plastic bottles and sent two red jets of tomato sauce arcing over the stage and into the front rows. There were shrieks and gasps and not much in the way of camera clicking.

Thor rolled onto his side, dead. Spartacus plucked the cow mask from his face.

"Our bloody sacrifice is made," he said. "Hoorah!"

The parents and younger siblings in the audience stared. There was a long silent pause, punctuated only by the plaintive cry of a frightened toddler.

Clovenhoof decided to get the applause rolling and clapped loudly.

No one joined in but he kept going undeterred.

CLOVENHOOF STOOD on the pavement just outside the school grounds and looked through the glass doors to reception, watching Nerys in conversation with Mrs Well-Dunn and the head teacher. The conversation went on for a very long time and there was some head shaking, some arm waving and even some poking.

Clovenhoof shifted from hoof to hoof and watched and waited with interest. At last, Nerys emerged, red-cheeked, walked out of the gates, past Clovenhoof and along the road without a word.

"Hey," said Clovenhoof, following close behind.

Nerys strode on, ignoring him.

"What did they say?" he called.

Still no response.

"Do they want me back on Monday?"

He trotted to catch up.

"Admit it," he said. "They liked it, didn't they?"

Nerys stopped stock still, then turned slowly and, as Clovenhoof came within range, punched him in the side of the head. He sat down clumsily on the wet pavement.

"Ow," he said, after a moment's thought.

"You vile colossal fuckwitted bastard!" she screeched. "How could you do that?"

"It was quite easy really. He just had ketchup bottles under his arms."

Nerys made a wordless shriek.

"It wasn't real blood," he protested.

"You've no idea what you've done, have you? You were meant to be in a warehouse position."

"Yeah, but I didn't fancy that."

Nerys towered over him and pointed a finger in his face.

"We told the school the person we were sending was a qualified teaching assistant. We told them they'd been checked for criminal records. You've broken the law. *I've* broken the law. The parents could sue the school if they wanted to."

"Look," said Clovenhoof with placatory hand gestures, "that ketchup will come right out. They just need to put their clothes on a hot wash cycle."

Nerys kicked him viciously in the shin.

"You don't understand," she hissed. "I hate you. I never want to see you again."

"An overreaction, surely?" he suggested but he was alone and talking to himself.

After a time, he picked himself up, brushed at the wet seat of his trousers and trudged down to the high street and the *Books 'n' Bobs* bookshop. In the empty shop, Ben was sorting through a box of new stock.

"Hey," said Clovenhoof.

"And to you," said Ben. "Look, I'm quite busy."

"I see."

"Room clearance after some ninety year old lady died up at the Willows. Got a box of first edition Barbara Cartlands."

"Really?"

"She was a keen glider pilot, you know."

"Is that how she died?"

Ben looked at Clovenhoof.

"I mean, ninety. That's a hell of an age to-"

Aren't you meant to be at work?" said Ben.

"Meh," said Clovenhoof, shrugging.

"What happened?"

"I've lost my job. Nerys shouted at me too."

"Did you deserve it?"

Clovenhoof scratched his beard as he thought.

"No. Not really. I just think I've had a run of bad luck. The job. Money worries. A less than successful meal out at the Karma Lounge with Blenda."

"Karma Lounge," said Ben with a frown. "Where have I seen that recently?"

"It's only just down the high street."

"No," he said and pulled a printed sheet from under the counter. "Here..."

"What's that?" said Clovenhoof and then saw the credit company logo on the top of the sheet.

Ben traced his finger down the list of payments.

"You went there last Friday," said Ben, "but my card was declined."

"What do you mean?" said Clovenhoof in exaggerated tones of innocence.

Ben looked at him squarely and at the shoelace with cow skull clasp around Clovenhoof's neck.

"Is that a bolo tie?" said Ben.

Clovenhoof fiddled with it but it failed to vanish.

"I can explain," he said. "There's a perfectly reasonable explanation for why I took your credit card."

"Really?"

"Yes. I had run out of money."

"And?"

"And?"

"And what?"

"That's it. It was either steal money from you or get a job."

"Four thousand pounds."

"Money isn't real, Ben."

"I can't believe you did that."

"It's a consensual illusion."

"I trusted you."

"I know. But you have to know I've never lied to you except when it was really necessary or convenient."

"I thought you were my..."

"What?"

Ben wiped his eyes with his sleeve and turned away.

"Get out," he said quietly.

"You want me to go?"

Ben went into the back room and shut the door.

"Right," said Clovenhoof to the empty shop. "That was a bit rude, wasn't it?"

He sauntered out of the shop, stopping only to flick through a book of Degas paintings and earmark the pages with the nudes on.

AT THE BOLDMERE OAK, Lennox refused to serve him.

"You owe me from earlier in the week," said the barman.

"Yeah, but I got fired."

"No money, no drink," said Lennox, not unkindly.

"Bugger."

"Here," said Blenda, stepping in with a twenty pound note.

Lennox gave her a look that suggested, again not unkindly, that she was being a fool but took the money anyway.

"You're a darling," said Clovenhoof.

"Come sit down," she told him. "I think you might need to tell me everything."

"Okay."

They sat down in a corner and Clovenhoof told her exactly why Nerys and Ben were angry with him. She had to ask a few questions to clarify the more obscure points but she let him tell his whole story without comment and judgement.

"And that's what happened," he said.

Blenda nodded.

"I like you, Jeremy."

"I like me too."

"You're funny. You're unpredictable. You make the world a more interesting place."

"Thank you."

"But that doesn't make you a good man, does it?"

"No."

Blenda sipped at her wine and looked briefly into its golden depths.

"Do you know what men want from women?" she asked. "Really, really want from them?"

"Constant sexual gratification?"

"Absolution."

"Absolution?"

"Men want someone to hold them, tell them everything's going to be all right and, ultimately, they want someone to forgive them."

"For what?"

"Everything, Jeremy. Everything."

"Okay," said Clovenhoof. "Good."

"But I'm not the one who has to forgive you."

"I don't want forgiveness."

A look passed across Blenda's face that Clovenhoof hadn't seen before.

"I can cope with you being a bastard but don't be a twat as well. The way I see it, you owe some sincere apologies to your friends and you owe one of them a ton of cash too."

"That's tough because I haven't got a job at the moment."

Blenda opened her purse and took from it a business card.

"Isn't it lucky then that I know someone who's hiring? Gordon Buford's a friend of a friend. He initially wanted someone with beauty therapy experience."

"Do I look like a beauty therapist?"

"There's nothing to it. Besides, Gordon's clients they're... not likely to complain."

She handed him the business card. Clovenhoof read it.

"You're kidding, aren't you?"

"Not at all. And Jeremy?"

"Yes?"

"Cock this job up and I will snap you like a twig."

GORDON BUFORD WAS a round and sanguine man with a disconcertingly tactile nature. He kept up a cheery, one-sided and mostly content-free conversation as he physically guided Clovenhoof through a tour of his business.

"And here," said Gordon, steering Clovenhoof through a set of double doors into a tiled room, "is where you're going to help prepare our clients for the big day, assuming we decide to take you on. Manpreet."

A tall, wide man in a plastic apron looked up from the gurney at which he was working.

"This is Jeremy," said Gordon. "We're considering him for the assistant position."

"Here," said Manpreet, drawing Jeremy up to the trolley

with a huge arm. Clearly, the touching was some sort of company policy. "This is Mrs Fincher."

Clovenhoof looked down at the pale, shrivelled corpse on the gurney.

"Until recently, a resident of the Willows Nursing Home," said Manpreet.

"Ninety years old," said Clovenhoof.

"Yes," said Manpreet surprised. "Now you see this wound here." He indicated a line of ruptured skin and bruising that ran down her face and onto her chest.

"Did she do that in the gliding accident?"

Manpreet frowned.

"No. When she had a heart attack and fell against a chest of drawers. Now, what we're going to do is use our range of pastes and cosmetics to fill in the wound and blend in with the rest of her lovely face."

"Right now?"

"Sure," said Gordon. "You've seen a corpse and kept your lunch down. That's good enough for me. Let's see how the rest of the day goes."

"Great," said Clovenhoof.

He looked down at the corpse once more.

"Hello, Mrs Fincher."

CLOVENHOOF TOOK a bunch of flowers up to Nerys's flat. He considered knocking but then decided against it; neither of them was quite ready for that. He left them leaning against the door. The attached message was short and to the point.

He hoped she noticed that they were expensive flowers and that he hadn't stolen them from a roadside accident black spot.

He returned to his flat, picked up an envelope containing half his week's wages and went out into the corridor so he could post them through Ben's door.

"What's this?" said Michael, lounging against the wall.

"Just some money I owe someone," said Clovenhoof.

"Wow. Settling debts. That's..." He waved the air for inspiration. "Mature. Noble even."

Clovenhoof shrugged.

"They're my friends. I want them to forgive me."

"Forgive?" said Michael as though he'd been burned.

"I want them to be my friends again."

"That is not like you," said Michael. It was more of an instruction than a statement.

"I thought you were big on penitence and forgiveness," said Clovenhoof.

"Well, yes, in a general sense. Of course we are. I mean, I am. But you're a special case."

"How am I a special case?"

"You rejected Him."

"Humans do it all the time."

"Knowing full well that He exists and that He is love, you rejected Him. There can be no greater separation between two individuals than there is between Him and you."

Clovenhoof stroked his beard.

"What about the prodigal son?"

"Please. Parables are open to so many interpretations. That's part of their quaint charm."

"There would be no greater celebration than the reconciliation between the father and his most wayward child."

"Come now," said Michael, loosening his shirt collar, which was suddenly too tight. "You cannot be forgiven unless you truly repent."

"Maybe I do."

"And you think you will be granted forgiveness?"

"The shepherd will sacrifice everything to rescue that one lost sheep."

"I think you're a bit more than a lost sheep," said Michael, his strangled voice shooting up an octave.

"His mercy knows no bounds."

"But you're..." He glanced about to see in anyone was in earshot. "You're the devil!"

"I am one of His creations."

"An angel. You do not have man's free will to sin or seek redemption."

"Either I have free will and can seek redemption or I have none and was never responsible for my actions. You can't have it both ways."

"Be reasonable, Jeremy, please."

"I am being reasonable, Michael."

Michael shook himself as though trying to wake himself from a terrible dream.

"All right," he said in controlled tones. "I'm big enough to take this."

"Thank you."

Michael constructed his best smile and placed a loving hand on Clovenhoof's shoulder.

"Do you, Lucifer, the Fallen One, confess all your sins and seek God's forgiveness?"

Clovenhoof met Michael's gaze and held onto the moment as long as he could.

"Fuck you, Gaylord," he said and winked.

Michael pulled away.

"You!"

"The look on your face," grinned Clovenhoof. "You fell for that."

"I did not."

"Hook, line and sinker."

"I was merely playing along," protested Michael.

"Balls you were."

"You took advantage of my good nature."

Clovenhoof pushed open Ben's letterbox and slid the envelope through.

"You tell Him from me," said Clovenhoof, "when *He* wants *my* forgiveness, then we'll talk."

He let the letterbox shut with a snap.

IN WHICH CLOVENHOOF HOSTS A DINNER PARTY, LETS SOMETHING SLIP AND STARTS A SMALL FIRE

Jeremy Clovenhoof requests your presence for a Candlelit Soirée on
the evening of June the Fourteenth.
Bring a guest.
Drinks from 7:30pm
To be followed by a Modest Supper
RSVP

A few hours after pushing the invitations through the doors of flats 2B and 3, Clovenhoof was pleased to get two responses. One came on lavender scented notepaper.

Jeremy, delighted to attend, Nerys. x.

THE OTHER CAME WRITTEN on the back of a takeaway menu.

Thanks mate, I'll be there. Haven't got a guest though, hope that's OK, Ben.

CLOVENHOOF WAS HELPING Manpreet to embalm the corpse of Mr Dienermann. Helping at the moment really meant turning the body when he was told to, and helping to wash it down. Manpreet was adamant that Clovenhoof would need to watch the embalming procedure quite a few times before he could attempt it himself, but Clovenhoof thought it looked pretty simple. Basically, it involved swapping the blood in the body with an arterial solution. All you had to do was insert the cannula into an artery and make sure that there weren't any holes in the corpse that would spring a leak. Then the machine pumped things around and did the rest.

"Will it be Findus Crispy Pancakes?" smirked Manpreet.

"What?"

"On your dinner party menu."

"I haven't really worked out the menu yet. What sort of thing would people eat at a dinner party?"

"You haven't got a menu yet? I thought you said it was tomorrow. Do you want to do the eyelids?"

Clovenhoof packed cotton wool under Mr Dienermann's eyelids to counter the shrinking of the eyes.

"Not too much," warned Manpreet.

"Okay, okay."

"He's not supposed to look like a frog, you know."

Clovenhoof adjusted his work and Manpreet nodded approval.

"Anyway," said Clovenhoof. "The dinner's tomorrow. No problem, I can go shopping later."

"Go shopping later?" Manpreet was spluttering.

"What's wrong with that?"

Manpreet poked Mr Dienermann's cheek as the active dyes in the fluid returned some colour to the man's flesh.

"Tell me. Why is it that you're having this dinner party? You want to impress someone?"

"Yeah. Sort of."

"Thought so."

"I want to show them all that I can behave properly, and I want them all to realise that Blenda and I are a couple, and, well you know..."

"You want to impress them." Manpreet shook his head as he worked on Mr Dienermann's jaw to fasten it shut. "Well, you need to try harder. If you're going to invite people round for a dinner party, you need to be giving them the very best that there is. I know quite a bit about food you know, and it can take me weeks to plan a dinner party. You have to source things."

"Is that like buying them?"

"Yes, but it means it's harder. That's the point. Let me think. Come and hold his head steady." Manpreet made a small incision in Mr Dienermann's neck and plumbed in the machine. "At the very least you need to make everything yourself. Have you even made the spun-sugar baskets to showcase your dessert?"

Clovenhoof shook his head in confusion

"You might be looking at an all-nighter if you want to get them just right," said Manpreet. "You'll need fresh berries for garnish. Make sure they're local."

"Why?"

"Oh, lots of people worry about food miles. If you want to impress people then make sure your ingredients are locally sourced where you can. There's a pick-your-own farm at Bassetts Pole, you could get there and back in a few hours. That leaves main course. Have you got any vegetarians, or people with allergies?"

"What?"

"You know, people who can't eat certain foods."

"No," lied Clovenhoof. He had no idea.

"That's easier then. You might want to think about some fish on your menu. People like it because it's healthy and it can make a stunning visual impact. You could have made a bouillabaisse, but I'm not sure you'd get the conger eel and the scorpion fish at such short notice. Oh, if you serve fish, try and get some samphire."

"What's samphire?"

"It's a plant that grows on the sea shore."

"Well that's not going to be local then," said Clovenhoof. "Sutton Coldfield's as far from the sea as you can get in this country."

"Ah but it's in season. You get points for seasonal too.

See?"

Clovenhoof didn't see. He was going to need some help.

"IF THEY DON'T HAVE it here, it doesn't exist," said Ben.

Clovenhoof pushed the trolley while Ben nodded appreciatively at Waitrose's array of groceries.

"Oh yeah. This is the place for posh food. Look at that, a whole row of shelves with different types of olive oil."

"Will I need some of that?" Clovenhoof asked.

"Probably," Ben said, "all upscale cooking's done with olive oil."

"What's wrong with lard?"

"I don't know. But it's wrong."

"Have you got a guest to bring with you tomorrow?"

"I don't have anyone I can bring."

"You must know someone."

Ben laughed mirthlessly.

"The only people I know are men, and I don't think any of them would last all through a meal in the company of strangers before they fainted or wet themselves."

Clovenhoof looked at Ben in disbelief.

"Okay. Well, get a prostitute then."

"Jeremy! I'm not coming if you're going to be like that."

"I'll book one for you if you like."

Ben stopped in the aisle.

"Look," he said testily. "I don't want to rush you, but I'm on my lunch hour."

"I've got to get this stuff."

"Then we'll ask for help."

Clovenhoof stopped a shelf-stacker with a left breast called Barbara.

"Where do I find the samphire?" he said.

"Sorry?" she said.

"Samphire."

Shelf-stacker Barbara looked uncertain, and then a smile lit her face.

"You mean saffron? A spice?"

"No, it's a plant that grows by the sea."

"Plants are by the entrance, with cut flowers."

"Er no. You eat it."

Various uncertain expressions played across her face like clouds over a hillside.

"No," she said eventually. "I don't think we have that."

Clovenhoof sighed and crossed it off his list.

"OK, what about scorpion fish and conger eel?"

"Well, they'd be on the fish counter if they're anywhere," Barbara ventured.

"If? So will they be there?" said Clovenhoof.

"They might be."

"But will they?"

"They don't sound very familiar to me. I don't think we stock them. The fish market in Birmingham's the place if you want unusual fish. Try there."

Clovenhoof left Barbara with his torn-up list raining down on her like confetti as he stormed from the shop. Ben ran to catch up.

∾

BACK IN *BOOK'S 'N' Bobs* bookshop, Clovenhoof added another volume to the pile of cookery books he had made on the counter.

The *Bloodthirsty Bullfighter's Book of Spanish Cookery* appealed to him because there was a close-up of a large angry bull on the front.

He searched the shelves for a book about cooking fish. *Got Any Crabs On Yer, Cock?* caught his eye. It was a publication commissioned by an eel and pie shop in London back in the seventies. He flipped through it, noting with pleasure that it contained many line drawings showing the correct ways to take a whole fish and reduce it to edible chunks.

He added *Cocktails: a Man's Guide* by Richard Harris to the pile and slid them over to Ben.

"Can I borrow these? I only want them until the dinner party's over."

"No," said Ben. "This isn't a library."

"You're right. Libraries have people in them."

Ben looked up at his empty bookshop.

"Okay. If you bring them back in the same condition, I'll refund you what you paid, minus a pound."

"Deal," said Clovenhoof, resolving to smear bogies on the middle pages before he brought them back.

THE FISH MARKET by the Birmingham Bullring was much more interesting than Clovenhoof had expected.

He found someone selling live prawns. He knew from the

cookbook that they were to be dropped into boiling water to cook. He couldn't miss an opportunity like that. He bought a large bag and sighed with pleasure.

He asked about conger eel, and was pointed to a stall that had one. He was brought up short when he saw it. Around eight feet long, with teeth that he knew would show no mercy. He'd enjoyed the ghoulish tales from the cookbook that described how a severed conger eel head had been known to bite off the arm of an unwary fisherman. Seeing it in the flesh, even though it was dead, filled him with admiration. He knew he could not cook this magnificent creature. He wanted to remember it as he saw it, arranged on ice, teeth bared at passers-by. He already had a pet in Herbert, but if asked about an ideal pet, he decided that a conger eel would be in the running. He turned on his heel and went away to re-plan his menu.

In the taxi home, Clovenhoof considered his successful mission and the still unfulfilled needs of his menu.

Unusual. Locally sourced. Clovenhoof's mind turned over the possibilities. He'd obviously have to be creative with just a few short hours to go. He had an idea about the star dish. Something that his guests would never have tasted before. He got out his pen and started to jot down ideas.

His mind though stayed with the fish in the market. He loved the look of them, laid out in ice. Some of the gaping mouths looked like souls in torment, which made him smile in recollection. There were, he admitted, still aspects of Hell he missed. He'd been proud of the work that they did there.

HELL

Michael flipped through the report as he and Satan walked on through the bowels of Hell.

"You can say what you like about them, those OFHEL guys are thorough. Look at this, they took the temperature from the lake of fire, in three different places. They sent out five hundred surveys to the damned to grade the level of suffering that they received. Mind you, it says that they only got back seventy of them. Why's that?"

"Oh, the others got eaten or burned up, I should imagine," Satan replied. "But a grade of 'improving' is good, right?"

"It shows we're doing the right things. I mean look at the entrance now. Can't believe it's the same place, can you?"

They watched the slick, multi-lane turnstiles, each manned by a pair of well-trained demons who jabbed at each person with a slickly orchestrated routine as they checked the computerised roster and showed them where to go.

"And the bridge over the Styx," added Satan. It had become one of his favourite places, with the views it offered.

"Yes, it's very efficient," agreed Michael, "but I'm rather keen to see the college, can we go and do the tour now?"

The Infernal College of Demon Training was the newest initiative, and promised every employee of Hell a personalised development programme.

They started the tour in one of the gym blocks, where an instructor was taking a class in Basic Pitchfork Techniques.

"Most of this is about control and stamina," Satan whispered to Michael as they watched. "You'll see that they barely pick up their pitchforks for the first few lessons. Frustrates the young ones like you wouldn't believe."

It was an inspiring sight to see forty young demons, perfectly synchronised, as they lunged forwards with a cry of "Hah!"

They moved on, and entered a laboratory.

"I think you'll be impressed with this," said Satan. "It's dedicated to the Infernal Innovation Programme. Let me introduce you to our head of research and development, Belphegor.

Michael shook the hand of the wizened demon sat in an elaborate wheelchair.

"So you're the brains of this enterprise?" Michael asked.

Belphegor cackled and pushed a large lever, which made his wheelchair lurch forwards in a noisy and jerky way.

"If I was the brains, I probably wouldn't have got in the

way of the bone-crusher that we used to make the foundations for this place."

"The foundations are made from bones?" Michael asked.

"The foundations, the walls, even the roof tiles. One of the areas we've had to develop most rapidly is the re-use of existing assets. If someone's a level seven damned, we use them for projects like this. It ensures that they don't run the risk of accidentally having any fun, and we save a fortune on materials."

"Can I ask, does your wheelchair run on clockwork?" said Michael.

"What a question! Oh dear me no. Clockwork's terribly old-fashioned, you know. This is steam-powered. My assistants will add more fuel every few hours."

Michael suddenly had an idea as to what the fuel might be and walked on in silence.

"We've got some exciting new developments for the humble pitchfork over here," said Belphegor. "It's a demon's hardest working asset, and we're trying to find ways to make them more efficient and durable. Replaceable tips are something that I'm certain will be popular. A demon wants reliable sharpness in his pitchfork. Hah! This one's fun. Do you want to pick up that pen, sir?"

He indicated to Michael, who picked up the pen.

"It looks very much like any ordinary pen. Now would you click the top please?"

Michael held it at arm's length as he clicked the top and the pen was somehow transformed into a lightweight pitchfork. He put it down hurriedly.

"Yes, very good. Very...innovative."

"Now, one of the goals of the Infernal Innovation Programme is to reduce the cost and time taken for quality torment of our clients. We've built a number of prototypes, which we're assessing in the lab. Would you like to see those?"

Michael nodded, not at all sure that he did. They followed Belphegor's wheelchair as it made its erratic, zigzagging way down a corridor, and emerged onto a gantry that looked across an enormous workshop.

The eye was drawn to the closest apparatus. It had the form of a huge wheel. There were people strapped to the outside of the wheel, their bottoms exposed. Inside the wheel, enthusiastic demons jogged continually, causing it to turn on its axle. As the wheel rotated, demons stationed on platforms around the outside wielded their pitchforks on the exposed bottoms. As they watched, a whistle was blown and the apparatus was stopped.

"What are they doing now?" Michael asked.

"Every fifteen minutes we take assessments of the level of torment. We measure this very scientifically. If we make some minor adjustments, we need to know how they are ultimately impacting the client experience."

Sure enough, a demon with a clipboard had a brief interchange with each human and circled a value on his sheet.

"What's that thing over there?" Michael asked, pointing at a large tunnel-like structure.

Belphegor smiled proudly.

"We're prototyping ways for the Lake of Fire experience to be delivered in a more efficient way. So that is our walk-through fire-wash. Burners on all sides ensure that clients can move through at speeds of up to three miles an hour and still be thoroughly charred."

"It'll never replace the real Lake of Fire," Satan said, "but it will enable the recovery of its delicate ecosystem, in time."

Michael gave a weak smile.

They said goodbye to Belphegor and moved onto the second floor of the college. There were smaller meeting rooms and classrooms off a long corridor.

"I thought we'd drop in on a performance management meeting." Satan said, "One of the senior demons, Toadpipe is reviewing Gutterscum. He's been underperforming. It's important that they follow the process, so we'll just sit quietly at the back and observe."

They entered the room in silence and took chairs at the back. Toadpipe and Gutterscum sat at either side of a table. Both had a copy of the review document. Toadpipe scanned through his copy, checking details. Gutterscum gnawed the corner of his copy, his eyes darting about nervously.

Toadpipe cleared his throat.

"Gutterscum, we've met before to talk about your performance, in fact I will record the fact that this is our twentieth meeting."

He made a note.

"So let's talk about the targets that you've been working towards. The first page of the document that you have there is the agreement that you signed when we set your objectives. You agreed at that time that you accepted the targets we came up with."

"You said I had to sign it," Gutterscum mumbled.

"Yes," said Toadpipe, glancing briefly at Satan and Michael. "I said that we needed to agree and we both had to sign to say so. We set you targets that were challenging but achievable. Let's take the first one. *Torment to achieve levels of misery of grade five or higher.* I have here the documented evidence that shows that your average level of torment is graded at misery level two."

"I work in the Pit of Masochists. They don't get miserable. They *love* being tormented," Gutterscum complained.

"You have similar working conditions to many other demons," Toadpipe said.

"But my victims can be really difficult! They try to trick me into giving them extra punishments."

"Clients, not victims. Remember that you had behavioural training to equip you with the correct language. It's important to remember that we're providing a service. Shall we move on to the next measure? *Rate of torment will not drop below twenty clients every hour.* We all know that this is an important measure, as it ensures that there is an optimum period of recovery and anticipation between intense periods of torment. The CIA provided us with lots of research for the optimisation that we've implemented. The records here show that your average rate of torment is eighteen clients per hour."

Gutterscum sighed and looked at the floor.

"Those masochists slow me down. They snatch my pitchfork so that they can stab themselves."

"We've given you lots of support in this area, Gutterscum. We've arranged for surprise inspections to observe your techniques. We've assigned you a mentor who meets with you twice a day."

"But that stuff just makes me get further behind."

"Now, Gutterscum. We've been over this in lots of these meetings. If you can't maintain a positive mental attitude, even after the behavioural training, then it's hardly surprising that you're struggling with your targets. I can see no option at this point other than putting you back into basic training here at the college."

Gutterscum nodded in easy-going acceptance.

"*After* a period of reflection," said Toadpipe.

Gutterscum's head snapped up.

"Er, what does that mean?" he asked.

"It means that we'll be cementing you into the foundations for a hundred years, so that you can think about your continued employment with our organisation."

Gutterscum's mouth moved wordlessly for a few moments and then he shrugged.

"Be nice to get away from those masochists."

Toadpipe stood and shook his hand.

"Good man. Well it's been nice helping you through your development."

"Yeah. Thanks," replied Gutterscum and two larger demons in work boots and hard hats appeared behind him.

Later, walking away from the college, Satan and Michael discussed what they had just observed.

"We've found that it's really helped with efficiency," Satan said. "Now everybody knows exactly what's expected of them. We can recognise who's doing a really good job, and give them more challenging tasks, and then we can weed out those who are just trying to get by with the bare minimum."

"I'm pleased that it's proving effective," Michael said.

"Oh yes," said Satan, "I will be doing the performance management reviews for Mulciber and Azazel next week."

"Well, that's a surprise," Michael said, turning and facing him. "I wasn't sure that you'd be quite so ready to apply these principles to your most senior colleagues."

"Oh I'm a firm believer in leading by example." To demonstrate this, Satan skewered the buttocks of a newly arrived client who was being used in a tug of war contest between the younger demon students. "Good work there. Pull a bit harder, we're looking for dislocations."

He smiled at the powerful effect of his intervention. They put in such efforts that they pulled one of the arms completely off the torso. Satan made a mental note to put them forward for a commendation.

BOLDMERE

There was a lip-smacking kissy noise that Aunt Molly used to summon her dog. Aunt Molly normally got to do it in the privacy of the flat. Nerys was less happy with having to do it Sutton Park.

"Twinkle!" she called in a high and enticing voice.

She took out her phone and looked at the time. She had been searching for three hours now. Aunt Molly would have already finished listening to the *Archers* omnibus and be wondering where her niece and her dog were.

She phoned Dave.

"Twinkle!" she bellowed while it rang out and went to answer phone for the fifth time.

"Dave," she spat, "are you even listening to your messages? Get here now!"

Ten minutes later, Dave jogged up to her, red-faced.

"What happened?" he asked.

She indicated the empty lead that she carried.

"Oh," he said.

"Aunt Molly's convinced he got out under the fence, but he's so fat with all the biscuits she gives him that he's more likely to have bounced over the top. I thought he might have come up here because he likes to chase the squirrels."

"Have you looked in those bushes?"

She fixed him with a stern gaze.

"Have you ever been called a 'paedo'?"

"Um."

"I heard a rustling and went to investigate. The two... amorous teenagers I found were quite rude. I mean, do I look like a paedophile?"

"I wouldn't know what one –"

"I was mortified. And Aunt Molly will be beside herself."

"Oh dear," said Dave. "Poor dear. I can see why you said it's an emergency."

"This?" She shook her head at his stupidity. "Oh no, this isn't the emergency. Here's something much more pressing."

She handed him Clovenhoof's invitation.

"This looks like, um, fun," said Dave handing it back.

Nerys rolled her eyes.

"Yes, but it's tonight and I don't have a date."

"I'm sure you know lots of men. I mean, when I say lots, I don't mean –"

"Graham and Mark. They're both busy. Nice guys. Gentlemen of reduced stature but I don't hold that against them. They're apparently working as extras in a film."

"Yes?"

"I phoned Trevor, I think that's his name, do you know it might be Stephen. Anyway, I got the impression that he was just making excuses. I think he's intimidated by strong women to be honest."

"Really?"

"And I went and spoke with that Doug down at the supermarket. He's a Libra but I'm not prejudiced. I know he was drawn to me, but I could see that he was fighting it. He's a very physical man, if you get what I mean. Anyway, he said he's on shift tonight." She blew out her cheeks. "There's nothing for it Dave, you'll have to come with me."

"Oh," said Dave. "Like a date, you mean?"

"No," Nerys said firmly. "Certainly not."

"Oh. Okay."

"Off you go now. You need to find something suitable to wear."

Dave looked down at his outfit.

"What's wrong with this?"

Nerys didn't even bother looking. She took a document wallet from her handbag and passed it to him. He flipped through. There were photographs taken from magazines, swatches of cloth, a list of dos and a longer list of don'ts.

"You know my inside leg measurement?" said Dave but Nerys had already moved on, making kissy noises.

7:30 pm

Ben waited for the second hand to reach the twelve and then knocked on the door of flat 2a. Clovenhoof opened the door, grinning enormously. He was wearing a luminous paisley smoking jacket that made Ben squint in pain.

Clovenhoof had pushed the easy chairs out of the way, and had set up a bar on one side of the room. A large table and chairs filled much of the remaining space. Candles burned in the centre of the table. They were the size of church candles although Ben doubted any church had black candles streaked with red.

Blenda came through from the kitchen, drying her hands on a tea towel.

"Ben? Nice to meet you at last."

Ben, never happy with social situations, was unsure whether to say, 'thank you' or 'nice to meet you too' or 'I've heard so much about you, Blenda' and plumped unwisely for, "I've heard thank you too."

"Are you going to be first to sample some of Jeremy's cocktails? He's pretty excited about some of them."

Ben looked at the bar and the array of drinks on the bar.

"Can I just have a cider and black?"

"Have a Pink Leopard, it's very similar," said Clovenhoof, upending bottles into a cocktail shaker at great speed. He launched into an ambitious routine of mixing the drink. Ben was impressed with the back-kick, particularly in such a confined space.

Ben took the sugar-frosted glass, and sipped the Pink Leopard.

"It tastes pretty strong."

Clovenhoof slapped him on the back, taking that as a compliment.

"So Ben," said Blenda, "I heard all about Jeremy's foolishness with your credit card."

"It's all forgotten about now," he said magnanimously.

"Is it?" said Clovenhoof.

"No."

"You've been a decent lad about the whole thing," said Blenda, squeezed his shoulder and headed back to the kitchen.

Ben turned back to see a man leant against Clovenhoof's bar wearing the kind of suit that probably cost more than a small car.

"I didn't see you there," said Ben.

The man smiled at him with such charm and warmth that Ben felt all strange and confused inside.

"I've seen you before somewhere, haven't I?" ventured Ben.

"I'm Michael. I meet so many people."

Clovenhoof sighed.

"Michael, this is Ben. Michael, you can be Ben's date for the evening. You can decide between you which one of you is the man."

"Now then, Jeremy, let's not be unkind," said Michael. "And, yes, I'll have one of whatever you're making."

"Is it the cocktails? Can you smell them from wherever it is you hang out?"

Michael picked up *Cocktails: a Man's Guide* by Richard Harris and flicked through it.

"Hmmm, very earthy. Hello, what's this?"

A printed page from the internet fluttered to the floor.

It was headed *Mind-Bending Cocktails for Students on a Budget*. Michael tutted gently.

"I'm not so sure that some of these things are suitable for consumption." He picked up a large container of what looked like pink hand-cleansing gel. "This came from a hospital didn't it?"

The doorbell rang. Michael put down the bottle, which was now quite clearly a pink lychee liqueur not hand-gel.

Nerys entered with Dave slightly behind, pulling unhappily at the tight collar of a new shirt.

"Jeremy!" declared Nerys as though she hadn't seen him in months and made mwah mwah noises at Clovenhoof's cheeks.

"Ben!"

She approached Ben with similar intention, but he flinched awkwardly, snagging his lips on her long, angular earring.

She turned to Michael.

"Well hello, I think I met you here once before?"

"I'm Michael."

He turned his perfect smile on. Clovenhoof stuck his fingers down his throat and made barfing noises, which he quickly turned into a cough when Michael looked round.

"Well, I'm Nerys. I'm sure you've heard about me." She gave him a conspiratorial wink. "Oh, and this is Dave, everyone."

"Hi," said Dave with a little wave.

"He is not my boyfriend or anything," said Nerys firmly.

"Nope," agreed Dave dutifully.

"We've met," said Clovenhoof. "Dave got me my first job."

Nerys froze for a moment, the smile on her face transforming into a feral snarl at the memory and then saw Ben's lip.

"Oh Ben, you're bleeding! Go and clean yourself up."

Blenda came in from the kitchen.

"Right, let's try those cocktails then, chuck. Jeremy's so excited to show you what he can do. Well I'm ready to be wowed with a Pink Leopard."

"You can't all have the same," complained Clovenhoof, "that's no fun. Let me check the book."

As Clovenhoof launched into his cocktail-shaking routine Ben went into the kitchen to get some tissue for his lip.

He stopped and stared at the counter. Lined up in the orderly manner of an operating theatre was a puzzling array of tools. Ben could just about imagine that the mallet, the saw and the goggles might be used in the preparation of food. As he looked at the grind wheel, the foot pump and the ladyshave, he gulped and backpedalled. He almost tripped over the belt-sander as he did so. There was an elaborate stand behind the door, supporting a muslin bag of red jelly-like substance that dripped slowly into a bowl placed beneath. He grabbed a piece of kitchen roll for his lip and walked quietly out, trying not to look at anything else.

"So, Ben, are you a Blues fan?" asked Dave.

"What?"

"Villa perhaps."

Ben's mind lurched into familiar unhappy territory: football. Dave was a man and men talked about football and Ben knew nothing about football.

"Er, no," he said.

"Not West Brom, surely?"

He wished he could say something knowledgeable and insightful about football, something that would make the conversation stop without revealing his ignorance. Perhaps there had been an important game earlier in the day. Was it even football season at the moment? He floundered and gave up.

"I'm sorry, I'm not into sport."

"Oh, right?" said Dave in a voice which was not condemning but politely interested in the curious notion that there were people who didn't like sport. Ben felt like a freak and felt the subsequent need to defend himself.

"I was put off it at school. I never liked PE."

"Shame. Exercise is a good thing."

Ben scoffed mentally. There wasn't much exercise in being stuffed in goal and used as a moving target by the taller, less clumsy boys.

"I think sports are elitist, a substitute for war," he said.

"Oh, I've always loved football," said Blenda.

Dave smiled at her, clearly relieved to be in the company of a normal human being.

"It's not even a sport though," said Ben. "The richest teams buy the best players. It's just a matter of who has the biggest bank balance."

"Oh," said Blenda in gentle disagreement. "There's nothing as good for the soul as a live match, I always say."

Dave beamed in approval at this.

"The roar of the crowd," he said.

"The team spirit," agreed Blenda.

The mindless conformity, thought Ben and sloped off towards the cocktail table. Clovenhoof gave him something called a Stinking Zombie. He downed it in one.

Clovenhoof raised his eyebrows.

"Can I get you another?"

"Whatever."

"Maybe you'd like something from my other, ah, reference work?"

Ben nodded and Clovenhoof eagerly scanned *Mind-Bending Cocktails for Students on a Budget*.

Ben couldn't keep up with the speed that Clovenhoof assembled the drink, but he sipped appreciatively.

"Interesting. Reminds me a bit of something else. Maybe that flavouring they put in cough mixture."

Clovenhoof grinned and pushed the bottle of linctus out of sight.

"Who else needs a top-up?"

Clovenhoof equipped Nerys with a Between the Sheets, which got him a nudge in the ribs. He made a Bosom Caresser for Blenda, which he delivered with a lewd wink. He made a Golden Daisy for Michael, which he handed over with an exaggerated moue of the lips.

"Jeremy, I'm surprised you haven't thrown away that filthy mess yet." Michael said, indicating the impressive bloom of mould that was thriving on Clovenhoof's mantelpiece.

"Herbert? Don't be ridiculous, I can't get rid of Herbert."

Michael touched the edge of the mould, which had mounted the rim of the cocktail glass and was reaching outward in plate-like layers. It seemed to be making a bid for freedom. Light-headed, Ben reckoned that given a month or two it would be out of the flat and making off down in the road in a stolen car.

"Honestly," said Michael, turning to Ben. "Such a childish thing to do."

"Hmmm?" said Ben.

"Herbert Dewsbury was the previous tenant of this flat, wasn't he?"

Ben blinked.

"You knew him?"

Michael nodded.

"I've worked with him. You knew him well?"

Ben blanched.

"Uh, he kept himself to himself. Didn't see all that much of him."

"Really? Come on. He wasn't exactly a quiet man. I think some people found his personality grating."

"I…"

"Maybe that's what got him killed in the end."

Ben whimpered in fright.

"Killed? No, I think he went away to…"

"No, no," said Michael with a terrifying finality. "Killed. Murdered."

Ben reached out behind him for a bottle, any bottle…

8:30PM

Nerys watched Michael over the rim of her glass as she sipped.

"Dave, I'm not sure who he is exactly, but I think Michael might be someone."

"Well obviously he's someone," said Dave with a knitted brow.

"I mean," said Nerys in the tone of a woman whose

previously paper-thin patience could now only be measured in microns, "that he's not just anyone, but *someone*. Someone of importance. You can tell."

"Oh, okay."

"So no more blathering on about football, for pity's sake."

"Right. What can I talk about then?"

Nerys counted on her fingers. "Travel, current events, weather, hobbies. But don't bring up hobbies if Ben's listening, obviously."

"Right, right." He looked at the empty glass in his hand. "Well I think I'd better mention to Jeremy about my food allergies."

"Oh, don't bother the man."

"I'll be back in a minute."

Dave went into the kitchen, brushing up against Blenda in the doorway.

"If you're looking for sanctuary, I'm not sure this is the place," said Blenda.

"No, no. It's not like that. I just need to talk to Jeremy."

He entered the kitchen and took in the sight of Clovenhoof wielding a cleaver on a bloodied carcase. He held the cleaver high above his head and brought it down onto the board with a cry of "Hi – YA!"

Clovenhoof brought the cleaver up for the next blow. A string of blood droplets splattered up the wall.

Dave clutched the doorframe to steady himself.

"What, ah" – he coughed -"what meat is that?"

Clovenhoof looked up, registering Dave's presence. He wiped the cleaver across his thigh, adding to a sinister, crusted stain.

"Hi, Dave. What's up?"

"It's just, I have some food allergies."

"What?"

"Um allergies."

"Like deadly ones?"

"Well, intolerances. I can't eat dairy or it gives me uncontrollable wind."

"Really? How interesting," smiled Clovenhoof. "Well, I'll be sure to point out anything that I think you shouldn't eat."

"Thanks."

Clovenhoof picked a scab of dried blood off his apron and popped it in his mouth.

9:00PM

Blenda ushered everyone to their places. Nerys wasn't overly impressed by the seating plan. There were certain rules of seating etiquette even with a dinner party of six. But she sat where she was told and commended herself on her tolerance and tact.

Blenda gently pried the absinthe from Ben's fingers. There was something seriously wrong with the man, as though the cocktails hadn't just gone to his head but also his brain, his spine and his limbs.

"We've got some wine now, chuck," said Blenda reassuringly.

"Wine?" said Ben. "Wine's good."

When everyone was seated, Clovenhoof came in.

"Ladies and gentlemen and Michael," he announced in

his loudest voice. "I present to you the first course. We will shortly be dining on gamberetti reclining in a warm love apple emulsion, surprised by insalata mista."

Clovenhoof took a deep bow. There were murmurs of interest. And, from the kitchen, Clovenhoof and Blenda produced their starters.

"Enjoy!" bellowed Clovenhoof, bowed once again for luck and took his own seat.

Nerys prodded her starter with a fork as Clovenhoof poured the wine.

"This looks just like prawn cocktail," she said.

"Indeed!" boomed Clovenhoof, whose voice, having slipped into circus ringmaster mode, seemed unable to change back. "But it's of such superlative quality. I have *sourced* those prawns!"

Nerys smiled and speared one with her fork.

"I boiled them myself as well," continued Clovenhoof plucking one from his glass with his fingers. "It's most fascinating. As you drop them alive into the boiling water, they turn from a translucent grey colour to a beautiful pinky colour. They also fold in half, as you see here. It's such a strong reflex that some of them pop straight out of the pan with the force of it. Not always dead by then either. And fear" – he fixed every person on the table with a roving eye – "is a powerful seasoning."

He jiggled the prawn next to his face.

"*No, please don't kill me, Mr Clovenhoof,*" he squeaked in a tiny high voice.

Clovenhoof looked at the prawn and addressed it sympathetically.

"I'm sorry, Mr Prawn, but I need to make a tasty starter for my friends."

"Please. Kill the others. They're fatter than me."

"Oh, I shall, Mr Prawn. But I need lots of you."

"No! Please, Mr Clovenhoof. Nooooooo."

The squeaky voice faded as Clovenhoof lowered the prawn down in the glass where it died a second death with an imaginary splash.

Nerys's fork had halted halfway to her mouth.

"Well, you get the idea," said Clovenhoof. "Tuck in."

Nerys selected a piece of lettuce and ate that instead. She looked across at Ben and noticed that he was unfazed by the grisly prawn murders. He did however seem to be having problems getting them onto his fork. Were his hands shaking? He tried a couple of times and then covered up one eye with his free hand. He swayed gently as his fork finally connected with something and pulled out a piece of beetroot.

"Ooh, beetroot," Ben said, as he gazed at the salad. "Gotta love beetroot, for making it through the digestive tract. It adds colour to your life today and tomorrow."

He gave a chuckle of silent laughter at his own joke.

"Ben, don't be so vulgar at the table," said Nerys. "Such talk of bodily functions, it's no wonder you don't have a girlfriend."

"I could have a girlfriend if I wanted," he replied. "S'personal choice thing."

"Really. Have you ever had a woman in your life?"

Ben stared at his starter and made another effort to snag a prawn.

"There was this one girl," he said. "Rose."

"Oh?" said Blenda encouragingly. "What was she like?"

"Beautiful. Brave. Smart."

Ben's fork chinked against something as he found another prawn. His wrist waggled drunkenly towards his mouth as his alcohol-clouded brain tried to plot a course.

"She travelled around with this guy. I think he had a thing for her but-"

Dave grabbed Ben's wrist.

"What's that on your fork?"

"Is that a razor blade?" said Michael.

Dave lifted the fork out of Ben's hand.

"How on earth does a razor blade get into a prawn cocktail?"

"Luck of the draw," Clovenhoof said. "I was using a razor blade to get all the hairs off the lettuce. My cooking's all about attention to detail. Anyway, I guess I was distracted."

Forks were set down around the table and there was a degree of surreptitious gazing into prawn cocktails.

"So what happened to this Rose then?" asked Dave.

Ben shrugged.

"Well, after the battle between the Daleks and the Cybermen, she got trapped on this parallel Earth and the Doctor got a new assistant."

There was a long silence in which Blenda began to tidy away the starters. Nerys waggled her glass for Dave to top her up.

"Ben, have you ever thought of swinging the other way?"

"Eh?"

"You're practically gay in other ways. I mean, all your friends are men."

"I'm not gay though," said Ben. "I'm straight."

"How do you know for sure unless you've tried it?"

"She's right," said Clovenhoof shovelling prawns from unattended glasses into his mouth.

"I don't think it works like that," said Dave but Nerys paid him no attention.

"Anyway," she said, "I think you could learn a lot from gay guys. Better grooming for instance."

"That's a stereotype," said Ben. "What about Greasy Bob in the chip shop? He's gay."

"No. He's just a pervert. Look, take Michael here for instance," Nerys continued. "His clothes. His hair. I would kill for nails like those. You guys don't seem to worry about that kind of detail. Terrible shame."

Clovenhoof snorted and opened another bottle of wine.

"So, Michael, what do you look for in a man?" Nerys asked.

Michael leaned forward and gave the question some thought.

"I've known many fine men over the years," he said, "and the ones I admire most of all are the ones who are brave-hearted but also humble and pious."

Nerys almost choked on her lettuce with laughter.

"And you still hang out with Jeremy? My God, he's got an ego the size of a planet!"

Michael nodded in agreement.

"A bit like his cookery book lists one hundred overblown ways to describe a prawn."

"He thinks humility is a measure of how much moisture there is in the air."

"A healthy ego is a good thing," said Clovenhoof diffidently.

Nerys waved him away and said to Michael, "This man causes chaos wherever he goes, like some vortex of confusion."

"I think that's unfair," said Ben.

"He stole thousands of pounds from *you*!"

Michael laughed.

"She's got you banged to rights, Jeremy."

"Well I think it's a good job that we're all different." said Blenda. "It would be a pretty boring world if we were all the same."

"That's the sort of self-denial you'd need to consort with the devil," said Michael.

"Consort with the devil, that's funny!" Nerys hooted.

Clovenhoof humphed.

"Tell me, Blenda," said Nerys, "what exactly do you see in him?"

Blenda answered unhurriedly.

"Life around Jeremy's never dull."

"That's one way of putting it."

"Sometimes he makes me laugh, sometimes he makes me scream, but he's never boring, never passive."

"But, honestly, can you see things working out with Jeremy in the long term?"

Blenda pulled a face.

"I've learned to take life as it comes. So what if it's not forever?"

"Here, here," said Dave, raising his glass.

"Shut up, Dave," said Nerys. "I know exactly what you need, Blenda."

"Really?"

"You need to put yourself out there more."

"Put myself..."

"You'd have your pick of men. Do what I do, keep a log of everyone you come into contact with, and give them a score on whether they'd be suitable boyfriend material. If they score highly enough, then you make an action plan."

"An action plan?"

"Yes, like, maybe you set up ways to bump into them, read up on subjects they're interested in, or brush up on sexual techniques."

Dave gulped some wine down the wrong way and choked until Ben slapped him on the back.

"You might need a spreadsheet to be properly organised," continued Nerys. "I tie mine into my electronic calendar too, so it prompts me for follow-ups."

"Oh Nerys," said Blenda who seemed unaccountably ill at ease. "I don't think I could ever be so calculating."

"It's not calculating. Well, it is, but in a *good* way."

"Are you sure that you're really doing the right thing?"

"I always do the right thing."

"I do wonder if maybe you're confused between love and lust."

Nerys bristled at the woman's naivety and rudeness.

"I'm sorry, *chuck*," she said quietly. "I didn't realise you were frigid."

Blenda's mouth dropped open.

Dave, glass in hand, cut across the table with a loud voice.

"Can I just say I think you're both very special ladies. I think we should celebrate our differences."

"Quite," said Blenda but Nerys could see the unjustified anger in her eyes.

"Now," said Dave, "why don't we try chatting about something different?" He nodded encouragingly to everyone. "Who here has got a hobby?"

9:45PM

"Main course coming up!" Clovenhoof boomed, entering from the kitchen.

Ben focused carefully on him through the gently lifting alcohol haze.

"For your enjoyment, I have prepared oven-dazzled medallions of beast flesh with an allium jus! Accompanied by patatas rosti, carote stufate and baby asparagus, garnished with nuggets of morcilla. With batter chapeaus on the side."

"Is that Italian for Findus Crispy Pancakes?" Nerys asked as Clovenhoof took his bow.

Clovenhoof and Blenda brought in the steaming plates.

Ben sniffed the air appreciatively and looked at the dish set down before him.

"Mate, you could have just said that it was meat and veg with Yorkshire pud and onion gravy." Ben had become quite animated and a little more sober during the discussion about hobbies.

"This looks great," said Dave.

"So Michael," said Ben, "you were just saying that you had actual experience commanding troops?"

"Yes," said Michael, "but I don't like to talk about my accomplishments."

Clovenhoof barked with laughter.

"I was the leader of a successful campaign," said Michael, with a mysterious smirk at Clovenhoof. "Mind you, some people would suggest that the enemy wasn't up to much."

"Brilliant," said Ben. "I've always wanted to meet a great military leader."

"But you'll have to settle for Michael," said Clovenhoof.

"How do you get respect from all those men?" said Ben.

"I like to think it's a mixture of personal charisma and making sure that they always know who's in charge. Being ruthless where necessary."

"Of course. But does that mean that you can't be one of the boys? You know, that they can't be your friends."

"Friends?"

"Yeah, all those men who've got to obey you without question."

Michael looked confused.

Clovenhoof, en route to the kitchen, was chuckling to himself.

"It's very much a full time job," Michael said, "socialising isn't really an option."

Ben nodded.

"Yeah, it's like I thought. A great military leader's got to be a lone wolf."

"Have you tried the asparagus with the – was it morcilla?" Dave asked. "I've no idea what morcilla is, but it's delicious."

Clovenhoof came in with another dish of Yorkshire puddings, which Dave and Ben fell upon with gusto.

"What's morcilla, Jeremy?" asked Dave, between mouthfuls.

"It's Spanish blood sausage. A bit like black pudding. A bit."

He went back out to the kitchen.

"Meat's good and rare, just how I like it," Nerys commented. "Little bones though. What is the meat, Jeremy?"

No answer came from the kitchen, but a loud sound started up, like a hammer drill.

10:15PM

It had been a mixed evening so far, Clovenhoof reflected in the kitchen. The main course had gone down a treat although he was disappointed that the starters had been left pretty much untouched, particularly after he had described all the individual sacrifices that had gone into making them.

As he laid out slices of dessert on the counter, Nerys spoke up from the other room.

"So Michael," she said, "there's something I'd love to know. How does it work out if you're gay in the military?"

"What?" said Michael.

Clovenhoof grinned to himself.

"Surely there must be issues with you all bunking together?"

"I'm not gay," said Michael.

"Oh, I'm sorry. I thought..."

"I mean, I've met a lot of homosexuals over the years."

Shortly before wiping their cities off the face of the Earth, thought Clovenhoof.

"I'm more what you might call celibate," said Michael.

"So am I," muttered Ben.

"Yes, but Michael's celibate by choice," said Nerys.

"And it's an interesting choice," said Blenda, "I think that more people should acknowledge that it's an acceptable idea. There's such pressure from society in general that you need a partner to be happy. In fact, I'm reading *Eat, Pray, Love* at the moment, and the author finds it really helpful on her journey to enlightenment to remove sex completely from the equation for a year of her life."

"New Age claptrap," said Michael dismissively.

"Excuse me," said Blenda loudly. "You can't just scoff at someone's path through life."

Clovenhoof shifted over to the doorway to pressurise the flamethrower tank and to peek at the goings-on in the dining room.

"People find happiness and spiritual meaning in so many different ways," said Blenda. "I say that if something offers you comfort and development, then you should work with it. I'm very keen on yoga, and I have some friends who practise distance healing. It really can work you know."

"Distance healing?" Michael snorted. "I can remember a time when you'd have been burned as a witch for spouting such rubbish!"

"I think you're being rather unfair," said Dave, "witch-burning belongs to a barbaric time. We've learned much more tolerance since then. It just so happens that I go to a yoga class, and I enjoy it on quite a few different levels."

"That's really interesting," said Blenda. "I bet it helps with the stress you get at work."

"Dave," said Nerys, "don't get drawn into defending silly things like this – Hang on, what stress?"

"Oh Nerys," said Blenda, "it's obvious these soothing, new age therapies are not for you. It's okay. We're all different."

"Bears," said Ben suddenly.

Everyone looked at him.

"Their world is divided into three things," he said. "Things to fight, things to fuck and food to eat." He pointed at Nerys with his half-full glass. "That's you. Maybe not the food bit."

"How dare you, Ben Kitchen!"

"I dunno," he shrugged and emptied his glass.

"Let's just be totally clear on one thing," said Michael, leaning forward and speaking with quiet authority. "There is only one truth, and that's God's truth. Anything else is just delusion."

There was a stunned and uncomfortable silence around the table at Michael's announcement.

"I have respect for all beliefs," said Blenda, "but to claim ownership of the one and only truth is..."

"Bigoted," said Dave helpfully.

"Thank you," Blenda said, giving Michael the look of someone facing a belligerent child who wants the bath filled with marshmallows. "There are many fine and intelligent people who don't believe in God."

"He believes in you," whispered Clovenhoof to himself.

"Truth is truth," said Michael. "Things are not true because they are nice or comforting or convenient. Your opinion on God's existence is immaterial."

"Religion is all fairy tales and mumbo jumbo," said Nerys.

Michael gave her a dangerous look.

"I'd like to remind you that you'll be judged on your actions in the afterlife. You might want to watch what you're saying."

His overly earnest warning had completely the opposite of the intended effect. Nerys gave out a hoot of laughter and the others fell in. Ben covered his mouth but made raspberry chuckles through his fingers.

"Right," laughed Nerys. "You're saying I'll go straight to Hell if I call you a bigot?"

"A fundamentalist bigot," added Dave.

Blenda squeezed his knee in merry agreement and tried and failed to stifle her laughs with a napkin.

Clovenhoof shook his head at the humans, four hairless apes mocking one of the most powerful beings in creation. Idiots. Idiots. Idiots. And the look on Michael's face. Clovenhoof had seen it before, just as the raindrops started pitter-pattering on Noah's ark.

Clovenhoof turned away and prepared to caramelise his Arctic Roll Alaskas. The recipe had said that a blowtorch would work better than the oven. Clovenhoof had reasoned that if a blowtorch was better, then a flamethrower would be superlative. He'd found the perfect thing on the back of a council truck that was resurfacing the road. The tank was primed, the pilot light was lit. He raised the nozzle and gave the row of desserts a healthy ten-second blast of flame.

"I'm sorry, Michael," he heard Blenda say, "but we can't help but find those kinds of ideas a little... quaint."

"Quaint?" said Michael

"Hellfire and brimstone," said Blenda.

Clovenhoof looked at his caramelised desserts. The plates and much of the kitchen counter and wall were now either brown or black. Each of the desserts had been reduced to a bubbling black tar-like blob. The air smelled of petroleum and vanilla.

"Balls," said Clovenhoof angrily.

"Yeah but imagine if there really was a hell," said Dave in the dining room, "I bet it would kick the coolest video game right into touch. Lakes of boiling oil and wailing orcs and everything."

"Orcs aren't from hell, you idiot!" Clovenhoof yelled through the wall.

He wondered desperately if he could hide the burnt puddings under layers of crème fraiche or custard. He poked one. It hissed and sank even further onto the plate.

"Orcs are bad guys, just the same," Ben was saying, "so they probably belong in hell. I guess we can have whatever we want there, it's all made-up anyway. You could have orcs, and cybermen and the Borg."

"And traffic wardens," said Nerys.

"And queue-jumpers," said Blenda.

"And football hooligans," said Dave.

"While we're making it up, how about putting Jeremy in charge?" giggled Nerys.

"Good one," said Ben.

"He'd be perfect if Satan wanted to take a holiday at any time."

Clovenhoof roared with anger and charged into the room, flamethrower aloft.

He was angry that Blenda and Dave had been pally all evening. Look, her hand was still on his knee. He was angry that Michael kept making small sarcastic comments and insulting his human friends. But most of all he was angry that his Arctic Roll Alaska, the crowning glory of his dinner party had been instantly cremated by the flamethrower.

"You have no idea, do you? Absolutely no fucking idea!"

They all fell silent, eyes on the flame that swung in time with Clovenhoof's agitation.

"Running an efficient Hell is the hardest thing you can imagine. Harder than getting Ben laid, even harder than getting Nerys to keep her knickers on. You can sit around mocking, but I've seen tough times like you'd never believe. Cleaning out the litter trays for Cerberus. Three mouths, one arse, it's not pretty! Up all night with the admissions during the World Wars. I even had to write a preparedness plan in case there was a bird flu pandemic."

"Put the flamethrower down, will you, chuck?" Blenda said.

Clovenhoof adjusted a switch and the yellow flame vanished, leaving only the tiny blue pilot light. Everyone breathed again.

"What are you trying to tell us?" said Nerys.

Clovenhoof groaned loudly between clenched teeth.

"I am Satan, you idiots! I am the devil. I am Lucifer. I am

the Adversary, the fallen one. Old Nick, Old Scratch, the Angel of the Bottomless Pit, Most Unclean, Son of Perdition. Can't you see my horns? My hooves?"

There was a long silence.

"Er," said Dave.

"He's not a well man," said Michael, to the others. "There's history of... you know." He tapped his skull.

"Those cocktails were very strong," said Ben.

"That's right," agreed Nerys hurriedly.

"And he's been over-worked recently," added Blenda.

"No!" Clovenhoof squealed. "I am Satan. I am God-damning bloody sodding Satan, you stupid twats!"

More silence followed, then there was a thumping sound from above.

"Ah," said Nerys, clearly glad for the excuse. "Aunt Molly wants me to put Twinkle's dinner out before it gets dark, to see if it'll bring him back."

Nerys stood up, took an automatic step towards the door and then slowly turned.

"Oh no," she said softly.

"What?" snapped Clovenhoof.

"Oh no, no, no. Jeremy. That roast dinner. The bones. You always hated that dog. Did you, did you...cook Twinkle?"

Clovenhoof rolled his eyes.

"No, I put him in next door's coal bunker because he kept sniffing round my prawns."

"Oh. What was the meat then?"

"Rabbit. From the market." he added. It was actually from the hutch two doors down but that was just a trifling detail.

There were exhalations of relief from everyone.

"And the morcilla?" asked Dave.

"Oh, that was Mr Dienermann," Clovenhoof said.

"Who?"

"He was in for an embalming. It seemed wrong to waste all the blood we pumped out so I brought it home in a bucket. Yummy, wasn't it?"

Blenda paled in an instant and vomited into Dave's lap.

The next moments were a scramble. Everyone wanted to get to the bathroom or the front door. They argued afterwards about who had knocked over the gently hissing flamethrower, but what is beyond doubt is that it quickly ignited the elegant draped tablecloth and then the curtains.

NERYS FORMED an impromptu action plan for the firemen who were called to the scene and gave a '*Nerys: Your Kind Of Woman*' flyer to each and every one of them.

Dave had rushed home, because he'd discovered that Clovenhoof's Yorkshire puddings contained milk, and he'd eaten at least six of them.

Ben had managed to snag the bottle of absinthe on the way out and sat in the garden taking hearty swigs and hoping that the flames and the fire fighters didn't reach his own flat.

Blenda released Twinkle from the coalbunker and reunited him with Molly who was wrapped in a blanket, sipping tea.

NOBODY KNEW where Clovenhoof had gone, but Michael stayed around long enough to assure the emergency services that he was not in danger. Betty and Doris stood beside Michael making clucking sounds as they watched the drama unfold.

"Well that depends how you define danger," said Doris. "He's going to have a bit of explaining to do after this."

"To his friends you mean?" asked Betty.

"Friends! You can call them that. For the time being," said Doris with a hollow laugh. "They might have other ideas after his latest antics."

"We don't know exactly what happened yet," said Betty. "All that we can be sure of is that he's had some kind of breakdown."

Doris stooped to pick up a charred piece of paper from the ground. *Mind-Bending Cocktails for Students on a Budget.*

"Lighter fluid cocktails?" she suggested.

"No," said Michael. "Someone kicked over the flamethrower."

"Flamethrower?" said Doris. "What was he doing with that?"

"Cooking," said Michael. "Obviously. There was a panic."

Doris scribbled in her notepad.

"So what was the thing that made people panic?" asked Betty.

"He'd used human remains in his haute cuisine," said Michael, lifting his eyes to Heaven.

"Oh dear. Oh deary me!" said Doris, scribbling gleefully.

"But he was making an effort, you say? Lovingly preparing a meal for his friends?" said Betty.

Michael thought for a minute.

"No," he said. "He was really just showing off I think."

Betty made a few notes of her own.

"It sounds as though he'd put a lot of effort into socialising though," she said. "Human remains or not."

"What kind of body parts did he cook?" asked Doris, eyes wide in anticipation.

"Sir!" said a fire fighter to Michael. "You might want to be careful about talking to reporters. It can start a lot of irresponsible speculation."

"Oh, I hardly think that these two are reporters. They're completely harmless," said Michael.

Another fire fighter ran up breathlessly.

"There's a woman across the road who swears she saw the silhouette of a man running through the flames."

"Really?" said Michael.

"She said it looked as though he was dancing."

"Dancing?" Michael gave him a supercilious look.

"Yeah, I know. Think she might be bats. Well, as long as everyone's accounted for, we just need to put that out."

He indicated the flames coming from the window of flat 2A. He turned back, but Michael was gone. Betty and Doris smiled at the fire fighters and continued to jot notes at a feverish pace.

HEAVEN

- Matters Arising
- Keep Heaven Holy
- The Throne
- Clovenhoof
- Festival
- AOB

Herbert, St Peter's flabby assistant, ensured that his *Keep Heaven Holy* presentation was understood by all.

He had produced a slide-by-slide computer presentation, had given annotated copies of the slides to all present and then read through each slide word for word, just in case anyone happened to have been struck blind. Mother Teresa dithered over whether to take minutes given that she had

Herbert's presentation notes in front of her and eventually plumped for copying them out onto parchment in her flowing golden script.

"In summary," said Herbert, clicking onto a slide that began with the words '*In summary*', "*Keep Heaven Holy* is designed to ensure that the moral rectitude demanded of the faithful on Earth is similarly demanded of all Heaven's inhabitants, present and future. Although 'Love God with all your heart and love your neighbour as you love yourself' remains the spirit of the law, the letter of the law must also be enforced."

"Enforced?" said Joan sceptically.

"We want the same Heaven you do," said Herbert. "You spoke of over-crowding and chaos. We want to sweep that away. Picture if you will... light open airy spaces, parks and flowers, amenities for all, venues for all manner of socially acceptable activities."

St Michael looked at the *Keep Heaven Holy* leaflet he had been given. The image on the front leaf depicted a long street of shops and houses beneath an azure sky, huge tubs planted with blousy flowers in pinks and purples, carefully spaced trees heavy with neatly pruned greenery. Michael realised that it was an idealised version of a street he had come to know very well over the last few months. Yes, here was the bank Clovenhoof had robbed, here Ben's bookshop (in the picture converted into a library), here a certain beauty therapist's now become a respectably austere barbershop.

"And what about animals?" said St Francis.

"Of course," said Herbert. "There will be a place for every lion to lie down with a lamb, a place for every donkey."

"It sounds wemarkable."

"Reminds me," said Gabriel. "The Wolf of Gubbio has been trying to eat people again."

"Impossible," said St Francis. "Bwother Wolf made an oath to me that he would never dine on human flesh."

"And when did he make that oath?" asked Pope Pius XII.

"1214," said St Francis. "Owiginally."

"What do you mean, originally?"

"It's a difficult oath for a giant, savage, man-eating wolf to keep. But he wenewed his oath here in Heaven in 1571."

"I see."

"And again in 1749."

"Yes."

St Francis raised his eyes in recollection.

"Again in 1838. Then 1884, 1905, 1916, 1922 and 1925."

"And since then?" asked Pius.

"We're on a sort of wolling pwobationawy contwact."

"Well, he's been trying to take bites out of people in that shanty town outside the ninth gate," said Gabriel.

"I will have words," said St Francis.

"What shanty town?" said Joan.

"They've grown up in the past months around the Celestial City," said Gabriel. "A sea of white tents."

"I thought I'd noticed fewer people coming in," said Joan. "Can't manage the traffic, Peter? There are twelve gates to Heaven and you only ever have the one open."

"There is no traffic issue," said St Peter. "I'm insulted by the notion."

"So?" Joan spread her hands. "What's going on?"

"I think we need to stick to the items on the agenda," said Michael.

"I can assure you," said Herbert from his position by the presentation screen, "those shanty towns will be dealt with once *Keep Heaven Holy* comes into effect."

"What do you mean, dealt with?"

"Perhaps now would be a good time to talk about your proposed festival, Joan," suggested Michael loudly.

"You're trying to change the subject," she said.

"You don't want to talk about the festival?"

Joan sighed angrily.

"I want these shanty towns on next meeting's agenda."

"Done," said Michael, nodding to Mother Teresa.

Evelyn passed Joan a large rolled up sheet of paper secured by an elastic band. Joan unrolled it on the table top and pinned down the corners with chalices.

"Here's the venue layout. We have three main stages here, here and here. We've got Johnny Cash, Lillie Langtry and Karen Carpenter headlining. George Handel and Glen Miller are putting together some fusion thing for the chill-out tent."

"Johnny Cash," said Pius. "Isn't he in Hell?"

"We got him on secondment."

"You've got the damned performing at our festival?"

"No, The Damned are still alive and touring down on Earth," said Joan, grinning.

No one else smiled.

"Whoosh," said Evelyn, passing a hand over her head.

"It was a joke," said Joan feebly. "Anyway, here we have the craft tents, the food courts, children's activities, beer tent-"

"Beer?" said St Peter.

"Not just beer. Wine, cider, stout, mead."

"I'm not sure if this is appropriate," said Michael.

"Drinking makes you loud and foolish," quoted St Paul.

"I should hope so," said Joan. "I picked this up from Michael's Recording Angels, Betty and Doris." She placed a damp and singed copy of *Cocktails: a Man's Guide* on the table. "I hear you enjoyed a Golden Daisy or two."

"I've been known to indulge, responsibly," said Michael.

"This looks huge," said St Francis looking at the festival plans.

Joan tilted her head.

"Well, we do have ten thousand years of musical history to showcase and a festival crowd of maybe ten billion."

"You're inviting everyone to this thing?" said Pius.

"Sure," shrugged Joan. "This is Heaven. Everyone's invited to the party."

"I think we can sort out something more practical," said St Peter. "A ticket system perhaps."

Joan shook her head.

"There's no privilege in Heaven. No elitism."

"Neither Jew nor Greek, slave nor free, man nor woman, for you are all one in Christ Jesus," quoted St Paul.

"Thank you," said Joan.

"I can't see where you're going to hold this thing," said St Peter.

"There are several pieces of parkland that are big enough."

"Not my pwotected animal sanctuawy?" said St Francis fearfully.

"Just think of the mess," said Herbert. "The litter. The noise."

"The music," said Joan.

"The shared experience," said Evelyn.

"The creative buzz."

"The meeting of different cultures and different peoples."

"What's this 'clouds and harps' zone?" said Pius, pointing hopefully to a spot on the plans.

"Exactly what it says, Eugene," said Joan.

He smiled and nodded approvingly.

"I still cannot see a place in Heaven that could be given over to this venture," said St Peter.

"Fine," said Joan. "Then we'll hold it outside."

"What?"

"There's a shanty town outside the ninth gate, I hear. We'll hold the festival out there."

"In Limbo?" said Michael.

"Tents and festivals go hand in hand," said Joan.

St Peter frowned, horribly confused.

"But this is a festival for Heaven's residents. And now you want to hold it *outside* Heaven? How will people attend?"

Joan gazed at St Peter levelly, the teenager in shining plate armour and the man who held the keys.

"Open the gates, Pete," she said. "Just open the gates."

9

IN WHICH CLOVENHOOF HAS HIS FORTUNE READ, GOES INTO THERAPY AND MEETS THE PREVIOUS TENANT

Clovenhoof stepped into *Boldmere Beauty* as Blenda prepared to shut up shop for the day. She looked round, pausing with a bottle of nail varnish in her hand.

"Oh, look. It's the Great Satan," she said and went back to her stacking.

"I've got news," said Clovenhoof. "I thought I'd pop in and... Well, not seen you in a while."

"Yes," she said. "That will happen if you've been dumped."

"Dumped?"

"Yes, Jeremy. It is still Jeremy, isn't it? It's not Beelzebub or Mephistopheles or something?"

"No, Jeremy's fine," he said, confused and eager to please. "Dumped?"

Blenda came down from her footstool and put her hands on her hips.

"I believe the exact words were, 'You fucking bastard. I don't want to see your face ever again.'"

Clovenhoof felt a lump of disappointment in his stomach.

"I thought you were just... you know."

"Over-reacting?"

"Joking."

Blenda shook her head.

"No, Jeremy. I wasn't joking. What's your news?"

"No, it's okay. It doesn't matter."

"Tell me."

He gave an awkward grin.

"I thought we should get matching tattoos. You know, his and hers. 'True Love... Forever.'"

"Really?" she said flatly.

"I made the appointment and everything."

She came over. He thought for a moment it might be to hug him, to tell him that this was another one of her brilliant jokes but it was only to step past him and flip the 'open' sign on the door to 'closed'.

"I need to change," she said and went into the back room. Clovenhoof passed the time reading the ingredient lists on shampoos, hair relaxers and exfoliants. Some of the chemical names were quite beautiful, reminding him of the names of his underlings in the Old Place.

"Those are truly awful shorts," said Blenda, reappearing, her white work tunic replaced by a scoop neck top.

Clovenhoof looked down at his yellow and blue Bermuda shorts.

"I thought they matched the shirt," he said, pulling at the hem of his purple and green Hawaiian shirt.

"They distract the eye from the horror of the shirt," said Blenda. "Like a clown at a train crash."

"And that's a good thing?"

"I made an error of judgement with you," she said. "There's a fine line between kooky and..."

"Irritating?"

"Total psycho nut-job. You served up a dead person at a dinner party."

"Only his blood."

"What do you think would happen if I told Gordon Buford?"

"He might commend me for taking my work home with me?"

"He would fire you. He would call the police. I could call the police. Without sounding horribly like an American, I could sue you. Out."

Clovenhoof obediently stepped out onto the pavement. Blenda followed and locked up. The summer sun was a fat orange ball settling over the rooftops.

"I told you that if you cocked up that job I got you, I would snap you like a twig."

"I remember," said Clovenhoof.

"Go get professional help," she said. "Get your head examined. You are not Satan. You are a man. Sometimes wonderful. Sometimes strange. Sometimes a total psycho nut-job. Sort yourself out or I *will* snap you like a twig. Got it?"

"Got it," he nodded.

"You live that way," she said, pointing down the street and walked off in the opposite direction.

BEN LEAPED into action at the sound of Clovenhoof's footsteps on the stairs. All the windows in the flat were wide open and he had four electric fans positioned around the kitchen and living area on full blast. He ran round, closing windows and turning the fans down to medium. He didn't want to arouse suspicion. Nonetheless, he left the twelve electric air fresheners plugged in and turned up to maximum, not that they were making much impact on the smell that permeated the sun-baked flat. The stink seemed to take the most violent notes of an open sewer, of spoiled food, of animal musk and released them as a Greatest Hits compilation.

Nothing would get rid of it and, much to his mounting horror and paranoia, his temporary flatmate didn't seem to notice it at all.

"Hi honey, I'm home!" called Clovenhoof.

Ben, having shut the last window in the bathroom, came out into the living room.

He wafted a hand in front of his nose.

"Sorry about the smell," he said with the kind of blokiness he had never actually felt and shut the bathroom door behind him. "I'd give it a few minutes if I were you, eh?"

Clovenhoof looked at him and shrugged.

"Do you think my shirt and shorts combo looks like a clown at a train crash?"

It was Ben's turn to shrug.

"Which one's the clown, which one's the train crash?"

"Not sure. Not gone to work again today?"

"How can I?" said Ben giving a cheery but false grin. "Got my favourite lodger to look after, haven't I? Thought I'd cook us up a nice spicy curry tonight. Extra strong."

"I prefer crispy pancakes," said Clovenhoof.

Ben made a noise in his throat.

"Any news on your flat?"

"I know they've stripped out the kitchen but there's some rebuilding work and painting still to do. I'll ask them tomorrow. They'd gone home by the time I got back."

"Do you think Nerys has scared them away?"

"I heard that," she said, walking in.

"Haven't you heard of knocking?"

"Haven't you heard of locking your own door?"

Ben looked at Clovenhoof.

"It's not my door," said Clovenhoof.

"We were just discussing dinner plans," said Ben. "Perhaps we should all go out."

"I've come to tell you that your flat stinks," said Nerys. "It's putting Aunt Molly off her toad in the hole."

"It's Ben. He's done a smelly shit," said Clovenhoof. "Secretly, I think he's quite proud."

"I'm not talking to you. I still haven't forgiven you for turning me into a cannibal."

"You're not a cannibal."

"I ate human flesh."

"Blood."

"Semantics."

"You're only a bit cannibal."

"You can't be *a bit* cannibal. You have defiled me. My body is a temple, you know."

"What? People have to take their shoes off before they're allowed inside?"

"I think," said Ben, cutting across them very loudly, "there might be a problem with the drains."

"Then get them looked at, Ben. Ask those builders downstairs to help."

Ben shivered at the thought of tradesmen coming into his home and poking around.

"I'll get it sorted."

"See that you do," she snapped. "It smells like you're living in an abattoir."

"I quite like it," said Clovenhoof.

THE ONE-EYED WOMAN in the *Skin Deep* tattoo parlour just off Birmingham Road sat at her small counter and played cards by herself under the bright glow of a circular magnifying lamp. She nodded at Clovenhoof as he entered. Tattoo templates hung on framed sheets on the walls. Clovenhoof had noticed with some pleasure that his likeness featured on more than a couple of them, although most of them were rather unflattering.

The woman leaned to one side and peered at a battered appointments book.

"Mr Clovenhoof," she said.

"Yes," he said.

"You're late."

"We had an eleven o'clock booking."

"But I expected you sooner. She's not coming, is she?"

"No."

"And you've come to cancel."

"Yes."

"Because who wants 'True Love Forever' on their arm when their true love has left them?"

"Who says I wanted it on my arm?"

She fixed him with her one good eye and took in his mischievous expression.

"I don't do short hand, Mr Clovenhoof," she said and he grinned.

She returned to her cards.

"Well," he said, "I can see you're rushed off your feet..."

He turned to go and a poster by the door caught his eye.

Tarot Readings
Questions Answered.
Problems Resolved.

Readings by Mistress Verthandi
(Tuesdays and Thursdays)

HE LAUGHED.

"What?" said the woman without looking up.

"She told me to seek help, get myself sorted out."

"There are worse kinds of help."

"Wednesday today."

"If only I weren't rushed off my feet."

She gathered the cards together in front of her and kicked a seat back for him to sit down.

"You're Mistress Verthandi?"

"On Tuesdays and Thursdays. Names are impermanent things. Ten quid for the basic reading. More if you have specific questions."

He sat down.

"Ever had a tarot reading before?" she asked.

"Nope."

She began to deal the cards out, face down, in an unobvious pattern on the counter between them.

"You ever see that James Bond film with the voodoo stuff?"

"I like James Bond movies."

"Good for you. Me and Jane Seymour use the same deck. This is the Celtic Cross spread. Standard stuff. I turn over the cards and they help us find answers to your personal questions."

"And does it work?"

"What do you mean?"

"I mean, do you believe in this stuff?"

She tapped her black eyepatch.

"Do you want me to tell you I traded this eye for the gift of second sight?"

"Did you?"

"Fact is, Mr Clovenhoof, it doesn't actually matter what *I* believe. You can say it's magic. You can say it's subconscious influences or the synchronicity of Jungian archetypes. You can say it's the work of the devil if you wish."

"Doubt that."

"It works. It helps people. Let's see." She turned over the first card. "Two of cups. Reversed. That indicates an instability in your relationships. We knew that anyway." She turned over another. "Here. The Knight of Swords. Again reversed. This represents the thing that opposes you. A skilful warrior. Guardian of the gateway. Interesting." She flipped over another card. "This one's interesting. The Ace of Coins. Two-faced. Man and woman in one. The duplicitous twins. Two people – two women or maybe not - in your life who are not what they seem."

"Who?"

"I couldn't say. Ah, but here. Look. The Fool."

Clovenhoof gazed at the picture, a young man with a pack over one shoulder and a rose in his hand.

"The fool is me?" he suggested.

"The fool is one who departs in search of answers. The sun behind him is divine wisdom, the thing that he seeks."

"He's going to walk off a cliff," Clovenhoof pointed out.

"He plays a dangerous game. This is a journey of the heart, not the mind. But he holds the rose, a precious thing of heavenly beauty in his hand. Maybe he doesn't appreciate what he already possesses."

"Interesting, What else?"

She turned over another card.

"Oh."

"Oh?"

She turned over further cards, a sixth, seventh and eighth. She gazed at them for a long time.

"What do they say?" asked Clovenhoof.

"Hmmm." She looked at the cards some more and turned over others.

"Problem?" said Clovenhoof.

"Depends."

There was a strange expression on her face. Looking at her, he saw a woman who was probably younger than Blenda but to whom time and fate had been less kind. Her face was heavily lined, her long grey hair pulled back into a severe ponytail. If she'd met her, Blenda might also have said something about the lack of a proper health and beauty regime or words to that effect.

"Depends on what?" said Clovenhoof.

"What kind of reading you were after. Whether you wanted some reassuring 'if you love her set her free' platitudes or some brutal honesty."

"Oh, I'm all for brutal honesty."

"You are surrounded by death, Mr Clovenhoof."

"Uh-huh," he nodded.

"I was perhaps expecting a stronger reaction from you."

"I work as an assistant mortician."

"I can see that, or something very much like it, here." She stabbed at a card. "But here" – and her hand waved across the entire spread – "death again."

"I held a rather unsuccessful dinner party the other week."

She looked at him and blinked (or was it winked?).

"And you're going to get a big surprise soon."

"How soon?"

"Very soon."

"What kind of surprise?"

She gave him a lopsided smile.

"Death, of course."

CLOVENHOOF LEFT *Skin Deep* with a spring in his step. The sun was out, Britain's brief summer now running into four consecutive days, he had killed two birds with one stone, cancelling the tattoo appointment and finding professional help in a single action and, furthermore, he had a big surprise and a death to look forward to, two things he was generally in favour of.

He trotted down Jockey Road onto the Chester Road and into the flats. The builders were making busy noises in flat 2a but he decided not to disturb them. He was sure they'd let him know when their work was done. He put his key in the lock to 2b but the door would only open a few inches.

"Hang on!" squealed a panicked voice from within.

"Ben?"

"Just a minute!"

"You've put the security chain on."

"Yes, just hang on!"

There was a plastic rustling sound and the hiss of aerosol.

"Why? Are you doing something sordid in there?"

"What?"

"Are you wearing women's clothing?"

"Yes! Yes! Go away. Come back later."

"Not a chance," grinned Clovenhoof, stepped back and barged the door. The security chain popped from its housing and he stumbled in.

Ben knelt in the short hallway between the door and the kitchen with the blue and brass trunk open next to him. Inside the base of the trunk, nestling in the folds of a large transparent plastic sheet was a dead body. It was definitely dead and clearly had been for a very long time. The flesh that remained on the corpse was brown, oozing and almost completely rotted away. The putrid juices had soaked through the body's clothing and much of it lay pooled in the base of the trunk.

Ben stared at Clovenhoof.

Clovenhoof stared at the body.

Well, it was a big surprise. And it was death. How brilliant.

"Surprise!" he shouted, wishing he had some party poppers or streamers to mark the occasion.

Ben burst into tears.

CLOVENHOOF SHUT THE DOOR, made tea for both of them, and tried to ignore Ben until he stopped crying. However, he unavoidably picked up some details that Ben wailed out between sobs.

Clovenhoof thrust a hot mug into Ben's hands and looked down at the stinking remains.

"So this is Mr Dewsbury?"

"Yes," sniffed Ben.

"The previous occupant of my flat?"

"Yes."

"And he's been in this chest for the past..."

"Year. Nearly two."

"And you've not shown him to me before?"

Clovenhoof was incredulous. A gruesome treat like this, hidden away. It was like keeping all the chocolate biscuits at the back of the cupboard and only offering visitors custard creams.

"He had awful taste in ornaments," said Clovenhoof.

Ben sipped the tea, winced at its heat and sobbed again.

"He was a horrible, annoying man. I used to dread bumping into him."

"Why?"

"He always had something to complain about. Totally OCD. Everything had to be just right, just so. You could never do anything right in his eyes."

"He's not your dad though, is he?"

Ben sniffed.

"Is he?" said Clovenhoof.

"No. But... he ran this poxy little campaign. *Keep Boldmere Beautiful.* He'd print up these leaflets and spend every weekend stuffing them through letterboxes. He'd badger the council to plant flowers or put in new litter bins. He protested against the building of Housing Association flats on Gate Lane. He'd patrol up and down the high street, checking tax discs, shouting at teenagers and accusing them of lowering the tone of the area. It was all just an excuse to be nosy, to get involved with other people's business."

"Sounds like an arse."

Ben gave a bitter mirthless laugh.

"You have no idea. He didn't like my shop."

"Why not?"

"It was a *second hand* bookshop for one thing. And he didn't like the name *Books 'n' Bobs*. He didn't like the use of '*n*' in signage. God, you ought to have seen what he was like with greengrocers who misused apostrophes. He was a punctuation fascist."

"I can see why you killed him."

"I didn't mean to! It just looks..."

Ben shook his head and wiped away fresh tears.

"He came up to see me one evening. I let him in. I didn't want to argue on the landing. I was polishing my Seleucid armour. I had my sword out."

"That's not a euphemism, is it?"

"Jeremy! This isn't easy."

"Sorry."

Ben sighed.

"We talked. We argued. No, he argued. I tried to ignore him. I turned." Ben looked at his curled fingers, seeing an imaginary sword in his grip. "I turned quickly. Maybe my hands were sweaty. Maybe there was polish on the handle."

He looked up at Clovenhoof.

"I didn't mean to kill him."

Clovenhoof looked at the body. There was a gore-soaked rip in Mr Dewsbury's jumper, just below the neck.

"Where's the sword now?" said Clovenhoof, looking over at the shield and helmet on the living room wall.

"I got rid of it. I had to. I just gave it away."

Clovenhoof nodded.

"What are you going to do?" said Ben.

"Do?"

Clovenhoof bent down and poked Mr Dewsbury's cheek with his fingertip. His finger went straight through the flesh, knuckle-deep into his mouth. He stood up and inspected the glistening liquid coating his finger.

"Are you going to call the police?" said Ben.

"Do you want me to?"

Ben seemed to give this some serious thought but eventually said, "I just want it all to go away."

"You want to get rid of it?"

"God, yes."

"Shame," said Clovenhoof wistfully. "Okay."

Ben sniffed noisily and wiped his nose.

"Okay?"

Clovenhoof nodded.

"Okay. I'll help you get rid of it."

"Why would you do that?"

Clovenhoof shrugged.

"Dunno. You're my friend, I guess."

Ben gave him a long appraising look.

"You're not the devil. You do know that."

Clovenhoof opened his mouth to answer but there was a sharp rap at the door. Clovenhoof and Ben looked at each other.

Clovenhoof nodded at the trunk. Ben swung the lid up and over to close it. The lid came down on Mr Dewsbury's wrist, neatly severing his hand, which dropped onto the carpet. Clovenhoof picked it up, spun round on the spot, opened the bread bin and stuffed the hand inside.

Ben grabbed one of the cans of air freshener he'd been using and began to spray the room.

The knock at the door came again, louder and more insistent.

"Hang on!" called Ben.

"There in a minute!" cried Clovenhoof, adding, "We're not wearing women's clothing!"

Ben pushed the trunk against the wall and threw the aerosol in the bin.

Clovenhoof wiped the liquid remains of Mr Dewsbury on his Hawaiian shirt and went to open the door.

Blenda stood there, a business card in her hand.

"I don't care if you are wearing women's – My God! What's that stench?"

Clovenhoof jerked a thumb over his shoulder.

"Ben's got a dicky tummy."

Ben, in the kitchen, pointed to his stomach and pulled a sad face. The sad face didn't require much effort.

Clovenhoof pointed to his brown-smeared shirt.

"And he's backed up the toilet. I've had to get" – he made complicated hand gestures – "physical. You know?"

Blenda grimaced and stepped back.

"I just came by to give you this." She handed him the card, making sure their fingers didn't touch. "Denise is a person-centred therapist. Your first appointment is on Friday."

"Actually," said Clovenhoof smugly, "I've already sought my own professional help."

"What from Shelly Greenaway and her tarot cards?"

"Mistress Verthandi, you mean. Hang on, how did you know?"

"Shelly Greenaway, a woman without a proper skincare routine."

"I thought you'd say that."

"A woman so lacking in common sense that she waited until her ex battered seven bells out of her and blinded her in one eye before deciding he might not be her ideal man."

"I thought she was very helpful."

Blenda flicked the card in Clovenhoof's hand.

"Get proper help. Friday. If I hear you haven't made your appointment, I'm calling the authorities."

"Authorities?" warbled Ben from the kitchen.

Blenda gave Clovenhoof a firm poke in the chest to make her point and then regarded the smear on her fingertip. She shuddered and went downstairs.

Clovenhoof closed the door and turned to Ben.

"She's going to call the authorities," said Ben.

"Don't worry," said Clovenhoof, wandering over to the window, card in hand. "It'll be fine."

He looked down at the street to see Blenda climbing into the passenger seat of a car. He couldn't make out anything of the driver apart from his unfortunate haircut.

DENISE, the person-centred therapist, had offices above a bridal wear shop on College Road.

"Must be handy," said Clovenhoof.

"How so?" asked Denise brightly.

"They send them off to get married. You counsel them through the divorce."

Denise smiled and held it for three seconds, then made a little noise of interest and sat back in her chair.

"I thought I'd get a couch to lie on," said Clovenhoof, patting the arms of his chunky armchair.

"And I'd have glasses and a beard and ask about your relationship with your mother?"

"Something like that."

"There won't be any Freudian analysis here, Jeremy. We're here just to talk. Any answers are going to come from you, not me."

"So what do you do?"

"I'm here to listen, to show a genuine interest in your thoughts and feelings."

"So you're going to do nothing?"

"I hope to create an unthreatening environment in which you can express yourself and come to grips with the issues that you are facing."

"What's with the severed head then?"

He pointed at the stone carving on the window sill.

"The Buddha was a great spiritual thinker," said Denise. "He uncovered important truths through mere thought and meditation."

"Before or after they chopped off his head?"

"He was a man of peace. It's a reminder that this is a safe place where you can say anything without fear of judgement."

"Anything?"

"Anything."

Clovenhoof raised his eyebrows.

"So, if I were to say to you that I am Satan, the devil himself...?"

Denise smiled for three seconds again. She seemed to do that every time she looked like she wanted to say something.

"I would ask you to continue, perhaps ask you to explain why you think that or feel the need to tell me about it."

"And you'd believe me?"

"I don't have to believe you to value your opinion. If you make such an assertion and you're being earnest and honest with me, then I'm not going to condemn you for it."

"Fascinating," said Clovenhoof, convinced that the woman was bonkers.

"So, tell me a little about yourself, Jeremy."

Clovenhoof blew out his cheeks.

"What do you want to know? I'm Jeremy. Satan if you will. Two arms, two legs, two horns. What else is there?"

"What about your personality, your goals, your aspirations?"

He reached for something witty to say but found nothing. He shrugged.

"You must have interests," said Denise. "What did you do last night, for example?"

"Ah, well..." said Clovenhoof.

THEY HAD PAUSED for breath in the dark alleyway that ran behind the house, the body wrapped in several bin bags. It had sagged in unpleasant ways that made Ben feel queasy. It had been especially distressing when they'd had to unwrap it to add the hand from the bread bin, which they'd nearly forgotten.

"Ready?" said Clovenhoof.

Ben hoisted his end of the plastic-wrapped bundle. He couldn't remember if he had the head or feet. He didn't want to remember.

"What's the hammer for?" he asked.

"To smash his teeth in before we bury him," said Clovenhoof. "We don't want the feds to be able to recognise him from his dental records."

"You can do that bit," said Ben.

"Ah, cheers, mate. Let's go."

They walked up the unpaved path between two houses to the main street.

Ben was frightened to step into the orange streetlight, to make himself visible to the world but Clovenhoof pulled him on.

"You shouldn't be wearing those Bermuda shorts," said Ben.

"Why not?"

"They're very... distinctive. Couldn't you have dressed a little darker?"

"You worry too much."

"What happens if we're stopped by the police?"

"We tell them it's a carpet."

"Why would we be carrying a carpet around at midnight?"

Clovenhoof was silent as he led them briskly up the road.

"Well, why?" said Ben.

"I'm thinking."

"Oh, God," whispered Ben.

"Come on it's not far to the park."

"It's too far."

Ben let himself be tugged along, floating in some horrible, sick nightmare world. If the police saw them he knew he would drop dead from the shock.

There was a tiny, scraping footstep behind him and he looked back.

"Twinkle."

The Yorkshire terrier was trotting up behind him.

"Go home," hissed Ben.

The tiny dog ducked through Ben's legs, gave a jump and sank his tiny jaws into the underside of their grisly package.

"For Pete's sake," said Ben. "Get off."

"Attracted by the smell," said Clovenhoof. "Hey, we could bury this runty mutt at the same time."

"What has Twinkle ever done to you?"

"It's not so much what he's done," said Clovenhoof philosophically. "It's more that he's an offence against Mother Nature."

They carried on, with the tenacious terrier dangling by his teeth from the sagging body and growling excitedly all the while.

They turned into Beech Road. A ten-minute walk to Short Heath Park, Ben told himself.

"There's another," said Clovenhoof, nodding across the road to where a shaggy-haired mongrel stood, watching them.

As if in response to the acknowledgement, the dog scampered across the road and sniffed at the body.

"Now, if we had a pack of ravenous dogs..." said Clovenhoof thoughtfully. "Chomp, chomp. This could be gone in seconds."

Twinkle growled louder at the newcomer whilst retaining his dangling death-hold on the corpse.

"If we bury this thing in the park," said Ben, "the local dogs are going to dig it up in seconds. Hang on..."

He looked forward to Clovenhoof.

"Where's the spade, Jeremy?"

"I don't have it."

"But you had it before."

"I told you to pick up the tools."

"I've got the hammer!"

"But what about the spade?"

"It must be back in the alley."

"Oh, look, a third."

A grizzle-chopped dog had joined Twinkle and the other dog, and a whine indicated another close behind.

"This isn't working," said Ben. "About turn. Now."

They hefted the load onto their other shoulders so that they could switch direction. As they did so, something fell from the wrapping onto the pavement. There was much growling and scuffling over this morsel, until one of the dogs broke free and raced away with the prize.

"What was that?" Ben said.

"No idea," said Clovenhoof. "Let's get back."

They began walking back. The two dogs underneath the corpse circled one another, sniffing and whining and ducking in and out of Ben's legs. At the corner of Beech Road, he tripped against one of them and stumbled. Twinkle growled. Ben, not able to see what was going on, heard a bark, the snap of teeth and a shrill yelp. After that it only got louder.

"On second thoughts, run," said Ben.

BEN all but slammed the trunk lid shut on Mr Dewsbury and stormed into the kitchen to wash his hands.

"I can't believe we weren't arrested," he muttered bitterly.

"I think it was a creditable first attempt," said Clovenhoof, pouring himself a glass of Lambrini.

"First attempt?" Ben squeaked. "How many times are we going to do this?"

"If at first you don't succeed..."

"Give up."

"Normally I'd agree with you, Ben, but we just have to learn our lesson and move on. Next time, we'll remember the shovel."

"I am not doing that again!"

"Okay. Then we think of something different. If we can't dispose of him all at once..."

"If I hear the word 'hacksaw' then I'm just going to turn myself in."

"No, I'm thinking of something a bit more refined. An acid bath."

"An acid bath!"

Ben wheeled on Clovenhoof to see that his eyes were closed, contemplating.

"Some chemical," said Clovenhoof. "Something to strip flesh from bones."

Ben looked at his hands, remembering the drain cleaner that had burned his hands four months before.

"Bleach?" said Ben.

"Not caustic enough." Clovenhoof opened his eyes and smiled. "Hair relaxer."

"What?"

"The stuff hairdressers use to straighten afro hair."

"We're going to perm him to death?"

"I was looking at a bottle the other day at Blenda's. Sodium hydroxide. Caustic soda. It burns organic material. Eats it."

"And then what do we do with the bones?"

"I've got an idea about that too."

Clovenhoof sipped his Lambrini. Ben wasn't sure he liked the look on his face.

"THAT'S IT," declared Nerys, standing up.

It was the third time she had declared that *that was it* in as many days but, although she had meant it the first and second times, she meant it most sincerely this time. *That* was definitely unequivocally undeniably *it*.

She could tolerate the odd smell. She lived with a dog and an elderly woman with an irritating cough and a taste for gassy food. Such things were to be expected. But the stink that was emanating from Ben's flat had a vibrant and vile life of its own. It had invaded her home, inhabited her clothes and hair and made her skin crawl.

She took her indignation down to 2b and thumped on the door. It swung open.

"Come in," called Clovenhoof.

She pressed a scented tissue to her nose and ventured inside. Clovenhoof was at the kitchen table, a wad of printed sheets spread out in front of him.

"Where's Ben?" she said.

"Out. Shopping errand. Got a cold?"

She held her nose all the tighter.

"How can you stand it?"

"Stand what?"

"The smell."

"What smell?"

She glared at him.

"You know," said Clovenhoof, tapping a pen against his teeth, "olfactory hallucinations are one of the first signs of schizophrenia. I read that."

"I thought Ben was going to get this sorted."

"He is. That's what the shopping errand's for."

"What? More air fresheners? You need to get the plumbers in."

Clovenhoof shrugged and returned his attention to the sheets in front of him.

"What are you doing?" asked Nerys, irritated that her righteous anger wasn't getting any results.

"Something my therapist gave me to do. They're like questions about your personality. Sort of fun. Do you want some? I have spares. It could help you discover who you really are."

"I know who I am," she snapped. "I'm the woman who's living above a flat that stinks worse than a Parisian sewer."

Clovenhoof gave the matter some thought.

"Do you think having a therapist makes me seem more mysterious and interesting?" he asked. "Am I an enigma to you?"

"No. You're a mad idiot, Jeremy."

"An enigmatic mad idiot?"

She gave a whole-body shudder of annoyance.

"If you clowns aren't going to sort this smell out then I am."

"Okay," he said happily and, when it was apparent that this was as much as she was going to get from him, she turned on her heel, marched out of 2b and across to the open door of 2a.

Following the fire, the renovators had removed and disposed of all the living room furniture, ripped up the carpets and repaired the walls. It looked clean and bright and, beneath the all-encompassing pong, carried a scent of fresh paint and promises. It was better than Clovenhoof deserved.

"Helloo," called Nerys softly, stepping inside.

There was the quiet whisper of a radio from the kitchen. She went through to find two strapping builders in paint-spattered gear tiling behind the sink and fixing doors on the cupboard units.

"Hi, there," she said.

The one at the sink turned round and gave her a cheery smile.

"Didn't hear you come in," he said. "You all right?"

"I wondered if you'd be able to help me," she said.

"How so?"

"You must have noticed that smell coming from 2b."

"Haven't we just?" said the builder and his mate, with his head and shoulders inside a cupboard, grunted in agreement.

"I wondered if you'd be able to come and have a look at it."

"I'm sorry?"

"Have a look. Poke around."

"You need a plumber," he said.

"That's what I told them," she said.

"And you were right."

He picked up a cloth and wiped tiling grout from his hands.

He might have been thinning on top and he might have been unshaven but his stubble gave him a rugged air and even his nascent baldness had a certain devil-may-care aspect to it. And he wore a belt to keep his trousers up. Such an uncommon quality in tradesmen.

"But if you could come and have a look..." Nerys suggested.

He grimaced politely.

"We've got a job to finish here."

"I understand," she said, "but I would be very grateful if you could have a peek, or even a poke."

"We're on contract," he said. "We can't do cash in hand."

In an action she had practised in front of a mirror, she bowed her head slightly, tilted it to the side and looked up at him demurely.

"I would be *very* grateful."

The builder frowned.

"Pardon?"

She leant her body against the doorframe, raising a leg to caress the doorjamb.

"Are you sure," she said archly, "I can't tempt you to a quick poke?"

The bloke in the cupboard abruptly developed an uncontrollable cough.

The builder's expression squirmed from confusion to embarrassment to something that looked like pity and eventually settled on something stony-faced and unfriendly.

"Listen," he said. "I don't know who you are but you're bang out of order."

"What?"

"We've got a deadline and I don't appreciate being propositioned by strange women who dress ten years too young and wear too much lippy."

"Who said I was proposi-"

"You've made a fool of yourself and embarrassed my mate." The coughing accelerated into a higher gear and Nerys realised it wasn't actually coughing. The builder kicked his mate to silence him.

Nerys felt a hot flush of shame.

"I think-"

"I think," said the builder, "you ought to go and rethink..."

He waved his hand to indicate her entire body, her entire being.

Nerys backed away, her emotional state ping-ponging between anger and utter mortification.

"And for your information," said the builder as she left, "I'm only interested in women who've got a bit of self-respect."

Nerys all but ran out, across the landing and into Ben's flat. She slammed the door behind her and put her back against it.

"Is that you, Ben?" called Clovenhoof.

Nerys shook her head, to herself not him, and walked silently into the kitchen.

"Is it time for Mr Dewsbury's bath?" said Clovenhoof and then looked up.

"Oh," he said. "Er. Mr Dewsbury is my pet name for my penis."

Nerys realised she was breathing hard. The sound was loud in her ears.

"Do I wear too much make up?"

"I don't know. Blenda seemed to think so."

"She did?" she breathed.

"Tarty. That was the word she used. Slatternly too."

"Oh."

"But I like it," he said casually. "I think it complements your..." – he waved his hand vaguely towards her – "tits?"

Nerys gasped.

"Do *you* think I have no self-respect?"

"Absolutely. That's what I like about you."

"I see."

"Is that the kind of answer you were looking for?" asked Clovenhoof.

She had nothing she could say.

"Good," said Clovenhoof, pleased to have been of help and returned to his forms as she stormed out.

Ben came in with a large cardboard box stacked high with small packages in his hands. He had a frown on his face.

"Problem at the wholesalers?" said Clovenhoof.

"No. I was on the landing and thought I could hear crying."

Clovenhoof listened out and heard nothing.

"Sounded like Nerys," said Ben.

"She was fine earlier," said Clovenhoof. "She took some of the self-evaluation questionnaires my therapist gave me. Do *you* think having a therapist makes me seem mysterious and interesting?"

"No, it makes you seem mad."

"You too, huh? Shall we crack on with the body disposal then?"

Ben nodded with grim reluctance.

With the door firmly locked (the security chain was still broken) they dragged the bin-bag-wrapped Mr Dewsbury into the bathroom and with a bit of tearing and yanking, managed to roll the corpse into the bath tub, leaving the gore-slimed bags in their hands.

"This is gross," said Ben.

"All part of the cleansing process, dear boy."

Mr Dewsbury was laid on his front, his head tilted backwards against the incline at the back of the bath.

"He looks uncomfortable," said Ben.

"Wherever this man is, he's not here now," said Clovenhoof.

While Ben went to dispose of the bin bags, Clovenhoof fetched the packets of hair relaxer. He ripped the top off the first and sprinkled the white powder over Mr Dewsbury's back. It fizzed on contact with liquid-sodden clothes.

"Nice," he smiled and set to with the other packets.

"There'll be bones left once the flesh is gone," said Ben.

"All sorted."

"How."

"I phoned our friend, Pitspawn, and asked him if he'd be interested in a replica human skeleton for his Satanic attic."

"But this is real."

"You have model paints don't you?"

"Yes, but..."

"I bet you can make a real bones look like fake ones."

"Oh, I don't know."

"I have faith in you, Ben. Now hand us that next packet."

Denise flicked through Clovenhoof's filled out forms. He found himself clutching his knees and hoping for approval.

"Question: If you were an animal, what animal would you be?" she read. "Answer: A goat – I'm already half goat and quite like it."

Clovenhoof smiled.

"It's great. I can read a newspaper and then eat it."

She read on.

"Question: Name a time when you were completely happy. Answer: 1493." She looked up at him. "1493?"

"Spanish Inquisition," said Clovenhoof. "Hilarious."

"Right," said Denise and smiled for three seconds but Clovenhoof could hear the weariness in her voice.

"Are you judging me?" he said.

"Who are you?" she replied.

"I'm Satan."

"Where were you born?"

"I wasn't."

"How old are you?"

"I'm older than time itself."

"If you're Satan, why are you in Sutton Coldfield?"

"I was evicted."

"Evicted?"

"I was made redundant."

HELL

Satan had beamed at the Performance Management Review panel. He'd agreed to have a performance review on himself, but he was pretty sure it would just be a formality.

Saint Peter sat in the centre. His assistant, Herbert fawned over him, arranging papers and topping up his water if he took a single sip. Michael, Azazel and Mulciber also sat on the panel. Satan couldn't seem to catch anyone's eye.

He shrugged. No worries.

"I'm quite looking forward to this," he said to them. "It gives me such a buzz to talk about the improvements that we've made."

The panel was silent, and still nobody met his eye. Peter cleared his throat.

"We'll be going through the objectives that are in the document. Everyone should have a copy."

Satan grinned at the papers before him. It would be

another testament to the glorious triumphs that he'd overseen. He didn't need to read it to know that he'd over-achieved in every respect.

"There are comments against the individual objectives," said Michael, "but we have found, overall, that the targets have not been met."

The smile dropped from Satan's face like a stone. He opened the document on the desk in front of him and scanned the words.

"What's going on?" he asked.

"Well if you'll read-"

"Things are so much better now! How can you say that I haven't achieved my objectives? The place is transformed."

Peter took off his glasses. Herbert immediately picked them up, polished the lenses and put them carefully into the case.

"We've seen improvements, certainly," said Peter, "but not on the scale that's needed, and we are of the belief that you were not instrumental in putting them into place."

"Not instrumental!" Satan spluttered, "Hello! I'm in charge! How did that stuff happen if I didn't say so?"

"We have a consistent, documented pattern," said Saint Peter, "of best efforts being implemented by your direct reports. I cannot fault the way that they have responded to immediate problems. What is lacking, in my opinion, is the leadership and vision from yourself, vision to have looked further ahead and addressed the bigger picture."

"That is the craziest thing I ever heard," said Satan. "I've got a master inventor, and a huge innovation programme.

The flow of clients through the system is better than it's been for years."

"The flow is adequate, for the moment, but what if there's a major war or a pandemic? You can't cater for the peaks that are needed. And we acknowledge your innovation programme, but it hasn't really delivered any tangible benefits yet, just lots of theories and papers."

"You can't be serious."

"I'm afraid we are serious," said Michael.

BOLDMERE

Clovenhoof blinked at Denise.

"It's all that bastard Michael's fault," he said and then something clicked. "The knight of swords. The warrior."

"Sorry?"

"Something my tarot reader told me."

Denise leaned over the side of her chair and picked up a fat file secured with an elastic band.

"Mr Michaels was good enough to drop off your case notes."

"*Mr* Michaels."

"I know you stopped working with him a few weeks ago. There's nothing wrong with that. There can't be a therapist-client relationship unless there's mutual trust and respect."

"He's not my therapist."

"He's not the Archangel Michael either."

Clovenhoof raised his fist to shake it at the heavens and then stopped.

"Case notes?"

Denise nodded.

"Going back seven, eight years. Mr Michaels was convinced that you were not mentally ill."

"I'm not!"

"I agree. There is a clear boundary between psychiatric delusions of grandeur and the kind of psychological self-delusion you enter into. This dissociative pseudomania."

"I can't believe this. He's stitched me up."

Denise patted the file.

"Over the course of years, you've chosen to adopt certain personas. Jim Morrison, Prince Rupert of the Rhine, Barbara Cartland –"

"She was a keen glider pilot, you know."

"Were you? I mean, was she?"

"I'm not Barbara Cartland."

"I know you're not. You're Satan, apparently. What next? God?"

"Let me see those notes."

Denise slipped the elastic band from the file.

"Your lies – they are lies, Jeremy – are simply a coping mechanism."

"Coping with what?"

He reached forward and pulled at the papers in the file. Sheets of scribbled notes, documents, bills and photos spilled out.

"You're avoiding the past, Jeremy."

"But I am Satan!" he exclaimed, feeling the whine creep into his voice. "Look at the hooves and the horns."

Denise picked up a photograph from the floor and showed it to him.

It was a Polaroid snap and clearly of him. But he was standing on a beach. He had never even seen the sea, let alone stood on a beach. And he was wearing clothes he had never seen before and there, sinking slightly into the sand, were his bare feet, his pink, fleshy feet.

"This is a fake," he whispered.

"It might be a good idea if you spent a few days on the psychiatric ward of Good Hope Hospital for a full evaluation, in a safe environment."

"But he did this."

"There's lots of evidence in here that Mr Michaels has been working hard to help you come to terms with this, I can assure you."

"Where is he? Get him here now," said Clovenhoof loudly. "I want to speak to Michael."

"He's left the area. He's moved away."

Clovenhoof stood up and shouted at the sky beyond the ceiling of the room.

"Michael! Get your conniving well-groomed arse down here right now!"

There was only silence.

"Michael!" he bellowed.

"Mr Clovenhoof, please," said Denise reasonably.

He looked down at her. She smiled, a reassuring smile. She held it for three seconds.

"I think this session is over," he said, grabbed up an

armful of papers, stuffed them back in the file and ran from the room.

Down on the street, he looked up at the darkening sky.

"Michael!" he screamed once more and scanned the heavens for a response.

When there was none, he sighed heavily and, with an earnest mutter of "Tits!", ran off down the road.

WITH A BANG AND A CLATTER, Clovenhoof spilled through the doors of the Lichfield Road police station and up to counter.

"All right there, sir," said the woman police officer behind the counter.

"I need to report a missing angel," Clovenhoof wheezed breathlessly. It had been a long run from Denise's office and his physique wasn't built for speed.

"I beg your pardon?"

A moustachioed officer passing through reception clocked Clovenhoof.

"It's Mr... Clovenhoof, isn't it?"

Clovenhoof gripped the man's wiry arms.

"Constable Pearson!" he declared. "Just the man!"

"Really?" said PC Pearson, gently disentangling himself. "You've not been assaulting Christmas trees again? Or aiding and abetting armed robbers?"

"No, but I am looking for Michael. Or maybe it's Mr Michaels."

"Michael Michaels?" The constable's face was blank for

second and then he smiled. "Your legal eagle with friends in high places?"

"You have no idea. I don't know where he is."

"Right. We are the police, Mr Clovenhoof. We solve crime. We don't keep tabs on where your friends are. We leave stuff like that to MI5 and Google."

"But he's gone, proper gone. And I think he might be someone other than he says he is."

PC Pearson nodded and put a comforting hand on Clovenhoof's shoulder.

"What I think you need, Mr Clovenhoof, is a nice sit down."

"I can't sit down. Can't you see? I'm being framed or set up or something."

"Framed for what?"

Clovenhoof produced a wiggly dance to explicate his inexplicable situation.

"Feet," he said eventually. "They're trying to make out I have feet."

PC Pearson seemed to understand.

"A nice cup of tea, perhaps?" he suggested. "Or a pint?"

"Pint!" squeaked Clovenhoof. "Of course."

"Not that beer is the answer to your problems, now."

"Lennox!" Clovenhoof exclaimed. "He knows who I am."

"That's nice," said PC Pearson but Clovenhoof was already barging his way out of the door and heading towards the street.

∼

It was a quiet night at the Boldmere Oak, a few of the old boys at the bar, folks sat in ones and twos at the tables.

Clovenhoof ran up to the bar.

"Hello, dear," said the barmaid. "What can I get you?"

"Where's Lennox?" he panted.

"He's had to go back to Trinidad. His grandma's poorly."

Clovenhoof looked at his watch.

"Will he be back soon?"

"That depends."

"On what?"

"On how poorly his grandma is I should think."

Clovenhoof gritted his teeth and groaned.

"But he's the only one who can see my horns."

"Not sure I want to know," said the barmaid with a mild air of disgust. "Now, can I get you anything or not?"

Clovenhoof started to give her a dismissive wave and then changed his mind.

"A Lambrini," he said. "Make it two."

As the barmaid poured and he looked round for a free table, Clovenhoof saw a solitary figure at a window table gazing blankly into her empty wine glass.

"And a large Chardonnay," said Clovenhoof, paid and carried the three drinks over.

Nerys was wearing jeans and a shapeless roll-neck sweater. It was not her usual attire. And there was something odd about her face, something apart from the fact that she looked like she had been crying for hours, a paleness of her cheeks, her lips and eyes.

"Aren't you wearing any make-up?" said Clovenhoof, putting a drink down in front of her.

She looked up at him.

"Who am I?" she said.

"Bloody hell, not you too."

Her lips trembled and she burst into fresh tears.

Clovenhoof downed one of his Lambrinis and then sat down opposite her with the other.

Nerys wiped her eyes with a tissue and took a gulp of her fresh glass of wine. She put her hand on the questionnaire sheets on the table. He recognised them as the ones Denise had given him.

"What kind of animal am I, Jeremy?" she said. "Am I a cow? Am I a stupid and ugly cow, swinging my udders for all to see? Am I? Am I one of those bonobo monkeys, frantically throwing myself at everyone and anyone in some desperate attempt to fit in?"

"Actually," Clovenhoof interjected, "I think they're apes, not monkeys."

"Is that what I do?" she said, ignoring him. "Wave my big swollen red arse at any passing male?"

"Do you really have a swollen red...? No, of course you don't."

Nerys drained her glass.

"What's wrong with me?"

Clovenhoof opened his mouth to answer – it was quite an easy question and one he was happy to answer – but, for once, recognised that this might be one of those hard to spot rhetorical questions.

"Is it because I have a narcissistic personality?" she sobbed. "Is it because my parents divorced? Am I repressed lesbian? A lapsed Catholic?"

"You're not a Catholic," said Clovenhoof.

"How do I know?" Nerys wailed.

"Hmmm," said Clovenhoof.

He looked at his second drink and then downed it, just so he could go to the bar and get another.

MR DEWSBURY WAS FIZZING VIOLENTLY to himself in the bath. Two dozen packets of caustic hair relaxer was working its way through his rotten fleshy layers with surprising speed, generated a soft but persistent sound like the murmurings of a distant crowd.

Ben looked in on him every few minutes and, as night fell, was unsure whether it was better to leave the bathroom light on or off. A weird subconscious part of him was worried Mr Dewsbury might not like being left alone in the dark.

He compromised and turned the light off but left the door open a crack so a little light fell in on him.

When the knock at the door came, Ben assumed it was Clovenhoof. It was late and he was overdue. Why he didn't let himself in with his own keys didn't occur to Ben.

"Is that you, Jeremy?" he called cautiously as he approached the door.

"Yes?" came the reply.

Ben unlocked the door.

"You're not Jeremy," said Ben hollowly.

The tall, lean copper on the landing gave a little apologetic hum and tucked his hat under his arm.

"No, I'm *looking* for Mr Clovenhoof."

A tiny terrified part of his brain wanted him to yell out, "You can't come in here without a search warrant!" but Ben clamped down on it.

"He's not here," he said instead.

"Is he not?" The policeman grimaced genially. "I went to his flat but I see the decorators are in. And I wondered..."

"No," said Ben firmly.

"He came to see me at the station and-"

"Why?"

"Oh, something was playing on his mind. I did a little digging this afternoon and, well, I thought I'd pop round to speak to him."

"He's not here."

"You said, sir." The policeman gave Ben a look. "Shame. But how have you been?"

Ben swallowed hard.

"Me?"

"Since that nasty business with the bank robber back in March. I remember your face."

"Oh," said Ben, filled with the horrible feeling that they were on the verge of a full-blown conversation when all he wanted was the man to go away and leave him. Could the copper hear the hissing fizz of Mr Dewsbury being consumed in the bath tub. Why did he leave the door open? Stupid idea.

"I'm fine," he managed to say.

"That's good to know," said the policeman. "Well..."

He rolled lazily on his heel to turn away.

"If you see him..."

"I'll tell him," said Ben.

"Good."

The policeman sniffed deeply, his moustache twitching.

"Got problems with the drains, sir?"

EIGHT WHITE WINES and eight Lambrinis had not managed to elucidate who either Clovenhoof or Nerys were, their deep and true identities that had seemed only accessible through vast quantities of alcohol, but by the time they stumbled out of the Boldmere Oak, arm in arm, who they were no longer seemed to matter quite so much.

"We can be whoever we want to be," said Nerys drunkenly as they walked up Chester Road.

"Yes, we can," agreed Clovenhoof. "I can be Barbara Cartland if I want to be."

Nerys poked him in the chest.

"You'd make a lovely Barbara Cartland."

"T'riffic glider pilot."

"Is she?"

Clovenhoof pressed his lips together, possibly to hold the contents of his stomach down.

"No. Dead now."

"Oh," said Nerys, then, "Don't be her. Don't be dead."

"No." Clovenhoof peered ahead. "S'lot of cars outside our house."

In fact, there were three police cars and one ambulance.

"Aunt Molly!" blurted Nerys.

"I don't think so," said Clovenhoof, putting a restraining hand on her arm.

Without the aid of any diabolical powers, all the alcohol drained from his system.

"It's Ben," he said.

And there he was, stepping out of the house, a police officer either side of him. Ben raised his head and looked in their direction, although he possibly couldn't see that it was them on that dark street, and then one of the police officers opened a car door for him and he was gone from sight.

10

IN WHICH CLOVENHOOF TRIES TO FIND HIS FEET, DUFFS UP AN OLD LADY AND PRACTISES THE DARK ARTS

Jeremy Clovenhoof woke slowly. Morning sunlight streamed through the net curtains over the window. The fresh paintwork on his bedroom walls gave the room a bright and clean air. The linen on his brand new bed was a beautiful light cream. All so clean and pleasant and yet...

He couldn't shake the feeling from his dream that the brightness of this world had once seemed so wrong and unfamiliar. He pulled back the duvet and stared hard at his feet. Were they two fleshy pink human feet or were they hooves? He flexed and twisted his legs to view them from other angles. He closed his eyes and opened them again. He turned his head away and squinted sideways, closing first one eye and then the other. He tried flexing his toes.

He couldn't tell. He could not be sure exactly what was at the end of his legs. He sighed and settled back onto the pillow. Had his mind really constructed such detailed recollections to support his delusions? Was it all just dreams and make-believe?

He just wasn't sure any more.

But he could wait.

He stared sullenly down the bed at his feet.

If he had to sit and stare all day, he'd work it out.

NERYS WOKE FROM A TROUBLED SLEEP. Molly's cough had woken her numerous times in the night. Twinkle was scratching the door, wanting his breakfast.

"All right, I'm coming."

She sat on the side of the bed feeling wretched. If only Molly would shake off the cough or have the decency to just die and give her some peace. At least the smell from downstairs had nearly faded away. She fed Twinkle then got Molly out of bed and settled her in front of the television.

She went back to her room to get dressed. She pulled garments out of the wardrobe one at a time, and discarded each of them, wincing at what they said about her. Did she own anything that wasn't slashed or slit to show inappropriate amounts of flesh?

"You're a slut, Nerys," she whispered to the mirror.

She eventually settled on a spangled, low-cut top and trousers, but fetched one of Molly's cardigans to cover up a bit. She stared at her more dowdy reflection in the mirror. Was this better, or did she just look like her normal slutty self wearing a cardigan in August?

She kept it on and went out. She hurried past Ben's flat,

still criss-crossed with police tape, and down to the ground floor. Mrs Astrakhan came out as she heard her on the stairs.

"I don't know, Nerys, I just don't know," said the old woman.

"No, I'm not sure I do either," said Nerys truthfully.

"Murders and bodies, police and goings-on at all hours. I'm really not sure my nerves can take much more. Goodness knows how poor Molly's managing. What does she make of all this?"

Nerys thought for a moment. She hadn't actually told Molly about the body in the chest and Ben's arrest. She didn't have the energy for repeating and explaining all of the details to a half-deaf old lady who would doubtless mix it all up with some Peter Sellers film from years ago.

"She's keeping a stiff upper lip, you know, she's made of stern stuff," Nerys said.

Mrs Astrakhan put a hand to her breast and blinked in admiration at Molly's resilience.

"Wonderful woman. You're so lucky to have such a role model."

"Yes, I'm truly blessed," muttered Nerys, made her escape and hurried off to work.

JASON WAS SMOKING his first fag of the day.

Ben had found that sharing a cell with a remand prisoner at Winson Green Prison was a lot like student accommodation. There was a single chipped table with a chair and a bunk each. Jason chose most of their television viewing and Ben got to use the table whenever he wanted to. While Jason smoked, Ben lay back down on his bottom bunk and read. When he had finished his cigarette, Jason wordlessly passed the filter tip to Ben.

"Cheers," said Ben, and leaned over to add it to a small collection on the corner of the table.

NERYS MADE coffee in the back room and stared through the door at her colleagues in the front office. She'd come in that morning and greeted them as she walked through. They had responded with automatic 'Good morning's without raising their eyes, without truly acknowledging her. Even Dave.

Not one had noticed or commented on the change in her appearance. She hadn't wanted to be noticed but she had expected it.

Most of them had never been particularly friendly to her but would it kill them to pass the time of day with her? Is this what it had always been like? How many times had she walked into a room when they were all sharing a story and it would stop dead, and there'd be a stony silence as she took her seat. Sure, there were the numerous occasions that she'd rolled her eyes and told them she wasn't interested in their gossip or their family news but that didn't mean she didn't *care*.

A lot of people put up with all of that rubbish just to be nice to each other, too polite to be honest. But maybe that was what made them friends.

Nerys wondered if there was anyone she could really

count as a friend. She'd always had *best friends* at school. A series of complicated affiliations that could change with a swift and crushing blow if one of them wore the wrong outfit or liked the wrong music. A couple of those friendships had lasted into her teens and she cursed herself for messing things up by sleeping with Claire's boyfriend. And Catherine's dad. She might have got away with it if they weren't both at the same time.

She's messed things up in the past. But, she reasoned, this current mess wasn't totally irretrievable.

"Dave!" she hissed round the corner.

"Yeah?" he said, not looking round.

"I'm making coffee."

"Uh huh," he grunted, typing at his workstation.

She coughed. "I'm making *coffee*." God! Did she have to spell everything out?

"No, I'm fine, thanks."

"Come here and talk to me!" she hissed.

"I can't, I'm busy," said Dave.

Nerys was outraged. He couldn't possibly be so absorbed by legitimate work. She carried her coffee back in.

"No, you're not. You're just browsing the internet."

It was a website for a country hotel. Dave clicked 'Book Now.'

"Busy," he said.

CLOVENHOOF MADE his way down the Chester Road trying to keep the shoes on his feet. Stupid, stupid things. They seemed to be too large. They slipped off continually, no matter how tightly he tied the laces. He grunted with frustration as he stopped again to put them back on. He really needed to get used to wearing them if he was going to get better.

It took him twice as long as usual to get to *Books 'n' Bobs* but he unlocked and put up the *Open* sign. He checked the shop's email to see whether any books had been sold and needed to be sent out. By half nine, satisfied that he was on top of the business while Ben was indisposed, he made a call to Gordon Buford, funeral director.

"We haven't seen you for a few days, Jeremy," said Gordon.

"No. I won't be able to come into work for a while. A few family problems. I need to look after my cousin's shop."

"Your cousin?"

"Yes," said Clovenhoof. "My cousin, Ben."

"Well, you'll find me as understanding of family emergencies as the next boss, Jeremy, but my patience is not limitless. Do I make myself clear?"

"Patience not limitless," nodded Clovenhoof.

"We're going to need you back at work soon."

"Yes, Gordon. Got to go. I've got a customer."

Clovenhoof hung up and tried his 'friendly shopkeeper' smile on the customer. Ben could do the smile, but it was a tricky thing. You had to look helpful and interested without looking like a serial killer. Clovenhoof had practised in the toilet mirror when he first opened the shop. This customer was a man who looked too old to have pimples, but someone had forgotten to tell his face.

"Have you got *Wyrd Sisters?*" asked the man.

Clovenhoof frowned at the question.

"No, I don't have any family." He fixed the man with a look. "You do know that this is a bookshop, don't you?"

The man wandered off, to browse the shelves, a confused expression on his pimples. Clovenhoof went back to the task of replying to emails. Ben got mail from people who would write and ask if he would take an offer of fifty pence on a book that was offered on the website for ninety-nine pence. Clovenhoof's first inclination was to write back and tell them that he'd sell them half of the book for that much, but he checked Ben's email history and copied a more moderate response to use instead.

"How about *Making Money*?" The pimpled one was back at the counter.

"Search me," Clovenhoof said. "I can only assume that the rent is very low on this place."

The man looked as though he was about to say something else, but then thought better of it.

Two more people came in and browsed, Clovenhoof was hoping for an all time high of five customers in the shop at the same time, but he already knew he was delusional.

He looked down at his shoes to see how they were staying on. One was facing backwards which didn't look right at all. He bent down to sort them out and when he came back up there was another customer standing there, holding a paperback.

"What do you reckon to *Being Human*?" asked the man.

Clovenhoof shook his head

"I wish I knew. To be honest if you'd asked me that

question a week ago, I'd have laughed and said that it was for losers, but I'm beginning to realise that being human mostly means being confused. And nobody's more confused than I am right now. I can get my head round the practical stuff. Well some of it, anyway, but I have these dreams. They're so vivid. It's like, which is the dream, and which is reality, you know?"

The man was backing away. Clovenhoof remembered the smile and restored it to his face.

"And what do you think about being human?" he asked.

"Well I was hoping to buy it and read it for myself," said the customer, "but if it's a bad time, I can leave it for now."

Clovenhoof looked at the paperback title and moved to the till, smile still fixed firmly in place.

Nerys waited until Dave went into the kitchen to wash his mug at the end of the day. Everyone else had gone and the night was drawing in. Nerys followed him in and stood in the doorway to make sure that he couldn't slip out easily.

"Dave."

"Uh-huh."

"Tell me honestly. Do you like me?"

He looked up.

"Like you, Nerys? Of course I do."

Nerys moved closer, trying to catch his eye as he scrubbed his mug.

"You said I was aggressive and vindictive once before."

"Did I?"

"I know you like my arse or whatever."

"I'm sorry about that."

"But am I a nice person?"

Dave gave a brittle laugh and worked up an excessive lather with his attentive scrubbing. She could almost hear him choosing his words with care.

"You're a nice person who sometimes does aggressive and vindictive things, let's leave it at that, shall we?"

"What do you mean by that?"

"What?"

"I need to understand."

Dave turned around with his clean mug and realised that Nerys had him trapped.

"Nerys. Really. I've got to go."

She made no move.

"Can I get past?" he asked. "Or do I have to bodily lift you out of the way?"

"Tell me first. Tell me what sort of a person I really am," she said.

Dave took hold of her upper arms and gently steered her away from the door.

"I don't have the time."

"Be quick," she suggested.

"Nerys, please. I'm going now."

"No!" She clutched his arm as he tried to walk away. A little voice in her head was saying, 'Wearing your aunt's cardigan, grabbing hold of men, making a scene. All part of the slow slide into madness,' but she ignored it.

"Please!" she said. "I'm not a monster, am I? I mean I

know I have my faults, but you like me, don't you? Maybe you even love me? I always thought-"

"Nerys, for God's sake!" he said angrily, shaking off her hand. "How can you not know what you're like? You make outrageous, bigoted judgements about everyone, but you really can't see your own flaws?"

She had never heard him raise his voice like that before. He was so forceful, so... manly.

"Well let's start with this," he said. "You have zero patience. You can't even wait and ask a question like this at the right time. You're completely intolerant of other people, and you're downright rude to them if they don't interest you. The way that you chase men is so calculating it makes me queasy and you never dress appropriately." He waved his hands at her, up and down. "You always look as though you're off to pull a man at a nightclub. Or worse."

Nerys pulled Molly's cardigan around her more tightly but Dave, on a roll, hadn't finished.

"You know what I think?" he said. "You act like a spoilt kid. Maybe daddy didn't buy you a pony or whatever, but at your age you should get over it and grow up."

Dave pushed past her and Nerys made no move to stop Dave as he strode forward through the office. He turned at the door.

"I'm going away for the weekend," he said, the anger waning. "See you Monday."

She moved forward and watched in silence as Dave climbed into the car waiting outside. Blenda was at the wheel. There were exchanged words. Blenda turned to look at Nerys with something like pity in her eyes and then put the car into gear and drove away.

CLOVENHOOF STOOD at the counter in the bookshop and flicked through the file that he'd taken from Denise. There were more photographs, showing him as a young man, and even as a child. He stared closely at the image of a skinny boy blowing out candles on a cake. A woman with backcombed hair and a batwing sweater stood to the side, clapping. This was his mother, apparently. He couldn't summon up even the slightest glimmer of recognition. His parents' whereabouts was not clear from the file. It indicated that as a young man, Jeremy had behaved so badly, during one of his *episodes* that they had moved away.

There was a paternal aunt living in Streetly. She lived alone, and took the Irish form of the family name, Clabhanhaugh, because she preferred it. Clovenhoof raised his eyebrows at the hint of a more distant lineage. How could the name Clovenhoof really be anything other than a reference to his hooves? It certainly didn't sound Irish. He checked again and saw a pair of skewed shoes below his trouser hems. Feet or hooves? Feet or hooves? He gave a deep sigh.

As he raised his eyes, he noticed a pair of Ben's miniature soldiers on a shelf below the counter. He put them both in front of him and pushed them together, hunkering down so that they were at eye level.

"Hello," he said, in a strangled falsetto. "My name is

Jeremy Clovenhoof, and I am terribly normal. I have shoes and cushions and house insurance. Can I please come into your nice shop and buy some kitchen accessories with pictures of cockerels on them?"

"Of course," said the other figure, in a deeper voice. "I have a great many kitchen accessories. Don't mind me asking, but do you have Irish blood?"

"How very perceptive of you!" said the screechy one. "Yes, it seems I do," then added, "Begorrah!" as an afterthought.

Clovenhoof was shocked to see the pimpled customer from hours ago emerge from behind a bookshelf. He'd thought that the shop was empty.

"Do you have *A Troubled Background*?" asked the man.

Clovenhoof sighed.

"Is that another book? Haven't you realised by now that I really don't have the faintest idea?"

"No," said the man, letting himself out of the front door. "It's not a book."

NERYS DROVE HOME, incredulous that Dave had taken up with Clovenhoof's ex. Who could be more desperate, Dave or Blenda? She laughed bitterly at her own mean-mindedness.

She entered her flat. Molly was sitting in front of the television. Nerys shouted a greeting and went to investigate the contents of the fridge.

"I'm doing the fish while it's still in date," she called. "Nice day for something light anyway, I've got some strawberries for afterwards." She closed the fridge. "Strange how I'm looking forward to strawberries more than I've looked forward to *anything* all day."

Nerys gave a deep sigh as she put the kettle on.

"You know that job gets me down sometimes," she said to her aunt. "It's like I'm trapped. I don't know how to do anything else, and I can't afford to take time to re-train. To be honest, I'm not even sure what I'd do. Maybe it's not the job so much as, oh I don't know. Everything."

Nerys put the knife down among the chopped carrots and examined her hands.

"I just don't have any idea what I want out of life anymore," she said. "Did you ever feel like that?"

She glanced over at Molly through the open doorway. Molly sat serene as ever.

"I'd love to know what you were like when you were my age," said Nerys. "Did you ever make a fool of yourself or get confused by life? I just can't imagine it. You always seem so content with the simple things. You watch some TV, you fuss Twinkle and play cards with the same old friends. How do you do it?"

Nerys realised her eyes were welling up and she passed a hand across her face in sadness and frustration.

"Molly, I... I probably never told you how much I think of you. Daft old pudding, but you're always there, always the same."

Nerys grabbed a piece of kitchen roll to wipe away tears and blow her nose.

"You know I love you, don't you?" she called.

She sniffed loudly, fanned her face and looked up into the light to still the flood of tears.

Eventually, she frowned, realising that this had been a rather one-sided outpouring of emotion.

"Did you hear what I said? I said I love you."

There was not reply.

"Molly?"

Nerys went over to the chair in the living room and peered at Molly. Her eyes were closed.

"Oh," said Nerys and then laughed at herself. "Thank God," she said, gently shaking her shoulder. "For a moment there you had me worried!"

Molly's head fell forward and she keeled over sideways against the winged back of the chair. As Nerys grabbed Molly's arms to steady her, she realised that they were cold, lifeless.

"Molly."

Something moved in the corner of her eye. Nerys opened her mouth to scream and then saw it was Twinkle, looking up at her, still sitting in his mistress's lap.

BEN TOOK his lunch tray and found a table by himself. The food in prison was really pretty good, and he looked forward to mealtimes. He'd noticed that there were tables he should definitely avoid. The tables against the back wall were favoured by some bald and tattooed gentlemen and he'd seen the way that they all turned and stared if you sat there. One new inmate had failed to notice, and had been given a soup shampoo before being propelled across the room. Ben had also seen small transactions taking place under the tables on that side of the room. A small man with a face like a rat seemed to be involved in most of those.

Ben noticed a wad of dried out gum on the leg of his table. He picked at it between mouthfuls and eventually dislodged it. He put it into his pocket with a small smile of satisfaction.

CLOVENHOOF ANSWERED the door with a spatula in his hand. He was cooking meatballs, in an attempt to be more normal. He really wasn't sure that they'd be as good as crispy pancakes, but he was prepared to give it a go.

Nerys stood on the landing, looking at some point in the middle distance. He waved a hand in front of her face to make her refocus.

"Molly's dead," she whispered.

Clovenhoof wondered what he was supposed to say. He decided that his best course of action was to say nothing. He guided Nerys to the sofa and sat her down. He'd had a phone installed when his flat was redecorated. As he picked up the receiver, he wondered if it was inappropriate to feel a small thrill at being able to dial 999 for his first call.

BEN SURVEYED the careful arrangement of cigarette filters, dried up gum and balls of scrunched-up fluff. They covered the surface of the table. He adjusted a couple then fetched the dice from his pocket.

"Well, here's a familiar face!" said a voice.

Ben looked up.

Cell doors were opened for part of the evening, so that prisoners could socialise. Ben pretty much ignored this and carried on much the same as when the door was closed. He hadn't even realised someone was there. In the doorway was indeed a familiar face.

"Hello," said Ben cautiously and then realised who it was.

The bank robber, the one who had forced his way into his flat and bound his burned hands with duct tape.

"Trey," said Ben, remembering.

"Daniels," said Trey and advanced into the room. "You and your stupid friends landed me in here."

"Definitely my friend. Not me," said Ben.

"I did all the hard work, got away with the money, then somehow, and I still don't understand it properly, you lot dropped me right in it."

Ben shrank back into his chair as Trey moved forward.

"I find it pleasing that you're in here. We can chat."

Ben was terrified by the prospect of a chat. Part of him just wanted the physical violence to be over with.

"Murder you're in for, isn't it?"

Ben nodded.

"Hmmm, never would have thought you'd got the balls to be honest. Well I only hope you killed that friend of yours, the clown who lumbered me with all of that stolen cash."

"No it wasn't him," said Ben. "And you did point a gun at him and tell him to give you the cash."

Trey raised his eyebrows.

"Attitude? Interesting." He glanced over to the door

where two large knuckle-draggers awaited his instructions. He seemed as though he was about to say something then he turned back to Ben.

"What are you doing with all of that rubbish?" He indicated the tables. "You haven't really been here long enough to be properly out of your tree."

"These are Romans," said Ben, indicating the filter tips, "and these are Gauls."

The Gauls were represented by gum, and fluff balls.

"Right," said Trey slowly. "But what are you *doing*?"

"I'm re-enacting the siege of Alesia," said Ben. "There are eighty thousand Gauls holed-up in the city, here." He indicated a rough circle, drawn with cigarette ash on the table's top. "And there are fifty thousand Roman soldiers deployed here, here and here in the hills surrounding the town."

"So what happens next?" asked Trey, moving closer.

"Well, one of the sides must make a move. Both armies are short of food. If you were the Gauls, what would you do?"

"I don't want to be the Gauls, I want to be the Romans," said Trey, pulling up Jason's chair.

"Okay, well decide what you're going to do, and then we'll use the dice to determine how successful you are. By the way, this circle is a defensive ditch with spikes in the bottom."

"Cool."

NERYS LOOKED around Saint Michael's church to see all of Molly's friends from the hairdressers and the endless whist games. How many people would be there if it were her own funeral? Nerys shivered, knowing that she'd be lucky to fill a single pew.

She sat next to her mother, who was dressed in the style that Nerys had long ago dubbed *Cruella*. She had added a vintage pillbox hat with a veil to her skirt suit and towering heels. She topped it off with a cloak, trimmed at the collar with rabbit fur. A cloak. Nerys shook her head.

"Aren't you warm in the cloak?" she asked.

"Darling, it may cloud over as we leave."

Nerys knew her mom had only worn it so that she could swish it around in a stylish and dramatic way.

"So many *old* people, look at them."

"Mom! What did you expect? Molly was old. You're old, for that matter."

"Yes, but you won't catch me dressing in horrible synthetics. Or elasticated waistbands. Mind you, Molly always was the plain one. I suppose it's only to be expected. And did you see that strange-looking man at the back? His shoes don't seem to fit him. I think he might be in the wrong place, you know."

"Mom, keep your voice down. Someone's going to hear you."

"Well why would I care about that? I didn't get where I am today by being a shrinking violet! You could do with being a bit more focussed, yourself, Nerys. You'd have a man by now if you did. Try being more like your sister."

Nerys hissed her breath out, in an effort to maintain her calm.

"Why didn't Catherine come today, anyway?" she asked.

"She's hosting a charity fashion show with some of the other players' wives. She couldn't possibly take time out at the moment. I can get you a ticket if you like. You look as if you could do with some new things yourself. Although most of the things are in smaller sizes."

Nerys had forgotten the power that her mother had to target her insecurities like a heat-seeking missile. She never failed to feel the tears pricking her eyes within ten minutes of her company. To cry in public would be the ultimate humiliation, so Nerys folded her hands into her lap and concentrated on the service. The new vicar ran through a brief history of Molly's life, some of which surprised Nerys.

"What is that strange man doing?" hissed her mom. "Look, he keeps staring up at that tapestry in the back there."

"He's a neighbour. Now, shush." Nerys said, trying to hear the vicar. "I didn't know Aunt Molly used to be a keen tennis player."

"Says who?"

"The vicar. Listen."

Afterwards, the congregation went outside for the committal. Nerys watched Molly's coffin lowered into the ground, and tried to ignore her mother's comments about her job, her hemline and everything else that she was getting wrong.

"There's that man again. He keeps hanging around. He's a bit creepy, if you ask me."

"You're right mom," said Nerys, "I'll go and get rid of him, shall I?"

Her mother looked mildly startled, but was soon distracted by Molly's hairdresser admiring her hat.

Nerys put her hand on Clovenhoof's arm.

"Jeremy, I need to get out of here. Now."

"Okay," said Clovenhoof. "Who's that woman you were with? She looks a bit like you, is she your sister?"

"Urgh! Come on."

AT THE HOUSE, Nerys stopped abruptly in the downstairs hallway.

"What's up?" said Clovenhoof.

"I really don't want to go into my flat just now," she said.

"You've got washing up to do?" said Clovenhoof.

"It's just so sad."

"Ah."

"Besides, my mom might find me."

"That was your mum? She doesn't look old enough."

"Jeremy. Shut up about my mom looking young."

"I'm just saying."

"Let's go to your flat. I hope you've got some drink."

"Depends how fussy you are," said Clovenhoof, following her upstairs. "I've got lots of Lambrini."

"Fussy? God, no. I mean it's not as if I'm an alcoholic or anything," she stopped and looked at him, "I'm not an alcoholic am I?"

"Well, if you're an alcoholic, then I definitely would be too. And I'm pretty sure I'm not."

"You're right," Nerys said, "we can stop any time we want."

"Except now."

"Hell yeah."

Clovenhoof unlocked the door to his flat. It still had the fresh air of a show apartment, apart from a dark red stain on the beige carpet.

"What's that?" said Nerys, touching the crusty stain with the tip of her shoe.

"Meatball," said Clovenhoof. "They roll."

Nerys flicked through the paperwork on the table while Clovenhoof fetched the glasses.

"What's this thing on the table?"

"Another meatball stain," he called. "They roll a long way. And bounce."

"I mean next to it."

"Oh, it's my file. My life's story."

"It's what?"

Clovenhoof came back through and they both drained a large glass of Lambrini. Clovenhoof smacked his lips and Nerys grimaced slightly. She held out her glass for a refill.

"My therapist gave it to me," he said, pouring. "Well, I sort of stole it. It seems that I'm so involved in my delusion that I forgot who I am. This file has my medical history. And also stuff about my family. My family that I have absolutely no memory of."

"Lucky you," murmured Nerys as she picked up a photo.

BEN WALKED between the tables in the recreation room, like a head gardener passing through his prize rose beds. He had a small but permanent smile on his face and his chest, small though it was, was puffed out in pride. He was overseeing the HMP Birmingham C Wing war-gaming tournament.

"No, you can't use guns," he told a Yardie gangster from Derby.

"Why not, man?"

"Because they hadn't been invented at the time, Jacob. Think about using landscape features, and sympathetic neighbours, remember you've got a weighting for each of those, if you look on the sheet I drew up for you."

Trey Daniels had made sure that they had plenty of plastic figures, proper dice and enthusiastic supporters. Ben was in demand for his experience and technical knowledge, and had gained a new level of respect as Trey's friend.

"Go Nero! Come on my son!" came the yell from a nearby table where a car thief was pitting his troops against those of a petty drug dealer.

As Ben walked over to take a look, a warden came up to him.

"You've got a visitor, Kitchen."

"I wasn't expecting one."

"But she's here now."

"It's not my mum again, is it?"

"Visitor, Kitchen. This way."

Ben, dragged away from his garden of budding flowers, was led reluctantly through to the visiting room, which was already filled with prisoners, their wives, girlfriends, extended family and generally shifting-looking friends.

BEN PLONKED himself down in the seat.

"This is a surprise," he said.

Nerys leant over and planted a sincere kiss on his cheek.

"Are you all right?" he said.

She smiled for only an instant and ignored his question.

"How are *you*?" she said. "We've all been so worried about you."

"Have you? I assumed you all hated me," said Ben.

"No, of course we don't. Jeremy's been tending your shop."

"Oh, God."

"No, he seems to be making a decent go at it."

"Really?"

"Well, the shop hasn't burned down or anything so that must be a good sign."

"I suppose."

"How's the food? And more importantly, have you been able to put up with the, ah, you know."

"The food's fine. But I'm not sure I know what you mean. Put up with what?"

"You know..."

"No."

"Oh, do I have to spell it out?" said Nerys. "Being used as a sex toy by huge men."

"That hasn't happened."

"Oh," said Nerys, trying not to sound disappointed.

"So, um, how are things with *you*, Nerys?"

"Oh, fine, fine," she said. She wasn't going to mention Molly, not now. "Your flat's still got all of the tape around the door. Mrs Astrakhan keeps going on about it all. Apparently it's affecting her nerves."

"Tell her I'm sorry. I didn't mean to upset her."

"I'm not sure getting personal messages from you would make her any happier."

"No. Sorry. How's Clovenhoof? I feel bad about him too. He tried so hard to help me with, um, you know."

Nerys nodded.

"He's a very confused man at the moment."

"Confused or confusing?"

"Both. He's been trying to understand his background. He got a file from his therapist, supposed to be his background and history. The thing is," Nerys looked into the corner, searching for the words, "the thing is, it seems kind of fake to me."

"What would make you say that?" asked Ben.

"I see lots of CVs at work. Sometimes I have to check the details on them as well. I know how they look and feel. No end of times you'll find that the dates people put are a little bit wrong. Not by much, but a bit out, because they can't quite remember. What *never* happens is that people put accurate dates for everything, like the actual day of the week that something happened. That would only happen if someone was recording every single thing as it happened and they wrote down the date."

"Some people have excellent memories," said Ben.

"Really? Can you remember the date of every exam you ever sat?"

Ben shook his head.

"No, you write down the year you did them," said Nerys. "Jeremy's file has a date against every single thing. Medical appointments I could understand, but there's dates against family holidays from his childhood, and when his parents moved house. *Actual* dates."

"Yeah, but why would someone fake a thing like that?" asked Ben.

"Absolutely no idea," said Nerys.

"He's not Satan you know."

"No, of course he's not," said Nerys. "That's crazy. I'm going to do a bit of digging though. He's supposed to have some family living locally."

Ben nodded. He almost jumped out of his skin when she placed a gentle hand over his.

"Nerys?" he said, alarmed.

"I just have to say," she said.

"What?"

"I never liked Herbert Dewsbury. He was a dreadful man. Rude, intolerant, always trying to tell people what to do."

She paused for a moment, wondering where she'd heard some of those words recently. Oh. Yes. Dave had used them about her. She sighed.

"Doesn't mean he deserved to die though," said Ben.

"No," she agreed.

Ben gently extricated his hand.

"There's something worthwhile, something good inside the most unlovable of people," he said.

"If you say so."

BACK ON C WING, a small man with the rat face gave Ben a wink from the corner.

"Psst, got that stuff you wanted."

Ben went over and a jiffy bag was thrust quickly at him. He passed a thin roll of notes to the man and walked casually away.

Back in his cell, he opened the bag, and carefully unwrapped the tissue from six Roman legionnaires. He clutched them to his chest with a small sigh of pleasure.

"WHAT IF I don't want to go for a drive?" Clovenhoof complained.

"Just come with me," said Nerys. "There'll be alcohol."

"I'm appalled that you think I can be persuaded by alcohol, particularly early in the morning! Do you really think I'm that shallow?"

"Yes Jeremy, I do. Now come on."

Clovenhoof shrugged and climbed into the passenger seat. Nerys drove for ten minutes and pulled up outside a semi-detached house. It was an affluent-looking street in Ward End and the house had a well-stocked rose garden in front of it.

"This was the house you lived in when you were a kid," Nerys said. "Does it look at all familiar?"

"No, not at all," said Clovenhoof, winding down the window to look out.

"Look!" she insisted. "Look at that window in the shape of a little circle. Are you sure you don't remember it? If I'd lived in that house when I was a kid I'd have spent the whole time with my face at that cute little window. What about the roses?"

"What about them?"

"Do you want to get out and smell them?"

"Do I what?"

"Smells are very good for triggering memories."

Clovenhoof gave her a withering look.

"If you think I'm going to go and sniff those roses you're out of your mind. I've never been here before. Ever."

Two old ladies stopped by the roses and inhaled deeply.

"Roses are nice," said Nerys, to herself more than anything. She put the car into gear and pulled away.

She drove them to a pub with a beer garden out front.

"This place looks nice, we can sit outside in the sun."

"As long as they have Lambrini."

They sat at a picnic table and Clovenhoof tried to keep the wasps from his Lambrini by batting them towards other people. Very soon, they had the beer garden almost to themselves. Nerys was deep in thought and sipped her drink, barely noticing.

"You're not wearing your Bermuda shorts," said Nerys. "Nice hot day like this."

"I'm going for the 'normal' look," said Clovenhoof.

"Brown corduroy trousers?"

"They're normal, aren't they?"

"Beyond normal and out the other side, Jeremy." She sipped her drink. "Things have been so strange lately. Ever since all the fuss about that idiot, Herbert Dewsbury, everything's gone wrong," she said.

Clovenhoof put down his drink heavily.

"Herbert Dewsbury?"

"Yes, the corpse, the ex-tenant. You haven't forgotten him too?"

"*Herbert* Dewsbury?"

"Yes!"

"*Herbert*? Was that his name?"

"Yes," she said. "Why?"

"I knew him."

"You did? And you've only just remembered?"

His brow furrowed.

"I didn't know his first name. Herbert. Scheming, weasely Herbert."

"That's him."

"The question I can't answer is what on earth that means."

"Oh look, now that's strange," said Nerys. "Those two old ladies were at your parents' old house. That must be five miles away, and here they are again."

She indicated the pair of women in thick coats over by the roadside. Clovenhoof stared at the two biddies who were intensely studying the bus stop timetable.

"I've seen them before," he said quietly.

"Maybe you've got stalkers," Nerys said and giggled into her glass. "No more drink for me. I'm driving."

Clovenhoof shook his head.

"I assumed they were..."

"What?"

"Part of my illness. But you can see them too?"

"Course I can. I'm not the one with – what was it? - dissociative pseudomania."

"I'm starting to get an idea of what they might really be."

"Not stalkers?" said Nerys.

"*The duplicitous twins.* The tarot reader said there would be a pair of women who were not what they seem. I think I know exactly what they are."

He stood up.

"Jeremy?"

"Hey, you," he called to one of the women. "You know your coat's a cotton and wool mix, don't you?"

The two women exchanged a glance and then the one that Clovenhoof had shouted at took off her coat and flung it to the floor as though it had burned her.

Clovenhoof grinned at Nerys. "Gotta love that crazy Leviticus; *neither shall a garment mingled of linen and woollen come upon thee.*"

He sprinted forwards, kicking off his shoes, vaulted the beer garden fence and punched the coatless woman in the face. The old woman flew backwards, hitting her head hard on the floor.

"What have you done?" yelled Nerys and then gasped as the old dear sprang to her feet in a single fluid movement that was straight out of a Jackie Chan movie.

"Angels!" growled Clovenhoof. "Twatting cockless bastards! I knew it!"

"Oh, my goodness," warbled the other biddy. "It's one of them young hooligans, Doris. Probably on drugs or-"

Clovenhoof silenced her with a fist to the chops. He followed it up with another punch and a swift hoof kick to the stomach. Yes! He had hooves! Of course he did!

"You must have been loving all this," he bellowed as he continued to beat her. "You made me think I was *human!*"

He drove the last word home with a vicious sidekick to the woman, sending her reeling into the road. The old dear turned around, dazed, and saw that she had dropped her collapsible brolly. She bent to pick it up and was immediately struck by a passing articulated lorry.

Nerys screamed loudly, but this was instantly reduced to a low mewling sound as she realised that all that remained in the road was a coat, woollen stockings, a pair of stout shoes and a sprinkling of golden light, like tinsel.

NERYS SAT at the picnic table, hugging herself and moaning softly. A hundred yards down the road, an ashen-faced haulier stood outside the open door of his cab, his whole body trembling. He was staring at the clothes lying limply in the middle of road and shaking his head numbly.

Clovenhoof dragged the remaining old woman by the collar of her cardigan over to the picnic table. Nerys whimpered as the woman was pushed down onto the seat.

"Lucky this place is quiet at the moment," growled Clovenhoof. "Angels popping up would raise a few eyebrows."

"Killing old ladies, you mean-"

Clovenhoof broke her nose with his fist. She clutched at it painfully.

"You can stop that right now," he said. "Show us your real form."

There was a brief pop, a miasma of yellow light, and the old lady was replaced by a beautiful youth in a white gown. He took his hands away from his face to reveal his nose was fully restored.

Clovenhoof broke it again. The youth pulled a sulky face.

"You really shouldn't have disincorporated Parvuil, you know," he said. "There'll be no end of trouble."

"Trouble! TROUBLE! The only trouble worth worrying about is the trouble I'm about to cause. Now listen to me you snivelling wretch – what's your name?"

"Doris. Vretil, I mean. But you can call me Doris if you want, I quite like it."

"Oh please," said Clovenhoof.

"What happened to the old lady?" whispered Nerys faintly. Clovenhoof ignored her.

"I want some answers out of you," Clovenhoof demanded. "What on earth is going on here?"

"We're Recording Angels."

Vretil indicated the notebook tucked into a fold of his gown.

Clovenhoof grabbed the notebook and flicked through the pages, looking at some of the entries.

HEAD-BUTTED SHOP ASSISTANT

Drunken behaviour (again)

Stole money from bank (query – did Michael authorise this?)

Unsuitable role model for children (see pictures from school assembly)

. . .

Clovenhoof tossed it aside.

"But why was I put into Herbert's old flat? Is he behind all of this?"

"Herbert's just a lackey," said Vretil, "but so am I. I'm just a Recording Angel. I was supposed to tell them what you were doing." He glanced at the discarded notebook on the grass. "We weren't doing any harm. We were only following orders."

"That is what I hate about you lot," said Clovenhoof. "It's what I've always hated."

He stood up and grabbed a heavy cast-iron parasol base. He brought it crashing down onto Vretil's head and sent him the same way as Parvuil.

Ben sat in front of a table, with three policemen on the other side, staring at him. He recognised PC Pearson, but he hadn't seen the other two before. One had a shock of white hair that stood up from his head like a brush, and the other one had terribly bloodshot eyes. He was the one asking most of the questions. Ben was getting fed up of his questions, because most of them were repeats. He'd seen them write down answers in their notebooks, but he'd ask the same question again, in a slightly different way, as if Ben would be dumb enough to answer differently.

"So, tell me again about the night Mr Dewsbury met his death. I'm interested in the weapon, and how you came to have it upon your person."

"I told you already," said Ben, "it was a replica sword, part of my Seleucid weaponry collection."

"A replica sword, not a real one?"

Ben sighed. "It's a replica of a sword that would have been used by a Seleucid soldier. It's a real sword though."

"Sharp then?"

"Yes, sharp. Really, really sharp, as it turns out." Ben shuddered at the memory.

"One might consider it an offensive weapon then?"

Ben shrugged. "I bought it from a specialist website. I'm fairly sure it was legal."

"Mr Kitchen," said the detective, "we'll see what the jury says about that. It's certainly an unusual thing to possess, and even more unusual to be handling it when receiving visitors."

"I wasn't receiving visitors, he just came to the door when I was cleaning it."

"Well, I think we've got a pattern of unusual behaviour here. For instance, you still haven't adequately explained why you have a woman's head in your wardrobe."

"Yes I did," said Ben. "It was a spare part for a doll."

"A *sex* doll?" asked the detective, leaning forward.

"Yes," said Ben, going red, "but I never actually slept with her."

"And you no longer have this doll in your possession?"

"No. I threw her, I mean it, away."

"Apart from the spare head, which you chose to keep in the wardrobe," said the detective, nodding to the other two, as if this proved he was right about everything. "You see I'm wondering whether you like to keep souvenirs. You've obviously kept Mr Dewsbury's hand for instance."

"No," said Ben, "I told you that dropped off when I tried to get rid of the body."

"Ah yes, when you tried to carry it off for burial. Interesting that. You know you don't look that strong."

"Sorry?" said Ben.

"To carry a body on your own. Did you have help from someone?"

"No, of course not!" said Ben. "Who would help me with a job like that?"

"Who indeed? Who indeed?" The detective with the bloodshot eyes was trying to annoy him, Ben was certain. Trying to get him to blurt out something stupid in a temper.

"So my last question is about this sword of yours," said the detective. "What did you do with it after the death of Mr Dewsbury?"

"I gave it away. I couldn't bear to have it around."

"You gave it away. And who did you give it to?"

"Some guy I met in a pub. I don't know his name."

The detective sat back in his chair and looked at Ben for a long moment before speaking.

"We've got your first appearance at the Crown Court this afternoon. You know, I think you might go to prison for a very long time, the way this is shaping up."

Ben nodded solemnly and tried to look unhappy at the prospect.

"I TOLD YOU, I've had a brainwave. You need to drive us," said Clovenhoof.

"I don't think I can't drive," said Nerys faintly, her mind a billion miles away as she looked back at the beer garden and tried to process what had just happened there. "You drive."

"Excuse me," said Clovenhoof irritably and pointed at his feet. "Hooves and pedals don't go."

"Oh," she said. "Of course."

As Clovenhoof directed her to Pitspawn's house, he chattered excitedly.

"I need to speak to Michael or Peter. I know they're behind this."

"Behind what?" said Nerys. It was an automatic question. It felt good to be driving, to be talking without thinking. It was better than doing nothing, better than actually thinking.

"I don't know," said Clovenhoof. "They're up to something but I've got no way to get hold of them at the moment."

"Do we have any alcohol?"

"What?"

"I need alcohol."

"Focus, Nerys. Turn right here. I do know *someone* who'll have answers."

"Who?"

"We need Pitspawn."

"Pitspawn has the answers?"

"No, but he can get hold of someone who does. Park here. Here."

As Nerys pulled up, Clovenhoof jumped out and hammered loudly on a house door. A woman with her grey hair tied back in a bun opened the door.

"Excuse me, Mrs Pitspawn," said Clovenhoof and barged past her.

The woman turned and called up the stairs.

"Darren! Your friend's here. Oh!" she exclaimed in surprise. "And a young lady as well!"

The woman beamed at Nerys. Nerys, despite her scrambled brains, managed a polite smile of greeting and followed Clovenhoof up the stairs at a trot and into dark attic bedroom which, from the look (and the smell of it) should have belonged to a teen metal-fan with no girlfriend but which apparently belonged to a forty-something with male pattern baldness and a fondness for unhealthy foods.

"Pitspawn!" said Clovenhoof breathlessly. "I need your help." He glanced over his shoulder. "Oh yeah, this is Nerys."

Pitspawn looked at Nerys, wide-eyed and fearful.

"He's terribly shy with girls, but he's a lovely lad," said the woman, Pitspawn's mom, coming up the stairs.

She entered the room and placed a hand on Nerys's shoulder.

"Well go on, Darren, say hello to the lovely young lady. You know any girl that gets to know you would realise how adorable you are!" She turned to Nerys. "He's very attentive. Kind generous nature-"

"Mom, please!" said Pitspawn, almost bent over with mortal embarrassment. "Can you leave us alone?"

Pitspawn's mom retreated reluctantly down the stairs, giving Nerys a little wave.

"*Very* attentive," she whispered to Nerys with a conspiratorial wink.

"I need a resurrection spell," said Clovenhoof to Pitspawn.

"What?"

"Resurrection spell. Now."

"Are you serious?"

"Look, I know it's in your book, you said it was last time." Clovenhoof hopped with anxiety. "Let's have a look, I'm sure we can figure it out."

"You really want to perform a resurrection."

"Yes. I said."

"It's not that easy to do. You need the body of the person." Pitspawn looked towards the staircase. "You didn't bring a body with you, did you?"

"No, the body's in the mortuary," said Clovenhoof, "but I bet the spell will work if we have some small part of it."

"Oh, please, no!" Nerys muttered. "I've had enough weird shit for one day."

"What part did you have in mind?" asked Pitspawn.

Clovenhoof went over to the wall and took down a sword.

"Ben gave you this, didn't he?"

"Yes," said Pitspawn. "I always wondered why he didn't want it any more. It's a lovely piece."

"This is the reason," said Clovenhoof, pointing to a brown smear near to the end, "it's the weapon that killed Herbert Dewsbury. This is his blood."

"No. Fucking. Way," said Pitspawn, a sudden and huge grin on his face. "You serious? This blade killed someone?"

Clovenhoof nodded.

"Cool," said Pitspawn.

"So you can do it?"

"The sword will have a lot of power if it's the thing that killed him," agreed Pitspawn. "Maybe we can do this."

"Excellent!" said Clovenhoof. "Where's the book? There's no time to lose."

"Uh, we might have a problem. Mom's been really funny about me using her crystal animals." He glanced at Nerys, coughed and looked at Clovenhoof. "I don't suppose your friend would go and ask my mom for her crystal animals, would she?"

"Crystal animals," said Nerys. "Makes perfect sense."

Nerys left Pitspawn and Clovenhoof consulting the details in a book and beginning to chalk an outline of the wooden floorboards.

Pitspawn's mom was waiting at the bottom of the stairs, making Nerys think that she'd been trying to listen in.

"Hello dear," she beamed. "What do you think of Darren then?"

"He seems like an interesting character," said Nerys. "I bet you're very proud of him."

"Oh yes, I am. He'll make someone a wonderful husband one day. It's a wonder he hasn't been snapped up already. There's not a thing he doesn't know about computers, you know. Shall I write down his phone number so that you can call him if you ever get stuck?"

"Actually, he sent me to ask you for the crystal animals. Do you think we could borrow them please?"

This caused Pitspawn's mom to frown, but then a thought occurred to her.

"Do you mean that he spoke to you?"

"Er, yes," said Nerys.

"Actually spoke to you?"

"Yes."

"Oh, that's wonderful! Yes. I'll get them for you right away. You make sure that he takes good care of them though, won't you?"

Nerys went back up with the crystal animals to find that the pentagram the pair of them were drawing was nearly complete, but that Pitspawn and Clovenhoof were arguing about some of the details.

"Look," said Pitspawn, "the diagram in the book is very clear. This power rune is supposed to look like a little lean-to greenhouse."

"I know what the book says," said Clovenhoof, "but take it from me, it's supposed to be symmetrical. Belphegor's dog, Bargest has them all around his dog bowl."

"What's a dog got to do with this?" asked Pitspawn.

"He's not just a dog, he's the Hound of Resurrection. I think it's Bargest that we'll summon with this ritual."

There was a small snort of derision from Nerys.

"So," she said, feeling her old self returning, through the long tunnel of madness and out into the tentative sanity beyond, "we've killed a pair of old ladies who turn out to be angels and we're now using a crystal dolphin to summon a Hell hound? And that's going to bring Herbert Dewsbury back to life."

"Angels?" said Pitspawn.

"Long story," said Clovenhoof.

"Good grief," said Nerys. "I don't know who's more bonkers, you for coming up with this stuff, or me for playing along with it."

"There, that's better," said Clovenhoof, ignoring her as he adjusted the rune. "Let's begin."

The joss sticks were lit, and Pitspawn began to intone the words from the page. Clovenhoof joined him in the capering, causing Nerys to get a brief fit of the giggles, until Clovenhoof commanded her to join in too. Reluctantly, Nerys joined the other two as they pranced around the pentagram, Pitspawn waggling the joss stick and droning the incantation.

"You are going to have to give me your therapist's number," she hissed to Clovenhoof.

"Dance," said Clovenhoof deadpan. "And concentrate."

Across the city, in the mortuary behind the coroner's office in Newton Street, an attendant was distracted from his lunch by noises coming from the long bank of refrigerated units. He got up from his desk to take a look.

In the centre of Pitspawn's room, something began to take shape amid the wisps of incense. Nerys blinked and wondered if she was imagining it but it was definitely there, indistinct but nonetheless real like a swarm of bees.

IN SUTTON PARK, the soil in a flowerbed began to shift and move. This went entirely unnoticed by anyone.

CLOVENHOOF, Pitspawn and Nerys stopped their dance and stared at the centre of the pentagram, where the form of a man was now complete. It was also screaming.

IN THE MORTUARY, the attendant frantically dialled the Deputy Coroner's number to report that the corpse drawer that was supposed to be holding the remains of Herbert Dewsbury was now unaccountably empty.

HERBERT DEWSBURY CONTINUED to scream as he got to his feet in Pitspawn's room.

"This isn't Heaven!" he screeched. "Where am I?"

He spun around and saw three people staring at him.

"Erdington," said the fat, balding one.

He recognised the other man instantly.

"Satan!" he yelled, pointing. "Clovenhoof! Whatever!"

"See?" said Clovenhoof, giving the woman a smug look. "I *am* Satan."

"Nerys?" said Herbert.

"Herbert," said Nerys.

Herbert's nostrils flared. He had no idea what was going on but he didn't like it one jot, not one iota.

"What do you think you're doing?" he demanded. "You're all going to be in such a lot of trouble for this!"

Clovenhoof rolled his eyes.

"Everyone's so worried about all the trouble I'm supposed to be in. What about you, Herbert?"

"What do you mean?" snapped Herbert.

"You haven't got your pal Peter to protect you now, and you're at my mercy. I'm going to get some answers out of you. Seems to me that you're in more trouble than I am, right now."

"I've done nothing wrong. I am a paragon of virtue."

"Really?" He pointed casually. "By the way, I'm not sure whether you noticed, but you're missing a hand as well."

Herbert looked down at the stump of his right hand, the sealed stub of flesh at his wrist, and began to scream once more.

HEAVEN

- Matters Arising
- The Throne
- Disbanding of Guardian Angel Scheme
- Clovenhoof
- Doctrinal Diligence Ministry
- Shanty towns
- Leasing of extra-celestial property
- AOB

"Item one, the Throne," said Joan of Arc.

"Ah, yes," said St Francis. "We've put it off long enough."

Michael made a noise in his throat.

"I seem to recall that I'm the chair of these meetings."

"But it's on the agenda," said St Francis.

"But St Peter is not here," said Michael, indicating the empty chair. "It would be a fruitless discussion without his input. We'll move onto the second item in his absence: the disbanding of the Guardian Angel scheme."

"Do we have to get rid of the Guardian Angels?" said Pius XII.

Michael shrugged.

"Demand is far outstripping supply."

"I did warn you," said Joan.

"There are a hundred million angels in the Heavens," said Pius.

"And over two billion faithful on Earth," said Michael. "That's one angel for every seventy people on Earth."

"And less than one angel for every hundred people in Heaven," added Joan.

Michael nodded in sad agreement.

"Long gone are the days when every one of the faithful could be assigned two Recording Angels, one for the good they do, one for the evil."

"And yet," said Joan of Arc, "you've got two angels following this Jeremy Clovenhoof character."

"Oh, yes," grinned Michael. "I was going to share this later but it's too good, too funny, to hold back on."

Michael opened the leather wallet on the table in front of him and produced a series of photographs.

At that moment, there was the slamming of a door and St Peter strode into the boardroom.

"You've not seen him, have you?" he said.

"Who?" said Pius.

"Herbert."

"Your servile little friend?"

"Yes! I can't find him anywhere."

"Well, he's got to be somewhere."

"But he's gone. Gone!"

"I'm sure he'll turn up," said Michael. "Now, take a look at these."

St Peter threw himself irritably into his chair.

"What is it?"

"Clovenhoof," said Michael simply as he dealt the photos out like cards to the board members. "We've beaten him."

Joan picked a couple up. One was a picture of the Clovenhoof man trudging along a dinky nowhere shopping parade. The other one showed the same man half-asleep behind the counter of a grubby shop, his head propped up by his hand.

"He thinks he's human," said Michael, savouring the words.

St Peter gripped a photo tightly, creasing it.

"Really? Are you sure?"

St Francis tittered.

"That howwible howwible man? Human?"

"He's wearing shoes!" said Gabriel.

"I wonder what the theological implications are?" said Pius.

"Who cares?" said Michael. "He's wearing shoes. He has no toes and he's trying to wear shoes! It's priceless."

"I know this man," Evelyn said to Joan.

"Who is he?" asked Joan.

"I don't know. He made a fuss at funeral. He once asked

me to exorcise him. A troubled individual. He..." She stopped. "He was the last person I spoke to before I died."

"Who is he?" Joan asked the general board.

The saints and angels along the table didn't respond, too busy clucking over this apparent success and making jokes. Even Mother Teresa had cracked a small, wrinkly smile and left her quill and parchment untouched while she looked at the photographs.

Joan stood with a clatter of armour.

"Excuse me," she said loudly. "Who is this man? Who is Clovenhoof?"

They stopped and looked at her.

Pius put a hand over his mouth to stop a smirk of laughter.

"Can't you see?" said Michael.

"It's some bloke," said Joan.

"No, it isn't. We put a glamour over him but..." He looked at her. "You've met him, Joan. He invited us into his domain and then we turfed him out."

She peered at it closely.

Michael waved a hand, making an invisible change.

"Satan?" said Joan, her voice little more than whisper.

"That's right," grinned Michael.

Joan shook her head.

"This is wrong."

"It is wrong the Adversary has been defeated?" said Gabriel.

"He was *always* defeated," said Joan. "Even before he rebelled, he had lost." Her face was filled with an expression of faint horror. "You've all done something terrible here. You've let the devil loose on Earth."

"But woe to the Earth," quoted St Paul, "because the devil had gone down to you."

"Thank you, Paul," said Joan.

"The Earth was always under the devil's sway," said Michael.

"Figuratively speaking perhaps but that didn't mean people had to have him as a next door neighbour."

"His new home was chosen with care," said St Peter. "Where *is* Herbert?"

"And what of Hell?" said Joan.

"What of it?" said Michael.

"Who is running Hell? Who is in charge?"

"The same people who were always running it, Joan." Michael spread his arms wide. "Since the beginning of time. Us."

"Did you have some burning desire to reclaim Hell?"

"There's a lot of... real estate down there," said Michael, giving her a meaningful look.

Joan stared at him, long and hard.

"Is it me?" she said. "Or has anyone else sensed that Heaven has been a little less crowded of late?"

"Just effective management," said St Peter.

"And the shanty towns?"

"They are recent phenomena. A feature of the transitional process."

"Transition," she repeated softly.

"*Keep Heaven Holy* is designed to ensure that the moral rectitude demanded of the faithful on Earth is similarly demanded of all Heaven's inhabitants, present and future," read Evelyn from a *Keep Heaven Holy* leaflet.

"Everyone's position in Heaven is under constant appraisal," said Michael. "Nobody here gets points for length of service."

"You're changing the entry criteria for Heaven," said Joan.

"Changed," said Michael.

"No," said Peter, disagreeing gently. "Not changed at all. We're merely enforcing it properly now as it was always meant to be enforced. We are doing a review of every individual in the Celestial City and grading them against fixed criteria. If they come up wanting..."

Michael had a long list in his hand.

"No one who has been emasculated by crushing or cutting shall enter the Kingdom of Heaven," he read.

"There were a couple of people surprised by that one," said St Peter.

"Then there's the dietary laws," said Michael. "We can start on the less obvious stuff: ostriches, lizards, bats."

"But the coming of Christ presented a new covenant, a new law," protested Evelyn.

St Paul shrugged.

"For I tell you," he quoted, "until Heaven and Earth disappear not the smallest letter, not the least stroke of a pen will by any means disappear from the Law until everything is accomplished."

"We can move onto those who have eaten shellfish," said St Peter. "Oh, and imagine if we invoke the law involving eating dairy and meat together. All those cheeseburgers! There won't be a single American left in Heaven."

There were intrigued and hopeful noises made by a number of those present.

"This is insane!" said Joan.

"Really?" said Michael.

"Does He approve?" said Joan.

"We are the board. We run things."

"But has this been taken before the Throne? Has the Lord himself condoned this?"

"Well," said Michael, putting on his best smile, "it's not as simple as that."

"The Thwone was on the agenda," said St Francis. "St Peter is here now."

"Shut it, Francis."

Joan stepped away from the table.

"This cannot be allowed. I'm going to speak to Him."

"There's no point," said St Peter.

"Why?" demanded Joan, her hand on the hilt of her sword.

There was a flare of golden light and an angel appeared in the room, staggered, straightened up and patted his chest as if to check it were whole and undamaged.

"Parvuil!" said Michael, shocked. "What are you doing here? Where's Doris – I mean Vretil?"

The Recording Angel gave Michael a wild and unhappy look.

"There's a problem, Archangel. A big problem."

11

IN WHICH CLOVENHOOF EXTRACTS A CONFESSION, FLICKS A SWITCH AND KILLS A FRIEND

I n Pitspawn's attic room, Herbert Dewsbury clutched at his right wrist and screamed. He was wearing the clothes he had died in, minus the blood and gore, although there was still a tear, the width of a sword blade, in the neck of his woolly jumper.

"Where is it?" he bawled. "What have you done with it?"

Herbert started to cast about the untidy room as though expecting to see his hand lying about somewhere.

Clovenhoof stroked his chin and then clicked his fingers.

"We chopped it off."

"What?" squealed Herbert.

"Well, Ben did," said Clovenhoof. "Shut the lid too quickly when my girlfriend came to the door. Ex-girlfriend now, I suppose."

"She's going out with Dave from the office," said Nerys conversationally.

"Is she?"

"Going away for a long weekend away together."

Clovenhoof frowned and stuck out his bottom lip.

"I wouldn't have imagined those two together," he said thoughtfully.

"That's what *I* thought," said Nerys, nodding in grim satisfaction at having her own opinions confirmed.

"You cut it off?" screamed Herbert.

"Yes, yes. Do keep up," said Clovenhoof. "We put it in the breadbin and then when we tried to take the corpse to the park to bury it we... well, we lost it."

"Lost it?" He howled in anguish. "I knew you were incompetent but..." He waved his stump at Clovenhoof. "It's my hand!"

There was light tap at the door.

"Darren?" said Pitspawn's mother, opening the door a crack. "You and your friends are making quite a bit of noise. I don't want it to bring on one of my migraines. And I do need you to help with the cleaning. Pelmets today."

Pitspawn, who had been sat dumbly on the floor ever since Herbert's appearance mumbled, "Just resurrected someone, mum."

Nerys leapt to the door, foot positioned to stop Pitspawn's mum opening it any further.

"Hi, Mrs Pitspawn," she said. "Sorry about the noise, it's –"

"Call me Phyllis, dear."

"Of course, Phyllis," she said. "Pitsp- Darren and I were just trying out some, er, primal scream therapy. You know, getting in touch with the inner animal. He's a very sensitive man, isn't he? Very much in touch with his... inner self."

"He was always a sensitive boy," agreed Pitspawn's mum.

Herbert opened his mouth, perhaps to call for help, perhaps to object to the codswallop Nerys was spouting. Clovenhoof kicked him violently, hoof connecting with knee with a pleasantly meaty thud. Herbert doubled up, howling in wordless pain.

"Good one, Darren," said Nerys. She smiled at Pitspawn's mum. "We're really connecting, you know. But we'll try to keep the noise down, Phyllis."

"Oh, okay," said the little woman and backed away. "But we do have the pelmets to dust before lunch."

Nerys closed the door.

"That should buy us a little time."

"What's a pelmet?" said Clovenhoof.

Nerys gestured with her hands in an attempt to mime a pelmet.

"It's like a mini skirt for a curtain rail."

"And do they need dusting?"

"Of course they do!" snapped Herbert. "I don't suppose you've so much as run a feather duster over mine, have you?"

"I tore one down and wiped my arse on it," said Clovenhoof. "And set fire to the other with a flamethrower."

Herbert gave an anguished groan and made to wring his hands but found that impossible to do with only one hand.

"But since you've finished screaming," said Clovenhoof, "we have some questions that need answering, starting with why in His name have I been living in your old flat for the last nine months?"

"I resurrected someone," said Pitspawn numbly. His

mind had decided to take a short vacation and, in its absence, his voice had slipped into autopilot.

"Don't worry," said Clovenhoof, scooping up Ben's Seleucid sword. "We can soon fix that."

"No need for violence," said Nerys.

"Really?" said Clovenhoof, disappointed.

"Not yet. Herbert, you are going to answer every one of Jeremy's questions."

"And why will I do that?" sneered Herbert. "Death holds no fears for me."

"Yeah?" said Nerys, stepping round Pitspawn on the floor to reach a chest of drawers under the window. "But what about socks?"

"Socks?" said Clovenhoof.

"Trust me," said Nerys and opened Pitspawn's underwear drawer.

BEHIND THE RAILINGS alongside Monmouth Drive, in a corner of Sutton Park much favoured by neighbourhood dogs, there was a planted border of mixed flowers and shrubs. In that thick soil, late summer had brought forth red-spiked salvia and silver-leafed lambs tongue and something entirely new. Emerging from a long sleep, returning to life in an unexpected form, Herbert Dewsbury's amputated right hand poked its index finger up through the soil and into the afternoon sunlight.

"So you expected my arrival to lead to Ben's arrest?" said Clovenhoof.

"No," said Herbert irritably. "I just wanted to inflict you as a punishment on those people who had given me so much pain and grief in life. I wanted to inflict you on the murderer, Ben Kitchen."

"He didn't mean to kill you."

"He had a sword in his hand. I didn't expect your moronic influence to lead directly to his arrest." Herbert smiled. "That was just good fortune."

"And that's what this is all about?" said Clovenhoof, frowning.

"Yes."

"The whole Satan on earth business? Revenge?"

"Yes."

Clovenhoof threw himself against a wall, deep in thought.

"He's lying," said Nerys.

"Me?" said Herbert indignantly, stump on heart. "Lie? I've told you everything. Now send me back."

Nerys looked down at the open sock drawer.

"Oh, look." She pulled out two pairs of socks. "Black socks. Blue socks."

She pulled the socks apart and then paired one black sock with one blue sock.

"That's better," she said.

Herbert twitched. It was bad enough that the socks were dusty and covered with lint. It was bad enough that the man, Pitspawn, had no system for organising his underwear and obviously had low standards of cleanliness and hygiene. But to mis-pair socks like that...

"No," said Herbert, warding her away. "I can ignore your attempts to upset me."

"Really?" said Nerys. "But I haven't put them back in the drawer yet."

"What?"

Nerys held the mismatched socks over the drawer.

"I'm going to put them back in, stick them right at the back. They could stay there, like that, for months."

Herbert shuddered and clutched at his stomach.

"That's... that's immoral."

"Is it?"

"Insane!"

"Then tell us."

"No!"

"Tell us everything."

"I can't."

"Fine," she shrugged and began pulling socks and pants out of the way to make room.

"Please!" whimpered Herbert, feeling the sickness and goosebumps crawl all over him. "They'll never forgive me."

"Who?" said Clovenhoof.

"Michael," said Herbert. "Michael and Peter."

Spartacus Wilson, seven-year-old scourge of St Michael's Primary School, kicked a pine cone at a squirrel but his heart wasn't in it and the pine cone missed by several feet. The squirrel looked at the pine cone, looked at him and then scampered off into the bushes.

If Spartacus had the courage and the words to admit it, he would admit that he wasn't enjoying his summer holiday half as much as he had expected. Six weeks of total freedom turned out to be six weeks without a captive audience for his wit, wisdom and acts of gymnastics and sleight of hand. It was six weeks without Mrs Well-Dunn. She had always been the Sheriff of Nottingham to his Robin Hood, the Jabba the Hutt to his Han Solo. Without an evil and incompetent tyrant to rail against, he had nothing. And, worse still, his year three teacher was going to be Mrs Sokolowski, who used to be a Russian spy, had eyes in the back of her head and ate naughty boys for breakfast.

He looked beyond the park fence, at the houses along Monmouth Drive. He seemed to recall that Melanonychia Brown from 2C lived around here somewhere. Maybe she'd like to come outside to have her pigtails pulled. That could be diverting, for a time at least.

A movement in the nearby flowerbeds caught his eye, something small making rapid movements in the dirt. For a split-second, he thought it might have been the squirrel, burying his nuts or whatever it was squirrels buried, but he instantly saw that this thing was too pink, too spindly to be a squirrel. It looked like the hairless offspring of a mole and a spider, a snuffling questing thing.

Spartacus edged closer and crouched.

"Hey there," he said gently and rubbed the fingers of his outstretched hand together as though he had food to offer it.

The creature turned, stepped up through the shrubbery

and onto the grass and Spartacus could see that it was, quite clearly, despite the mud that covered its skin and nails, a human hand.

"Cool," said Spartacus with a crooked smile.

The summer holidays had taken a sudden turn for the better.

Herbert sat on the floor, doing his best to properly re-pair a dozen socks with only one hand.

"So Heaven's in just as big a mess as Hell," said Clovenhoof.

Herbert nodded.

"But this is Heaven we're talking about," said Nerys.

"So?"

"Heaven. God. The Almighty. How can it be anything other than perfect?" She shook her head. "Why am I even asking these kinds of questions?"

"Heaven and Hell are ruled by the Other Guy, sure," said Clovenhoof, "but they're also bound by scripture."

"What? So just because some first century fruitcake declares Heaven is a certain size then it must be so?"

"Scripture is written by men," said Clovenhoof, "but ratified in Heaven."

"As it is on Earth, so shall it be in Heaven," said Herbert who had now resorted to using his teeth in his sock-pairing frenzy.

"Exactly," said Clovenhoof. "Heaven is over-crowded. They need to turf some people out."

"The *Keep Heaven Holy* initiative will soon remove those residents who should never have been admitted in the first place."

Nerys abruptly remembered Herbert's *Keep Boldmere Beautiful* campaign and laughed in recognition.

"Clearly your idea," she said.

"I came up with the name," Herbert admitted.

"Do you hand out leaflets and window stickers?"

"Cultivating conformity through gentle encouragement is one strand of the programme," said Herbert with a flickering pout of annoyance. "We will use force on those who won't comply. However, the first stage of the programme is to ensure that the entry requirements for Heaven are strictly enforced."

"Eh?"

"We're not letting in any more riff-raff."

Something occurred to Nerys.

"What about my Aunt Molly?"

Herbert gave her a scornful glare.

"I think if she's planning on popping her clogs any time soon she might need to do some serious re-evaluation of her moral st-"

"She died three weeks ago."

"Oh. My condolences." A smile played over Herbert's lips. "Well, I do recall she did complain about the cold a lot. She'll be somewhere warm right now."

"Bastard!" she yelled and leapt at Herbert, snatching the sword off Clovenhoof in the process.

Herbert stumbled as she swung the blade at him. The sword passed over his head, decapitated a statue of Shalbriri, demon of blindness, and embedded itself in the plaster wall. As shards of cast resin cascaded down on him, Herbert ducked under Nerys's arm and dashed for the door. Clovenhoof lunged after him and immediately tripped over Pitspawn. Nerys took a second to yank the sword from the wall and by the time she was at the door, Herbert was down the stairs and out of the front door.

"Oh my," said Pitspawn's mum, Phyllis, watching from the hallway. "Another friend?"

She came to the foot of the stairs.

"Nerys dear, could you tell Darren that I *do* need a hand with the dusting now." She then took in the sword in Nerys's hand and the snarl of rage fixed on her face. "Maybe later then," said Phyllis and took herself off to the kitchen.

Nerys slammed the door behind her and threw the sword on the floor.

"Forget him," said Clovenhoof. "He's told us all we need to know."

"Really?"

"This business, me being here, is all a set up. They want me out of the way so they can shunt their cast-offs into Hell."

"Including my Aunt Molly."

Clovenhoof nodded grimly.

"I resurrected someone," said Pitspawn.

"Yes, yes. Be quiet, Pitspawn," said Clovenhoof. "I'm thinking. We need to get into Heaven."

"You mean, like, *now*?" said Nerys.

"As soon as possible."

"Can't you... devil yourself there?"

"I have been stripped of all my powers. And I certainly

don't meet their general entry requirements." He raised his eyebrows at Nerys. "It'll have to be you."

"You want me to go to Heaven?" Nerys put her hands on her hips and threw her eyes to the ceiling. "This is madness."

"Yup," agreed Clovenhoof. "But, you know what, it's either you or the mumbling moron here."

Nerys looked at Pitspawn, sat cross-legged like a child in the ruins of his summoning pentagram.

"And even though, despite the evidence of this room, I suspect his sins are fewer than yours," said Clovenhoof, "he's in no fit state to articulate them and seek forgiveness."

"You want me to confess my sins?" said Nerys.

"Yes."

"All of them?"

"Pretty much."

Nerys stared at him.

"Perhaps we'd better sit down. This might take a while."

HERBERT'S HAND nestled contentedly in Spartacus's arms. Spartacus stroked it and picked a flake of dried mud from between its third and fourth fingers.

"I think we'd best keep you hidden," said Spartacus. "I bet grown ups will only want to lock you in a cage and do experiments on you and stuff."

The hand bedded itself down further in the crook of Spartacus's arms, understanding fully.

"Doesn't mean we can't have some fun though," said the boy.

The hand was in total agreement.

In Spartacus Wilson, this would-be villain of a boy, it sensed a kindred spirit. The hand might once have belonged to the law-abiding and sanctimonious Herbert Dewsbury but now it was a free agent. And although Herbert's mouth might have spoken of goodness and forgiveness, his mind might have been filled with noble deeds and his heart home to the occasionally charitable feeling, it had been his hands, and this hand in particular, which had led the way in every wicked deed he had done.

The hand liked the idea of 'fun'.

"THERE WAS the time I pulled all the stuffing out of my sister's teddy bear," said Nerys. "I also threw her piggy bank downstairs once. And then her, in a cardboard box."

"Really?" said Clovenhoof with a smile.

"I told her it would be like tobogganing. I stole money from my mum's purse when I was ten. Several times. And from Mrs Hughes, my form tutor at Greenhill secondary school."

"Okay," said Clovenhoof. He went over to the chest of drawers and unplugged the table lamp that stood on top of it.

"Secondary school," said Nerys, deep in thought.

Clovenhoof sat down with the lamp and inspected how the electrical lead connected to the lamp base.

"Did you commit any sins at secondary school?"

Nerys grimaced.

"Does... messing around with boys count as sinful?"

"Not in my book but what do you mean by messing around?"

Nerys made a variety of hand gestures. Pitspawn, still circling the drain of potential madness, made a strangled noise in his throat.

Clovenhoof nodded solemnly.

"I think we'd better hear it all, just to be on the safe side."

"Right," said Nerys. "Then we'll start with Owen Sellers and the art cupboard."

Clovenhoof wrapped a length of flex around his hand and forcibly ripped the electrical lead from the base of the lamp.

BEN SAT in the back of the security truck, staring at nothing, letting the sway of the vehicle rock him back and forth on the bench. There were four prisoners in the truck. The one in the cage next to him, a lifer from Nuneaton called Winston, leant his head towards the dividing mesh.

"What have you got today?" he asked.

"Preliminary hearing," said Ben.

Winston nodded.

"You?" said Ben out of politeness.

"Sentencing."

"I thought you'd been sentenced."

Winston chuckled dryly.

"The Crown Prosecution Service asked if I'd like some other offences to be 'taken into account.'"

"What does that mean?"

"They wanted me to confess to some extra stuff, stuff from way back when. Help tidy up some cold cases. You nervous?"

Ben nodded.

"Worried my mum and dad are going to be there."

"Ashamed?"

Ben shrugged.

"I just want it to be over," he said.

"Good luck with that," said Winston.

Ben looked down at his feet.

"These crimes," he said. "The ones you're confessing to."

"What about them?" said Winston.

"Did you do them?"

Winston chuckled.

"This thing." He raised his hands to indicate the cage and all it implied. "It's never over. Ever."

"AND AGAIN WITH Adam Davies in the park. Same bush. I only did it because he'd failed his driving test and was really upset and I wanted to put a smile on his face."

Nerys paused to take stock and count on her fingers although, truth be told, she had run out of fingers quite some time ago. Clovenhoof pulled at the plastic covering over the lamp flex with his teeth while he listened.

"University," said Nerys, stating it as a title, a new chapter heading in her litany of sins. "Freshers' week. That was a busy seven days. There was Damon. Adrian. Twice. Harjeet.

That one with the goatee beard. Can't remember his name. Jeremy?"

Clovenhoof looked up. He had ripped back the white outer covering and was now paring down the brown plastic within to expose two strands of copper wiring.

"Yes?"

"Does it count as a sin if you were too drunk to properly remember it?"

Clovenhoof paused to give it some thought.

"I think it might actually be worse," he said.

"Right," said Nerys, giving up counting on her fingers. "Then there were certainly some extras in there. Maybe I should just give you the highlights."

"I think the important thing is that you recognise what you have done wrong and wish to atone for it."

"That would include paying someone to write my dissertation for me?"

"You paid someone to do your degree dissertation for you?"

"I paid in... services. Yes."

"Mmmm," nodded Clovenhoof. Happy with the wires, he levered the three-amp fuse out of the lamp plug and replaced it with a paperclip he had found on the floor.

HERBERT OPENED the door of the sub-divided house on Chester Road. His flat keys had been in his pocket when he had appeared in that fat occultist's bedroom, along with the few coins and the bus ticket he'd used on the day he'd died.

It had been two years since he had last stood in the place, but being in the old building brought back so many memories and emotions.

There was that corner of carpet which the property management company promised they would nail down and hadn't. There was that patch of mildew under the stairs they should also have dealt with. And there was Mrs Astrakhan's brolly and boots outside her door. He had told her so often that they were a trip hazard but the woman had failed to take action. Herbert suspected her truculence stemmed from being a bit simple.

He took himself upstairs to the first floor and saw the blue and white police tape criss-crossed over Ben Kitchen's front door. It struck him like a physical blow. That was the flat in which he had died, in which that strange young man had murdered him.

Herbert sighed deeply and mournfully.

He had been a fool to miss the signs: the grubby, poorly managed bookshop, the indifference to personal appearance and grooming, that strange obsession with toy soldiers, the utter lack of interest in finding himself a young woman. Herbert should have recognised him for the psychotic killer he was.

Herbert turned away and went to unlock the door of his own flat. The key stuck in the lock.

Of course, they had moved that satanic fool into his flat. On *his* recommendation. But he was back now. Surely, it was his flat once more. The fact that his keys didn't automatically fit the lock annoyed him intensely. He would have to have *words* with someone.

Not overly sure where he was going, he stomped downstairs once more. Mrs Astrakhan was at the open door of her flat, slipping on her boots.

"They're a trip hazard, Mrs Astrakhan," said Herbert, glad he had caught her in the act.

The woman looked up at him, stunned and speechless.

"This is a communal area," he said, gesturing to the length of the hall, "and we shouldn't be cluttering it up with personal items. We've spoken about this before, haven't we?"

Mrs Astrakhan's face had drained of all colour, her eyes wide with shock.

"So we won't be leaving them here again, will we?" said Herbert with what he considered an avuncular smile.

"No, Mr Dewsbury," said Mrs Astrakhan, her voice reduced to a stunned whisper.

"Good. I see no one's taken the landlords to task over the loose carpet in my absence. Everyone leaves it for muggins here to sort out."

"But Mr Dewsbury," said Mrs Astrakhan.

"Yes?"

She prodded him cautiously on the arm to check that he was really there.

"You're meant to be dead," she said.

"I know," he said. "It's all very inconvenient."

"But that lad's up in crown court today for *killing* you."

"Today?" said Herbert.

"THEN AFTER MARK and Graham there was Trevor. Or was it Stephen? It didn't end happily with him. Apparently, he's become celibate and he's thinking of joining an order of monks. I've been pretty much celibate myself since then, not for want of trying."

"Hold this," said Clovenhoof and placed a long strand of copper wire in each of Nerys's hands. "I always thought you and Dave... you know."

Nerys shook her head.

"I never really considered him as a sexual being. More like a Labrador, really." She made a noise to herself. "I was never particularly nice to him. I abused his friendship all the time and only realised he was a good friend when I lost him. And Blenda..."

"What about her?"

"I thought some very uncharitable thoughts about her. I imagined bad things happening to her. I've imagined that about a lot of people. My daydreams haven't been nice things. I've not been a very nice person at all, have I?"

"No," agreed Clovenhoof, turning off the switch beside a nearby power socket and plugging in the lamp plug.

"I'm rude to you and Ben," said Nerys. "And my work colleagues. And I've driven away pretty much every friend I've ever had. I don't even love my own family. And I was never the niece Molly deserved to have. I'm a horrible person."

"And do you wish you had been a better person?"

"Of course I do," said Nerys, eyes glistening wetly.

"Are you sorry for all those bad things you've done?"

She nodded, sending a tear running down the side of her nose.

"Then we're ready," said Clovenhoof. "Once you're in Heaven, you've got to find one of the unattended gates and open it up and find a way of pulling me through."

"And how exactly am I meant to do that?"

"I trust you to think of something."

"And how will I get there? Some sort of magic spell?"

"Not quite."

He flicked the switch on the plug socket. Nerys's hands involuntarily convulsed, gripping the lengths of copper wire tighter. Her eyes went wide, her teeth slammed together and a strange rasping sound emerged from her tightened throat. Clovenhoof shuffled out of the way as her legs spasmed and kicked.

He watched her the entire time and, when he judged the job to be done, turned the plug socket off again. Nerys crumpled up like a doll, upper body slumping down over her legs, her arms tucked untidily beneath her.

Clovenhoof moved closer and felt for a pulse.

On the floor, Pitspawn made a wordless mewling sound and pointed weakly at Nerys's body. Clovenhoof frowned at him.

"Of course," he said. "Your lamp. Did you mind me using it? Was it valuable?"

Pitspawn shook his head and began to cry.

"Okay," said Spartacus, leaning against the wall outside the Newsmarket paper shop. "Let's go over it one more time."

He unwrapped the cube of bubblegum, popped it into his mouth and wafted the wrapper in front of his pet hand's forefinger, which seemed to act as the creature's nose.

"We'll both go in the shop. I'll distract the shopkeeper with some chitter-chatter and you grab as many of these as you can. Got it?"

The forefinger waggled happily.

"Good," said Spartacus and threw the wrapper on the floor.

"Pick that up!"

Spartacus looked up to see a dishevelled and harassed-looking man striding up the street.

"I said pick that up," said the man, stopping, red in the face and very much out of breath. The old guy had a scruffy rip in the top of his jumper and had his right forearm tucked under his left armpit as though he had hurt his hand.

"What?" said Spartacus, encircling the hand with his arm, hiding it.

"That wrapper," said the man irritably. "You're littering!"

"*That* wrapper? I didn't drop it."

"Yes, you did."

"No, I didn't."

"I just saw you do it," spat the man, regaining his breath but now red in the face for an entirely different reason.

"No, you didn't," said Spartacus, "cos I didn't drop it. Are you all right, mate?"

"Mate? *Mate?* I am not your mate, sunshine."

"I'm not your sunshine either. I'm Spartacus."

"No, I'm Spartacus," muttered an old codger, stepping past them to get into the paper shop.

"Young man," said the red-faced busybody. "I'm your elder and better and you should show a bit more respect."

"You're a window licker, that's what you are," said Spartacus.

"What?"

"Is your mini bus around here somewhere, waiting to take you back to the home?"

"I have never known such rudeness!"

"Really?" Spartacus felt a thrill of pride. "I'm only warming up to be honest."

"Pick that up now or else," shrieked the man.

"Or else what?" Spartacus turned to shout into the shop "Ow! Don't hurt me mister!"

The weirdo took a step away and scowled at Spartacus.

"I don't have time for this," he said.

"Okay."

"But when I see a police officer... not that there are any on the beat these days... always doing bloody admin they reckon."

With that, the man stomped off in the direction of the town centre, waving frantically at a passing taxi.

Spartacus carefully opened his arm to reveal his pet hand.

"You all right?"

The hand ran an appreciative knuckle against Spartacus's arm in response. Spartacus looked along the path to where the angry man was striding away, talking about "political correctness gone mad" to no one in particular.

"You ought to be glad you don't belong to someone like that," said Spartacus.

The hand pressed itself against him in full agreement.

THE QUEUE MOVED FORWARD a couple of feet and Nerys shuffled forward with it. The ground beneath her feet was like hard packed sand. The sky above was a very pale blue and the summer light that warmed her skin seemed to be coming from nowhere in particular.

The queue crept forward a little more. To her left and right were row upon row of white tents and even though she couldn't see beyond the third or fourth row, the sound of voices, activity and music from both sides suggested that she was walking through a makeshift canvas city. The tents billowed softly, more like bedsheets drying on a clothesline than any practical camping tent. She recalled then an afternoon from her distant childhood, making a den with her sister from an old bed sheet and their mother's clotheshorse.

Nerys laughed at the memory and only then realised that she was meant to be in Pitspawn's bedroom, had been telling Clovenhoof all the regrettable sins of her life, had thoughtlessly held onto those pieces of wire when...

"Oh."

Up ahead, at an unguessable distance was a wall of white stone. It ran up into the sky, storey upon impossible storey until it became one with the pale sky. It ran equally, left and right, over the flat landscape until it was lost in the haze.

An angel came walking down the line. It was obviously an angel. It was wearing a white robe, had a huge pair of wings sprouting from its back and a golden halo of sourceless light surrounded its head. The fact that the angel was carrying a huge grille-fronted stage amplifier in its hands did throw her at first but this oddity seemed to be answered by the arrival of a man.

The big bear of a man wore a long scraggly beard, sunglasses and a red bandana around his forehead. He waved a fat hand at the angel.

"Eh, mate. You're goin' the wrong way with that. You need to take it through there for the Robert Johnson and John Lee Hooker set. Ask Red Dog Campbell where to put it. Do *not* try to rig it up yourself."

"Yes, Mr Roadkill," said the angel and departed down a row of tents.

"Excuse me," said Nerys as the roadie was about to depart.

"What is it, love?"

"Are we...?" She pointed to the wall ahead of them.

"'Bout half a mile from the first gate. Not long to go now. That's if you get in."

"If?"

The roadie shrugged.

"Don't sweat it. Either way you should come to the festival when it kicks off. Jimi and Janis are gonna be doin' a jammin' session with Fats Waller and Thelonius Monk. It's gonna be awesome."

"I'll be sure to check it out."

Roadkill pointed at her and clicked his tongue.

"Diggin' the dress, love," he said and went off in the same direction as the angel.

Nerys looked down at her clothes. She was no longer wearing the top, trousers and cardigan she had been wearing at Pitspawn's but a babydoll dress and black tights. She ran her hands down her sides and at once realised that she had also lost several pounds in weight. She looked at her hands, the now taut and blemish-free skin. It was if...

"Catherine's eighteenth birthday," she whispered.

These were the clothes she had worn to that party all those years ago. She had looked at herself in the mirror just before heading off to the party and thinking – knowing – that this was as good as it was ever going to get. Even though the evening had ended with a most unfortunate threesome, for those few golden hours she had loved and been in love with who she was.

"You don't need to queue, Nerys."

A dark-haired woman in a short white dress and plimsolls took hold of her hand and pulled her from the shuffling ranks.

"Don't I?" said Nerys.

"No," said the woman, giving her a cheeky grin. "I've come to fetch you."

IN THE LABYRINTH of corridors and rooms beneath Birmingham Crown Court, Ben was relieved to see the familiar face of Mr Devereaux, his barrister. Mr Devereaux shook his hand.

"Bearing up, Mr Kitchen?"

Ben nodded glumly.

"Nothing to worry about today," said the barrister. "This isn't the trial. You'll only need to stand there and answer some basic questions. Name, address, et cetera."

"I understand," said Ben.

A young man came up behind Mr Devereaux and, standing on tiptoe, whispered something in the barrister's ear. Ben couldn't hear what was said but saw the man's eyes widen. The barrister was silent for a while.

"Tell me, Mr Kitchen," he said. "Have you heard of the concept of *habeas corpus*?"

THE WOMAN in white led Nerys onward at a brisk pace, overtaking the wide, slow queue of people waiting to get to the gate.

"Are you sure we're allowed to do this?" said Nerys. "I have very specific views about queue jumping."

"I know you do," said the woman in white.

"There was this time at Disneyland Paris... Europeans have no notion of how to queue."

"It's what makes us British," said the woman.

"Exactly," said Nerys and then wondered if the woman was making fun of her.

Up ahead was a tall pair of gates, wrought from a brilliant white material and criss-crossed with intricate filigree.

"The pearly gates?" said Nerys.

"One of twelve," said the woman.

Nearer to the gates, wooden barriers divided the queue into channels that herded and corralled those hoping to get into Heaven. At the gate itself was a checkpoint and a turnstile which seemed thoroughly modern.

The angels at the gate allowed some people through but a significant number were herded away through a covered walkway that disappeared into the city of tents.

"Herbert said the entry requirements were being tightened," said Nerys.

"They've turned it into a bureaucratic nightmare," said a blonde woman stepping in beside them.

Nerys looked at her frowning and then realised why she recognised her.

"You're the vicar of St Michael's."

"Was. Evelyn Steed."

"Nerys," said Nerys. "I'm sorry you died."

"Ditto," said Evelyn.

"I thought you did a lovely job with Briony's funeral. Even if Jeremy did his best to ruin it."

"Quite," said the woman in white.

They had slowed their pace as they approached the gate.

"They're turning people away on the flimsiest of excuses," said Evelyn. "I saw them turn a farmer away for keeping two different breeds of cattle in the same field."

"That's a sin?" said Nerys.

"If you look hard enough, you can find anything you like in scripture. I hear they might turn on people with flat noses next."

"You're having me on."

The woman in white shushed them with a wave of her hand.

"We've got to time this perfectly."

"What are we doing?" whispered Nerys.

"Sneaking you in. We've just got to wait for Joan to distract him."

They were maybe fifty yards from the gates and up ahead, at the checkpoint, a man with what appeared to be a computer tablet in his hand was deep in heated discussion with a teenager wearing heavy plate armour.

"Joan *of Arc*?" said Nerys.

Evelyn nodded.

"You'll like her. Beneath that armour is one hell of a party girl."

A gaggle of hopeful entrants into Heaven had clustered around Joan and Peter, joining their voices to the argument that was going on.

They approached the barriers to the left of the gate. The nearest angel casually looked their way. Nerys smiled automatically.

"He's going to stop us," said Evelyn out of the corner of her mouth

"Just keep walking," said the woman in white.

Suddenly, Joan of Arc pointed off to the right.

"Oh, my goodness!" she shouted. "A rampaging elephant!"

Angels and humans turned to look. The crowd around the gate swelled and shifted. There were shouts and cries as people alternately hurried to get away or get a better view.

Evelyn pushed Nerys under the barrier. The woman in

white hopped over it nimbly. They walked on briskly, past the turned backs of angels and to the open gate.

Behind them, the man with the tablet PC shouted for order. Nerys did not look back. They went through the gate and into a wide city boulevard lined with yellow-flowered acacias and thronging with crowds.

"That went better than expected," said Evelyn with a relieved laugh.

A hand came down heavily on Nerys's shoulder. She gasped.

"So pleased to meet you, Nerys," said Joan of Arc.

"Er, yes. And you," said Nerys. "Nice armour."

Joan gave an ambivalent tilt of her head.

"I'm thinking of changing my image to be honest. It's not very practical. Or fashionable. Whereas you..."

Joan gestured at Nerys's party outfit.

"This old thing?" said Nerys.

"And that basque and stockings thing you wore for the Devil Preacher concert."

"Um," said Nerys, not sure if that kind of attire was suitable conversation material in Heaven.

"Do you think it would suit me?" said Joan.

THE BUSINESS of establishing the most obvious details of Ben's upcoming trial seemed to take an impossibly long time. Across court number one, between defence and prosecution, court clerks and judge, empty words went back and forth, names and dates and addresses and legal formalities. Ben, in the dock, felt a desperate need to be somewhere else and yet did not want to miss a word of what was being said, particularly after what Mr Devereaux had suggested to him less than an hour before. When it did come, Ben was so wrapped up in nerves and distracted thoughts that he almost missed it.

Mr Devereaux got to his feet.

"I do have one matter that I wish to bring to your honour's attention," he said.

The bewigged judge, Judge Arbuthnot, looked meaningfully at the clock.

"Make it quick."

"It regards the body of the alleged deceased," said Mr Devereaux.

"*Alleged* deceased?" said Judge Arbuthnot.

"Quite, your honour. A source has informed me that the city coroner's office appear to have mislaid the body."

Arbuthnot looked to the prosecution and the representatives from the Crown Prosecution Service.

"Is this so?"

"A clerical oversight," said the barrister for the prosecution.

"You knew of this?"

"They assure me that it will turn up."

"Turn up? It's not a TV remote or a pen to be lost down the back of the settee!"

"Indeed, your honour," interjected Mr Devereaux. "A search has been made of the mortuary and the body of Herbert Dewsbury cannot be found."

"I have never heard of such a thing," said Judge Arbuthnot.

"And may I suggest, your honour," said Mr Devereaux lightly, "that without a body there cannot be a murder trial."

THE DISNEYLAND METAPHOR seemed increasingly apt to Nerys. The cobbled streets were spotless. The angelic staff were all smiles and helpful comments. The spires of beautiful white towers rose in the distance like an infinitely more tasteful version of the Magic Kingdom's castle. And yet, like the very worst theme parks, the place was overcrowded, noisy and seemed unreal, ready to crack at the seams.

Joan seemed to read her mind.

"Over ten billion people crammed into a cube not big enough to contain them. We're not at saturation point yet but it's not far off."

"A lot of people sleep rough in the parks," said Evelyn. "Someone started up a free blankets programme but that was stopped by the KHH squads."

"KHH," nodded Nerys. "*Keep Heaven Holy.*"

"All overseen by the Doctrinal Diligence Ministry with the Archangel Michael as its figurehead."

"One moral slip-up and you're out," said Joan.

"I think I've met Michael," said Nerys. "Several times. I suspect he might be a complete git."

"The worst kind. He thinks he's doing the right thing. Now we've got to get you to the next gate so you can let your friend, Clovenhoof, in."

"You want to help me?"

"Of course," said the woman in white.

"But he's the devil."

"And he was an angel," said Evelyn. "*The* angel, in fact."

"Heaven has a problem," said Joan, "and I think we need his help to fix it."

"How far away is the next gate?" said Nerys.

"Five hundred miles along the wall."

"Five hundred miles? Can we... fly?"

"Don't be silly. We'll take the monorail."

"Monorail. Of course," said Nerys. What theme park would be complete without its own monorail?

"The monorail station-" began Evelyn but had the words knocked from her as Joan suddenly pushed the three women through an open doorway and into a gallery hung with illuminated manuscripts.

Nerys looked around.

"What are we...?"

"Shush," said Joan and looked out through the doorway. A quartet of figures, two angelic, two human, all wearing a purple sash strode past.

"KHH squad," said Joan.

"Are they looking for us?" said Nerys.

"If not already, they will be," said Joan. "Particularly when they find out we've got these."

She raised a pair of large keys in her hand.

"Are they St Peter's keys?" said Evelyn.

"Uh-huh. I picked his pocket when his back was turned." She slipped them back beneath her breastplate. "And that's not easy to do while wearing gauntlets, I can tell you."

JUDGE ARBUTHNOT STARED at Mr Devereaux over steepled fingers.

"Are you trying to suggest that Mr Dewsbury, the alleged deceased is not, in fact, dead?"

"I don't think I would be quite so presumptuous," Mr Devereaux replied.

"I think that to make such comments would be upsetting to the deceased's family." The judge raised his eyes to the public gallery, looking for a grieving wife or, at least, some misty-eyed friends but found none. "And it would be time-wasting flimflammery of the highest order," he added.

"I present these facts to you with an open mind, your honour," said Mr Devereaux.

"We are all in agreement are we not that a man has died and that that man is Herbert Dewsbury?"

"Of course we are, your honour," said the barrister for the prosecution.

"Except..." said Mr Devereaux.

Judge Arbuthnot cleared his throat.

"Except what, counsel?"

"There have been some issues with the forensic evidence also."

The judge glared at him.

"Do tell, Mr Devereaux. Speak plainly, omit nothing and, above all, do be quick about it. This is my court, not yours, so stop playing to it."

Mr Devereaux consulted his notes.

"A number of samples taken from the scene of the crime

have gone missing. To be plain and omitting nothing, the West Midlands Police forensic service have no blood, tissue samples or other genetic material belonging to Mr Dewsbury."

"Another clerical error?" said Judge Arbuthnot.

The barrister for the prosecution shrugged.

"They have the bags, beakers or whatever it's stored in," said Mr Devereaux, "but they are empty."

"How is this possible?"

"I do not know, your honour, but may I submit to you that, while the coroner's office and police force put their house in order, it would be illegal to keep a man imprisoned for a crime that may never have happened."

HEAVEN'S MONORAIL WAS SILENT, fast, efficient and clean and bore no relation to any British form of public transport Nerys had ridden on. It was however crowded and most people had to travel standing up, making it very much like the best of British transportation. Despite making stops every few minutes, it had apparently covered most of the five hundred miles to the next gate in less than half an hour.

The elevated monorail presented an excellent viewpoint of the Celestial City. Leaning over a seated couple who were conversing in what appeared to be Latin, Nerys watched the vast cityscape roll past. She was no expert on architecture but Nerys could see that the city was an unplanned mish-mash of building styles. Red brick apartment blocks and mansions of stone stood beside long wooden halls and rude earthen huts. Among the stout temples and soaring cathedrals were white wooden churches and squat stone chapels. Domes, ziggurats, minarets, towers and spires, any of which might have ranked among the wonders of the mortal world, were commonplace.

"It's not as green as I'd expected," said Nerys. "Those Jehovah's Witness leaflets painted a false picture."

"There's no room for green spaces," said Evelyn.

Joan consulted the route map on the carriage wall for the umpteenth time.

"Speaking of which," she said, tapping the stop labelled 'Blessed Animal Sanctuary', "we can get off at the next stop."

"About time," said Evelyn, stretching as much as she could in the crowded carriage.

"It might not be soon enough," said the woman in white.

Nerys followed her gaze along the carriage to the furthest door. Nerys saw the purple sashes.

"But are they specifically looking for us?" said Nerys. "Let's just act casual. Wing it."

"It's not as simple as that," said Joan.

The *Keep Heaven Holy* squad were working their way down the carriage, speaking to every person in turn.

"What is everyone showing them?" said Nerys. "Were we meant to buy tickets?"

Evelyn produced a laminated card from her pocket. Nerys peered at it. It had Evelyn's photo on it, a date of death and a complicated paragraph of words that might have been an address.

"Residency permit?" read Nerys.

Joan and the woman in white had cards also.

The KHH squad were coming closer. By unspoken agreement, the four women began moving along the carriage, away from the sashes. Nerys apologised repeatedly as she squeeze through the press of bodies.

"So Heaven is a totalitarian state," she said to Joan.

"Always was," said Joan. "Just used to be a benign one."

"And God allows this?"

"Who knows? Access to the Empyrium is restricted."

"The what?"

"Empyrium. The seat of the Holy Throne. Where God lives."

They had reached the end of the carriage with no way to progress further. They positioned themselves at the door with the other three women arranged in front of Nerys.

"I thought God was everywhere," said Nerys.

"Yes, he is. And he's in the Empyrium."

Evelyn looked ahead along the track.

"Not far to the station," she said.

"Too far," whispered Joan and then gave a cheesy grin to the sash-wearing man who was now standing before her.

"Permits," he said flatly.

"This is mine," said Joan loudly and thrust her card in his face.

The man gave it a cursory glance and tried to pass it back to her.

"Do you think that picture does me justice?" said Joan.

"Your card, madam."

The man pressed the card against Joan's breastplate and let it drop. He clicked his fingers for the others to pass theirs over.

The three other KHH sashes had finished with the other passengers and now approached the women. The woman in white made a big show of searching herself for her permit.

"I've only been here three weeks," she said, grinning. "I'm sure it's here somewhere."

"For your sake it had better be," said an angel.

Three weeks, thought Nerys.

"We're coming into the station," said Evelyn.

"Permits," said the angelic sash and held out his hand to receive them.

"Here it is," said the woman in white and held it up for inspection.

"Got mine here," said Evelyn and waved it vaguely at them while she looked out of the window.

Nerys could feel the monorail slowing.

"Your card, madam," said a sash and, without looking, Nerys knew he was talking to her.

"This is hers," said the woman in white, passing her own card over again.

"No," said the man. "This is yours."

There was a platform beside the door now but the monorail had not yet stopped.

"Do you want to see my card again?" said Joan and thrust it into one of the angel's faces.

"Madam," he said, looking past Joan at Nerys, his sandy hair ablaze with light, "your permit. Now."

"I'm over six hundred years old but I think I can still pass for nineteen, don't you think?" said Joan.

The angel stretched an arm forward and gently but implacably swept Joan aside.

"Hey," she said, "you can't push me around."

As the monorail came to a halt, the angel gave the French martyr a contemptuous look.

"Why not?"

"Because," said Joan and rammed a gauntleted fist into his nose, flattening it against his face.

The automatic doors shushed open and Nerys leapt out onto the platform, followed rapidly by her three friends and, shortly after, by four KHH sashes, one of them clutching his smashed nose.

"Stop!" yelled one of the sashes.

"No!" yelled Joan and the four women ran.

"No, your honour," said Mr Devereaux. "I am not offering an opinion on whether Mr Dewsbury is dead or alive. What I can say is that the Crown Prosecution Service holds no evidence to suggest that any corpse was found in Mr Kitchen's flat."

"With your permission, your honour," said the prosecution barrister, "there is the photographic evidence. The scenes of crime officers took many photographs of the body."

"And have these photographs been mislaid as well?" asked Judge Arbuthnot, a little giddily.

"No," the prosecution assured him. "I even have copies here with me."

"He does indeed, your honour," said Mr Devereaux. "Photographs of what appears to be a human corpse."

"Appears?" said Judge Arbuthnot, his voice shooting up halfway through the word.

"Mr Kitchen is a gifted model maker. My learned friend's photographs will no doubt feature the paints and model-making materials that Mr Kitchen has throughout his flat."

"Is this so?" said Judge Arbuthnot and Ben, who had been watching the proceedings with an anxious detachment, realised that this question was addressed to him. "Was the corpse in the trunk a model?"

"Jeremy told me to make it as a model for Pitspawn," Ben heard himself say.

"Please, your honour," said the prosecution barrister. "Mr Kitchen readily confessed to the murder. Without prompting."

"As might any man in Mr Kitchen's fragile state of mind," said Mr Devereaux.

"Fragile?" said Ben.

AT THE BASE of the stairs leading down from the monorail station was a narrow street, a row of closed up buildings and a wrought iron gate leading into a park area. Nerys grasped the gate, pushed and then saw the padlock and chain.

"They're coming!" yelled the woman in white.

Nerys read the wooden sign pinned to the gate.

"Sanctuary for Blessed Animals. Closed for Redevelopment."

"Duck!" shouted Joan.

Nerys turned as one of an angel with a broken nose came

swooping down on an eight-foot long wingspan. Joan stepped forward and swung her broadsword upward, neatly clipping the angel's wing and sending it slamming face first into the wall next to the gate. She turned and, continuing the same stroke, brought the sword down on the chain securing the gate. The chain shattered.

They barrelled through into the park and ran on towards the colossal wall that marked the city limits. As she ran, Nerys realised that the body she had possessed as an eighteen year old, the body she now possessed, was far fitter than the one she had left behind on the floor of Pitspawn's room. Sprinting through the parkland, past animal enclosures and pastures, was an almost enjoyable experience.

An angel in a purple sash landed with a thump on the path ahead of them. He pointed a silver spear towards the women.

"Through here," said Joan, vaulted a fence to the side, sliced through a wire mesh fence and ran on through a herd of pure white horses. She slapped one on its hindquarters with the flat of her blade to scatter the herd.

"Joan's enjoying herself," said Nerys as they followed in the wake of the now stampeding horses.

"I don't think she gets out much," replied Evelyn.

"Over there," said the woman in white, pointing.

Nerys looked.

"Are those lions and lambs lying down together?" she said.

"Mmmm," nodded the woman in white. "Do the lambs look nervous to you?"

"Through here," cried Joan.

Nerys glimpsed a larger group of purple sashes off to the left but was distracted by events over to the right where the stampeding horses had crashed into an enclosure for large mammals. A great animal cry went up.

"We're not exactly being subtle," said Nerys.

"Can't be helped," cried Joan, skirting a deep fishpond and joining a path that ran towards the city wall.

A man in a brown robe with what appeared to be a giant grizzled wolf on a lead was hurrying towards them along the path. Nerys couldn't be sure if he was hurrying to intercept them or hurrying because the snarling beast on the lead was pretty much dragging him along.

"Twespassers! Vandals!" he cried. "The sanctuawy is closed!"

The shadow of an angel passed over Nerys.

Joan ducked sideways and leaped into another enclosure. Nerys leaped after her. Something squeaked and slipped beneath her feet.

"Not the wabbits!" cried the robed man. "Have you no wegard for your fellow cweatures?"

"Sorry, Frank!" called Joan, kicking aside a fat white ball of fur.

They scrambled up an embankment at the far side of the rabbit enclosure. In the distance, the lisping curator was berating someone else. There was a cry of "mind the whinocewos" and then an almighty bellow of animal, human and angel voices.

Evelyn pointed.

"There's the gate."

It was a gate very much like the one by which Nerys had entered Heaven albeit closed and unattended.

They put in a final sprint to the gate and, with the sounds of animal confusion fading behind them, it seemed that they had left their pursuers far behind. But then, emerging from behind a row of trees, came a band of half a dozen KHH sashes, and at their head was a man Nerys had glimpsed less than an hour before, although he hadn't been wearing such an expression of fury before.

Joan skidded to a stop.

"St Peter," said the woman in white, almost running into the back of her.

"Do you think he wants his keys back?" said Evelyn.

"Mr Kitchen has had a traumatic year," explained Mr Devereaux, "and has had a number of stressful encounters with the law."

Ben felt the urge to ask his barrister what on earth he was on about but, since the man was apparently working for his benefit, he did his best to nod in mournful agreement.

Mr Devereux picked up a sheet of paper and read.

"He was briefly detained following a police raid on a rock concert at the beginning of the year and although no charges were brought, your honour, I believe the incident had a profound effect on him. Only a few months later, he was captured and tortured by a known bank robber in a case of mistaken identity. The police arrested him yet again and, once again, he was released without charge."

"Are you suggesting Mr Kitchen is being persecuted by the police?" said Judge Arbuthnot.

"I'm painting a picture, your honour." Mr Devereaux consulted his notes. "Then there was the nasty business of the house fire."

"Is this relevant?"

"Mere scenery, your honour. Mr Kitchen has obviously been under a lot of pressure and has been caused a great deal of embarrassment of late. Shall I mention the woman's head?"

"Woman's head?"

"Found in his wardrobe by the police. Not a real head of course, your honour. It was part of a – how shall I put it? – a mannequin. A marital aid, if you will."

Now genuinely traumatised and mortified by embarrassment, Ben looked away. He began to think that spending twenty-five years in prison might be preferable to hearing a crown court judge discuss the dismembered sex doll in his wardrobe.

He looked aside at the public gallery, maybe a dozen faces, all entranced by the exchange going on between barrister and judge. At least, he noticed, none of his family were among them. Although he was surprised and mildly disappointed to see neither Nerys nor Clovenhoof among them.

He froze. Not all of the faces were turned to the barrister and judge. One particular pair of eyes was fixed on him, brows screwed up in an expression of malevolent hatred.

Herbert Dewsbury silently shook an angry fist at him.

"Herbert?" said Ben.

Herbert twitched.

"Mr Kitchen," said Judge Arbuthnot sternly. "I must ask that you remain silent unless questioned."

Ben pointed uncertainly at Herbert.

"Can *you* see him?" he asked the judge uncertainly.

"Mr Kitchen!"

Ben looked to the gallery.

"What are you doing here, Herbert?"

"Mr Kitchen! I will have you removed from the court!"

"Take him away!" blurted Herbert. "Lock him up! Send him to the gallows!"

"Order!" cried Judge Arbuthnot.

"He did it!" replied Herbert, pointing furiously. "He killed me!"

"Order!"

"I was there! I saw everything!"

The judge pounded his table with his fist.

"What is going on here?" he demanded.

Mr Devereaux paused a moment, his lips frozen on the cusp of forming words.

"Your honour," he said, finding his tongue, "I believe it is the murder victim."

St Peter shook his head in patronising disapproval.

"I have no idea what you hope to achieve, Joan," he said. "But it stops here."

Joan passed her sword from one hand to other and then back again.

"Just give up," said Peter. "You are one woman against all of us."

"Ahem," said Evelyn loudly.

"Sorry," said Peter. "You have your trendy vicar, tennis girl and – what?" He waved a hand at Nerys. "A go-go dancer?"

Nerys was in a mind to object to the accusation but was distracted by the realisation that the woman in white was indeed dressed for a tennis match, albeit one from fifty odd years ago. It stirred some vague memory within her but she couldn't put her finger on it.

"I'm almost glad you've chosen to rebel in this way," Peter said to Joan. "You are nothing but a rabble-rouser. A troublemaker. This act of treason gives me the justification to have you removed from the Celestial City."

"You do not rule this city," said Joan between clenched teeth.

Peter raised his eyebrows.

"You give me back my keys and we'll see about that."

Joan tightened her grip on her blade and then abruptly let it drop.

"Oh, my goodness!" she shouted, pointing. "A rampaging elephant!"

"Please," said Peter wearily. "Am I going to fall f-"

His words were lost in a thunder of feet and tusks as a blessed grey mountain of African elephant led a stampeding menagerie through the *Keep Heaven Holy* squad.

"Now!" yelled Joan and led the women forward, through the dust clouds and lumbering tail end of the stampede.

She plucked the keys from beneath her breastplate and

tossed them to Nerys. Nerys caught them and ran forward. Joan spun on her toes to defend the rear.

"Oh, my poor cweatures!" came a plaintive cry from behind. "What have they done? Peter, are you all wight?"

There was a growl and the sound of violence.

"Bwother wolf! No! Leave! Put him down!"

PITSPAWN HAD PUSHED himself into the corner of his room, wedging himself into the corner between two walls.

His conscious mind had resurfaced from the shock of discovering that his resurrection spell had worked and now fervently wished it could sink back into the depths of delirium. Not only had he successfully brought someone back from the dead but he was now in a room with a man who claimed to be Satan and the woman he had murdered.

After killing the woman, Clovenhoof / Satan (whoever he was) had become deeply bored. He spent several minutes rearranging the corpse. First of all, he laid it out, arms crossed over the chest. Bored with that, he stuck one of the woman's fingers up her own nose and then two. This amused him only momentarily.

He then sat her upright and tried to compose her into the pose of Rodin's *Thinker*. The floppy corpse was quite uncooperative in this endeavour and he settled for sitting her on the bed next to him and holding her head upright with his hand.

"Pitspawn?" he said.

"Nng," said Pitspawn.

"Do you think a spot of ventriloquism would be vulgar and tasteless?"

Pitspawn couldn't find an appropriate response. What he wanted was for the dead woman to vanish, taking the insane Clovenhoof with him.

As though in response to this wish, a mote of light appeared in the centre of the room and expanded rapidly to become a large glittering tear in mid air. Through the soft-edged portal, Pitspawn could see a bright and beautiful sky, white stonework and a trio of women gazing through at him.

"Is that Heaven?" he managed to say.

"About time," said Clovenhoof, cast the corpse aside and leapt head first through the hole.

The portal shimmered and then vanished in a flash of light. Pitspawn blinked. Clovenhoof was gone and, he noticed, the woman's body too.

Pitspawn whimpered, struggling to control his own body, thrust his hands together and tried to remember the first words of the Lord's Prayer.

CLOVENHOOF LANDED on something soft and not at all unpleasant. Coughing away the dust that seemed to be enveloping him, he put his hands down to raise himself up. He encountered more soft pleasantness.

"Excuse me," said the young woman in white beneath him.

"Oh, hello!" he said, removing his hands and getting to his knees. "Fancy seeing you here."

Nerys hooked a hand under his elbow and lifted him up.

"You know her?" she said.

The woman in tennis whites gave the pair of them an admonishing look.

"He tried to sell me on E-Bay."

Nerys stared.

"Molly?"

Molly rolled her eyes and smiled.

"Took you long enough," she said.

12

IN WHICH CLOVENHOOF SETTLES AN OLD SCORE, MEETS HIS MAKER AND GREETS HIS NEW NEIGHBOUR

C lovenhoof dusted himself down and raised his eyes to the city in front of him.

"Bloody hell," he said. "This place has changed. I remember when it was nothing but gleaming spires of silver and glass and a hundred million idiots singing His eternal praises. What's all this?" He waved his hand to take in the parkland, the grass, the looping monorail, the hodgepodge of buildings. "It's bloody people, isn't it? Cluttering things up. Making things... messy."

"Whereas you are well known for bringing stability and order," said the French girl in knight's armour.

"It's all I've ever wanted," said Clovenhoof with such profound sincerity that he wasn't even sure himself whether he was being sarcastic or not.

"Reverend!" he shouted gleefully, recognising the blonde woman.

"Still think you've got no friends who care about you?" smiled Evelyn.

Clovenhoof looked to Nerys. Nerys and Molly were locked in a tight embrace, Nerys's fingers clutching at Molly's back, tears in her eyes. Clovenhoof wondered if he was in for an unexpected display of incestuous girl-on-girl action but sadly doubted it.

"No, I have friends," he said and then turned to face the woozy and staggering assemblage of angels and blessed dead who, it appeared, had just been trampled by a herd of wild beasts. "Oh. And enemies."

"Where's St Peter?" said Joan. "He's gone."

"Peter?" said Clovenhoof. "Gone? Fled like a coward? Abandoning his friends? Really? That's not like him at all. No, wait. Silly me. It is."

The angels and humans with purple sashes rearranged their robes and readied their weapons. Clovenhoof grinned. His infernal power, his one-time angelic power, wasn't a form of energy. It was something that formed his very being, gave him reality and presence. He felt it returning to him now, making him feel larger and stronger than he had felt in ages.

"Once an angel, always an angel," he whispered to himself.

He looked down at himself, his eyes particularly dwelling on the brown corduroy trousers that, not so very long ago, seemed like a wise fashion decision. He could click his fingers and throw off this body and becoming the angel Lucifer, the Bringer of Light, once more. He could magic away these clothes and becoming a towering goat-demon, all hairy balls and horns. Neither seemed quite right...

Clovenhoof clicked his fingers.

"Better," he said and strode to meet Heaven's forces in red velvet trousers, cravat and a quilted smoking jacket.

A sash-wearing man came running at him with a spear.

"Bekele," he greeted the man. "Liked to poke children with sharp sticks."

Clovenhoof stuck out an arm, which caught the man under his neck, sending him cartwheeling feet first through the air.

Another man tried to catch him unawares with a sword.

"Ernest," said Clovenhoof, caught the blade between the palms of his hands, twisted it out of Ernest's grip and knocked him out with the sword hilt. "My! Some very inventive sexual fantasies involving sandpaper and superglue. Dirty boy."

An angel with what appeared to be a broken nose and a shredded wing, came at Clovenhoof.

"Look in my heart, demon. You'll find only love there."

"I know," said Clovenhoof. "You and Feruzial. Up in the clerestory when you think no one's looking."

The angel looked sheepishly aside at one of the other angels. Clovenhoof used the distraction to plant a powerful punch on his chin and lay him out on the ground.

"Jian! Paulo! Belaphron!" cried Clovenhoof and leapt into the group of men and angels, lashing out joyously with fists, hooves, horns and an endless list of individuals' transgressions.

∼

"I WAS AN AWFUL NIECE," said Nerys, rubbing her eyes.

"Is that so?" said Molly. "How many nieces do I have?"

Nerys thought.

"Four."

"And how many of them cooked for me, cleaned for me, escorted me to every bloody whist drive I wanted to go to?"

"Yeah, but..."

She turned away, to see Clovenhoof emerge, beaming like a happy fool, from amongst the still and scattered bodies of the *Keep Heaven Holy* squad.

"I don't think I did any of it out of love," said Nerys.

Molly took hold of Nerys's hand.

"What we do and what we intend to do. Families." She squeezed Nerys's hand. "It's all relative."

"Okay, ladies," said Clovenhoof, clapping his hands together. "I've come here for some answers. Who's going to help me get them?"

"It's Michael's committee that kicked you out of Hell," said Joan.

"And started all this *Keep Heaven Holy* nonsense," said Evelyn.

"That was Herbert's idea," said Nerys.

"He's just a pawn," said Clovenhoof. "I always thought Michael was a brainless doofus but I guess he's the game player here."

"The power behind the Throne," said Joan and then frowned. "Michael has been very cagey about talking about the Throne of late."

"The Throne?" said Nerys.

"Where God sits," said Evelyn.

"I thought you said he was in the Imperial something or other."

"The Empyrium," said Joan. "On the Throne in the Throne Room in the Empyrium."

"Yes," said Clovenhoof grimly. "The Other Guy and I haven't spoken in ages. Maybe it's time for a little chat."

"So where's this Empyrium place?" asked Nerys.

Clovenhoof shook his head at her.

"Nerys, God isn't in just one place. God is everywhere."

He drew a rectangle in the air with his finger and a doorway appeared.

LAYERS OF CURTAINS in the richest of colours were draped from the hands of gilded cherubs. Chandeliers were suspended from a frescoed ceiling and the walls were lined with pleated silk in jewel colours.

"I don't want to be rude," said Nerys, "but I always imagined God would have better taste than this."

"It's like the castle of Gilles de Rais," said Joan.

"Reminds me of Brighton Pavilion," said Molly.

"Oh, we went on that coach trip for the day, didn't we?" said Nerys.

"Far too much queuing," said Molly. "And those seagulls!"

Clovenhoof growled in his throat.

"Do you think the Empyrium really looks like this?" he said irritably. "Do you think this is actually a physical place? That we are actually walking along a corridor?"

"Er, we're not?" said Nerys.

"Humans," he said. "I could learn to hate them all over again."

"Now, now," said Evelyn, patting his arm. "You're doing really well. Don't spoil it now."

They passed through a gothic archway, hung with swags of heavy, tasselled damask, and into a large hall. The walls were hung with panels of crushed velvet with quilted gold accents. It was uncannily like Clovenhoof's outfit.

The Archangel Michael stood in the centre of the room, his Italian suits now sacrificed for the more traditional robes, angelic wings and golden lance. Clovenhoof involuntarily touched his side, remembering what the tip of that lance had felt like, what it had done to him.

Behind Michael, hovering in tiered rows that stretched up to the high ceiling, were rank upon rank of angels.

"Oh, it's Michael," said Nerys.

"Have I met him?" said Molly.

"Possibly. He's Jeremy's I'm-definitely-not-gay friend."

"He's got lovely hair."

"You ought to see his nails. Keeps them perfectly tri-"

"Not another step," said Michael loudly, cutting across the women.

Clovenhoof clip-clopped forward an inch on the marble floor.

"Or what?" he said.

Michael pouted at him.

"Be serious for once, Jeremy."

Clovenhoof wrinkled his nose.

"You don't want me to be serious, Michael. Me serious is me angry. Very very angry."

Michael lifted himself up on his tiptoes and floated up into the air.

"I don't care how angry you are," he said. "I don't care about your petty grievances. You should not be here."

"You had me fired."

"You got yourself fired."

"You organised it, arranged it. You teased me out like a winkle from its shell and cast me down to Earth. And then – and *then* – you tried to make me think I was human."

Michael shrugged.

"So? No one cares what happens to you. You are the fallen one, the Angel of the Bottomless Pit. You are the Great Dragon. I threw you down once and I will throw you down again."

"*That* was an unfair fight," said Clovenhoof, wagging a finger at the angel.

"*It wasn't a fair fight*," said Michael in a high-pitched mocking voice. "*I had the sun in my eyes. I couldn't see. You had all the best soldiers.*" Michael shook his head and his halo shone fiercely. "Change the record, Jeremy. We fought. I won. You lost."

"Come down here and say that!" shouted Clovenhoof.

Michael's lips curled in the faintest of smiles. He looked round at the angelic host about him to share his amusement.

"You honestly want me to do that?" he said to Clovenhoof.

"Absolutely."

"You want to be beaten and humiliated again?"

"I won't."

Michael slowly drifted down.

"I was going to let you return to Earth and your sordid little suburban life but you would rather take the pain, be thrown down into another pit of torment, one which you will never leave?"

"Bring it on," said Clovenhoof.

Michael's bare feet touched the ground and he walked slowly towards Clovenhoof, like a big cat approaching its wounded prey. He stopped a few feet from Clovenhoof.

"Last chance," he said with a triumphant twinkle in his eye. "Do you really want to do this?"

"Yes," said Clovenhoof and then, "Oh, just one question, Michael."

"Yes?"

Clovenhoof smiled.

"Do you honestly think that was the *sun* in my eyes?"

Michael frowned and Clovenhoof head-butted him in the face. Michael staggered back.

"The light that blinded me," said Clovenhoof as he advanced on Michael. "That brilliance. That glory. You think that was the sun?"

Michael swung at him awkwardly with his lance. Clovenhoof ducked and stamped a hoof down on Michael's foot. Michael fell to one knee.

"You think that *you* threw me down?" said Clovenhoof. "You conceited, idiotic fool."

He snatched Michael's lance from his hand. Michael resisted but Clovenhoof kneed him in the mouth and sent him flying back. Clovenhoof snapped the lance in two and threw the pieces aside.

"There was only one power that could defeat me," he

said, addressing the host above him. "And I can't see that power here."

Michael was crawling on the floor, apparently trying to pick up some of his teeth. Clovenhoof twisted a handful of cloth at the neck of his gown and yanked him upwards. Michael tried to say something but it was weak and muffled by blood and the lack of teeth. Clovenhoof kicked him viciously in the ribs to silence him.

"My friends and I are going to see the Throne," he told the host. "If anyone has an issue with that, I'm right here."

The angels stayed exactly where they were. In fact, Clovenhoof thought that some nearer the ground were slowly distancing themselves from him.

"Good."

He looked back at Nerys, Evelyn, Molly and Joan.

"Come on, girls."

He led the way, dragging Michael face down with him and leaving a fine trail of blood and teeth in his wake. They passed beneath the angels, through a tall archway and into a grand high-vaulted corridor with double doors at its end.

"It's like that bit in Wizard of Oz," said Molly as they walked.

"Where they go to see the wizard in the Emerald City," agreed Nerys.

"Yeah," said Evelyn, "but if this wizard turns out to be a man behind a curtain, I'm going to be seriously put out."

"Joan can be the tin man," said Molly.

"I have no idea what you're on about," said Joan.

"Jeremy can be the cowardly lion," said Nerys.

"Cowardly?" said Molly.

"Well, he's hairy enough."

"The brainless scarecrow," said Evelyn, pointing at the limp form of Michael.

"Good call."

"That just leaves Dorothy," said Molly.

"Well, I'm the youngest," said Nerys.

"I played Dorothy in a school play," argued Evelyn.

"What about me?" said Molly.

"You can be my Aunty Em," said Nerys.

"Excuse me!" said Molly, pretending to be offended.

Clovenhoof stopped at the double doors and turned.

"Ladies," he said sternly. "We are about to go through those doors and step into the presence of the Almighty Himself. Your mortal eyes are about to look upon His heavenly Throne, the most spectacular and transforming sight in all creation." He eyed each of them in turn. "I somehow think it inappropriate for you to spend these last few moments arguing over which of you is most like Judy Garland!"

"Sorry, Jeremy," said Nerys.

"Sorry," said Molly.

"Point taken," said Evelyn contritely.

"Right," said Jeremy, placing his hands on the doors. "Now. Behold!"

He gave a push and flung the great doors wide open.

The room beyond was an enormous white cube of a hall. At the far end, on top of a dais with more than a hundred steps, was a stone seat with a back as high and as intricately carved as any church spire. And sat on the Throne was... no one.

"Oh shit," said Clovenhoof.

"Wow!" said Nerys in dutiful appreciation. "And, um, where is God?"

"This is wrong," said Clovenhoof and ran forward, still dragging Michael along with him. He abandoned the battered archangel at the bottom of the steps and scrambled up as fast as he could.

"Is everything all right?" Nerys shouted after him.

"Very very wrong," Clovenhoof muttered to himself as he climbed.

At the top there was someone waiting for him, leaning against the arm of the Throne.

"Weren't expecting this, were you?" said St Peter.

For some reason, the divine apostle's robes were ripped along the hem and there were what appeared to be bloody teeth marks in his lower leg.

"What have you done?" said Clovenhoof.

"Not me," said Peter. "It's what He's done."

Clovenhoof stared at him blankly.

"God has gone," said Peter. "He is no longer here."

"But... but why?"

Peter shrugged.

"You want me to second-guess the motives of the ineffable Lord? What can I say? He moves in mysterious ways and He moved out something like three hundred years ago."

Clovenhoof stepped back, stunned.

"So, who's been running Heaven in all that time?"

Peter tapped his own chest modestly.

"Who do you think?"

"I thought Michael..." He gestured down the steps to

where the archangel was slowly picking himself up off the floor. The four women stood beside him, gazing upward at the Throne.

"Michael?" Peter scoffed. "He's a complete doofus. Are you familiar with Dante's *Paradiso*?"

"Italian poetry?" sneered Clovenhoof. "Can't get enough of it."

"Dante Alighieri compared Heaven to a rose, with the faithful dead as the petals and the angels as bees, buzzing back and forth, labouring out of love for Him. Poetic twaddle but he was right about one thing. They are like bees and, with no queen bee in the hive, they are nothing but powerful morons. They are very good at following orders even when they don't realise that's what they're doing."

"I can't believe this has happened."

"Believe it," said Peter, standing upright and pacing around the Throne. "We've struggled on for three hundred years, keeping His absence a secret to avoid panic. The dead keep coming and Heaven stays the same. I recognised the population problem decades before Joan of Arc publicly raised it. Joan wasn't in full possession of the facts. Without Him, without a divine contradiction of divine scripture, Heaven cannot expand. We needed a solution and now we're putting it into place."

"Randomly casting out Heaven's residents into Limbo?"

"Wrong," said Peter, mildly annoyed. "Wrong on two counts. Firstly, our *Keep Heaven Holy* programme is not random. It targets those who fail to demonstrate the moral rectitude that Heaven demands. This Celestial City will be the abode of the best, the most righteous, the most morally upstanding."

"As decided by you?"

"As dictated by scripture, Lucifer. You're also wrong about sending them out into Limbo. Those camps of asylum seekers outside our gates will not be tolerated for long. Those people will be relocated soon enough."

"To Hell," Clovenhoof nodded. "Pack 'em in, stack 'em high."

"Hell is more... amorphous than Heaven," Peter agreed. "Its dimensions are more malleable. We'll make room."

"You'll damn millions, billions even, just to get a bit more breathing space, a little more *lebensraum*."

"Lucifer, please. Don't cheapen this conversation with tacky metaphor. Hell does not have to be a terrible place. We can provide the displaced with a tolerable, almost pleasant existence. It will require significant reorganisation but it can be done."

"And that's why you wanted me out of the way," said Clovenhoof.

Peter made a seesaw motion with his hand.

"Oh, partly. The main reason – and it is unfortunate that it's come to pass – is that I wanted to avoid this exact situation."

Clovenhoof gave him a puzzled look. Peter sighed.

"An empty Throne. And you."

"Oh, I see. You think I might try to take it for myself. As job moves go, it's a natural progression."

Clovenhoof took a step towards the throne. Peter moved sideways to stand in the way.

"I had hoped that being on Earth you would be out of the way, eternally oblivious to the situation," said Peter, tutting at himself.

"Yeah, that's not really worked out for you, has it?"

"It just means I have to put other plans into motion a little sooner than expected." With that, Peter sat down on the Throne.

Clovenhoof did a double take.

"What are you doing?"

Peter ran his hands along the arms of the Throne, trying it on for size.

"I had planned to steer the committee toward appointing me to this position but, since you've forced my hand..."

"You're taking over the Throne?" said Clovenhoof, astounded.

"I've had centuries of experience standing in for Him."

"So, you are promoting yourself to – what? – God?"

Peter smiled.

"Blessed am I, Simon son of Jonah. I am Peter, the rock on which the church is built and the powers of Hell will not prevail against me. To me is given the keys to the kingdom of Heaven and whatever I bind in Heaven shall be bound on Earth and whatever I loose in Heaven shall be loosed on Earth."

Clovenhoof recognised the mangled quotation.

"You think that just because you were pope, that makes you the ideal candidate for the job?"

"It is a matter of dogma that anything a pope says *ex cathedra*, from the Throne, is true."

"I don't think it meant *this* Throne."

"It does now," said Peter and a crackle of light ran along the throne where he touched it and a distant boom echoed around the high ceiling. Peter giggled and stared at his hands, the power they now contained. He caught Clovenhoof's eye.

"Sorry," he said and coughed. "Should a bit more solemn. Dignified."

"Regal," said Clovenhoof derisively.

"Indeed." Peter placed his arms firmly back on the Throne. "And now, Lucifer, you will bow before me."

"I will not," said Clovenhoof.

"Bow before me," Peter commanded and, as the light fizzed through the stone and the room echoed to deep rumblings, Clovenhoof found his knees and waist bending of their own accord.

He fought it and, with a monumental effort, was able to hold it in check.

"You rebelled aeons ago for refusing to bow down to man, His greatest creation."

"He was making a mistake," spat Clovenhoof through clenched teeth as he battled against the forces bearing down on him. "You're just proving me fucking right."

"He should have forced you to comply. Now, bow!"

It was as though a great weight had slammed down on him. Clovenhoof dropped to his hands and knees, coughing.

"He wanted me to rebel," gasped Clovenhoof.

"Really?"

"No. He wanted me to have the freedom to rebel. He wanted to see what I would do. He wanted to see the choices I would make."

He coughed again and, as a thought struck him, the cough became a laugh.

"Damn it. The fool."

"Who?" said Peter. "Me?"

"You. Me. Him. A tarot card."

"What are you babbling about?"

"The fool with the sun at his back and the rose in his hand. The rose of Heaven."

"You really aren't making sense."

"You told me God had gone and I almost believed you."

"Oh, but He has."

"Why?" Clovenhoof looked up. "Because you can't see Him?" He found himself to be grinning. "I think He would have liked your *Keep Heaven Holy* idea. What was it? To ensure Heaven is only for those who demonstrate *moral rectitude*? And how would God test that if He's looking over your shoulder all the time? He had to give you the freedom to do wrong, to see if you are truly worthy of Heaven. *That's* what He's been doing for the last three hundred years!"

"But he's not here!" insisted Peter.

"Do you think He would let Heaven slip from His hand for a single moment? Do you think He ever left?"

"You lie, Lucifer!"

"Maybe. But I tell you what, you were right to fear this situation. The Throne. And me."

"Why?"

"Because even if he had gone away there would be one thing that would bring him racing back, one thing he would not be willing to tolerate."

Clovenhoof leant forward and placed a hand on the Throne.

"He wouldn't like that at all," said Clovenhoof.

Light exploded from behind the Throne, a supernova that blasted the walls and ceiling and came rebounding back in amplified glory. A long way off, Clovenhoof could hear Nerys swearing.

The light of Heavenly wonder washed over the Throne and cascaded down the stairs. The Throne itself began to glow.

"Clue's in the name," said Clovenhoof, finding he was able to get to his feet once more. "Bringer of light, that's me."

The Throne had turned a radiant, retina-burning white. Peter, transfixed, seemingly unable to lift his arms or body, stared in horror at the seat he had taken and wailed. Screaming, burning, he sank into the enveloping light. Clovenhoof backed to the edge of the dais, forced to turn his head away.

Down below him, Michael attempted to hide his eyes from the glare.

Above Peter's screams and the roar of God's splendour, Clovenhoof just managed to hear Michael plead.

"Lord, I was only doing what I thought was right."

"Doofus," grinned Clovenhoof and gave the pitiful archangel the finger.

On the blazing Throne, Peter's cry reached a crescendo in both pitch and volume and was then abruptly halted by an all-engulfing thunderclap, an explosion that pitched Clovenhoof off the dais completely and sent him rolling down the steps, bouncing and cursing all the way.

He landed heavily on his side and stumbled to his feet, cradling a bashed elbow.

Michael had vanished. So had Nerys, Molly, Evelyn and Joan. Atop the dais, the Throne was buried at the heart of a light greater than that of the sun.

"Good to see you again," Clovenhoof called out, shielding his eyes with his hand. "You're looking well. You've lost weight?"

The light shimmered and span. Ineffable truths swam in its depths.

"Humans, eh?" said Clovenhoof. "I told you there'd be trouble. Look what it's led to."

He tried to discern answers in the blinding radiance.

"So, this is the bit where you put everything right," he went on. "*Deus Ex Machina.* Clue's in the name and all that."

He waited for a response.

"Do I have to click my heels together three times and say, 'There's no place like home'?" he suggested.

Something boiled and flared, a new brightness: a question.

PC MATTHEW PEARSON put the polystyrene cup of vending machine coffee down on the table in front of Mr Dewsbury and sat down opposite him.

"Well, you'll be pleased to hear that there won't be any charges brought against you, sir?"

"Against me?"

"Perverting the course of justice. But, no, no charges."

The one-handed man stared at him in desperation.

"But what about my flat? What about my hand?"

PC Pearson tried a sympathetic smile.

"You have been out of the country for nearly two years." He looked at the documents that the passport service had faxed through to him. "And, obviously, what happened in France is a little outside our jurisdiction."

"But, I... I..."

Tears welled in the man's eyes.

"Now, do you have somewhere to stay?" asked PC Pearson. "I know the number of a nice B and B." He dipped his hand into an inside pocket and produced a business card. "And may I suggest giving this woman, Denise, a call. She's a therapist."

"A therapist?"

"Helped me a lot after the divorce. You know, if you feel you need someone to talk to."

Herbert numbly accepted the card and stared at it and wept.

EVELYN FOUND herself walking through the gardens of the Celestial City's sanctuary for blessed animals, Molly to one side of her, Joan of Arc to the other. Up ahead, St Francis of Assisi harangued a band of angels as they attempted to herd the large African mammals back into their enclosure.

St Francis spotted the women and strode over, the Wolf of Gubbio constantly straining at his leash. The wolf had a tuft of white fur between his teeth.

"Such weckless wegard for animal life!" squealed the indignant saint.

"Sorry, Frank," said Joan, holding up her hands in apology. "We were sort of in a hurry."

"The wabbits are absolutely besides themselves."

Evelyn could hear a rumbling sound. It was just on the cusp of audibility, not because it was quiet but because the sound was so deep.

"Can anyone else hear that?"

"And poor Woberta. I don't think she'll ever be the same again."

The Wolf of Gubbio whimpered.

"You *should* be sowwy, Bwother Wolf," said Francis. "When Woberta finally emerges from your fundament you will apologise."

The rumbling was growing and Evelyn could now feel it reverberating through her legs. She looked up to see if there was a monorail passing overhead but she already knew there wasn't.

"What is that?" said Molly.

The ground shook. The Wolf of Gubbio hid its head between its paws.

And then something happened that made Evelyn's brain throb. She could only comprehend it in terms of that cinematic trick where the camera panned in and zoomed out at the same time so that everything stayed exactly where it was and simultaneously moved away from everything else. The distant spires of the city, the tower blocks and temples, without moving, sped away from one another, creating huge open spaces between them that (and this was the bit Evelyn struggled with) *had always been there.*

"Problem solved," said Molly.

There followed another sound, smaller and more distant but clear nonetheless. The sound of twelve sets of pearly gates slamming open.

Joan grinned with child-like joy, reminding Evelyn just how young the Frenchwoman was.

"I seem to recall," she said, her eyes alight, "that we have a festival to organise."

SPARTACUS WILSON SLEPT UNEASILY beneath a thin quilt.

The only light in the room came from luminous stars, moons and spaceships stuck to his bedroom ceiling. A copy of Commando comic lay open on his bed where he had dropped it. From downstairs came the sounds of a reality television programme and the raised voices of his mum and her boyfriend. The voices filtered into his sleeping mind and his nightmares, in which Mrs Sokolowski was preparing to eat him for her breaktime snack.

Spartacus moaned.

Herbert Dewsbury's hand crawled from beneath the bed and scampered up to the boy's pillow. It tucked a strand of hair behind the boy's ear and gently stroked his forehead until the boy quietened and settled into happier dreams. The hand snuggled into the hollow of Spartacus's neck and, as much as a hand could, it too slept.

BEN STEPPED into the Boldmere Oak. It felt odd to be back on the streets again, back in public. At his core, he had the unshakeable feeling that this was somehow wrong, some sort of mistake, that he was walking through a dream or that the police would swoop down on him at any moment to correct their mistake and whisk him off to prison once more.

He had left the courthouse that evening a free man and returned home to his flat. He had wandered around his home, touching things that he had left behind all those weeks ago. The half-painted soldiers from Antiochus's Indian campaign. The now dried and crusted plates waiting to be washed in the sink. He had gone to Clovenhoof's flat and Nerys's to tell them that he was back but he got no response from either flat apart from a frenetic yapping from Twinkle behind Nerys's door.

Put out that his friends were not only too self-interested to come see him in court but also had the cheek to be out when he called, he put on his coat, went out onto the street and walked to the pub.

The place was crowded and Ben had to weave his way to the bar, hoping that no one would recognise him, ask him awkward questions or try to start something with him. He got to the bar and found that the barman, Lennox, had already poured him a pint of cider and black.

"On the house," said Lennox. "I think you deserve it."

"Thank you," said Ben, mildly uncomfortable with the generous gesture.

"So, it turned out to be a model corpse all along."

Ben smiled politely.

"I did try to tell them. It's amazing that it took Herbert returning from France to show his face in court to convince them I'm not a murderer. My neighbour, Mrs Astrakhan, was apparently so traumatised by the event that she's run off to her sister's in Shropshire, vowing never to return."

Ben paused. Yes, it did seem amazing, implausible, even impossible. The whole business seemed incredible but that was the truth of the matter. Perhaps he would stick to miniature models from now on.

"Now the pint is free," said Lennox, "but if you'd do me a favour."

"Sure."

Lennox pointed across the room to a chair by the window.

"Your friend there has been sleeping off the booze all evening. Can you see that she gets home safely?"

Ben looked, saw and then walked over. Nerys was slumped in a chair. A trio of wine glasses stood on the table in front of her. He sat down across from her and poked her on the shoulder until she stirred.

"Probably not the best place to sleep," he said.

Nerys looked at him blearily.

"Ben?"

He spread his arms.

"Ta-dah. Sprung from jail by the slow-moving cogs of justice."

She sat upright and touched her fingertips to her cheeks. They were wet.

"Crying in my sleep," she said. "I had the strangest dream."

"A sad dream?" said Ben.

"No." She gazed at the table, trying and failing to remember. "Not at all."

DAVE CAME through from the hotel bedroom to the balcony overlooking the sea.

"You'll get cold," he said wrapping his arms around Blenda's shoulders from behind.

She leaned back against him.

"I'm fine," she said and then, "I'm very happy."

Dave looked at a far off light in the darkness, wondering if it was a boat.

"Back to grimy Sutton tomorrow," he said.

She shrugged.

"A nice full English and a leisurely drive. It'll be nice." She chuckled to herself. "Might skip the black pudding. Still can't face the stuff."

"Do you think about him a lot?" said Dave.

She tilted her head back and pecked him on the cheek.

"Nope. Maybe we'll just skip breakfast and have a nice long lie in."

"Sounds good. Peace, quiet and a long lie in."

She turned to face him, staying within his embrace.

"I didn't say it was going to be a quiet lie in."

CLOVENHOOF WENT UP to the bar.

"Lambrini?" said Lennox.

"The same," said Clovenhoof. "How's your grandma?"

Lennox laughed.

"False alarm. She'll bury us all yet."

Clovenhoof saw Ben and Nerys by the window.

"And the usual for those two reprobates."

"No problem, boss."

Lennox put the drinks on a tray and Clovenhoof was surprised to discover he actually had the money in his pocket to pay for them. When the barman passed him his change, Clovenhoof pointed to his head.

"The horns. Can you still...?"

Lennox grinned.

"Still there. Still ugly."

Clovenhoof carried the drinks across to his friends.

"At last he appears," said Ben, gladly taking his next drink. "Where have you been?"

"Here and there," said Clovenhoof. "Mostly there. And how are you?"

"Fine," said Nerys. "Why?"

"No lasting effects from the electric shock?"

"Electric shock?"

"At Pitspawn's?"

"Who?"

"Nothing," said Clovenhoof, sitting down. "Nothing."

Nerys stared at the palm of her hands and then prodded at one as though expecting to see something.

"It was a dream."

"What was?" said Clovenhoof innocently.

Nerys looked at him for the longest time.

"Nothing," she said and reached for the wine.

DARREN POTTERSMORE (formerly known as Pitspawn) sat upright in bed, reading from his mum's copy of the King James Bible. The naked bulb hanging in the middle of the room filled the room with stark, unloving light.

The room had been stripped almost bare. Darren had boxed and bagged up his entire collection of occult books. He had torn down his posters and pentagram. He had binned the statues, jewellery and candles. Even the satanic chair covers his mum had knitted for him had been removed and binned.

The only reminder of his lamentable time as a Satanist was the black paint on his walls. Darren, hours from ever finding sleep, had already made plans to go out the following morning and buy some tins of cleansing white emulsion. And maybe some crucifixes.

THEY TOTTERED HOME DRUNKENLY, arm in arm.

On one side of Clovenhoof, Nerys was explaining the importance of female empowerment and how women through the ages had expressed that through clothing. On the other side of him, Ben laboured under the false impression that his friends were interested in his opinion of the effectiveness of the Greeks as a fighting force.

"Take Joan of Arc," said Nerys.

"Take her where?" said Clovenhoof.

"She wasn't Greek," said Ben.

"Tiny slip of a thing," said Nerys, "but put her in a suit of armour and the English were quaking in their boots."

"No women allowed in the army," said Ben. "Weren't allowed out of the house in fact."

"And here's our house," said Clovenhoof, fumbling in his pocket for his keys.

"All I'm saying... all I'm saying is that this..." She poked at her breasts although she might have been aiming for her spangly low-cut top. "This is my armour. See?"

Clovenhoof turned the key and fell in.

"Rubbish armour," burbled Ben. "Doesn't cover anything."

"I was being meta... metaphysical," she said, struggling to get her foot on the bottom step of the stairs. Ben put his hands on her shoulders and pushed her upstairs ahead of him.

Clovenhoof lay on the floor and briefly debated spending the night there. Ultimately deciding against it, he climbed to his feet and leaned against the door of flat 1a, which promptly swung open, spilling him into Mrs Astrakhan's living room.

The lights were on but he dimly recalled Ben saying that Mrs Astrakhan had gone, left forever.

"Helloo," he called in a drunken singsong voice.

There was a sound from further within the flat, the

movement of furniture. Clovenhoof navigated his way round Mrs Astrakhan's three piece suite and into the master bedroom. There was an old-fashioned boxy suitcase open on the bed. The Archangel Michael, wearing a modest linen suit, was unpacking pants and transferring them to a chest of drawers.

"You're not Mrs Astrakhan," said Clovenhoof.

Michael gave him a stony look of miserable self-pity. There was something *diminished* about him, less magnificent and more... human.

"Don't utter a word," warned Michael.

Clovenhoof looked round.

"You? Here?"

"I go where He sends me," Michael sniffed, returning to his unpacking.

"But here? Permanently?"

"I *don't* want to talk about it."

Clovenhoof nodded and then, without warning, the laughter burst from within him.

"Jeremy!"

"Michael," snorted Clovenhoof, doubling up in hysterics. "Neighbour!"

"Not by choice!"

Clovenhoof howled.

"Have you no sympathy?" whined the earthbound angel.

Clovenhoof shook his head and collapsed into a fit of giggles.

HELL

Saint Peter found himself sitting in another seat. It wasn't a throne but it was a tall chair and positioned at the head of a long table in a dim, redly lit room. There was smell in the air, something faint and not quite identifiable but certainly not very pleasant.

The chairs along the length of the table were filled with, well not people but... individuals. Peter was surprised to see he recognised most of them. Azazel looked at him with penetrating eyes, a needle-sharp quill poised in his hand. Berith had the hindquarters of some small animal stuffed in his huge mouth. He gave Peter a friendly wave. Directly to Peter's left, the demon Belphegor sat in his puttering steam-powered wheelchair. To his right, the fallen angel Mulciber presented Peter with a stack of parchment over two feet in height.

"What's this?" said Peter.

"We have a very long agenda to get through today, your lordship."

Peter stared at Mulciber blankly.

The former angel gave the former saint a not unkindly smile.

"They say it's better to reign in Hell than to serve in Heaven, eh?"

Peter tentatively reached for the first sheet of parchment and began to read.

AFTERWORD

Many thanks for reading book one in the Clovenhoof series. You can find the link to book two in the coming pages.

We're grateful to all of the readers who continue to support our work and help us to keep writing.

If you can find the time to share your thoughts in a review, it not only helps us, but it helps other readers too.

We're very busy writing new books, so if you want to keep up to date with our work, you could subscribe to our newsletter. Sign up at www.pigeonparkpress.com

Heide and Iain

ABOUT THE AUTHORS

Heide and Iain are married, but not to each other.

Heide lives in North Warwickshire with her husband and children.

Iain lives in south Birmingham with his wife and two daughters.

ALSO BY HEIDE GOODY AND IAIN GRANT

Pigeonwings (book 2 in the Clovenhoof series)

As punishment for his part in an attempted coup in Heaven, the Archangel Michael is banished to Earth. The holiest of the angelic host has to learn to live as a mortal, not an easy job when you've got Satan as a next-door neighbour.

Michael soon finds that being a good person involves more than helping out at Sunday school and attending church coffee mornings. He has to find his purpose in life, deal with earthly temptations and solve a mystery involving some unusual monks and a jar of very dangerous jam.

Heide Goody and Iain Grant have written a wild comedy that features spear-wielding cub scouts, King Arthur, a super-intelligent sheepdog, hallucinogenic snacks, evil peacocks, old ladies with biscuits, naked paintball, stolen tractors, clairvoyant computers, the Women's Institute, and way too much alcohol.

Pigeonwings

Oddjobs

Unstoppable horrors from beyond are poised to invade and literally create Hell on Earth.

It's the end of the world as we know it, but someone still needs to do the paperwork.

Morag Murray works for the secret government organisation responsible for making sure the apocalypse goes as smoothly and as quietly as possible.

Trouble is, Morag's got a temper problem and, after angering the wrong alien god, she's been sent to another city where she won't cause so much trouble.

But Morag's got her work cut out for her. She has to deal with a man-eating starfish, solve a supernatural murder and, if she's got time, prevent her own inevitable death.

If you like The Laundry Files, The Chronicles of St Mary's or Men in Black, you'll love the Oddjobs series.

"If Jodi Taylor wrote a Laundry Files novel set it in Birmingham... A hilarious dose of bleak existential despair. With added tentacles! And bureaucracy!" – Charles Stross, author of The Laundry Files series.

Oddjobs

Sealfinger

Meet Sam Applewhite, security consultant for DefCon4's east coast office. .

She's clever, inventive and adaptable. In her job she has to be.

Now, she's facing an impossible mystery.

A client has gone missing and no one else seems to care.

Who would want to kill an old and lonely woman whose only sins are having a sharp tongue and a belief in ghosts? Could her death be linked to the new building project out on the dunes?

Can Sam find out the truth, even if it puts her friends' and family's lives at risk?

Sealfinger

Printed in Great Britain
by Amazon